DIANNE OREN

Fake It Till You Make It

A sweet romantic comedy

First published by Dianne Oren Books 2025

This novel is entirely a work of fiction. The names, characters, and incidents portrayed in it are the work of the author's imagination. Any resemblance to actual persons, living or dead, events, or localities is entirely coincidental.

Dianne Oren asserts the moral right to be identified as the author of this work.

First edition

ISBN (paperback): 979-8-9920634-3-1
ISBN (hardcover): 979-8-9920634-4-8

This book was professionally typeset on Reedsy.
Find out more at reedsy.com

To Mrs. Vanderkam.

Thanks for inspiring my nine year old heart so many years ago. You, and so many teachers like you, are the reason Ashley is a teacher in this book.

Contents

Acknowledgments

My first thanks is to *you*, the reader who is reading this book. You bought my book and you're reading it, and so you have my heartfelt thanks for supporting my dream of telling stories. Thank you so much.

Humble thanks to my husband, Kevin, and my family members all across the country. I appreciate the love and support more than you know. To my friends and colleagues, you are the absolute best. Thank you for buying my books, for telling other people about them, and for supporting me with your unending friendship and love.

To my beta readers, aka the Dragons…ladies, I love you so much. My beta team is comprised of four badasses who get to read these books eight chapters at a time, never complain, always answer all my questions, and send me hysterically funny messages in the middle of the night. I dubbed them the Mermaids when I was writing "How to Date a Mermaid" and they decided their group name needed to change with every book. So they're the Dragons in these acknowledgments because Ashley calls herself the Dragon Lady in this book. Linda B, Linda M, Tammi D, and Tammy C…thank you from the bottom of my heart for your willingness to read my work and give me meaningful feedback.

Victoria Straw, my editor, you've done it again. You've polished up my baby and made it shine beautifully. Thank you for your collaboration and professionalism. You are amazing to work with!

And to my ARC Team…wow! Y'all jumped on this train so fast…I love you. Thank you so much for everything you're doing to support me in my efforts to fill the world with swoons…with aahs…and with so many forehead kisses.

Finally, to Emma St. Clair, Aven Ellis, and Tomi Tabb…for just being the all-around badass, amazing authors/mentors you are. For answering my weird questions, holding my hand through mistakes, and being guiding lights in the chaos for a baby author like me. You're the bombdiggity.

Content Warning

This is a sweet, clean romantic comedy. You're getting a feel-good, fun, romantic story with kissing only and a huge happily ever after. I want all my readers to have a positive experience, so here are a few trigger warnings:

Loss of parent to cancer (past/off page)
Heart attack (past/off page)
Processing grief from loss of parent throughout
Anxiety attack (on page)
Ex-fiance/narcissistic weasel who can't let go mentioned throughout

Chapter 1

Ashley

I watch the too-perfect, too-handsome, well-dressed stranger retreat to the bar to lick his wounds, giving his friends a disappointed head shake as he sits down. Another victim of the Dragon Lady. #SorryNotSorry

"Time?" Scarlet asks from our booth in the stylish restaurant.

Merry looks up from the stopwatch app on her phone, flipping her dark brown hair over her shoulder.

"Twenty-two seconds. A new record."

I smirk.

They can tease me all they want, but after my fiancé stomped all over my heart last year and made me question my ability to judge good humans from bad ones, the whole Dragon Lady thing has worked well for me. I don't see the sense in even letting them get a complete sentence out of their slick-talking mouths when it's not going to do any good. I think this one got four words out before I shut him down.

My friend Marina, the one we're celebrating tonight, nudges me from her seat to my right. She's fighting back a shocked grin.

"You can let some of them get a whole sentence out, can't you?"

I shrug. "Why? When they're not going to get anywhere? It's better to put them out of their misery quickly."

Merry holds her drink up in a salute. "Smashed like a bug on a windshield!"

We all burst into laughter, and I look up to see how my latest admirer is doing. He's already off to another table, where a very pretty brunette smiles up at him like she's the luckiest woman on Earth. All is well. They'll probably toast to me at their wedding.

At the risk of sounding completely full of myself, I'm very blessed when it comes to good looks. I'm really *not* full of myself - but when you're born the only child of parents who look like they won some kind of genetic lottery, well...I definitely benefited from it. I remember the first time a stranger approached my parents in a restaurant, presenting a business card from a modeling agency and asking if I had representation. It only got worse as I got older. I've always gotten attention from strangers for my looks, and I'm pretty used to it at twenty-five. Looking back, it never really bothered me before Greg broke my heart. I always took it as a compliment when I was approached by men before, but something changed in me when Greg broke up with me the *second* time. I got...mad. And I can't seem to get *un*mad. So until I figure this out, I'll keep guarding my heart like a dragon guards treasure.

"Anyway, tonight is not about me," I begin, holding my drink in the air. "Tonight, we're celebrating Marina and Zach's engagement. To true love and mermaid tails!"

Marina laughs softly as we all clink our glasses together in her honor. She's glowing with happiness, and my heart is full just looking at her. A few days ago, we helped her fiancé pull off the ultimate surprise engagement right in the middle of the Golden Gate Bridge. There were times when I thought Marina's fear of going against her rigid rules would derail the relationship before it even started, but I was wrong. Zach charmed her right off her feet—or, I should say, mermaid tail.

We were all dressed up in costume that day, having just come from a singing gig at an engagement party, when we met him. Marina was dressed as a mermaid. And now, since Zach is a world-famous rock star, she'll never have to wear that mermaid tail again. Ever since she and Zach were in a viral video, she's too famous to wear it. And we only do the singing gigs occasionally now, but if she shows up anywhere in that tail, I think the whole world will stop to record it.

"I'm so happy for you guys," Merry says wistfully.

She's our little ray of sunshine, forever positive. Always looking on the bright side. It's all rainbows and unicorns in Merry's world, and we love her for it. She was born on Christmas day, so I'm pretty sure it's in her DNA.

"I'm super happy for you and just a little jealous," Scarlet chimes in with a laugh, taking another swig of her mojito.

She's the realist. If you want honesty, you go to Scarlet.

"I think that's the first time anyone's ever been jealous of me," Marina replies with a head tilt in Scarlet's direction.

Scarlet shakes her head. "Not just you. I'm jealous of Ashley, too."

My eyebrows shoot up to my hairline in surprise. "Why me?"

"You get to be maid of honor," she replies, sagging her shoulders dramatically. "I've never been one!"

Merry nudges her shoulder. "Stop whining, Scarlet…you can be mine."

She sits straight up with a wide grin. "Oh! Well, okay then."

I look at Marina and smile. "So when do we get to go dress shopping?"

Merry lights up like a Christmas tree. "Oooh, yes! I can't wait to see you trying on all those dresses!"

"You'll be gorgeous no matter what you pick," Scarlet says as she takes another sip of her drink.

Indeed. With Marina's beautiful, long red hair and startling green eyes, she could wear a burlap sack down the aisle and look like a queen. It won't matter, but we'll have fun shopping anyway. We always do.

"More importantly," I say lightly, "what color are you making us wear?"

She laughs. "With Merry's dark hair and you two blondes, I think some kind of blue or purple is a safe bet. But I want to see what we think when we start looking at dresses."

"And for you?" I ask.

Marina shrugs. "I'm not sure if I'll even wear a proper wedding dress," she says softly. "It might be just a nice dress. I don't want a big wedding."

"You can wear a proper dress and have a small wedding," Merry says, sitting up straight. "But definitely have the wedding you want, and don't be pressured into doing anything else."

"No pressure happening," Marina says with a glint in her eyes. "Everyone's been wonderful, but I should probably give you guys one tiny detail right away."

That's enough to silence the table. No sips are taken, no rolls are buttered. We're all watching Marina expectantly.

"I didn't grow up going to church or anything," she begins. "So there's no place that's special to me in that way. I'm marrying the right man, and that's really all I care about, but Zach grew up—"

"Oh my God!" I exclaim.

I look around the table and can see by Merry and Scarlet's expressions they've made the same realization.

Marina laughs. "So, yeah, I'd like for us to get married in England," she says. "It means a lot to Zach."

Scarlet, Merry and I exchange excited looks. We're completely speechless.

"Zach is paying for everyone's travel expenses because he's…him," she says with a smile. "So get those passports, ladies."

"This is amazing!" Merry cries excitedly. "How exciting!"

Marina nods. "I'm definitely excited. And his mom has been so sweet. She's over the moon about it all, and she's going to be such a help from a planning aspect."

"Who did Zach choose for his best man?" Merry asks.

I know the answer without having to hear Marina say it. Rick—a present-day Viking god and Zach's best friend. The lead guitarist for their world-famous band, The Royal Rebels, Rick, is six feet two inches of luxurious blond mane and gorgeous muscles. He and Zach write most of the songs the Rebels perform. And despite his rock star status, he's a really nice guy. I know because I asked Zach to come speak to my third graders last year during music week at school, but there was a scheduling conflict, and Rick very graciously volunteered to take his place.

The kids loved every minute of their time with him. He made sure every child had time to hold his guitar and try it out, and he brought guitar picks for all the kids to keep. Finally, he played a couple acoustic versions of Rebels songs for the class and…wow. As much as I've shoved every man I meet into the friend zone, Rick was dangerously close to breaking out of it that day. I've managed to keep him contained, but he's…beautiful. And sexy as hell.

"Ash?" Marina asks, bringing me out of my thoughts.

Everyone is looking at me, waiting for an answer. Answer to what?

"Sorry?" I say quickly.

Merry gives me a knowing look. "Marina jokingly asked if you'd find it terribly trying, working with Rick on the wedding, but we all know the answer to that question now."

I scoff. "Oh, please," I answer lightly. "I consider Rick a friend, nothing more. And it won't be terrible at all. He's super sweet."

I avoid eye contact with Merry, who is obviously not convinced.

"A friend?" Marina asks.

I shrug. "We text each other once in a while," I explain, leaving out the fact that our banter borders on flirty more often than not and my pulse hammers like crazy any time his name appears in my incoming messages. "He was so great with my third graders last year."

Merry levels her stare at me. "So, you text each other about your third graders?"

I smirk at her. "Of course not. But once in a while, he'll see something funny and text it to me or something. I do the same. It's meaningless. Just silly things."

Like the time I got a random text from him telling me that no one can hear a pterodactyl use the bathroom because the p is silent. I got the giggles so bad I had to step outside my classroom for a few minutes.

"I think it's sweet that you keep in touch," Marina says, giving me a little squeeze on my hand. "I'm glad to see you're getting to know him better."

I level my gaze at her. "Don't get your hopes up, Marina. Rick will remain firmly in the friend zone."

Marina gives me a look I can't quite identify. I'm not sure if she's accepting my words or taking the whole thing as some kind of challenge.

"Even Rick? Seriously?" Scarlet scoffs, shaking her head at me.

Merry laughs out loud, which of course only encourages Scarlet further.

"I mean…look at him," she says boldly. "And look at you! You both look like supermodels. Think of the gorgeous kids you'd have."

"Oh, yes, please!" Merry sighs as if Rick and I are already walking down the aisle.

Just as I'm about to say enough is enough, another man steps over to our table and right into my space. Too close. I nearly choke on the cloud of Axe body spray that hits my nostrils as he settles his gaze on me. I feel my skin crawl.

"Hey, ther—"

"Don't speak," I say sharply, jabbing him hard with my index finger. "And step back."

He takes a step back in surprise, and I hear Merry suppress a nervous chuckle.

"No," I say emphatically. "Not interested."

He opens his mouth to argue, and I hold up a hand.

"Bye bye now."

He rolls his eyes at me and walks away. I turn back to my friends to see them all watching me with wary expressions. Merry speaks first, eyes wide.

"I didn't even have a chance to time that one."

Scarlet giggles and gestures at the man's retreating form. "Look at the poor guy. Walking away with the air of a man sentenced to prison."

Marina shakes her head at me. "And what was his crime?"

Scarlet answers before I can. "Not being Rick."

I swipe my hand at her playfully. "Stop making something from nothing. Rick is a friend."

Merry wiggles her eyebrows at me. "The only friend of the male persuasion you're nice to."

I point a finger at her. "Not true. I'm nice to Zach."

Marina smiles. "And thanks for that."

Scarlet is undaunted. "The only single man friend—"

"Okay, enough!" I scold them, trying to keep a straight face. As ridiculous as they're being, I definitely need to nip this in the bud. Out of the corner of my eye, I can see Marina trying to hide a smile.

"They're not wrong," she mutters. "You *are* nice to him. It's not a bad thing. And you two look really good together."

"Back to the wedding preparations," I say slowly, giving everyone a warning look. "Have you decided where you're having the engagement party?"

Merry snorts. "Oh, she didn't get to decide that."

Marina laughs. "I sure didn't. The party will be at Nonno's. It's not in my heart to tell him no, even if I wanted to. He's so excited for us."

Merry's grandfather, Nonno, is really a grandfather to all of us. He's full of nothing but love and joy, although I have seen him yelling in Italian at some of the kitchen staff a time or two. Most of them are Merry's cousins. His restaurant serves the best Italian food in San Francisco, and it's the perfect place for our group of friends and family to celebrate Marina and Zach.

"Well, we all know how hyper-organized you are," I say to Marina. "So my job as maid of honor will probably be easier than most. But tell me when you need help with something, okay? Whatever it is."

I'm rewarded with a side hug as the waiter comes swooping in with our plates. Once everyone is served, a comfortable silence settles over us as we dig into our entrées. I try to shove all thoughts of Rick out of my head, but they keep rolling back in. Rick with the kids at my school. Rick on stage performing with Zach and the band. Rick smiling at me while we're talking. He really does have a gorgeous smile.

Get out of my head, you huge, perfect Viking god.

"How's your dad doing, Ash?" Merry asks as we eat.

I finish the absolutely perfect bite of steak in my mouth.

"He's good," I offer. "His doctor says there's no evidence he ever had a heart attack. And he's keeping me busy with that fundraiser dinner party for his 'Have a Heart Foundation'. He may have gone a little overboard."

"In what way?" Scarlet asks.

"Well, it's a foundation for heart patients…on Valentine's day, so he wants a Valentine-themed dinner," I explain. "Hearts everywhere."

Merry lights up. "That doesn't seem overboard. It sounds perfect."

I tilt my head at her. "Yes, but I'm the one coordinating this thing, and I really hate Valentine's day right now."

Merry sticks her lower lip out at me. "C'mon, Dragon Lady, that cold heart has to soften up someday. You liked Valentine's Day last year!"

"Don't remind me," I grumble. "My plan is to just focus on the task at hand and be there for my dad, but I dread being at the dinner. I don't want to be surrounded by hearts and flowers right now. We're having lunch tomorrow, and I just know we're gonna talk about it."

"Of course he'll want you there," Marina chimes in. "He's proud of you. And you've worked really hard to create this charity dinner. You know he'll want to acknowledge you."

In our friend group, my dad is everyone's dad, just like Nonno is our grandpa and Scarlet's mom is the mom. My mom passed when I was still in high school. Merry's parents live in Silicon Valley and are not very present in her life. But everyone knows my dad well, and I'm afraid Marina is right. He will definitely want me sitting there with him, surrounded by all the ridiculous reminders of Valentine's Day. Ugh.

"I know, I know," I moan over my plate. "I just don't feel very Valentiney this year."

Marina nudges me and whispers, "Sorry, girl."

I busy myself with buttering a roll while I try to get myself in the right mindset. Greg broke up with me a little over a year ago. The hurt has faded, but the anger remains. Anger at myself, not Greg. He was just being who he really is, and I was looking at the whole thing through rose-colored glasses. He works at the investment firm that's been in my family for generations, and we met at the company retreat two years ago. He was quickly becoming a sales superstar, and he ended up being paired with me at the retreat's golf tournament. He was handsome, witty, and showered me with attention. I was swept off my feet so fast I failed to see a lot of red flags. I feel like that meme that says, "Didn't you see the red flags?" and the woman is gasping, "I thought it was a parade!"

What upset me most about the Greg red flag parade is that I really thought I loved him, but when I look back, I can see he never really loved me. He just wanted the boss's daughter. I was just another goal to achieve, and when he had me, he got bored. My instincts were so off track that it was laughable, so my plan is to just be the Dragon Lady and keep them all away until I figure myself out. Like the Taylor Swift song says, I'm the problem. It's me.

Marina gasps, and I look over to see her smiling down at her phone. She looks up to find all of us watching her curiously.

"The guys got home early!" she says with a huge, disgustingly sappy grin.

Merry tilts her head. "Aww, you're so in love. It's gross!"

We all laugh…mostly because it's adorably true. They are so in love it's enough to make me want to sing show tunes and throw flowers whenever I'm near them. They're the cutest thing ever, and I'm so happy for my friend. Friends, actually. Zach has been fully integrated and I consider him a friend as well. He'll either be in our apartment when we get home, or she'll run straight up to his. We're all under the same roof, so to speak.

Last year, when Zach and Marina became a couple, he bought a building. Yep, a whole building. Because that's what multi-millionaires do, I guess. Even my dad, who is also extremely wealthy, has never bought a whole building, but he's not a rock star in love with my best friend.

It's four stories of classic Victorian architecture that was in dire need of some love. So Zach had the ground floor turned into offices for The Mermaid Foundation, Marina's charity that supports families in crisis. The second floor was made into two temporary apartments for said families. The third floor was transformed into an apartment for Marina and me, and Zach took the top floor for his own apartment. I thought it might be weird at first, but it's actually been really great. For one thing, Marina is at Zach's half the time, and it's almost like I live on my own. And I love me some quiet time!

I nudge Marina. "If he's going to be at our place when we get home, can you get him to make those cheese chip things?"

"Done!" she replies, pulling up her phone and tapping a message on the screen.

"Thanks," I say with a quick nod. "I love those things, and I can't figure out what I'm doing wrong when I try to make them."

"Hey, Scarlet's got a great plan for the San Francisco Beautiful Home competition," Merry brags.

We all turn to Scarlet.

"Tell us," Marina says with a smile.

Scarlet wiggles her eyebrows excitedly. "I got my mom to let me redecorate her office, so that'll be the project I show on my application this year. I feel like the faux corner window I designed last year wasn't enough. Hopefully, this is enough of a boost to get me on the show."

We'll all be cheering her on, too. Scarlet is an interior designer, and she's laser-focused on getting a spot as a contestant on the Decorator's Showcase television show. The winner gets $250,000, and Scarlet has her eye on the prize.

I wink at Scarlet. "You got this."

She winks back, and she thrills us with her ideas to make her mom's office the most gorgeous space in the city. The conversation shifts to Merry's mission to rediscover her beloved Nonna's cookie recipe, and before we know it, the check is paid, and we're hugging each other goodbye on the sidewalk outside.

The restaurant isn't far from our apartment, so Marina and I walked here. We fall into step beside each other, chatting easily about her wedding plans as we cover the three blocks home. There's a chill in the air and I didn't bring a coat, which I'm really regretting in the damp San Francisco night air. There's a thick fog rolling in off the bay. I thought this sweater dress would be enough, especially with boots. So wrong, but kind of a thing I do frequently. Someone's always scolding me for forgetting a coat. Just a little further and I can curl up with a hot cup of tea and get warm.

"You're freezing, aren't you?" Marina guesses correctly from under her warm coat.

"Of course. But I look cute, so there's that."

Marina nudges my shoulder with hers. "You always look cute."

I stop abruptly just before we start up the steps of our building.

"Maybe that's it!" I exclaim. "Next time we go out, I'm putting my hair in a messy wad on top of my head, not wearing make-up, and wearing baggy, mismatched clothes."

Marina rolls her eyes at me, then grabs my elbow and pulls me up the stairs to the front door. She puts her key in the lock, and I keep going.

"Too bad it's not Halloween. I could buy some fake warts at one of those costume shops that pop up all over town."

"Wow," she says coolly. "I almost wish I could see that. But you'd need about thirty-seven fake warts to scare most men away. You're just that gorgeous."

We step inside and take the stairs up to our apartment.

"I don't think that's true, but thanks for the compliment, girl."

As soon as Marina opens the door to our apartment, she runs to Zach. He's in the kitchen, making the aforementioned cheese crisps

I can't stay away from. Snacks for tomorrow. Yay! I look over at my friends with a huge grin. Zach has cow print oven mitts on his hands as he scoops Marina into his arms and kisses her passionately. Freaking adorable.

I rub my hands together as I step into the apartment, averting my eyes from the display of affection in the kitchen. A tiny ping of longing knocks against the iron door to my Dragon Lady heart. I miss that feeling, even knowing what Greg and I had wasn't real. My head was full of home decor ideas and naming our children when I should have been focused on the fact that Greg's actions and words didn't line up. He knew how to say all the right words, but he just wasn't present. And I guess that's the biggest lesson I learned from him. I want someone who cares enough to show up for me. In all the ways a person can show up for another person.

I walk across the expanse of our generous living room, decorated in cream and rose, and start down the hall to my room so I can put my bag away. While I'm there, I shimmy out of my sweater dress, ditch the boots, and throw on some cozy gray leggings, my favorite pink over-sized sweater, and a pair of fuzzy socks before darting back out to hang out with Zach and Marina. Right after I grab a big steaming mug of spiced chai tea, of course. I pad down the hallway and hear Marina laughing.

"All right," I call out before I'm even in sight of the kitchen. "Don't block my kettle with your make-out session, I'm freez—"

I skid to a halt as I get to the kitchen. My jaw drops open in surprise. Because there, standing in the kitchen next to my tea kettle, is the Viking god himself...holding my favorite mug out to me and flashing me a knowing grin that makes my pulse jump.

"You forgot your coat again, didn't you, Ash?"

Chapter 2

Ashley

The Viking god in front of me flashes a cocky grin and wiggles my favorite mug at me, steam billowing from within to indicate he's already prepared my tea. I don't even have to look at it to know he's made it to my exact specifications. Rick is never less than perfect. Spiced chai with milk. We had a whole conversation about it once. I even forced him to take a sip when his lip curled up because I put milk in my tea.

Rick visits Zach and Marina a lot, so he knows his way around our kitchen. He's wearing a dark blue waffle-knit long-sleeved Henley with blue jeans and brown boots, so there's a bit of a lumberjack vibe going on as well. He looks like the perfect thing to cuddle up with on a rainy day. The universe is testing me. If I'm being honest, it's hard not to stare. He looks really cozy. And gorgeous. And warm. I kind of want to climb up into his arms and set up camp right now. I bet I'd warm up really fast.

Instead, I step forward, roll my eyes, and carefully take the mug from his hand. Our fingers brush, and the heat coming off his fingers sends little electric sparks dancing along my skin. Can you hold hands with a guy in the friend zone without giving him the wrong idea? Pretty sure that's a no, but those massive hands could warm up my freezing fingers so fast.

I step back immediately and climb onto the nearest stool at our kitchen island. I haven't figured out if it's cologne or just the soap he uses, but he has a whole piney woods mixed with raw sex appeal thing going on, and I can't get too close to that. When he finished teaching the kids in my class last year, he came over to my desk and leaned on it to chat with me. Suddenly, the air around me was filled with this subtle sexy pine tree scent and, before I knew it, I got caught staring at his lips.

I mutter my thanks and dip my head to blow the steam off my tea, taking a minute to slip the Dragon Lady mask back on. I wrap my fingers around the warm mug and close my eyes. When I open them again, my expression is schooled into one of indifference. I catch Marina watching me from behind Zach. She's frowning at me. She can scold me all she wants, but it wasn't long ago when she was holding every man on the planet at arm's length as well—including Zach. She'll just have to understand.

Zach growls and whirls around, scooping Marina into his arms. I've lost count of the number of swoons these two have wrung from me. I love how in love they are, especially Marina. She deserves this kind of happiness. Is it a little hard to take sometimes because of my present circumstances? Yeah, a little. Sometimes the wound Greg left behind starts to sting a little. But it's my fault it's there, so I just lean into it and call out the Dragon Lady. To be honest, I'm not able to conjure her a hundred percent tonight. I'd really rather take my tea to my bedroom and be alone, but that would be a little rude. Especially when I smell Zach's cheese things in the oven, which I asked him to make.

"Hey, hey, hey," I tease, pointing a finger between Rick and me, who has wandered dangerously close again. "Not in front of the kids."

Zach laughs and pulls a cookie sheet out of the oven. It's covered in lightly seasoned cheese melts that he somehow turns into crackers. I don't know how he does it. He gave me the recipe and I can't do it, and I'm pretty good in the kitchen. I look at the bubbling cheesy squares with a predatory glint in my eyes. Zach wags a finger at me.

"Let them cool first, and don't eat them all in one sitting this time," he scolds.

I flash Zach a smile as I giggle. Yep. I sure did do that. They were *that* good.

"Thanks for making those, my friend," I say enthusiastically. "I promise I won't touch. Now I have my favorite snack for work tomorrow."

Zach winks at me. "My pleasure, Ash."

Marina moves towards the living room and motions for all of us to follow.

"C'mon, guys, let's get comfy," she says, dragging Zach by the hand and curling up on the couch with him.

I grab my mug of tea, accidentally making eye contact with Rick's deep blue eyes. The corners of his mouth tip up as he gestures for me to go ahead of him.

Danger, danger.

I shuffle ahead of him, suddenly very aware of the fuzzy pink socks I'm wearing and feeling a little silly. I normally prefer to stretch out on our love seat, but that might invite Rick to sit next to me. Too tempting. I plop down in the leather chair next to the love seat, prompting Rick to look down at me with a confused scowl.

"Why are you sitting there?"

I shrug. "It was close, and I'm lazy?"

He tilts his head, pointing at the love seat. "That's your favorite spot."

I blink up at him. Does the man notice *everything?* He steps aside and motions for me to take the love seat.

"Go on," he says with a knowing expression. "I won't crowd you. I'll take the chair."

All eyes are on me now, so I quickly get up and flop onto the love seat as Rick takes the chair. Without a word, he leans over and grabs my favorite throw from the basket next to his chair and hands it to me before I can even reach for it. I stare for a minute.

"You must be freezing, Little Miss Forgot Her Jacket Again."

Even a dragon has to admit when they're out-witted. I can't compete with Rick's uncanny ability to notice every single little thing about me. I nod my thanks as I take the throw from him, using one hand to spread it across my lap and legs while I try not to splash my tea. Most of me is covered and getting warmer. If I try too hard, I'll end up spilling tea everywhere, so I snuggle back against the cushions.

"So, how was dinner?" Zach asks, his gaze moving between Marina and me.

"Too good," I say, pushing out my stomach and patting it loudly. "I have a food baby."

"Me too," Marina says with a laugh. "Totally worth it, though."

Rick leans over and grabs a corner of the throw, tugging it so both my feet are covered, then sits back in his chair and takes a swig of his water. I give him half a smile.

"Thanks."

He nods, and I'm suddenly aware of Marina's attention.

"See?" Marina says with a pointed look. "You *can* be nice to men sometimes."

Zach and Rick look at me curiously.

"Ash," Rick teases. "Were you mean to another boy?"

I feign an evil grin, a little proud of my Dragon Lady persona. "I'm not mean. I'm spicy nice."

I'm rewarded with a collective laugh from our little group.

"Well," Rick says with a smirk, "thanks for not being spicy nice to *me*."

I wave him off with a flick of my hand, but inside I feel little flutters of nervous energy when his eyes rake over me. I'm spicy nice to strange men. Rude men. Boys in men's bodies, really. I can't imagine Rick ever provoking such a response from me. From the moment I met him, he's only ever been kind. He's a little soft-spoken for someone with an appearance that, let's face it, is pretty breathtaking. He has a way of looking at me that makes me feel like every cell in my body is awake and alive and reaching out for him. And his eyes...

"Ash?"

I jump in my seat as Marina calls my name, instantly feeling like some kind of love-struck teenager getting caught staring at her crush. What is with me today?

"Yeah? Yep?" I stammer quickly.

Smooth, Ash.

I watch a slow, knowing smile spread across my friend's face. "Never mind. Your mind was somewhere else."

I feel a blush slowly crawl up my cheeks. So that's fun for later. Marina saw me staring at the Viking god. Great.

I'm about to change the subject when Zach lets out a huge yawn. I'm surprised it didn't shake the building. We all look over at him in wonder.

"Sorry, guys," he grumbles, standing up and stretching. "I've got to get some sleep. Today was a long day."

Marina stands up too, waving a hand at us when we move to get up.

"You two stay and catch up," she says, thinking she's being nonchalant. She's so not. "I'm going to get Zach upstairs so he can get some rest."

Zach moves pretty fast for someone so exhausted, and Marina is right on his tail.

"See you tomorrow, Ash!" she calls as the door closes behind them both.

In tandem, Rick and I turn to face each other and burst into laughter together.

"Did they think they were being subtle?" I ask, nearly spilling my tea from laughing so hard.

Rick turns those deep blue eyes on me. "I think so! I guess they're in love, so they want everyone else to fall in love too."

I roll my eyes. "That would be sweet if it wasn't so annoying."

"I'm sorry, Ash," Rick says lowly, looking a little guilty when he has no reason to be.

I frown, studying him for a few seconds. "Why do you say that?"

He shrugs. "Because I know you hate it."

I soften my expression and nudge him with one fuzzy sock covered foot.

"I hate getting hit on in bars or when I'm out to dinner with the girls. But I don't hate *you*. You're my friend. In fact, I think you may be the only man I know who *hasn't* hit on me—so thanks for that!"

He holds his hands up in surrender. "I know better than to play with dragons."

I roll my eyes again and burrow further under the blanket.

"I'm sure you understand more than you're letting on," I say with a hint of curiosity. "You're the lead guitarist for The Royal Rebels. A rock star in your own right. And you…"

I catch myself, but too late. I was about to point out his obvious good looks, but I don't want to seem like I'm making a move. Now I'm stuck.

Rick raises his eyebrows. "I…what?"

I laugh self-consciously, pointing at him and waving my finger in a circle. "You're all…you."

He shakes his head at me as if he doesn't know what I mean, but the devilish grin on his face tells me he knows exactly what he's doing. There's no way he's not aware of his own hotness. That's completely impossible. He's messing with me, and I kind of respect him for it because I would absolutely do the same to him.

I gesture at him again, swiping my hand at him from head to toe. "Have you looked in a mirror? You're basically a Viking god in human form. Women must go crazy for you."

He shrugs. "Yeah, they do."

I nod and take a sip of my tea. "Doesn't that drive you nuts? Or do you like that kind of thing?"

There's no ego about him. He's never given me that impression. Given his near-perfect appearance and the whole rock star thing, he gives off a pretty normal vibe.

He crosses one leg over the other and turns to face me. "If I answer that honestly, will you promise not to judge me too harshly?"

I nod again. "I would never judge you anyway."

"I'm well aware of what I look like," he begins. "I'm used to getting a lot of attention, mainly from women. I don't let it get to me. Naturally, because of the fame from being in the Rebels, I meet a lot of women who see a pleasing face and a big bank account. I'm always polite, but I'm not interested. I want something real with someone who sees me for who I am and not what I can give them."

His response hits home, and I realize I wish I had that. I wish I could find that with someone. I just don't trust myself. I wonder what it would be like to have that with Rick, and alarm bells begin to go off in my head. That's all I need. Let Rick out of the friend zone and then mess it up. I'd be signed up for a lifetime of awkward moments because our best friends are getting married.

"Do you think you'll ever meet her?"

He smiles softly. There's an almost secretive look about him. "Who says I haven't already?"

My eyebrows shoot straight up into my hairline. "Are you holding out on me? Did you meet someone?"

My heart sinks at the idea that he's found someone, and instant guilt consumes me. Why should I want to deny a friend something I'd love to have myself? I should be happy for him if he's found that, but somehow, I don't feel happy at the thought of his huge, muscular arms wrapped around anyone who isn't me. I'm going to have to figure out how to keep this attraction in check.

He makes a motion over his lips like he's locking them up and throwing away the key.

I laugh softly.

"Friends tell friends, you know."

He shakes his head. "There's nothing to tell. She doesn't see me."

My brow furrows in confusion. Who wouldn't notice Rick? I'm about to press him for more details when he changes the subject.

"Can we talk about the wedding for a minute?" he asks with a pensive tone.

I take another sip of my tea and nod. "Of course! I'm so excited for them. I've already started planning."

He looks sheepish.

"Yeah, that's the thing. I don't really understand everything that a best man does. I'm a little lost."

"You've never been in a wedding before?"

He shakes his head. "I've never even been *to* a wedding before, and from what I've seen on TV, it's planning a bachelor party and going to a strip club."

"You better not take him to a strip club!" I exclaim, swatting at him in the air.

He playfully grabs for my hand and misses.

"Don't worry, Ash," he says. "We're not like that anyway. I have a feeling we'll end up at his place watching a Lord of the Rings marathon and eating pizza. The media likes to make us sound much more exciting than we are."

"Okay," I say, shooting him a mock warning glare. "Then I'm happy to help you with your best man duties."

He smiles. "Thanks, Ash."

I can't deny that I'm more than a little happy at the chance to get to spend more time with Rick. Viking god status aside, I find myself missing male companionship. I'm not ready to trust myself to make romantic decisions yet, but Rick is a nice guy and seems content in the friend zone. It would be good to hang out with him more. I just need to keep the physical attraction thing in check.

"Our first big event will be the engagement party next weekend," I explain. "As the best man and maid of honor, we should give a toast to Marina and Zach."

"Okay. That doesn't sound too hard."

"Do you think we should do something more, though? They're our best friends, and their story is so special. Are we going to settle for a regular toast?"

He grins mischievously. "You wanna kick it up a notch?"

I smile back at him. "Yeah. I'm just not sure how, though. I need to think about it for a little while."

He nods, contemplating. "Okay, what else?"

"I put together a little gift basket for Marina," I say excitedly. "A cute tank that says 'bride' in rhinestones, a pretty journal, some beauty products from this really bougie spa. Have you gotten anything for Zach?"

Rick's eyebrows make a slow crawl upwards. "I didn't know I needed to. What should I get him?"

I pause, realizing I've proposed a particularly difficult challenge. What do you get a rock star millionaire who has everything already?

Rick's face falls, and I sit up, instinctively placing my hand on his.

"Hey," I say gently. "I'm helping you, remember? I'll make sure you have a spot in the best man hall of fame by the time we're done."

I'm rewarded with a laugh and I sit back and start thinking.

"Maybe some cuff links? Or a gift card for a massage he can use the week before the wedding."

"Maybe," he says. "I have some ideas, but those are good to fall back on. I'll check some options tomorrow."

I raise my eyebrows and take a sip of my tea. Warmth runs through me like a wave. I close my eyes and sink into the cushions again, pulling the blanket up over my nose until only my eyes and the top of my head are visible. Rick's soft laughter warms me further.

"Why do you always forget your coat, Ash?" he asks, watching me with a fond smile.

I smile back, even though it's hidden under the blanket.

"I don't mean to forget it," I say through a yawn. "I just get pre-occupied sometimes."

He mulls that over for a moment, then looks at me with a serious expression.

"What are you so pre-occupied with?"

"This benefit dinner I'm organizing for my dad."

He raises an eyebrow. "What's that about?"

"When Dad had his heart attack last year, he shared a room in the hospital with a man who wasn't as well off as Dad is. The man didn't receive the same treatment as my Dad because his insurance wasn't as good, and it really bothered my softy of a father. So he created a foundation to help heart patients bridge the gap so they have access to better treatments…and here we are."

Rick remains silent for a long moment, so I keep sipping at my tea and watching his thought process play across his handsome face. He slowly shakes his head.

"Now it makes sense," he says quietly. "Where you get your passion from."

I nearly spill my tea in my lap. "What?"

He grins at me. "You get your fire from your dad, Dragon Lady. He saw something to fight for, and now look at him. He's using his wealth to build something for people less fortunate."

I nod. "He's amazing. I don't see what that has to do with me, though."

Rick gives me an incredulous look.

"You fight for your friends, even when you think they're wrong. Marina told me how hard you worked to get her to see sense when she was trying to kick Zach to the curb."

I smile slowly. Yep. I sure did that, didn't I.

"You fought for your own dreams," he continues. "Anyone else in your position might have taken an easy job at Daddy's investment firm. Not you."

My smile spreads until my cheeks hurt. "Not me."

"You wanted to work with kids, so you became a teacher."

My heart swells at the admiration in Rick's voice, and I feel a blush crawling up my neck. I nod.

"Kids are the best," I say softly. "I love my job."

He nods, a subtle smile playing on his full lips. "I know."

My gaze finds his. His eyes are a deep, rich blue like the Pacific Ocean. I can't look away, and I don't want to. Something about the energy in the room changes. It feels like we're flirting, but we're not. It feels like something is happening, but I'm not sure what. We're just sitting here in some sort of sexy staring contest, waiting for the other one to blink. Since I can't risk letting Rick out of the friend zone, I shrug and laugh softly.

"Well, I guess it's a good thing I'm the Dragon Lady," I say lightly, "since you say I get my fire from my dad."

I wait for him to laugh, but he doesn't. He stares for a few beats more.

"You know you don't have to do that with me," he says softly, almost a whisper. "You don't have to bring out the Dragon Lady to keep me at arm's length."

I blink back my surprise, and he laughs.

"I just mean that I know you don't want anything but friendship," he clarifies. "Any man with a brain can read that message loud and clear, so I don't want you to feel like you have to be on guard with me. I know where the line is. I won't cross it."

My pulse quickens. If he only knew the truth: that I'm on guard because I'm afraid I'll be the one who'll cross the line. I look down into my mug, feigning interest in my tea bag. Rick sees a lot, and I have to give him credit for it. But why do I feel a little sadness hanging in the air when he tells me he won't cross any lines? I find myself wondering what it would be like for Rick to get out a giant eraser and wipe that line out of existence.

"Hey."

I look up quickly. Rick watches me carefully, concern brewing in those stormy blue eyes.

"You okay?"

My smile is automatic. I don't really feel it.

"Yep. I'm good."

Rick looks skeptical, but doesn't argue.

"It's okay if you're not, you know. Friends tell friends."

I smile genuinely when he uses my own words against me. His eyes twinkle as he takes a final swig from his water bottle, then gets up to toss it into the recycle bin in the kitchen. I watch silently, taking a moment to appreciate how perfect he looks in that Henley.

"I'm heading home," he says, pulling his keys from his pocket. "I owe you one for helping me with all the best man stuff. I'll text you if that gift idea falls flat, okay?"

I nod. "I'll be ready with ideas. I've got you."

His gaze holds mine, and he smirks at me, the cocky rock star returning. Something in me stirs.

"You do."

There's something hidden there, some meaning I know I'm not quite picking up on. My jaw drops open briefly.

What did that mean?

Before I have a chance to say anything, he crosses the expanse of the living room, opens the apartment door, and steps through it.

"Make sure you lock this behind me," he calls as he closes the door and heads downstairs and out of the building, leaving me to wonder what on earth just happened.

Chapter 3

Marina is happily puttering around our kitchen by the time I'm dressed for work and ready for breakfast.

"Good morning," I greet her as she passes me an empty bowl and my favorite boxed cereal.

I grab a bar stool and sit down at the island, watching her get the rest of our breakfast items together. She's humming softly as she pulls a carton of milk out of the fridge and slides it across the marble counter top to me. After being roommates for so many years, our breakfast routine almost looks like an intricately choreographed ballet as we move around the kitchen and dip in and out of the refrigerator and various cabinets and drawers.

"Morning, Ash. How'd you sleep?"

I grumble. "Not great. There's a lot going on in my head right now."

My friend shoots me an empathetic look. "Anything I can help with?"

I shrug. "It's mostly just this benefit dinner for Dad. I want to do a great job for him, but I'm just really not in the mood for all the Valentine's Day stuff."

She settles on the bar stool next to me, regarding me for a few moments with her emerald green eyes. I know that look. She's contemplating whether she's going to get real or keep things light.

"Are you ever going to forgive yourself, Ash?"

We're getting real then. Okay.

I shrug. I truly don't know. I want to stop being angry at myself, but I can't seem to do it. Maybe I could forgive myself if I'd only fallen for Greg once, but that's not what happened. I fell for him once, and then he got bored and dumped me. About three months later, he came crawling back, and I actually fell for it again. Because I saw a handsome face. A well-dressed, successful man…and I believed everything that came out of his mouth. Then he got bored again, so I got hurt. Again.

"I'm not trying to pressure you, truly," she says gently as I focus too hard on my cereal bowl. "But it's been over a year. I think it's okay to give yourself a little grace."

I bite my lower lip as I meet her eyes. "I'm not sure I know how. I keep thinking about how stupid I was to fall for his same old tired lines again."

Marina tilts her head. "Not stupid at all. Ashley, you've always been such a passionate, vivacious person. I hate that he took that away from you. You're angry at yourself for having a loving heart while he has been an absolute jerk. Any fault lies with him, not you."

I consider her words. I want them to be true, but I still feel like the guilt is mine to own. I'm the one who lost my head and stopped thinking, awe-struck by a wolf in sheep's clothing. I'm still so ashamed of my ridiculous behavior. I dreamed of a life I would never have had with Greg, but that didn't stop me from plowing forward anyway. I was dragging the both of us toward the picket fence, the kids, the whole nine yards.

I shake my head. "Maybe. The first time. But I never would've gotten hurt again if I hadn't run back to him as soon as he crooked his stupid finger at me."

Emotion clogs my throat as the stupidity of the situation hits me once more. Disappointment. Anger. Guilt. They're all there, like old friends popping up to say hello whenever I think about Greg.

I hear an exasperated sigh spill out of my best friend, and I shoot her a regretful glance. She eyes me with too much sympathy in her eyes.

"Just promise me you'll be nicer to my best friend Ashley, okay?" she says, giving me a nudge.

I nudge her back and force a half smile. "Done. Now, can we talk about something else, please?"

Marina gulps down the last of her cereal and slides off the bar stool. "Gladly. How about home decor?"

I frown. "That's oddly specific. Sure."

Marina laughs to herself as she flips the faucet on and rinses out her bowl. I finish the last spoonful of my cereal and hand her the bowl, which she makes quick work of.

"Remember the bookcases I was thinking about for the living room?"

I nod. Our new apartment is huge, and the living room has plenty of space. Marina has always wanted a wall lined with bookcases, but she wasn't sure she wanted to do that when the building was being renovated.

"Work starts today," she says with a little squeal. "I'm so excited!"

Even as I try not to make a face, I know I'm making one. Marina misses nothing.

"And before you start up about strangers working in the apartment while we're both at work, I've found the perfect solution."

I raise my eyebrows expectantly. "Yeah?"

She nods and offers me a wicked grin. The grin she only wears when she's up to something.

"Rick."

My pulse quickens at the mere mention of his name. It should annoy me, but can I really blame myself? He is perfect. I'd be dead if I didn't notice. Does that make me feel any better about the fact that he'll be in my apartment every day? No. No, it does not.

I clear my throat. "Rick?"

"He likes to tinker around with wood sometimes," Marina explains lightly.

"Tinker?" I parrot. "Maybe we don't want someone who *tinkers* in charge of large, heavy furniture that can land on top of us. You know…in a city where earthquakes happen."

Marina scoffs. "If you'd seen the bookcases he built for his house, you wouldn't say that."

Okay, so maybe it's not the tinkering thing I'm worried about. Maybe I don't want to get used to a six-foot-two-inch Viking god muscling around my living room every day. How will I focus on grading papers and planning lessons with Rick here?

"How long will the work take?"

She shrugs. "I'm not sure. The Rebels are done recording their new album, but they might have to go back to the studio to fine-tune some things. And they're doing some publicity. They're trying to take some time off, though, so it shouldn't be too much. I don't want to hit him with a hard deadline, so I asked him to just fit it in around whatever plans he has."

She finishes rinsing out the dishes and loads them in the dishwasher, flipping the door closed with an excited flourish. My phone buzzes inside my bag, and I retrieve it to find a text from my dad.

Dad: Hey, baby girl. I found a box in the attic last night. Looks like some of your mom's things. Can you help me look through it in the next week or two? I don't want to do it without you.

A familiar wave of regret and longing passes through me. My mom died of cancer when I was thirteen. Eleven years later, I still think of her every day and feel the sting of grief whenever things like this surface. Marina watches me curiously, noticing my sobered expression. I hold my phone up.

"Dad found some of my mom's stuff."

Marina rounds the kitchen island and gently places a hand on my arm as she reads Dad's text. She gives my arm a little squeeze, and I look up to find her looking at me with heartfelt empathy. Marina lost her mom at the same age, so we've shared a bond over that from the day we met in college. I was lucky enough to still have my Dad. Marina and her brother Max went into foster care.

"You okay?" she asks in a quiet tone.

I close my eyes for a moment and breathe deeply. It's a practice my therapist taught me back when we first lost my Mom, which I do whenever it feels like my feelings might overwhelm me. It's been at least eight years since Dad and I let go of the last of Mom's things. It feels unreal that there is suddenly more to go through, almost as if she were reaching down from heaven to send us a message. I open my eyes and look at my friend.

"I think so," I say hesitantly, my voice thick with emotion. "It's... unexpected."

Marina steps to my side and wraps an arm around my shoulders. I take another big breath.

"I mean, what is it? Is it something that's going to make me cry? How will my dad react? I want to know what it is, but I also kind of don't."

"What will you do?" she asks softly.

I shrug in resignation. "There's only one thing to do. I have to be there for Dad. And I *do* want to know what's in the boxes, but I'd prefer not to do it right now. With Dad's big benefit dinner coming up, I'm already feeling a little overwhelmed."

"You could postpone it."

I shake my head. "No, I can't. I won't think about anything else until we open it. I'll just keep over-thinking."

Marina smirks and squeezes me around my shoulders. "I can relate."

Her response makes me laugh under my breath. We're so similar in some ways. I pull my phone up and start typing out a response to Dad.

Ashley: Can we do it Saturday? Before Marina's engagement party?

I look up to see Marina watching me with compassion.

"Will you promise me something?"

I nod.

Dad is typing...

"If you need to talk at any time," she begins gently, "before or after you open the box, promise you'll come to me? I don't want you to feel like you can't come to me about anything because of the wedding."

I pop up off the bar stool and hug Marina. My friend's arms wrap around me and we squeeze each other hard. Our inner circle believes in the power of a great hug, and we give the best ones. She smiles at me when we let each other go.

"Of course I will," I say lightly. "I don't feel like I can't come to you, I promise. I just...I don't know."

She watches me with interest, giving me the space I need to form my thoughts. I throw my head back for a moment and let out an exasperated sigh.

"I'm just going through some stuff right now. Ever since that whole mess with Greg, I just don't quite feel like myself."

Marina nods as she reaches into a cupboard for a travel mug, then grabs a ginger and turmeric tea bag from the drawer and passes them both to me. My phone pings.

Dad: Sure, honey. Let's talk about it at lunch tomorrow.

Right. Our weekly meet-up slipped my mind somehow. All this

talk about Rick actually had me focusing on something else.

"Okay," Marina says as she reaches over to flick on the electric kettle to boil water. "Well, I know two things. First, you'll be late for school if you don't make your tea and get going."

I look at my watch and throw my tote bag over my shoulder.

She's right.

"And what's the second thing?"

Marina leans over the counter and levels her emerald green gaze at me.

"And second," she says with a grin, "you, my friend, are amazing… and you'll figure it all out. There's no doubt in my mind."

With that, she walks out of the kitchen and heads for her bedroom, leaving me to wait for the water to boil and wonder what's in that box of Mom's.

***

Rick

I don't know how many t-shirts I have to try on in order to be okay with how I look, but I know it's not seven. I yank number seven over my head and toss it aside, mentally cursing myself for caring this much. I'm literally just building some bookcases. It's a job I know well, even though woodworking is just a hobby. I've built them for my mom, for my sister…for myself, and a few others. But in all the times I've built them before, I've never built them for my best friend's fiancé and her best friend…the Dragon Lady of San Francisco.

Ashley. The five-foot-nine-inch breathtakingly beautiful source of all my angst, complete with an adorable personality and a penchant for giving her heart to the wrong guy. Twice. Since the day I met her, I get a lump in my chest when she's near. And that's saying something because she was dressed up like a sailor when we met.

Her hair is the color of morning sunlight, buttery and warm. Her eyes are the exact same blue as the hydrangeas that grow in my mom's garden. And when she's not being the Dragon Lady…well, God help me. She has a power over me. I'd do anything to get half of a smile from her.

When I find a woman attractive on this level, things usually get easier for me as I get to know them. I relax more when I see they're not perfect. But with Ashley, she's still perfect. There's literally nothing I don't like about her. Well, I didn't like the fact that she was engaged when I met her, but that's changed. The idiot let her go. The more I get to know her, the more I shake my head at the level of idiocy he displayed when he dumped her. I hate that he hurt her, but he didn't deserve her. She should be with someone who appreciates her for everything she is, and I thought I might get a chance at being that person someday. Until Ashley opened the door to the friend zone and shoved me through it. As soon as the idiot…Greg is his name, apparently, dumped Ashley, she proclaimed herself the Dragon Lady, and here we are.

As desolate as it sounds, there are perks to being in Ashley's friend zone. For one, I'm the only resident. The place is mine and mine alone since all other men she's come across have been borderline creepy or have provoked the dragon's wrath in other ways. Some have just given up hope and left. According to her. Zach is her friend too, of course, but isn't the friend zone reserved for single, unattached members of the opposite sex? I think so. And my best friend Zach is most definitely attached to Ashley's best friend, Marina.

I flip back through my closet again as if I expect new choices to materialize. Finally, my hand stops on a vintage t-shirt with The Royal Rebels logo on it. It's well worn, but I look good in it…and since I'll just be inside Ashley and Marina's apartment all day, it's not like I'll be recognized somewhere. I already have everything I need loaded in my truck, so I grab my cell phone and head for the door. It's a twenty-five-minute drive from my house in Mill Valley to their place in the city, and I need to get moving. I turn off the lights in the kitchen and walk through the atrium on my way to my garage, inhaling deeply as I look at the green woods I see out the wall of windows.

I loved this house the moment I walked in the front door. Settled up against the woods, it feels like I'm the only person out here. There are only five houses on this street, all huge and built on substantial lots. I've never even heard one of my neighbors start their cars in the morning. It's very secluded and serene. Nothing like the busy city of San Francisco I'm about to head for. It suits me perfectly.

I climb into my truck and pull my phone out to text Zach, then grab a hair tie from the console and pull my long blond hair away from my face.

Rick: Hey, bud, you up? Want me to pick up breakfast on the way in?

It's 10 am, which isn't early for most people, but our schedules can be erratic at times. I settle my phone into the holder on the dashboard and start the truck, then pull down the long driveway that descends to the secluded street below. My phone pings just as I pull onto the street, so I brake and take a look.

Zach: Come up to my place first. I'll have breakfast going when you get here, mate.

Excellent. I don't really like driving in the city, so I'm happy not to have to navigate in and out of crowded shopping centers to grab a fast food breakfast. Another win from Zach and Marina's relationship. Zach has become quite domesticated and loves to cook. I love watching him fawning all over Marina, and now that I know Marina better I'm super excited to see her so happy. It'll be a challenge, though, to be there for my best friend as he marries his love…who happens to be best friends with the lyrically beautiful Dragon Lady I can't get out of my mind. And who wants nothing to do with me. I move the truck forward with a scowl on my face, mulling over this impossible situation.

Ashley knows her own mind, but I don't think she realizes the severity of the hurt she endured when Mr. Low Life broke her heart. She's blaming it on herself, which is not helpful and probably not too healthy from an emotional standpoint. It's been going on too long. I know Marina is concerned. I can see it in her face whenever Ashley pulls out the Dragon Lady persona.

I check my blind spot as I merge onto the highway, pulling into the steady stream of traffic. It's a beautiful day today, but there's a cloud over me. Because, just to complicate things further, yeah…I'm interested. Ashley is beautiful and fun and so talented. I don't even have to talk to her. I'm happy just being in the same room with her. Straight up, asking her out isn't the answer. She'd just shoot me down and then distance herself, which would only make things awkward between us while we're helping with Zach and Marina's wedding. I've thought about it for a while and I just can't see my way out of the friend zone.

Traffic moves at a steady pace, and I settle into it, letting my mind mull over the problem at hand. Yep. I've got a problem. With a dragon. I laugh under my breath at how ridiculous that sounds as traffic slows to a crawl. I pull up behind a moving van with a cartoon bee lounging inside a well-appointed bee hive, a big smile on his face. A banner underneath reads, "Busy bees trust us to get their hive cozy and move-in ready". There's a cute little lady bee looking in the window, obviously smitten with the bee lounging comfortably in his new domain.

None of this makes any sense, of course, because don't bees have a queen? And wouldn't she be pretty upset to find one of her guys just lounging around instead of doing his work? It doesn't matter. I don't care about the sexual politics of bees, but this absolutely gives me an idea. Maybe a good one.

Maybe I don't need to spend any more energy thinking up ways to get out of the friend zone. I don't need to break out. I need Ashley to unlock the door, so maybe I need to make it my own. I'm gonna own the friend zone. I'll set up house in there. I'll hang curtains, buy new furniture. I'll make it look like I'm having so much fun in her friend zone maybe she'll wonder why I'm not trying to get out. I'll be like my buddy the bee here—lounging around and having a great time until maybe I find Ashley looking in the window at me realizing I'm the thing she's missing. I can't decide whether it's completely brilliant or absolutely crazy, but the very idea has me smiling ear to ear in bumper-to-bumper traffic as I work out all the possibilities.

***

Ashley

I'm still wondering about the box of my mom's things as I walk up to the front of Wahoo Tacos at Fisherman's Wharf, which is my dad's favorite place to eat in the entire universe. He's already seated at our usual table on the patio, and he waves at me as a huge grin spreads across his face. I smile and wave back, then swing open the door and step inside. I nod hello to our favorite waitress, Patti, and make my way through the crowded restaurant to the patio in the back. I step outside and straight into my Dad's arms for a hug.

"There's my beautiful girl."

His rich, deep voice vibrates against my cheek as I'm crushed by his big arms. All my stress melts away for a few moments.

"Hi, Daddy," I mumble against his shirt, wrapping my arms around him and giving him a squeeze.

He squeezes me so hard that my face smushes against his white shirt, and I'm immediately glad I decided not to bother with make-up this morning. I let go, but he holds me tight until I begin to giggle, then he releases me. We settle into our chairs, and I inhale the fresh San Francisco Bay air.

"What's up, kid?" Dad asks as he eyes me curiously. "You only call me Daddy when you're worried about something."

I smirk. That's not entirely true, but it is today.

"Just thinking about Mom's stuff," I say quietly as Patti appears at our table with a bright smile.

"Good morning, friends," she greets with her usual sunshine, setting a glass of ice water in front of me and putting a steaming cup of coffee in front of Dad. "The usual?"

We both nod, and she disappears again. Dad's expression sobers.

"Sorry, kiddo," he says as he shifts in his seat. "I was poking around up there, and it took me by surprise. I thought it might be some old toys of yours, but I looked inside and saw some of your Mom's things. It didn't feel right to go through it without you there."

I nod. "And you shouldn't have to. What if there's something in there to upset you?"

His eyes meet mine, and my heart hurts over the sadness I find.

"She could be gone a hundred years, and I'll still miss her like it happened yesterday."

Silver lines my eyes, but I silently will the tears not to fall. I nod.

"Me too," I mutter, trying to force a smile. "But we'll get through it. We've got each other."

The corners of his mouth turn up slightly. "We sure do."

I turn my face into the sun's warmth and sigh contentedly. We're blessed with another beautiful day. I let the sun's warmth wash away the worry.

"Hey," Dad whispers. "Let's look at it in a different light."

I smile. "Yeah?"

He nods. "The only thing I saw was a ball of yarn, but there could be a whole lot of happy memories in there that we get to find."

I reach out and cover one of Dad's hands with my own.

"You're right," I say lightly. "I mean, it's not like we'll find anything dark and disturbing. It's Mom's stuff. She was all light and love."

Dad squeezes my hand. "Just like you, my girl."

Guilt tugs at me. I haven't felt very light and loving lately, I realize. Greg really knocked me off course.

We chit chat for a bit about everything under the sun. His right hand man at work just became a grandfather. I update him on Marina's wedding. It's nice to catch up.

"Here we are, friends!" Patti says as she breezes in with her arms loaded down with plates. She sets our entrées down, then leaves condiments and more napkins before barreling back through the door.

"Thanks, Patti!" I call out just as she disappears again.

The heavenly smell of freshly grilled fish tacos hits my nostrils and everything is rosy in my world again. I pick one up and take a big bite, audibly groaning over how good it is. Dad chuckles as he digs into his fajitas.

"So what's new?" he asks with renewed gusto.

I shrug casually. "We text each other every day, Dad. Nothing new going on in my world since two o'clock yesterday."

He raises his eyebrows. "You never know. You could have bought a new dress or made a new friend. New boyfriend, even."

I nearly drop my taco. "No, thanks."

Dad puts his fork down. Uh oh. Incoming lecture in three...two....

"Honey, it's been more than a year."

I shrug again. "I'm not ready."

I look up in surprise when he mutters a curse under his breath. "I should've fired his sorry—"

"Dad!" I scold. "You can't just fire someone because they hurt my feelings."

Now it's Dad's turn to shrug like it's no big deal to fire someone for such a reason, and I fight back a laugh. I love that he's my biggest fan, but sometimes he can be unreasonable. I never should have dated Greg. It's my fault. I take another bite, even though I've lost my appetite.

"I never should have allowed it," he growls. "I knew he wasn't good enough for you. You just seemed so happy."

I think about his words while I chew, nodding. "I was happy for a while. But then I wasn't. So I have to work on that."

"Have to work on what? He's a jerk," Dad argues. "He's the one who needs to work on himself. You're perfect."

I laugh out loud. "Dad, c'mon. I think you might be a little biased."

He grins at me. "A little. Maybe. But he's still an idiot."

I nod. No dispute. But he isn't the only one.

"Actually, we need to talk about him," Dad hedges.

I look up immediately. "Why? We're eating. He's gross."

Dad nods. "Definitely gross, kiddo, but I need to warn you about something."

Okay, now I'm really not hungry. I put my hands in my lap and sit up straight, watching Dad expectantly.

"Tammi assumed I'd want the usual incentives for the sales team for the heart foundation fundraiser," he begins, looking guilty. "She's been my assistant so long I don't really check in on her. She knows to come to me if she needs to."

"Out with it, Dad."

"She let the sales team set a competition for a special bonus," he begins slowly. "The prize was two tickets to the fundraiser."

A wave of dread hits me. I know exactly where this is going. I close my eyes.

"Greg won the contest," Dad says heavily. "And he'll be sitting at our table."

Chapter 4

Dad's words echo in my head as if we were in a scene from a movie. Greg won tickets to the dinner. Greg, Destroyer of Hearts, is coming to the cardiac foundation dinner that I've organized for my Dad. My vision blurs as I look down at my plate and shake my head. Greg. The last person I ever wanted to see again.

"Honey, I'm so sorry."

I blink back tears and look up at my Dad, who looks like he'd love to crawl into a crack in the ground rather than have this conversation with me. Bad news like this used to make me fly off the handle right away, but when Dad had his heart attack, I learned to chill out a bit more. Over-dramatic Ashley doesn't make as many appearances now. I take a deep breath and consider the possibilities or lack thereof. I *have* to be there. I planned the entire event as a favor to Dad. I can't phone it in, nor would I want to—even if it means having to deal with someone Taylor Swift describes perfectly as The Smallest Man Who Ever Lived. Dad has built this business up into a highly successful investment firm. There are appearances to consider, not to mention the rules of running a business. He can't just take away the tickets

Greg earned, fair and square. I'm stuck, and I know it. Something inside me clicks into place.

"It's okay, Daddy," I say calmly.

He looks at me with regret etched on his face. I know in my heart he'd make the whole situation better if he could. He's stuck, just like me. And I'm not sure where it comes from, but I smile. I almost feel like I'm channeling my friend Merry, who always, *always* finds the best outlook for every situation. Or maybe it's Mom reaching down from heaven to say *Ashley Marie Roberts, I didn't raise you to have a one-woman pity party for yourself. You stand, and you deal.* Whatever it is, I feel my backbone beginning to grow a core of steel, and I sit up a little straighter.

"Maybe this is a test," I offer. "I just need to try to look at this a different way."

Dad raises his eyebrows but remains speechless.

"We can't change it. What did Mom used to say?"

Dad's eyes glisten, and he nods. "The only way out is through."

I stand and take a step over to Dad, planting a kiss on his cheek, then take my seat again.

"It'll be okay, Daddy," I say with renewed confidence. "We'll make it okay."

He smiles at me, and something like fatherly pride shines in his eyes. Since my appetite seems to have returned with my backbone, I pick up a taco and dig in.

"Okay, tough guy," Dad says, watching me with admiration. "Tell me how you're doing with the dinner then. What's the latest?"

"It's a week away. It's pretty much done, although I wish I had a few more big items for the silent auction."

He shrugs. "I'm sure it'll be great, honey. I know how hard you've worked on this for me. You're a wonder."

I smile sweetly and take another bite. This fundraising dinner is going to be great. He really has no idea. Marina's friend and events manager at The Mermaid Foundation, Hillary, helped me bling it all up nicely. I've invited the usual supporters. High-profile clients. Investors. Politicians. Philanthropists. Sitting here at Wahoo Tacos, you'd never know my Dad ran in the same social circles as the San Francisco elite, but he does. He's spent a lifetime forging those relationships, and I intend to leverage that.

I've hired professional photographers, and Dad's marketing team is doing all the public relations, but since it's a foundation that will raise money for heart health and Valentine's day is that same weekend, I wanted it to be extra special. The decor will be next level, and I can't wait for Dad to see it all come to life. Now Greg will be there. A wave of dread threatens to creep in, but I mentally shove it away. Fear isn't going to help me with this. I do need support, though, and there's only one thing to do about it. Well, two things. First, I'm going shopping after this so I can avoid the presence of a certain Viking god in my apartment. I need to think, and I can't think with him around. Second, I pull my phone out and open our girlfriend group chat as Dad excuses himself to go to the restroom.

Ashley: Emergency Conclave tonight. 7 pm. My place.

Merry: Chinese or do you want me to bring Nonno's?

Scarlet: You okay? Good news or bad news?

Marina: Does it matter? She called a conclave!

Scarlet: Just trying to figure out if I need to bring extra tissues. Or maybe a shovel and some rope.

I laugh at Scarlet. She totally would bring a shovel if I needed her to.

Ashley: Nonno's sounds great. I need help with a plan, ladies. Greg won a contest at work and now he's coming to the fundraiser.

Merry: Oh, crud! I'm adding cannoli. We're gonna need it.

Marina: We got this, Ash. See you tonight!

***

"Girl, you have nothing to worry about," Scarlet assures me from her perch on the floor. "When he sees you in that dress, you'll get your revenge for sure."

"What dress?" Marina cries. "I want to see it. Go put it on."

I toss a wadded-up napkin at Scarlet and shake my head at Marina before I grab at the last bread stick.

"First of all, I don't want revenge," I clarify adamantly, pointing the bread stick like a weapon. "Second, I am not putting on any dresses right now. We need to focus."

We've been talking for hours, and so far, the only thing we've decided is that Nonno's bread sticks could bring about world peace. But we already knew that.

Scarlet raises an eyebrow at me. "You don't want even a little revenge?"

"No! I just…I don't want to look like I haven't moved on from Greg."

"Dude, you *haven't* moved on," she deadpans.

Merry gasps. "Yes, she has!"

I hold up a hand. "I don't think she meant that I'm still pining over Greg, but she's right about the fact that I haven't *dated* anyone since Greg. I have no plus-one. Greg won two tickets. Odds are he has a plus-one."

"So we're talking about optics?" Marina asks. "That's not so hard."

"I can't fall madly in love with a guy in a week," I grumble, taking another sip of my wine. I'm starting to get that woozy, boneless feeling that tells me I need to put down the wine glass and pick up a bottle of water.

"Merry could," Scarlet jabs.

Merry huffs and throws a sock at her.

"It doesn't have to be real," Marina says with a mischievous grin. "It just has to *look* real."

My brows knit together in confusion. "What?"

"Get a male friend to go to the dinner with you so you can hang all over him and put Greg in his place," she says matter-of-factly.

Scarlet frowns. "She doesn't have any male friends. They can't get past the Dragon Lady long enough to be anything but a sad little pile of ash."

I open my mouth to object, then close it. I really can't argue about that. Some guys do try to stick it out in the hopes they'll escape the friend zone, but they all give up eventually.

Marina raises an eyebrow. "She does too have a male friend."

"Zach doesn't count. And he's too famous. Everyone knows who he is and that he's madly in love with you," Merry croons with a silly grin.

Marina aims a determined gaze at me. "Okay, she has *two* male friends. I wasn't talking about Zach."

It takes me about two seconds to get her point, and then I hold both hands up as if I'm warding off an attack.

"No way!"

She nods. "Yes way."

I shake my head. "I can't do that. I can't ask Rick."

Merry gasps. "Oh, he's perfect!"

I nod, wide-eyed. "Yes, he is. Exactly. He's too perfect. I can't ask him."

"Would he do it?" Scarlet asks Marina as if I'm not even in the room objecting to the idea.

Marina nods. "In a heartbeat."

"He would not, and I'm not going to ask him. It's too much."

Marina grins knowingly. "Which part?"

I raise my eyebrows in question.

"It's too much to ask? Of a friend? That's ridiculous. He'd totally do it," she says, tilting her head at me curiously. "Or is it too much of something else?"

I give her a knowing look. "Yes. It's too much to ask, and he's too…much."

"Well, since you've scared all the other boys away, it looks like he's your only choice," Scarlet chimes in. "Poor thing. You have to go on a fake date with a hot guy."

I shake my head. "No."

Marina throws her hands up. "It's one date! It's the perfect solution."

I look at Merry for support, but she just smiles and nods in agreement with Marina and Scarlet.

"Rick's a good guy," Marina presses. "And a loyal friend. You know him. He's not some schmoozy creep who will use the situation to his advantage. He would totally help you."

Her words finally give me pause. She's right about that. He isn't some creep from a bar just looking for a way to get close to me. In fact, he's had plenty of chances to press his advantage, but he hasn't. He's clearly fine with being in the friend zone. Considering all the perfect-looking women that must throw themselves in his path, he's probably not attracted to me at all—and for some reason, the idea rubs me the wrong way. I look up to find Marina looking at me like she knows exactly what I'm thinking.

"Okay, yeah," I groan. "You're right. He would do it. I just hate asking for favors."

Scarlet scoffs. "Dude, am I ever going to get my blue scarf back?"

"Yeah, you borrow my stuff all the time," Merry chimes in.

Marina giggles and raises a hand. "I could say the same. Is it just Rick you don't want to ask for a favor? I wonder why that is…"

"All right!" I yell, throwing my hands up in surrender. I shoot

Marina a withering look. "I'll ask him."

My three enabling girlfriends cheer, and I laugh under my breath. This is a disaster in the making. They may think I've made the right decision, but I have a rap sheet full of bad decisions when it comes to men. I'm going to end up looking like a complete idiot. Or hurt. I nudge Scarlet with my foot.

"Hand over the cannoli."

Scarlet grins and does as she's told. Merry gets up and starts gathering takeout containers.

"You guys and your man problems," she teases. "You should take after me. Go on lots of first dates, and that's all. They can't tie you up in knots if you only see them once."

Marina laughs from the kitchen as she begins washing wine glasses. "Worked out okay for me."

"I'm too busy to obsess over some guy tying me up in knots," Scarlet offers.

I stand up and stretch, facing my friends. "You're all blowing this out of proportion. Rick doesn't tie me up in knots."

That didn't come out like I meant it to, but I take a bite of my cannoli and chew with renewed determination.

Scarlet raises an eyebrow. "Maybe he should."

Merry bursts out laughing, and I roll my eyes.

"No, I mean…I…"

I take a deep breath and gather my frazzled thoughts. Yep, one too many glasses of wine. Maybe two.

"Okay, I just can't trust myself. Happy now? I make horrible decisions when it comes to men. And Rick? He's not just some guy. He's cute. Actually, he's more than cute. He's perfect. And he's my friend. My beautiful, hot, perfect man-friend. So I don't want to screw this up and make things funky between us by asking him a favor and making things weird…and now I'm babbling. I'm babbling. Like an idiot."

In fact, I'm so busy babbling that I don't realize Marina, Scarlet, and Merry aren't looking at me anymore. They're looking at something behind me. Or...someone, I realize, just as I hear Rick's voice behind my left ear.

"What favor?"

Zach passes me and heads straight for Marina in the kitchen. As if on cue, Scarlet and Merry grab their purses and coats.

"Oh geez, look at the time, gotta run!" Merry yelps as she tries to run over Scarlet, who isn't much better.

"Yeah, I gotta see a man about a horse..." she mutters.

"Stop!" I yell just as Scarlet's hand hits the door knob.

Everyone freezes. Everyone except Rick, who steps around to stand in front of me, looking down at me with those perfectly beautiful ocean-blue eyes. Eyes full of concern. I steal a glance and then turn to face my friends at the door.

"Get back here."

Eyes-wide, they both turn away from the door and walk back into the living room. Now, everyone is quiet and staring at me, waiting to see what my next move is. And now I've made it weird. Is that going to stop me? Nope. I look around at everyone, hoping I'm giving them a look of stern warning but feeling like I might just look deranged. I take a deep breath.

"No one is sprinting out of this apartment like I didn't just make a complete idiot of myself," I declare, instantly regretting it. What is my point right now?

Scarlet furrows her brow. "So...we're gonna openly talk about you making an idiot of yourself instead?"

Merry smacks her on the arm.

I heave a heavy sigh and look up at Rick, who is still looking at me with concern, but I also suspect he's fighting back laughter. I snap my fingers at everyone else.

"You guys carry on with your evening," I order, then turn to face Rick. "We just need a minute."

I grab Rick's huge Viking hand and pull him down the hall towards my bedroom, leaving everyone else slack-jawed where they stand. Meanwhile, I can't…absolutely can't ignore the fact that my entire hand disappears into his as he wraps his hand around mine. It feels too good. Too natural.

I don't stop pulling Rick behind me until I get him through my bedroom door, but I let go too soon and go spiraling towards the dresser. Rick lunges forward and catches me before I crash into it, carefully making sure I have my balance before letting me go. When he releases me, I'm instantly cold where his hands were touching and I want them back.

"Ash, are you okay?" Rick asks quietly. "How many glasses of wine did you drink?"

Does he notice *everything?* I can feel over-dramatic Ashley taking hold as I stomp my foot.

"Stop acting like you know me!" I whisper-yell.

He frowns, looking at me like I'm crazy. "I *do* know you."

I roll on my feet, and he catches me again, but this time he doesn't let me go. The heat from his hands on my shoulders threatens to melt me where I stand, and I finally realize I'm in way over my head here. I pinch the bridge of my nose between two fingers.

"Why don't you sit, Ash? Then we can talk," Rick says gently, turning me around and walking me to my bed. I plop down in defeat.

"I don't want to talk," I mutter.

Rick takes a step back, regarding me with widening eyes. "What? Ash, you can't be that drunk…"

"No!" I cry out. "Um…that's not what I meant. Oh my gosh, I dragged you into my bedroom and said I don't want to talk, implying—

I just did that, didn't I? Sorry. I'm not making any moves."

Rick laughs softly. "Calm down, Ash. It's okay. I get hit on a lot."

"No, oh my gosh, Rick! I'm not hitting on you, I swear!"

Now he's just full-out laughing. I squint up at him.

"You're teasing me."

He nods solemnly, the corners of his mouth turned up just slightly. "I'm teasing you. But it probably wasn't very nice. I apologize."

I shrug, resignation pressing on me. "It's okay. I'm ridiculous right now."

"You're *not* ridiculous. You're just a little tipsy. And wired up. It's kind of fun seeing you like this."

I look up at my beautiful, hot, perfect man-friend. I didn't say that out loud, did I? I can't remember. His expression is soft as he watches me.

"Fun?"

He smiles. "The Dragon Lady never lets go like this."

I raise my eyebrows in question, but he changes the subject.

"Didn't you say you wanted to ask me something? A favor?"

I nod slowly. "I do, but I think my mouth has done enough damage for one day."

He squats down in front of me, his eyes roaming over my face.

"I'll be over tomorrow to start work on the bookcases. How about then?"

"Okay," I reply in surrender as much as resignation, forcing myself to keep eye contact despite my embarrassment.

"Okay," he parrots, putting one of his large hands over mine and squeezing. "Are you gonna be okay? Should I send the girls in?"

I huff and shake my head. "No, I'm just going to crawl into bed and try to forget the last thirty minutes happened."

Rick laughs softly as he stands. He ruffles my hair and then heads for the doorway.

"Don't worry, Ash, I'll remind you of all the gory details tomorrow."

I groan and throw myself back onto the mattress. I have no doubt there's a ton of teasing coming my way tomorrow. I know because I would do exactly the same thing.

"Hey, Ash?" Rick's voice floats toward me from the doorway.

I don't look up. "Yeah?"

"Whatever the favor, the answer will be yes. See you tomorrow."

By the time I look up, he's gone.

***

Rick

Ashley thinks I'm hot. No, not just hot. What did she call me? Her beautiful, hot, perfect man-friend. I'm making the drive back to Mill Valley with the biggest, dumbest smile on my face. I mean, I shouldn't. It doesn't mean anything. She was pretty toasted. But I think it also means a little something.

I don't even know why I'm this happy about it. I've always been pretty content in life without anything but a casual relationship once in a while. But something shifted in me the minute I saw Ashley for the first time, and it has stayed with me. She pulls my attention whenever she's near. Even if we're not in the same conversation. I'm aware of her. I hear her laugh from across the room and lose track of what I'm saying. I didn't think much about it at first because she was engaged. End of story. Now, she isn't, but there's the Dragon Lady to contend with. I do see the real Ashley from time to time. Since I'm Zach's best friend, I'm around a lot…and when Ashley lets her guard down it's like the whole room lights up. I love trying to make her laugh for just that reason.

I chew on my lip as I wait for the light to change. I always assumed it was easy for Ash to keep me in the friend zone because she didn't find me attractive. Now? Well, now I'm her beautiful, hot, perfect man-friend. Sure, some of that was just Ashley's sass…which I think is adorable and fun. The biggest take away here is that she does find me attractive, and that's huge. Has the Dragon Lady gone? No. Is that going to stop me? Also no. The light turns green, and I pull my truck forward onto the road that will take me over the Golden Gate Bridge. I let the steady rhythm of the bridge panels thumping under my tires lull me into a deep, ruminative state.

I still like my original plan. Move into the friend zone, set up house, and show her what she's missing. With the added confirmation that she does find me attractive, it almost feels like I have a shot. I wish I knew what the favor is that she wanted to ask, but Marina wouldn't tell me when I asked on my way out. Their inner circle is tight, so I didn't even try to argue. Besides, Zach was getting an ear full from Marina about learning to call first before barging in on one of their conclaves. I said goodnight and headed home. I needed time to think, anyway, and I might throw some laundry in the washing machine before I go to bed. Because this beautiful, hot, perfect man-friend needs to look good tomorrow. I'm building bookshelves and granting favors.

Whatever this favor is…it's hanging in the air all around me. Ash prides herself on her independence. Except for her inner circle, she doesn't ask others for things—so she must be desperate. My gut twitches at the thought of her needing something that bad. She should have whatever she needs, so I meant what I said. Whatever it is, my answer is yes. I just really wish I knew what it is. It might help me prepare. Like, is it a huge favor? It can't be money. Her dad is wealthy. It's got to be something else. Something she can't get from her inner circle. Or Zach.

Before I know it, I'm rolling up my long driveway and pulling into my garage. I get out of the truck and key in the code for my alarm system on the panel next to the door, then step into the kitchen. The inside of the house is dark, so the woods outside are illuminated by my landscape lighting. It looks beautiful and serene, and I find myself wondering what Ash would think of it. I'm not sure how any of this will play out at this point, but I know one thing—I definitely want to see where it goes.

Chapter 5

Ashley

I pull my car into the garage and immediately note that the lumber pile Rick deposited in here a few days ago is noticeably smaller. That means there's a Viking god in my living room right now. I'm careful to avoid the various power tools he has set up around the perimeter of the garage as I maneuver the car all the way in and put it in park.

I grab my purse and tote bag out of the car and go inside, mentally noting that it's just after 4 pm. Marina won't be upstairs for about two and a half hours, so if I don't want an audience when I ask Rick to go on a fake date with me, I need to do it soon. I still feel a little weird about it, but I've just spent the last recess at school trying to get little Timmy Nolan to stop licking all the playground equipment, so asking Rick for this favor doesn't put me in a panic like it did yesterday.

I step into the first-floor lobby and check our mailbox, then climb the stairs to our apartment, juggling a few magazines, my keys, and my bags. Once I'm inside, I toss my keys into the bowl on the entry table and plop the magazines next to it.

"Ash?" Rick calls, his deep, rich voice reaching through the apartment to find me.

My pulse picks up at the sound of his voice, and I follow it to the living room. I am completely unprepared for lumberjack Rick. All the air leaves my lungs like the time I landed wrong coming down the big kid's slide at the school where I work. I was trying to show a little girl that the slide was fun and ended up landing hard on my butt and knocking the wind out of myself. That's how I feel in this moment: knocked on my butt, no air.

Rick is wearing jeans that seem to have been hand-stitched onto his body by fairies. The fit is so perfect it should be illegal. And he's wearing another Henley, this one is smoky gray and brings out the deep blue of his eyes. A small band of leather is around his wrist, and his hair is pulled into a knot at the back of his head. He's holding a drill in his hand and smiling at me as he sweeps a hand back toward a wall in the living room.

"Come and see," he says, stepping back.

I step past him, just catching a whiff of that sexy pine tree scent as I walk into the living room. The main wall of the living room is a long wall of exposed brick, against which sits our flat screen TV, various potted plants, and art…all lovingly chosen by Scarlet when she decorated for us. The adjacent wall has been cleared of furniture and decor, and Rick has already constructed the bones of a floor-to-ceiling bookcase. We have high ceilings, and the best word I can use to describe it is…epic. It's already amazing, and it's not even finished. I take it all in, imagining what it'll look like when the build is finished, and it's filled with books and decor.

"Wow."

Rick steps alongside me. So close that I can feel the heat from his body radiating out to my arm. My skin tingles lightly in response. I look up at him and find him watching me. I smile when our eyes meet.

"Is there nothing you can't do?"

He laughs softly and nudges me with an elbow. "Plenty. But thanks for the compliment, Ash."

I turn my attention back to the wall.

"Marina's the real book lover, but I get a few shelves. We talked about it."

"What books will you put on them?"

I adjust my tote bag on my shoulder.

"Scrapbooks, actually. I have a ton of them that my Mom made before she died, and I don't have a bookcase in my room. And maybe a few actual books."

Rick offers me a soft smile, but doesn't reply. Those deep blue eyes start pulling me in. Honestly, I think I could just stare at him all day long. That'd make things weird, though. I pry my eyes away and take a few steps toward my bedroom.

"I'll just go put my bags away," I say quickly, retreating down the hall to the safety of my room and shutting the door behind me.

I toss my bags on the chair by the window and flop on my bed.

Wow.

That wasn't weird at all, Ash.

I close my eyes against the wave of panic that threatens to make me completely lose my cool. This would be so much easier if Rick was unattractive. With warts. Maybe even a zit. But I honestly can't picture Rick looking anything but perfect. I'll bet he never even needed braces as a teenager.

I sit up.

This is ridiculous.

What is my issue here, exactly? Rick is my friend, and I have a problem. I need help. This is no different from asking anyone in my inner circle for help. Except he's a guy. No, that's not it. I'm fine around a lot of guys. I'm even spicy nice when needed. Rick is different, and it comes back to the fear that if I screw up with him,

I can't just shut him out of my life like anyone else. He'll be around Zach…and Zach is marrying Marina. We'll be friends-in-law for life.

I get up, pull my top off, and toss it into the hamper in my bathroom. Sweet little Rowan Carpenter accidentally smeared me with paste while we were working on our art projects today, and I reek of it. Thankfully, nothing got on my jeans. Right now, I just want to be comfortable if I'm going to have to humble myself to the Viking god, so I rifle through my closet until I find my favorite t-shirt. I yank it off the hanger, throw it over my head and comb through my long, wavy blond hair on the way to the kitchen. Rick is putting his tools away as I come back down the hallway.

"All done for the day?" I ask breezily, whisking into the kitchen and pulling out what I need to make dinner.

Rick puts his work bag in the entry by the door, then comes over and sits at the kitchen island. He doesn't seem very talkative right now, and I wonder if it's because he's waiting for me to ask The Favor or if I made things weird last night, and I can't remember.

"Pretty much," he replies with a nod. "The framing is finished and I want to try to be done with all the hammering by the time you get home from work every day. No one wants to hear that."

I busy myself by pulling out my big baking dish and all the prep tools I'll need, and I try to ignore the fact that Rick's eyes follow me wherever I go.

"Are you making something?"

I set the last dish down and open the fridge to start pulling out ingredients.

"It's my night to make dinner," I answer, shuffling back to the counter with an arm load of stuff.

Rick nods. "What do you do on Marina's night to cook? Zach told me she doesn't really cook."

I laugh. "No, but she's great at ordering takeout or heating frozen meals or leftovers."

He grins at me. "I guess we all have our strengths."

I nod and point to the baking dish in front of me. "And one of my strengths is my lasagna."

His face lights up. "Yeah?"

"You're welcome to stay for dinner. Marina and Zach won't be upstairs until around 7 pm, so if you stay, I'm going to put you to work."

He stands quickly and takes a bow. "I'm all yours."

Oof.

I'll take Things You Shouldn't Say to Ashley for $5,000, Alex.

I knit my brows together.

"How good are you at browning Italian sausage?" I ask with a hand on my hip.

He scoffs. "The best."

I step back and gesture at the stovetop, and he jumps into action. I grab the pasta pot and fill it with water.

"How was work today?" he asks easily as he starts breaking up the sausage in the pan.

"Oh, it was okay. One of the kids smeared me with paste pretty well, but otherwise it was uneventful."

Rick's rich laugh fills the kitchen.

"So that's why you changed your shirt."

I nod. "Guilty. I didn't want to smell like paste for one more minute."

"Can't blame you for that," he says, giving me a curious look when I perch on one of the bar stools to watch him work.

I point to the pasta pot on the stove top. "I can't do anything else 'til that boils. You got the short end of the stick, my friend."

He turns away from the pan to face me for a minute, a mischievous grin slowly spreading on his face.

"Friend? Don't you mean 'beautiful, hot, perfect man-friend'?"

The horror is instantaneous, and it hits me like one of those instant replay slow-motion shots in sports. My face gets hotter and hotter. I want to crawl under the kitchen island and never be found.

No, no, no.

I didn't say that in front of him, did I?

I did, though. I know it. I felt the truth of it in that evil grin of his. My hands fly up to my cheeks.

"Oh, no," I mutter, slowly lowering my head to the kitchen island.

The marble top is cool against my cheek, which is good because I plan to stay here.

"Oh, Rick, please tell me I'm dreaming. Or having a nightmare. I did not say that to you, did I?"

He turns back to the pan, the grin still plastered on his perfect face, nodding.

"Do you know how much it's been killing me to keep that inside?"

I pull myself back up to a sitting position and cover my face with my hands. I can never look at him again. I'll never live this down. Ever.

"I'm so, so sorry," I say through my hands. "In my defense, I—"

I smell his piney woods scent a split second before I feel the warmth of his hands wrap around my wrists. I look up through two barely separated fingers. I didn't even hear him move.

"Hey," he says gently. "There's no reason for a defense. I was only teasing."

I go back to hiding my face. "Yes, there is."

He brushes his fingers down my arm, and my skin erupts in goosebumps.

"Ash," he says softly.

I peek up through my fingers to find him watching me with concern.

"I'm sorry I teased you. C'mon. We can act like it didn't happen."

I shake my head. "I'm so sorry, Rick. Was it bad? I honestly don't remember. Did I make you feel uncomfortable?"

His hands gently pull my hands away from my face. He doesn't let go. His grip is strong and reassuring as he looks into my eyes. This is more than embarrassment. I don't want Rick to look at me differently. He's literally the only guy who behaves normally around me.

"Of course not."

He pulls me up off the bar stool, so I'm standing in front of him, clasping our hands together. I'm trying and failing to ignore how nice it feels as I look into his face.

"You had a little too much wine and some things came out of your mouth that I know you probably never would have shared. That's all. You weren't weird or inappropriate. You were actually very cute about it. Okay?"

I look at him hesitantly for a few moments. I know he's sincere, but I still feel terrible. I squeeze his hands.

"If you're sure…"

He squeezes back. "I'm sure. We're still friends. You're still my best man coach, right? In fact, didn't you have a favor you wanted to ask me? I owe you one anyway."

Nope! Not happening. I look away and shake my head. Ask him for a fake date after I basically confessed my attraction for him? He'll think the fake date is just a ploy to get closer to him.

"I can't ask it now."

"Yes, you can. It must be important. You don't usually ask for favors."

I close my eyes for a moment and try to evaluate which is worse. Asking Rick for this favor or showing up dateless to Dad's dinner, knowing that Greg will absolutely do everything he can to show me how awful my life is without him. The answer is pretty clear. Greg is the jerk who broke my heart twice and is not to be trusted. Rick is my friend, who has never hurt me and is an all-around good guy. So, baring my soul to ask this favor is the path with the least risk. I open my eyes, reaching deep to scrounge up every bit of courage I can muster. He smiles down at me warmly.

"If it helps, I already told you I'd say yes."

Something behind his eyes brings my sass back to life. I smirk at him.

"Yeah? What if I need a million dollars?"

He smirks back. "We both know your Dad can handle that. Try again."

I think for a moment, looking him up and down as if I'm trying to figure out what'll make him say no. He squints at me and lifts his chin, challenging me. Game on.

"I need a partner for bull riding lessons."

He nods. "Okay, sure. But that's not it."

I sigh. "I'm going to start medical school, and I need someone to practice drawing blood."

He leans forward a little, and I suddenly remember we're still holding hands. I start to pull them away, but he squeezes my hands and shakes his head.

"Not letting go until you tell me what it is."

Okay. Courage. I lick my lips subconsciously and squeeze his hands for support.

"You can totally say no, and I won't be upset," I begin. "After the whole beautiful, hot, perfect man-friend thing, I would completely understand."

He nods and waits.

"Do you remember my fiancé, Greg?"

Rick makes a face like someone served him pickle-covered chocolate chip cookies.

"I never had the displeasure of meeting the moron, but yes. I remember him."

My eyebrows nearly hit my hairline in surprise.

"I think that's the meanest thing I've ever heard you say!"

He squeezes my hands again. "I'm not mean. I'm spicy nice."

Laughter bubbles up out of me, and I throw my head back and just let it out. I may be getting some kind of contact high from being this close to Rick for so long. I feel myself letting go a little, and, for once, it's not scary. I focus back on the task at hand.

"I found out yesterday that he's going to be at Dad's dinner."

Again, with the sour expression. He gets it. He gets me, I think.

"Yeah," I continue. "He won two tickets in a sales contest at work, which means he's bringing a date."

I see it click immediately in Rick's expression.

"I can see why that would suck," he says flatly. "That was the reason for the emergency conclave last night?"

I nod. "And the solution we came up with is…well, I was wondering if you would consider going with me?"

The corners of his mouth slowly turn up. "Ash, please tell me you weren't this scared to ask me for a date."

"Fake date," I interject quickly. "And you can totally say no. I don't want you to feel awkward or uncomfortable after…what I said last night."

He squeezes my hands once more and then lets me go. Bummer. Then he puts his hands on my shoulders. Better.

"First of all, it was a compliment," he says sweetly. "I'm flattered to be your beautiful, hot, perfect man-friend—although I'm far from perfect. And you didn't, and never could, make me feel uncomfortable, Ash."

He says it with such gentle conviction I finally believe it. And I'm filled with gratitude. I realize that gratitude has everything to do with the fact that our friendship is still intact and nothing to do with me being a complete idiot and him still saying yes. I think I need to unpack this later when I have a moment.

"And second of all?" I prompt with a smile.

"Yes, I will absolutely be your fake date."

Before I talk myself out of it, I throw my arms around Rick's neck and hug him as hard as I can. I feel his arms wrap around my waist, and, wow, this is the best hug I've ever had in my whole life. Our first hug, and now I'm addicted. There absolutely will be more hugs. I can't go back to living in a world with no Rick hugs. No bueno. I pull away, and he lets go.

"Thank you so much, Rick."

He nods, and I suddenly realize we are cooking dinner when I nearly meltdown from embarrassment.

"The pasta!" I cry out, running around him to get back in the kitchen.

Thankfully, the water is boiling and Rick had the good sense to take the pan off the burner so the sausage doesn't burn. I grab the box of lasagna noodles and open it, then drop them into the water carefully. I lean over and set the timer for the pasta. Rick follows me into the kitchen and moves the pan back to the burner.

"So when is this big dinner thing?"

"Next Saturday," I reply, turning away from the pasta pot and leaning a hip against the counter. "Valentine's Day weekend. And it's kind of fancy. Is that okay?"

"No problem," he says easily. "I have a few suits. I just don't wear them much."

I nod. "Great. Thanks again."

I grab the other ingredients and start blending the cheese mixture while Rick continues cooking the sausage. We work quietly for a few minutes. It's nice to just hang out together, especially now that I don't have the pressure of the unasked favor hanging over me.

"So tell me more about this dinner," Rick says as he gives the sausage a stir.

"It's a fundraiser for a charity my Dad started," I explain. "His assistant would normally coordinate something like this for him, but he has her on so many other projects he asked me for help."

"Sounds like a big job."

I nod. "It is, but I've done this kind of thing for him before. Besides, I could never tell him no."

"You guys seem really close."

"He's the best," I say with a smile. "What about you? Are you close with your family?"

Rick scoops the cooked sausage onto a paper towel for draining, then sets the pan aside to cool before turning to me.

"Not close to my dad," Rick says quietly. "He left when I was pretty young. He's on his third wife. But I'm pretty tight with my mom and sister."

"Was it hard to grow up without your dad? I can't imagine not having mine."

He shrugs. "It's hard to miss something you never really had. He still taught me things, but most of it was what kind of man I didn't want to be."

The frankness of his reply reaches right through my ribs and tugs at my heart. I've always liked Rick because he's a nice guy and, let's face it, what's not to like? But I realize now that there are qualities about him I've overlooked. He has a quiet consistency about him that I have a new appreciation for. And he's one hundred percent different from the average guy who hits on women like me in bars and restaurants. I don't just like him. I *really* like him. No wonder he pulls my attention any time he's near.

"What are you thinking about so sternly?" he asks. "Did I make things too serious?"

I give the cheese mixture a final stir and shake my head at him.

"Not at all. I just wish more men were like you."

Yikes. Did I just say that out loud?

He watches me curiously.

"Yeah? Care to elaborate?"

I grab the lasagna pan as the timer for the pasta ticks closer to zero, and I shrug.

"You're a gentleman, for one. And the world needs more of you."

"Thank you," he says with a warm smile that makes my pulse quicken. "I try to be."

I drain the pasta, thankful to have something to focus on other than those deep blue eyes watching me. We work in tandem, assembling the lasagna like we're just any couple making dinner together on a random weeknight. It's so nice, and I realize Greg and I never had times like this. He was all about fine dining and expensive wine. I realize I'm staring at Rick again, so I grab the assembled lasagna and nod at Rick to open the oven door.

"Well, let's get this in the oven so it's ready when Zach and Marina get here."

Rick opens the oven door for me, and I slide the pan inside just as my phone rings. Rick closes the oven door, then jumps and pulls his phone from his pocket. He holds it up for me to see that Zach is calling him. I grab my phone off the counter. Marina is calling. I swipe my finger across the screen to answer.

"Hey, girl. Dinner will be ready—"

"Ash, hey! I just called to tell you I won't be up for dinner. Hillary and I have to take care of something, and I'm not sure how long it'll take."

I look up at Rick, who is busy talking.

"Uh...okay," I say quietly so Rick doesn't overhear. "Rick is here... Zach is still coming for dinner, right?"

"I've got to run, Ash. See you soon!"

Click.

She hung up?

She hung up.

I stare at my phone, dumbfounded.

"What?" Rick mutters into his phone. "That makes no sense. Well, no. I guess if you can't, you can't. Okay, see you later."

Rick hangs up and smiles at me sheepishly.

"That was Zach. He's skipping out on dinner."

I frown, instantly suspicious. What is going on here…

"Same for Marina."

Rick smirks. "Smooth."

I laugh softly, relieved that he's just as suspicious as I am. Whatever they're up to, I should put a stop to it immediately. But I don't want to. It's nice having Rick here, and it wouldn't be very polite if I let him help me make dinner and then kicked him out the door, would it? No. It sure wouldn't.

"I guess it's just us then," I say pensively, watching his expression for a glimpse of how he feels about that. "If you'd still like to stay for dinner, that is."

I'm rewarded with a handsome smile. "I'd love to stay. Thanks, Ash."

I nod and pull a baking sheet out of the cabinet so I can make some bread sticks.

"Wait," Rick says. "On one condition."

I freeze, watching him in anticipation. What possible condition could he have? I can't think of a thing.

He levels his gaze at me. "I'll stay as long as you promise to keep the Dragon Lady locked up. I want to spend the evening with my friend Ashley without the fear of getting scalded by dragon fire. How about it?"

Chapter 6

Rick

Ashley looks up at me in surprise, and a little pride wells up in me for having caught her off guard. I raise an eyebrow as I wait for her reply. A challenge. She stands up a little straighter as she faces me.

"I've never turned the Dragon Lady on you."

I nod. "True, but I can count on one hand the number of times we've been alone together. I don't want you to get the wrong idea from me and suddenly bring the Dragon Lady out."

She laughs but looks chagrined. "No need to worry, Rick. You're safe with me."

Wrong. I'm not safe at all, I can feel it. It would be so easy to fall for her and I'm not sure what I'm going to do about it. I just need to stick to the plan right now—let her see that I'm completely content in her friend zone.

"Good," I say quickly. "Because there's nothing between us, right?"

She looks at me in confusion, and I swear I think I see a little disappointment. Maybe that's just foolish hope talking. I decide to double down.

"You don't want anything from me," I say pointedly. "Except for friendship, of course."

She blinks a few times. "Yes, of course."

I hold my hand out to her, and she looks down at it as if she's not sure what to do. Our eyes meet, and I smile softly.

"Shake on it?"

She gives me an approving smile and puts her hand in mine. I marvel at how delicate and small her hand is as I close my fingers around it and shake, trying to ignore the ridiculous level of joy I feel at this slight contact. It's a bread crumb compared to what we could have together if she would let me in, but I'll take it. Gladly. I let go of her hand, and she pulls away quickly to set the timer on the oven.

"What would you like to drink?" she asks, moving to the refrigerator. "Wine? Beer? Soda? We have everything."

I step over to the fridge and lean just slightly into her space, reaching for a bottle of soda from behind her. She turns in surprise, and those bright blue eyes meet mine. Her gaze flicks briefly to my mouth, then back up again. She smells like some kind of flower I can't quite identify. And sunshine, if it had a fragrance. I smile down at her.

"You don't have to play hostess, Ash," I say quietly. "I know my way around here pretty well."

She clears her throat and grabs a diet soda before closing the fridge, and the spell is broken. She eyes me curiously.

"You don't have to fuss over me. That's all I meant."

She shrugs. "What if I want to fuss over you?"

Now, it's my turn to look curious. I wait for an explanation.

"Going to this dinner with me is a huge favor," she clarifies. "You deserve some fussing."

I shake my head. "You're my best man coach. You're doing me a favor too."

I loop an arm through hers and start coaxing her into the living room. She smirks up at me.

"Rescuing me from looking like a fool in front of my ex-fiancé isn't the same as helping you with your best man duties."

She plops into her favorite spot on the love seat, already pulling the throw out of the basket so she can burrow underneath like an adorable mole. I sit in the chair as usual and set my drink down on the end table. She takes a sip of her diet soda and I shake my head at her.

"He's the fool, not you."

Her eyebrows shoot up at my words, and a charged silence hangs between us. I just wait, wondering if she's going to ask me what I mean. She nods and presses her lips into a thin line as she suppresses a smile.

"No wine for you either?" I ask with a grin.

I'm driving later, but she's home. She can drink what she wants.

She shakes her head. "After what I said to you the last time? Precautions must be made."

I chuckle and twist the cap off my soda.

"Give yourself a break, Ash. I told you it was a compliment, and there's no harm done."

She laughs self-consciously, then tucks her legs underneath her. I reach forward and grab the end of the throw, wrapping it around her and tucking it in so she's completely covered. Snug. I feel her eyes watching me as I tuck her in, a slow smile spreading across her face.

"You don't have to fuss over me," she says with a secret smile, teasing.

I raise my chin. "What if I want to fuss over you?"

She smirks and shakes her head. "Change of subject. I know what we can do to kick up the engagement party."

I sit up at the edge of my chair. "Spill it."

"Four words: bridal party flash mob."

"Yeah?"

Not gonna lie. I'm intrigued. And impressed. I love her imagination and passion for the people she loves.

She nods excitedly. "Think about it. When we're done with dinner and, people are walking around chatting with each other, and the music starts. They'll start looking around, wondering what's up. Then I pop up and start singing the first verse while you grab your guitar. You sing the second verse, and we keep trading off."

I fall back in my chair. I love this idea. It's a perfect tribute to our best friends. And I can't lie…the idea of singing with Ashley is all kinds of fun. I nod my approval.

"I'm in. What are we singing?"

Her whole face lights up when I say I'm on board. My heart skips a beat just seeing it. She really is such a beauty, especially when her guard is down.

"Marry You!" she exclaims.

A slow grin spreads on my face. "Bruno Mars. It's perfect, Ash."

"Do you think we can get Jimmy and Sam to play? I can guarantee Merry and Scarlet on backup vocals," she says excitedly.

Jimmy and Sam are the other two members of our band, and I know they'll jump at the chance to add this personal touch to Zach and Marina's engagement party. The four of us are more like brothers than band mates.

"For sure," I confirm, earning a sweet smile from Ashley.

"You're singing the chorus with me, right? Together?" she asks, her teeth biting her lower lip.

I grin mischievously. "Absolutely. I can't have you hogging all the fame and fortune for yourself."

She lets out a lyrical, hearty laugh and I feel way too much pride over the fact that I made it happen.

"No chance of that," she says with a shrug. "Marina has the real voice. I'm only okay. But I'm confident enough to know I can handle this."

I'm tempted to argue with her. She has a beautiful singing voice, different from Marina's but just as strong and pleasing to the ear. I'm still testing the boundaries of the friend zone, though, and I don't want to end up looking like I'm trying to flatter her too much.

"Okay, I'll tell Jimmy and Sam. Anything else?"

She's thoughtful for a moment, chewing at her bottom lip.

"What are you wearing to the party?" she asks.

I don't miss that she looks me over, and her eyes linger a little too long on my shoulders. Her question also confirms I'm in a little over my head with this whole best man thing. Musicians don't really have to think about dress codes.

"Um…" I hedge. "Whatever you tell me to wear?"

The smile I get in reply could light up the sun.

"How about cocktail attire? Does that help?"

I heave a huge sigh of relief. "Okay, good. No tie then."

"You hate ties?"

I purse my lips in thought. "Hate is probably a strong word. I prefer not to wear them, but I will. I'd rather be comfortable."

She nods. "Well, I can't think of anything else you need to think of right now. Most best man duties happen closer to the wedding. I'll be on maid of honor duty for a whole year. You're getting off easy."

I tilt my head at her. "That doesn't seem fair. Need any help?"

"Oh, I've got this," she says, waving a hand in the air. "It's all dress shopping and favor making. Things like that."

I gently nudge her leg with my foot. "I owe you, then. For best man job training."

She raises an eyebrow. "You don't. You're doing me a favor too. A bigger one."

I shake my head firmly. "This'll be easy and, quite frankly, a pleasure to kick Greg down a notch or two."

She looks surprised. "Why do you dislike him so much? You never even met him."

I know I can't tell her why. Not really.

"It's not something I can put into words right now," I say, treading carefully. "I just don't like anyone who hurts my friends."

Her blue eyes flick to mine in a mixture of sadness and gratitude. I can't figure her out. She's the only woman I've ever met who constantly surprises me. I decide not to spend this rare time with Ashley alone to worry about what's in her head or her heart. I'm simply going to enjoy the time we have, but I do need to ask a few questions.

"So I think we should talk about rules," I say, prompting a curious look from Ashley. "What's okay and not okay in fake dating?"

"Oh, I guess that's smart. Yes, let's. What's okay?"

I shake my head. "This is your fake date. You're the boss."

She grins. "Ooh, I like being the boss."

"Holding hands?"

She doesn't even have to consider that one.

"Of course. Also hugs. Wrapping your arm around me. All okay."

I nod. "Good. What about other physical touches?"

She looks confused. There's an adorable crinkle right between her eyebrows.

"If you were my girlfriend and we were out somewhere, I might reach over and put a hand on your leg if we're sitting close. Or I might kiss the top of your head. Or just…hold you."

She chews on her lower lip for several seconds, then pulls the blanket off her lap and sits up.

"You do those things?" she asks in a voice that has an almost imperceptible wobble.

"Sure. But then…I'm a hugger. I'm physically affectionate. I'm sure some other guys are different."

"They sure are," she mutters, focusing on the rug.

Something about her changes, and I wonder if I've said too much. I nudge her leg with my foot, and she looks up at me.

"You okay?"

Her eyes drift back to the spot on the carpet that's fascinating her so much.

"Greg never did any of those things."

I hesitate for a moment, suddenly aware that something I said hit a nerve.

"Well, I think we've established that he was a huge jerk. Right?"

She nods, still staring.

"I'm just realizing…I like all those things," she says in a hushed voice. "Holding hands. Sitting close. Just being held. Those things are all really nice."

I smile softly. "They are."

"It just clicked in my head when you were talking that Greg only did those things when other people were around to see it."

I have to use every muscle in my body to keep myself in this chair. I want to get up right now, scoop Ashley up, and hold her in my arms until she can't even remember who that idiot Greg is. I lean forward in my chair and take her hand in mine.

"Ash, I'm sorry," I say quietly. "You deserve so much better than that. So much more."

She nods. "I do, don't I?"

I squeeze her hand. "Absolutely you do. And you'll find it someday."

She rolls her eyes and laughs. "Everyone says that."

I laugh softly and nudge her again. "You can do anything you set your mind to. But maybe it's time to think about retiring the Dragon Lady, huh?"

She shrugs. "Maybe. But maybe the right guy won't bring out the Dragon Lady either."

I grin, knowing I'm the only guy she knows who hasn't provoked the Dragon Lady. I wonder if she realizes it too.

***

Ashley

I pull into Dad's driveway on Saturday afternoon and park the car. I don't get out right away. I'm too busy staring at the dashboard, wondering how I drove almost 15 miles without realizing it. If I had an x-ray of my brain right now, I know exactly what it would show.

Rick.

After Marina and Zach ditched us the other night, we had a great dinner together. The conversation was light and easy, and I found myself relaxing for once and just enjoying his company. And that part about physical touches and fake dating? I'm surprised I didn't steam up the apartment windows from my reaction to hearing him talk about kissing the top of my head or holding me in his arms. But in my defense, his arms are pretty spectacular.

He's been in the apartment when I've gotten home from work every day since, and I've found that I've looked forward to going home even more. It's even helped me to not obsess about this box of Mom's stuff we're about to poke through. Rick's presence has made things lighter in a way I didn't expect.

I shake myself from my Rick stupor, grab my purse and pull myself out of the car. The air is still crisp, even in the warmer afternoon hours, and I hurry to the door because, yes, I forgot my jacket. I'm just reaching for the door with the key in my hand when Dad opens it, and I'm instantly enveloped in a big Dad hug. I squeeze back as best I can with my purse dangling from my arm and my keys in my other hand.

"Hi, Daddy."

He lets go so I can step inside, then closes the door behind us.

"Hey, my beauty," he croons with affection. "I brought the box down and put it in the living room. Should we just go for it?"

I smile at him warmly. "We're not likely to find anything else of hers, so yes…let's do it."

I put my purse on the table in the entry and follow Dad to the living room, where a fairly decent-sized box sits on the coffee table. It's covered in colorful flowers, and everything about it reminds me of my mom. She loved to organize things and never turned down a chance to buy these in her favorite department store. Dad comes to stand beside me, and we look at each other for a moment before he nods at me.

"Go ahead, honey," he says gently. "You do the honors."

I mentally brush away a fleeting sense of dread as I reach for the lid of the box. There's nothing here that can hurt me. It's Mom's stuff. Finding something of hers we haven't been through before is bringing up our loss and making it new all over again, and I know that's at the core of what's making me so edgy right now. I lift the lid off and toss it to the side.

Instant memories flood over me as I look into the box and see at least a dozen skeins of yarn and a coffee cup containing several sizes of crochet hooks. It looks like there are some magazines tucked in one side, with who knows what buried underneath all the skeins.

"Oh!" I exclaim softly, smiling up at Dad. "I'd forgotten that she used to crochet."

I reach into the box and start pulling out the skeins. The yarn is soft and good quality and doesn't appear to have suffered from living in Dad's attic. I count fifteen skeins total and five magazines with a few pages marked with sticky notes. I leave the coffee mug with the crochet hooks and pull out a large, sealed plastic bag. Turning it over in my hands, I can see that it's some kind of project she was working on at some point. I hold it up so Dad can see, and he forces a smile.

I want to know what it is, and I know Dad does, too, but it also feels a little weird. Whatever this is, Mom must have been working on it when she got sick. I feel like I'm holding a snapshot of her life in my hands, from before cancer took her from us. With one last look at Dad, I open the bag and pull out the contents.

There are two pieces, actually. There's a pink scarf she must have been working on when she put these things away. There's a crochet hook still attached to the section she was working on. There's also a finished scarf made of deep navy blue yarn, obviously for Dad. I hold it out for him, and he takes it from me, holding it with reverence.

"Well," Dad whispers as he looks at the scarf with a soft smile. "Hello, Maggie."

I feel tears well up in my eyes, but I'm smiling ear to ear as Dad wraps the scarf around his neck and grins at me. We both laugh softly, amazed and grateful for such a wonderful surprise.

"You look very handsome," I say, adjusting the scarf on Dad's neck.

I wipe a tear away as Dad holds one end of the scarf in his hands, studying the perfect work with misty eyes.

"She must have boxed this up soon after her diagnosis," Dad muses. "What a wonderful, wonderful gift to find after all these years."

I shake my head in wonder as I stroke a hand over the soft pink scarf. "She did such beautiful work, didn't she?"

Dad nods. "She always did. I'm sorry yours isn't finished, honey."

I smile. "It doesn't matter. I love it anyway."

He wraps an arm around my shoulder and gives me a little squeeze. "I don't suppose you ever learned how to crochet?"

I shake my head again. "She tried to teach me when I was about twelve, but I had no patience for it."

Dad gives me another squeeze. "Well, you were just a kid. And none of us knew what was coming our way."

I nod. "Well, there's no time like the present."

Dad looks at me curiously.

"I'm going to teach myself to crochet," I say with conviction.

"Yeah?"

I smile up at Dad. "A good friend recently told me I can do anything I set my mind to. I think it's time for me to make some changes. Try new things. This seems like a good place to start."

Chapter 7

Ashley

The first thing I hear when I walk into the back entrance of Nonno's is Scarlet and Merry laughing.

"He's gonna die. It's just that awesome!" Merry says excitedly.

"I love it."

I freeze in my tracks. That was Rick's voice. What's he doing here so early?

"Ashley, I know those footsteps," Scarlet calls out. "Get in here, girl!"

I hurry along and find my friends clustered together in the front entrance to Nonno's, looking at some huge cardboard thing.

"Sorry, guys," I say as I come up behind them to see what they're looking at. "I—"

I'm rendered speechless at the sight before me. My hands drift up to my cheeks as the first wave of laughter hits. Merry, Scarlet and Rick back up so I can get the full view. I don't know how they did it, but there is a life-sized cardboard cutout of Marina in the mermaid suit. It's from a photo that was widely circulated on social media after our spontaneous concert on the Golden Gate Bridge a year ago, although she's no longer sitting on the hood of my car. Someone has superimposed a rock in there, so she looks like she's in the middle of the surf…and Zach is in a sailor suit, floating in the ocean. The love-struck look on his face is perfect. It's equal parts ridiculous and awesome. My eyes dart to Merry first.

"This is epic! How did you—"

Merry grins from ear to ear. "Scarlet's got some mad skills with her computer."

I look to Scarlet, who bows and turns back to her masterpiece. They've added some tissue paper sea urchins and colorful starfish from a craft store to give it a more three-dimensional feel. It's absolutely hysterical. Laughter bubbles out of me freely now. Marina's going to kill us, but it's totally worth it.

"Oh, wow, Ash!" Merry gasps, stepping over to look at my dress. "You look so pretty!"

I spin around so she can see the whole thing. I'm wearing a navy blue satin sheath dress with little navy rhinestones glistening all over it. My hair is in a soft updo accented with tiny navy and clear rhinestones. Little silver heart stud earrings match my silver strappy heels.

"Thanks, Merry. And thanks to you both for decorating so I could go to Dad's first."

Scarlet points at Rick. "The Viking god helped too."

I turn to Rick and…wow. *Wow.* He's wearing a charcoal sport coat over a white dress shirt and black jeans. Wow. The shirt stretches perfectly across his muscled chest, and the jeans fit so well they make his legs look a mile long. He really is a Viking god. My beautiful, hot, perfect man-friend.

"Hi," I say dumbly, but it comes out as more of a hoarse squeak.

The corner of his mouth tilts up. "Hi."

Scarlet and Merry look from one of us to the other and back again. Finally, Scarlet claps her hands together and breaks the spell.

"Right! You two catch up. Merry and I need to go change."

I'm barely aware of them as they scamper off. Rick closes the distance between us in three slow, deliberate steps. His eyes rove over my hair, my face. My dress.

"You clean up pretty good, Dragon Lady," he says as he pulls me in for a quick hug.

Too quick. I smile up at him.

"I thought I wasn't allowed to be the Dragon Lady around you?"

He frowns, thoughtful for a moment.

"You're allowed to be whoever you want to be," he clarifies, a teasing lilt to his voice. "I just don't want to be roasted into a pile of ash if I displease you."

I scoff. "As if you could ever displease me, my beautiful, hot, perfect man-friend."

He laughs wholeheartedly, and I feel it lift my spirits instantly. I look around the restaurant for the first time and gasp. Scarlet and Merry have outdone themselves. Iridescent bubbles of varying sizes dangle from the ceiling in random clusters, giving off an under-the-sea vibe. The tables are covered in white tablecloths with sparkly lavender runners going down the center. White candles in glass containers of different sizes adorn all the tables. Everything looks so beautiful. I shake my head in wonder.

"You guys did an amazing job," I say quietly, then turn to face Rick. "I didn't know you were coming early. Thank you."

He shrugs. "Marina suggested I might be helpful handling the DJ when he gets here, so you three are free to handle everything else."

As if he were magically summoned, the DJ pushes through the front door with a cart full of equipment. He takes two steps in the door and gives me a look I know all too well. Great.

"Hey there," he drawls as he offers me what I'm sure he thinks is a charming smile. "I'm Danny. Who are you, precious?"

I open my mouth to reply, ready to hit him with the Dragon Lady and Rick steps close to me. He reaches out to shake Danny the DJ's hand.

"Why don't we start over with better manners," he says with calm authority. "Her name isn't precious. Okay, Danny?"

Judging by the trembling smile on Danny's face, I'm guessing Rick's handshake is pretty firm. I stifle a laugh. Three seconds after Rick lets go, Danny's face lights up in recognition.

"Oh wow, you're Rick Archer from The Royal Rebels!"

Rick nods. Danny's eyes cut back and forth between Rick and me for a few seconds, and then he steps back.

"Oh, hey, man, I'm sorry. I didn't mean to hit on your girlfriend."

Before Rick can object, I wrap my arm around his waist and lean in.

"We'll forgive you if you set up quickly and do a great job tonight," I say sweetly.

Rick wraps a casual arm around my shoulders and gives me a squeeze. That familiar sexy pine scent washes over me, and I'm pulled into the warmth of his body like a moth to a flame. He's so warm and solid. I don't want to let go, but I do after a few seconds of sheer bliss.

Danny snaps back into DJ mode in a heartbeat, unloading the cart and setting up equipment after I show him to a spot against the wall with power outlets. I look at the clock on the wall and realize we have about twenty minutes before the first guests begin to arrive.

"Ashley bella!" Merry's grandfather, Nonno, bellows as he pushes through the door from the kitchen.

I gasp with joy and give Rick a glance when I hear him chuckle. Everyone loves Nonno. There's nothing not to love. The man is a ball of joy, and he's like a grandfather to all of us. He gestures wildly at my appearance and makes a chef's kiss with his hands, then pulls me into a hug. I hug back with all my heart.

"Nonno, it's so great to see you!"

He plants a loud kiss on my cheek and steps back to look at me again. I spin, and he applauds, making me laugh out loud.

"You are such a beauty, my girl!"

I take in Nonno's appearance. For once, he's not wearing the chef's whites we're used to seeing. He's wearing a white dress shirt, dress pants and shiny black shoes.

"And you are so handsome, Nonno! I don't think I've ever seen you in a suit before."

He scoffs. "Maybe you would if more of you girls would get married, huh?"

I laugh. I walked right into that one.

"Well, I tried. It didn't work out."

Nonno swipes a dismissive hand in the air.

"Bah! That Greg was a boy, not a man. He didn't deserve you."

"Couldn't have said it better myself, Nonno," Rick chimes in.

The clicking of high heels coming down the back hallway announces Merry and Scarlet's arrival. They both look amazing. Scarlet is wearing a beautiful beaded black cocktail dress with satin black stiletto pumps. Her hair is styled in her usual blond bob, just as sassy as her spirit. Merry is a vision in a turquoise blue dress made of layers of chiffon. The skirt seems to float around her knees like a cloud, and her hair is pulled up off her neck and secured with pearl pins that contrast beautifully with her chestnut brown locks.

"Oh!" Nonno exclaims as he makes a bee line for Merry. "Look at my baby Merry! So bella!"

Merry beams at her grandfather and laughs softly.

"Thanks, Nonno," she mutters as she gives him a light kiss on the cheek.

I love their relationship so much. Merry's parents are Silicon Valley executives who aren't very present in her life, so Nonno is more of a father to her than her own dad. Of course, Nonno is such a force to be reckoned with only he could be enough to replace both parents.

Merry has always been very content with Nonno and about a million cousins here in the city.

"And Scarlet," Nonno says with adoration. "Look at you…my little ball of sass. That dress will make every man at Nonno's want your phone number. I'll have all you girls married by Christmas."

Merry scoffs. "Nonno! Enough. Where's your tie and your jacket?"

Nonno wags a finger at Merry. "Don't try to change subjects on me, young lady. We're finding you a good man tonight."

"I go on plenty of dates, Nonno," Merry argues. "I don't need any help, thank you."

Now it's Nonno's turn to scoff. "Dates with *boys*. And only first dates, never any second dates. Why? Because they're boys, not men. You need to find a real man like Ashley found Rick!"

I nearly jump out of my skin. Scarlet busts into a full-out laugh, and I shoot her a warning glare. Merry's barely holding back her laughter, grateful the attention has turned to me. Rick is behind me, so I can't see his expression, but I'm betting he's as shocked as I am.

"No, Nonno, it's not like that. We're only—"

"Bah! I know what I see. You can't tell Nonno otherwise."

Merry raises her eyebrows as her gaze flicks between me and Rick. She has that look she gets when she's ready to instigate something.

"Really, Nonno?" she says in a tone just dripping with feigned innocence. "What do you see?"

Rick chuckles behind me and I turn my head to shoot him a withering look. I turn back to my friends.

"Merry, what time is Bob getting here? He's your date tonight, right?"

If looks could kill, I'd be dead on the floor. Instead, I hold back a smirk as a confused Scarlet looks at me and mouths *Who's Bob?*

News flash: there is no Bob. Mess with the bull and get the horns, Merry.

"Bob? Is he a boy or a man, my girl?" Nonno demands, linking an arm through Merry's and hauling her away from us. "We go find my tie and you tell me all about this Bob."

Merry shoots me a warning glare just as she disappears into the back room with Nonno and I finally let out the laugh I've been holding in.

"You're going to pay for that later," Rick says as he steps to my side.

"I'd say you'll protect me, but you weren't much help when Nonno was nearly walking us down the aisle."

Rick's eyes widen. "No one argues with Nonno. What was I supposed to say?"

***

Rick

Merry's cousins whip around the dining room and clear all the dishes from the dinner service. Nonno and Merry make their rounds around the room with coffee and the most beautiful tiramisu I've ever seen. Ashley and I both nod enthusiastically when it's our turn, although Merry only fills Ashley's coffee cup half full. I frown at her cup.

"She barely filled it. Do you want some of mine?"

Ashley laughs softly, picking up the small pitcher of creamer Merry left her, and shakes her head as she pours in nearly all of it. My eyes go as round as saucers.

"Wow."

Ashley shrugs. "Merry knows I'm a tea person. But I do love a little taste of coffee after a good meal."

I nod at her cup. "A *little* being the key word."

"Oh, you ain't seen nothin' yet," she says as she takes two packets of sugar, tears them open, then dumps them into her cup and stirs it in.

She raises her eyebrows at me as if to challenge my next words, and I laugh out loud.

"Well, I guess you're going to need the sugar kick pretty soon."

We share a secret smile. I love her spirit. She has such joy about her, especially when she's with the people she loves. I watch as she glances over at the instruments the guys and I set up in the corner. Zach noticed it fairly quick on arrival, and I told him it was a surprise for later. He was content to let it lie.

As if on cue, Jimmy taps me on the shoulder. I turn my chair around so I can see him, and Ashley swivels in her seat.

"You guys just about ready?" Jimmy asks in a conspiratorial tone.

"Ash?" I ask quietly, keeping an eye on Zach and Marina.

They're busy chatting with Scarlet's mom. Jimmy discreetly passes us two clip-on mics with battery packs.

Ashley nods. "Five minutes?"

Jimmy grins and gives her a fist bump, then walks away to tell Sam.

Ashley takes a long sip of her coffee and wiggles excitedly in her seat. Something tugs at my heart. She's wearing a simple cocktail dress in a deep blue that brings out the color of her eyes beautifully. Her hair is up, arranged in a soft bun with little sparkly pins dotted throughout. The whole effect has had me entranced all night.

"You know what I love?" she says huskily, training those beautiful blue eyes on me.

"What do you love?" I ask quietly, turning to face her squarely.

I resist the urge to lean closer and inhale her intoxicating scent.

"Moments like this one," she says cryptically, taking another sip of coffee and nodding at Zach and Marina. "They have no idea what's about to happen. No one does outside of our little bridal party."

I smile down at her, not sure I'm getting it. She laughs softly and wags a finger between us.

"We have a secret, Rick," she continues, leaning in close and giving me a radiant smile. "We're about to unleash a ton of awesomeness in this place and they have no idea. It's kind of thrilling, don't you think?"

My gaze drops briefly from her eyes to her mouth, so tantalizingly close, and suddenly, my throat is dry. Thrilling is the right word, but I wouldn't be talking about a flash mob. My eyes dart from the top of her head to her toes and back to her eyes again. The corners of my mouth tip up just slightly as I hold her gaze.

"Thrilling is the perfect word for this."

A slight blush creeps up her cheeks, and she laughs softly. She holds her mic pack low under the table so only I can see it.

"How does this work? What do I do?"

I tap the battery pack with my finger.

"Clip this inside your dress and then tuck the wire behind your ear when you put the ear piece on."

She looks down at the front of her dress while I try not to stare. There's not a lot of room up front, and something coils low in my gut as I predict what's coming. She opens her hand and offers me the battery pack.

"Would you mind? Just clip it in the center of the back."

She turns her back to me as I clear my throat.

"Sure," I mutter, stealing another glance at Zach and Marina, still chatting away in happy oblivion.

I turn in my chair so I'm facing her back, then reach up with gentle fingers and just slightly pull the edge of her dress out so I can tuck the pack in. My fingers graze her soft skin, and I get a heady sense of satisfaction from the little shiver that runs through her. I can't resist leaning in close enough to whisper behind her right ear.

"Sorry."

Another little shiver. I make sure the clip is secure, and then I pass the ear piece over her shoulder. She reaches up to take it from me, then turns her head to give me a look, which tells me she knows exactly what I just did.

"Do you need any help with yours, beautiful, hot, perfect man-friend?" she asks with a smirk.

I throw my head back and laugh as I shrug out of my sports coat and hand it to her.

"Can you hold this for a minute?"

She smiles and takes it from me. I clip the pack onto the waistband of my jeans, then attach the ear piece and throw the cord over my shoulder. Ashley hands my coat back to me, and I pull it on.

"It seems like you've made peace with the whole beautiful, hot, perfect man-friend thing. Am I right?"

She shrugs. "I've decided to lean into it."

I grin. "Good."

Something behind me gets Ashley's attention, and she gasps. Then, she looks up at me with a beautiful gleam in her eyes.

"Jimmy just gave the signal," she whispers excitedly. "Are you ready?"

I nod. "Ready, boss."

Her smile reaches through my ribs and straight into my heart. Yeah, I'm in a little trouble.

"Turn my pack on," she says, turning away so I can reach it.

I turn hers on, then reach back to get mine. She turns to me with a conspiratorial grin.

"Show time."

I laugh softly. "Show time."

We sit together for a few more seconds before Jimmy and Sam begin playing the intro. That gets everyone's attention. The rest of us continue sitting, acting as surprised as everyone else, until Ashley pops up and starts singing the first verse.

Marina gasps in delight as she realizes what's happening, and Zach bursts out laughing. Ashley dances towards them, singing to them as I stand and quickly make my way over to the guys and my guitar. I throw my guitar strap over my shoulder and start playing just as Merry and Scarlet pop up and begin dancing over to the area just in front of us. Our rendition of Bruno Mars' "Marry You" fills the entire restaurant, thanks to the mics and speakers.

I sing the second verse, and Ashley dances her way closer. I smile at Zach and Marina as I sing, knowing in my heart we're hitting it out of the park based on the look of utter joy on their faces. Especially Marina, who watches with tear-filled eyes. This is one of those moments when everything in the world feels perfect and right.

Ashley and I sing the chorus together, with Merry and Scarlet starting a rhythmic hand clapping that really gets the audience going. I watch Ashley dance towards me, and I'm mesmerized by her spirit and effervescence. Our eyes meet, and I can't look away. I don't even care if someone reads the feelings my expression has right now. It's impossible not to smile at this woman while she's dancing all over the restaurant. She's a natural performer, and the entire audience is having a great time.

With Merry and Scarlet dancing all around between the tables and engaging with guests, Ashley turns her attention to me. The air between us is electrified with energy as we sing to each other, throwing ourselves into the spirit of the song. She's beside me as we sing the last verse together, our faces inches apart and smiling ear to ear. The room bursts into cheers and applause as we finish, and I quickly remove my guitar so I can applaud for Ashley, Merry and Scarlet. They're all pointing at us in the band and applauding for us in turn.

Ashley grabs the girls by the hands and they run up to us so we can all take one final bow. This crowd will not stop cheering, mostly because Zach and Marina are egging them on. Ashley turns to me, positively glowing with pride, and before I even know what hits me, she throws herself into my arms. I lift her completely off the floor without hesitation, spinning her around until she squeals. She moves her lips close to my ear as I lower her to the floor.

"That was amazing!" she says, giving me a smile that feels like it's only for me.

She doesn't step away when I set her down. Instead, she raises up on her toes and plants a kiss on my cheek. I fold her back into my arms for another hug, and she stays. Her arms wrap around my waist, and when she presses her cheek to my chest. A sigh shudders through her as she squeezes me harder. Everything about this feels one hundred percent right. On every level. Something reaches down deep into my heart and hits me with all the feels. I want more of this. More smiles, more laughs, and definitely more of these hugs. But I also want soft, long kisses and secret glances and…just more of this incredible woman in my arms.

Ashley pulls away to hug her friends, giving me one more radiant smile for the road. I hate the empty feeling in my arms as she walks away. Merry and Scarlet exchange high-fives with her as Marina makes her way through the party guests. She's half way to us when her eyes lock with mine. I smile warmly, still reveling in the joy we brought our friends tonight. Marina is swiftly pulled into a hug by Ashley, Merry, and Scarlet—but her gaze doesn't break from mine. Instead, she mouths *I've got you*, and winks at me. And just like that, the odds have shifted in my favor.

I have an ally.

***

Ashley

Marina steps back with a gasp, running her fingers along the red chiffon that makes up the top layer of my dress for the fundraiser. It's a sleeveless A-line dress that dips low in front, perfect for my shape. A ruffle runs along the edge of the neckline and up over the shoulders.

"It's perfect!" she says excitedly. "And you always look amazing in red. Greg won't know what hit him."

I roll my eyes. "Yuck."

Marina laughs softly. "I agree, but we know how he is. He's going to do everything he can to show you what you're missing. He'll be speechless when he sees you in this."

I grin. "A speechless Greg is wishful thinking. He likes to hear himself talk too much."

She shrugs. "Still. Nothing wrong with taking him down a peg or two."

"No, there sure isn't," I say with a shake of my head.

"Show me the shoes. I know you picked something next level."

I don't even try to suppress the huge smile on my face as I duck into my closet and pull out the shoes I chose for this dress. I hold the gold metallic strappy heels in front of Marina and wiggle them around. She literally squeals.

"Wow," she says reverently, taking them in her hands. "These are beautiful! First dibs on borrowing these some day."

I giggle. "Deal. They're perfect, aren't they?"

She nods. "Forget Greg. Rick is a goner too. You're going to be absolutely breathtaking."

I shake my head. "Rick is just doing me a favor."

Marina studies me wide-eyed. "So? He's a man, isn't he? Besides… have you seen the way he looks at you sometimes?"

Again with the head shakes. "He just thinks I'm funny. Or maybe crazy because of the whole Dragon Lady thing. Either way, he doesn't think about me like that."

My friend looks at me incredulously. "Is that what you think?"

"It's what I *know*," I say emphatically. "He's a rich, famous guy. He dates models and actresses."

Marina makes a face. "Are we talking about the same Rick?"

I jog over to my closet and put the shoes back, then come back and flop on my bed.

"You know what I mean. He could have *anyone*. He's not going to settle for a fourth-grade teacher who—"

Marina holds up a hand. "Stop right there. Did you just say settle? *Settle?* Any man would be lucky to have you. Including Rick, so don't talk smack about my friend Ashley…got it?"

I smile at my friend, a fierce fighter for everyone she loves. "Got it."

She puts her hand down and comes over to sit next to me.

"While I'm defending my friends, though, I want to say something about Rick."

I'm all ears. I nod at her to go on.

"Rick is also my friend," she begins gently. "And while he has never stayed up all night with me to help me study for a test and never had to fight me as I tried to dump the love of my life, he is very special to me."

I put my hand on Marina's and squeeze. "I know. He's special to me too."

"Do you know? Really?" she asks cryptically. "You've had a rough time lately, and you're giving yourself too much grief because you loved someone who didn't deserve you. Rick isn't just a friend. Rick is a good man. And he has feelings for you, I'm sure of it."

I open my mouth to protest, but Marina's hand flies up again, and my self-preservation instincts kick in. I close my mouth.

"If you start listing all the reasons you don't measure up to Rick's type again, I will scream," Marina declares.

Yikes.

"When you are in the room, he is aware of every move you make. He tries to hide it, but I see it. He looks at you like Greg should have looked at you all along: like you are precious."

I shake my head. "He's never said anything to me about it, Marina. I think you're mistaken."

"He's never said anything because you are the Dragon Lady any time a man gets near you."

I scoff. "I've never done that to Rick. He's always been a gentleman."

She nods and waves her hand at me like I'm stating the obvious. "Because he *is* one. And he sees what happens to men who approach you. So what does a smart, good man do when the woman he's attracted to melts prospective suitors in her dragon fire?"

A giggle bubbles out of me, and Marina gives me a warning look.

"Sorry," I say quickly. "I know you're being serious, and I'm listening, but the whole dragon fire thing just hit me funny."

"Look," Marina says as she smooths her palms over the tops of her thighs. "I'm not telling you to go for it and I'm not trying to tell you what to do with your life. I'm only trying to shine the light on the gorgeous, good man who is clearly attracted to you. And, just like I would want to smack anyone who hurt you, the same goes for Rick. I don't want him hurt. So you do you, my friend…but please have a care for my friend Rick. I don't want him caught in the crossfire of your…"

I smirk. "Dragon fire?"

She laughs softly. "Do you understand, Ash?"

I reach over and wrap my arms around my best friend. She squeezes me back and all is right in the world. We've been through thick and thin together. We're sisters more than friends.

"I understand," I say solemnly. "And I promise to be careful with Rick. I care about him as well."

Marina nods, then shoots me a wry smile. "I see that too."

Chapter 8

Less than a week later, I'm standing in front of the mirror in my bedroom, smoothing a hand over the red chiffon of the dress and checking my reflection for the millionth time. I look down at these amazing gold, strappy heels in wonder. I thought they might be a bit uncomfortable, but they're not at all. After trying a few different hairstyles that didn't look right, I opted to leave my long blonde hair down. I put some waves in it, and now it flows when I move, just like the dress. Fourth-grade teachers don't get many chances to dress up this fancy, and I feel like a princess in a fairy tale tonight. All that's left is for my fake Prince Charming to come pick me up.

Except he's not fake at all. He's very real, and absolutely charming. A gentleman in every way. He's also a really good friend to do this for me. I just can't see the attraction Marina is so certain of. Rick is only being kind. I don't think he looks at me as anything but a friend. Even if he did feel some kind of attraction to me, I'm still afraid of what happens if I screw this up, and we're doomed to see each other for all eternity after I made everything unbearably awkward.

I check my make-up one more time, then grab the little gold evening bag I bought with these shoes and head out to the living room. I hear

Marina's soft laughter and smile to myself. Zach must already be here. Zach bought a table at the fundraiser, so he and Marina are going. The tables seat six, so they invited Jimmy, Sam, Scarlet and Merry. The whole gang will be there tonight, which gives me added confidence.

I see Marina first, and she's a vision in her dark blue satin cocktail dress that looks like the night sky. Little rhinestones are sprayed everywhere, looking like stars. It's breathtaking.

"Oh, Marina!" I gasp as I hurry up to hug her. "You look so beautiful!"

She smiles but shakes her head as she gestures at me. "Not compared to this, my friend. You're going to be the belle of the ball."

I twirl around, and Zach applauds. "You look amazing, Ash."

Zach is wearing a midnight blue suit that perfectly coordinates with Marina's incredible dress. Because of course it does. I grin at them both.

"Thanks. You guys look incredible," I say, not missing the complete adoration in Zach's eyes as he looks at Marina. They're so beautiful together.

A knock sounds at the door, and my pulse goes crazy. We all know who it is. Marina grins widely.

"Your date's here," she whispers.

I laugh as I walk to the door. "It's not real."

I swing the door open and find a very real, very sexy Viking god in a beautiful, perfectly tailored charcoal gray suit. His hair is pulled back in his usual man bun, and the stubble on his chin is precision trimmed. I fight the urge to stand on my tip toes and rub my face against it. His eyes meet mine, then his gaze drifts down. He steps back so he can see the whole picture and lets out a low whistle.

"All right, enough," I say quietly, feeling bashful. I step aside to let him in. "Come on in."

"You are the picture of perfection, my friend," Zach says, bringing

Rick in for a man hug.

Marina reaches up and gives Rick a hug. "You look fabulous."

Rick turns to me, holding up a beautiful bouquet of white roses. "For the lady."

"Oh, they're so pretty!"

How did I not see the bouquet? Probably because I was gawking at the gorgeous man. Pretty sure.

I reach for the flowers and wrap him in a hug. I can't resist pressing a quick kiss to his cheek as I let him go.

"Thank you so much, Rick. Let me just go put these in water."

I escape to the kitchen, grateful to have a moment away from everyone so I can compose myself. I wonder how I will get through the night, making sure the fundraiser is a success while avoiding my ex and trying not to catch feelings for the Viking god. How did I get myself into this mess?

Once in the kitchen, I open the cupboard where we keep the vases and select a clear glass cylinder that's a great size and shape for this bouquet. I turn to the sink to fill it with water and see Rick approaching. My heart thuds against my ribs so hard I'm sure he can hear it. He smiles softly as he approaches.

"You doing okay, Ash?"

I nod but busy myself with arranging the roses in the vase.

"A little nervous, just hoping the fundraiser goes well," I confess, wringing my hands with nervous energy. "I'll relax once we get there and I check on everything."

He reaches for my hands, holding them firmly as his deep blue eyes meet mine.

"You look absolutely beautiful," he says lowly. "You've worked really hard to create this night for your dad's cause, and it's going to be perfect. All your friends are with you. You'll be surrounded by people who love you. And I plan to be the best fake date you've ever had."

I laugh quietly, stealing a glance at Marina and Zach. They're busy chatting in the entryway.

"I'm not looking forward to seeing Greg again," I confess.

Rick nods in understanding. "Stay close to me if he bothers you. I'll make sure he behaves like a nice, respectful boy."

I laugh in earnest, letting go of his hands and wrapping him in a hug. Those huge, strong bands of steel wrap around me, and I instantly relax. Everything is okay now. Too bad he can't just haul me around the fundraiser like this. I wouldn't feel any stress at all. Nothing can harm me here. Reluctantly, I let him go and step back.

"All right, my beautiful, hot, perfect man-friend," I say as I nudge him toward the door. "Let's do this."

He gives me the side eye as we move toward the door.

"I'm not sure I like having a nickname if I don't get to give you one," he teases.

"Well, maybe you'll come up with one for me tonight."

Rick laughs softly. "The night is young. You never know."

*****

Two hours later, I'm seated at our table as tuxedo clad waitstaff move swiftly about the room to deliver dessert and coffee to our guests. Every element of the evening has been beautifully orchestrated by Hillary, and I'm not sure how I'll ever repay her for such a job well done. She is truly a wonder.

As soon as guests enter, they walk under a beautiful archway made of iridescent white and pearl balloons. Red heart-shaped balloons are tucked in randomly to give it contrast, and the entire arrangement is backlit with tiny white fairy lights. The tables are covered in white linen with gold, glittering runners going down the middle. Fine white china dinner plates sit atop red chargers, and beautiful floral centerpieces of roses and lilies sit at the center of each table. Lillies were my Mom's favorite, and I knew I'd hit the mark when Dad pulled me into a hug with tears in his eyes.

A dance floor is laid out in front of the stage, and tables running along the back wall showcase all the items included in the silent auction. All through the night, guests excitedly perused the auction items and bid generously but I'm still not sure we've hit our goal. Bidding ended thirty minutes ago, and Hillary is sequestered somewhere with one of Dad's friends as they tally it all up.

Overall, I wouldn't change anything about this evening—including the moment when Greg showed up with his beautiful girlfriend, Janine. Always picture-perfect, he walked straight up to Dad to gush all over him. Even though I know he saw me, he tried to act like he just noticed me standing there…right next to my father…the entire time. I smiled graciously and introduced myself to Janine, not faltering in the slightest even when Greg not-so-discreetly whispered *the ex* to her. I was rewarded for my patience when Rick appeared at my side, introducing himself with a handshake so fierce I saw tears form in Greg's eyes. Karma can be a wonderful thing.

Since then, he's kept to himself—although I've seen him watching a few times as Rick leaned over to whisper something in my ear to make me laugh or to hold my hand, or pay me any kind of attention. He was right. He has been the best fake date ever. Actually, and sadly, he's been my best date ever. Out of all of them. He's attentive and kind and so incredibly sexy. The longer the night goes on, the more I dread waking up tomorrow in a world without him looking at me like I'm the only woman on the planet. It's like a drug, and I just want more.

"Hey you," Rick whispers as he leans in close.

Little sparks dance along my neck where his breath warms my skin.

"Hey," I say quietly, smiling because I just can't help myself.

Rick scoots his chair closer, then turns in his seat to face me. He braces an arm across the back of my chair as his eyes flick over my face for a moment.

"Tonight has gone so well. You should be proud."

I nod. "I'm pretty happy right now. And I couldn't have done any of it without Hillary. I need to figure out something big to do as a thank you."

"You'll think of something."

He reaches out a hand and brushes his fingers down my bare arm. I feel Greg's eyes on us, and I lean in. Rick pulls me close until I'm cradled against his chest. I nuzzle my face into his neck and inhale that sexy pine scent. It's heaven, and I can't resist it even though I know I should.

Hillary appears again, this time whispering to Dad and running off again before I can ask whether we hit our goal. The lights dim slightly as Dad excuses himself and stands, walking up to the stage as the room bursts into applause. He smiles his thanks at the audience and looks across the room soberly.

"Just about a year ago today, I was laying in a hospital bed after having a massive heart attack," he says sternly. "Luckily for me, I had a great doctor. More than that, I had the best insurance money can buy. That isn't true for all patients, so I created the Have a Heart Foundation to bridge the gap between what insurance covers and the life-saving treatments and therapies some patients just can't afford. From the bottom of my now-healed heart, I thank you for being here tonight and helping those less fortunate in our community."

The dining room erupts in applause again, including Rick and me. As soon as it dies down, Rick reaches out and pulls me back against his chest again. My heart makes a million swoony flops against my rib cage as I snuggle in.

"Before we let the DJ get the real party started, I have a few people to thank," Dad says with a bright smile. "And the first person I want to thank is also my favorite person in the whole world."

Rick lowers his lips to my ear. "I wonder who that might be."

I laugh softly and gently pull away, knowing my Dad is going to make me stand up so people can applaud.

"My beautiful daughter, Ashley, pulled this dinner together for the foundation, and I have to say…I don't think it's possible for a father to be prouder of his daughter in any moment. Ashley, please stand up so these nice people can thank you."

I stand as the whole room turns its attention on me. I wave and smile, then blow a kiss at my Dad as the audience cheers. There's one table that's obnoxiously loud, and that is, of course, all of my friends. I break into nervous giggles and wave once more before sitting down again.

Rick's hand warms my back immediately, and I turn and wrap my arms around his waist. He pulls me in again, and I rest my head on his shoulder with a shudder.

"Are you cold?" he asks with concern.

I shake my head. "No, that was just a lot of attention. Now I want to disappear."

I feel him frown against my hair. "You could never disappear. And you were great."

"Please also help me thank Hillary Grammer, on loan to us from the Mermaid Foundation, for making tonight a huge success."

More applause as Hillary pops out to wave, then disappears into the shadows again.

"And finally, before I turn it all over to the DJ, I'm proud to share that we have, in fact, hit our goal of five million dollars tonight!"

Deafening cheers now from the audience, and our entire table joins in. I scream at the top of my lungs and look up at Rick excitedly as he applauds and whistles in celebration. Dad holds his hands up to quiet the crowd.

"As a special favor, I hope you'll let me have this first dance," he says into the mic with a wobbly voice, "with my best girl, as we celebrate the wonderful and generous hearts in this room tonight. Thank you so much."

Emotion wells up in my throat as Rick gently lets me go, and the DJ begins playing the familiar opening strains of "My Girl" by the Temptations. I'm vaguely aware of Rick standing and pulling me out of my chair, then escorting me to the edge of the dance floor where my Dad now waits. He softly kisses my cheek and returns to our table. I look up at Dad with teary eyes and wrap him in a hug as muted applause sprinkles out from the audience. We walk to the center of the room and begin the most special father-daughter dance I've ever had.

"Well," Dad says as we dance, "I think maybe you should start an event business because tonight has been perfect in every way."

I throw my head back and laugh. "Nope," I say quickly. "Not happening. I'm sticking with my fourth graders."

Dad chuckles and nods. "Lucky kids."

I love that my Dad has always been accepting of my desire to carve my own path and do what fulfills me in life. I'm so grateful to him for letting me be me and not trying to mold me into something different. Finance and numbers are just something I've never been interested in, but helping to shape children's lives? Bringing out their potential so they can be the best version of themselves? That's something I'm passionate about.

About halfway through the song, we begin gesturing for other couples to join us on the dance floor, and they do. I see Mayor Williams and his wife get up to join us, along with several people from Dad's firm and, of course, Zach and Marina. When the song is over, Dad gives me another big hug, and I send him off to visit with his guests. I head back to Rick with a heart full of conflict. Half of me wants to curl up in his arms, and the other half is dreading going back to a life without my fake boyfriend. I'm beginning to wonder how smart of an idea this actually was.

Rick stands as I approach, holding out my chair for me so I can sit. I smile up at him as I notice Greg rolling his eyes. I really can't remember what I ever saw in him. Greg gets up from his seat and I almost breathe a sigh of relief that he's leaving, but he turns our way instead and comes to sit in Dad's chair next to me. He winks at Rick, and my skin crawls.

"Congratulations, Ash," he says with an incredibly fake smile. "You finally got your dance. You were cute out there."

I offer a polite smile. "Thanks."

Rick reaches over and laces our fingers together in my lap, anchoring me. I know he's just doing it because Greg is here, and he wants to help, but I find myself not caring as much about what Greg thinks as I care about how the man next to me makes me feel. Still, Greg is reminding me of another facet of our relationship that should have shown me that he wasn't the one for me.

Greg smirks. "I'm afraid I was always a huge disappointment to Ashley on a dance floor," he shares, dripping with sarcasm. "I just don't see the sense of it."

I fight back the nasty retort on the tip of my tongue, and bob my head in Janine's direction.

"You're neglecting your girlfriend," I say pointedly, turning my back to Greg and focusing my attention on Rick.

I'm rewarded with a sexy grin. I hear Greg's exasperated sigh behind me, and I can tell by Rick's expression that he's gone back to Janine. Rick reaches up and brushes his fingers over my long waves.

"I didn't know you like to dance."

I nod. "A mutual friend bought us salsa dance lessons for an engagement present. I had to fight just to get him to go, and he only participated in one class. I spent the rest of the time dancing with the instructor while Greg sat in the corner with his cell phone."

Rick grumbles in disgust. "You dodged a bullet, Ash. Please tell me you know that."

I nod. "I absolutely do. I think maybe tonight has helped me get a better perspective."

A muscle feathers in his jaw as he shakes his head. "He should have taken every chance there was to dance with you."

I laugh softly and smile up at Rick. "Well, that's his loss."

He smiles softly. "No doubt about that."

The DJ fades the current song out and I hear the distinctive opening strains of Pitbull's "Fireball" start up. There are only a handful of couples dancing on the floor, and I wonder how many of them will stay and try to keep pace with it. The DJ is obviously trying to get people excited. I love this song.

Rick's gaze flicks over to the dance floor when he hears the music as well, and then he nudges me.

"How much do you trust me, Ash?"

I blink back my surprise. I wasn't expecting a question like that at all.

"You've never given me any reason not to trust you. Why?"

He looks over my shoulder at the dance floor again, then pushes up out of his chair and offers me his hand.

"Shall we?"

My heart hammers against my ribcage as I place my hand in his and stand. My inner control freak wants to ask a million questions before we hit the dance floor.

Do you know how fast this song is? Are you sure you know what you're doing? Am I going to slip and fall on my butt?

But those questions die in my throat as Rick laces our fingers together and tows me behind him.

I catch Marina's excited stare as we step onto the dance floor and we turn to face each other as if in slow motion. Pitbull is babbling through the final stages of the intro as I look up into Rick's eyes with an excited grin.

"Are you sure you know what you're doing?" I tease lightly. "This song isn't for the faint-hearted."

Aware that there are several sets of eyes on us at this point, including Greg's, Rick makes a show of leaning over to kiss the back of my hand. He looks at me with a challenge in his eyes.

"I guess you better try to keep up then," he growls with a sexy grin.

With the grace of a ballroom dancer, Rick tugs on my hand and steps into my space, placing his palm at my waist and holding my other hand out to the side. In that one movement, I understand the message clearly. He knows *exactly* what he's doing, and we're about to put on a hell of a show. And just as Pitbull growls out the word *Fireball*, we explode on the dance floor.

I hear the distinctive sound of Merry squealing in delight as we move across the floor, and I laugh openly. Rick isn't just a good dancer. He's a *great* dancer. I'm dumbfounded that someone with his stature is so graceful and smooth on the dance floor, but to my everlasting joy…he is. I easily follow his lead, and he quickly learns that he can push me into turns and I can spin my heart out and still stop on a dime. He grins at me as we match each other's movements.

Eventually, the other couples on the dance floor move to the edge to watch us, clapping along with the music. For once, I don't care that I'm the center of attention. I only care that I'm the center of Rick's attention. I beam up at him as we keep pace with each other to the delight of the crowd. As the song builds to the conclusion, I'm positively giddy as we move together.

As the final verse of the song plays out, Rick steers us toward the center of the dance floor. I follow him with expert precision, and he's basically throwing me around the floor at this point. We're both smiling ear to ear. The absolute joy I feel in this moment is unlike anything I've ever felt in my life.

"Heads up," he warns. "I'm sooo gonna dip you."

And five seconds later, he does exactly that as I shriek at the top of my lungs. The entire room erupts into applause and cheers as he holds me there for a moment. His arms are wrapped around me and I feel completely safe in this position, laughing with him as he looks into my eyes. He lowers his lips to my ear.

"Hey, Fireball," he says hoarsely, and I throw my head back and laugh.

I have a nickname, and I love it.

He pulls me up and crushes me in his arms. I wrap my arms around his neck, and we kind of dance around in this full-body hug until he lifts me up and spins us around. By the time he sets me down on my feet, the room is still thundering in applause as the DJ transitions to another fast-paced dance number. Twice the number of couples hit the floor as Rick takes my hand and leads me to the side of the dance floor.

"Where did you learn to dance like that!" I asked breathlessly.

Rick chuckles and pulls me in for another hug.

"I took dance lessons one summer as a surprise for my Mom for Mother's Day," he explains. "She loves to dance. Since my Dad was never around and she wasn't interested in dating anyone, it seemed like the best gift I could give her. So I learned, and I've made a point ever since to make sure she gets to go out and dance whenever I'm home."

My hand flutters up to my heart as I try to catch my breath. Rick looks behind me at the dance floor.

"Do you want to keep going?"

I laugh and shake my head. "I need a minute to recover from that," I say hoarsely. "But I am definitely going to let you push me around the dance floor again."

Rick links our hands again and leads me back to our table, where Dad is waiting to greet us with exaggerated applause. We both laugh and take a mock bow, then Rick pulls my chair out for me and takes a seat close beside me.

"Well done!" Dad says loudly. "I'm thoroughly impressed."

I don't miss the fact that Greg rolls his eyes again. I also don't care. Rick pours me a glass of water from the pitcher on the table, and I smile my thanks.

"Yes, well done," Greg cheers, raising his glass to us. "I didn't realize there would be a show as well as a silent auction."

Dad slaps Greg on the back a little too hard, and I nearly choke as I take a sip of water.

"Lighten up, Greg. No one likes a sore loser."

I laugh under my breath at Dad's stinging retort, but it seems Greg is unfazed.

"I can't wait to see what you two have in store for the company retreat," he fires back. "I can't imagine topping this."

Rick raises his eyebrows. "Company retreat?"

Greg's eyes dart to me, his expression curious.

"You're not bringing him?"

My pulse picks up again at his unexpected line of questioning. I shake my head.

"Rick has to do some publicity that weekend," I hedge, feeling him tense beside me. "He can't come."

Greg's smile is predatory. "What a shame. Then maybe you and I—"

"No, baby, that's rescheduled," Rick says calmly, placing a gentle kiss on my temple as he gives Greg an icy stare. "I'll be there."

I look up at Rick in total surprise. "What?" I gasp, then lower my voice so only he can hear me. "You don't have to do this."

Rick pulls me closer and I sink into his warmth as he grins at Greg. "I wouldn't miss it for the world."

Chapter 9

Rick

I hope I didn't just make a huge mistake. I may have overplayed my hand. There's something about this simpering little man-boy I can't stand, and I'm pretty sure he was going to suggest that he'd show Ashley a good time at this company retreat thing. And he was going to say it in front of his own girlfriend. What do women see in this guy?

I can see Ashley watching me closely from her perch on the chair next to me, and it's taking all the resolve I have not to turn my head and finally bring our lips together. That dance just now. That dance was everything. I could tell she was worried at first, but as soon as I pulled her to me she understood the game…and she played. The moment we started dancing, Ashley came alive. It was incredible to see. She threw herself into the dance, giving me flirty looks, showing all kinds of sass, and just being Ashley again. Fireball is the perfect nickname for her because that's what she's always been. And then Greg broke her heart and the Dragon Lady was born.

"Let's talk about it tomorrow," she says softly, so close that I can feel her breath on my jaw. "I don't want you to feel obligated."

I look into her bright blue eyes and smile softly. "When I do something for you, Ash, it's because I want to. Never out of obligation. But yes, let's talk tomorrow when we don't have an audience."

That earns me a relaxed smile that reaches into my gut and stirs everything up. She is absolutely breathtaking tonight. Her red dress made our salsa episode on the dance floor even more dramatic as it flowed around her like a sparkling red cloud. And the sheer joy on her face as we danced… priceless.

She settles against me, and I wrap my arm tighter around her shoulders. Something inside me changed on that dance floor. I felt it as if it was a physical thing. I want more of her. I need to re-evaluate my plan, so I'm glad tomorrow is Sunday. There's nothing on my schedule for once, so I will stay home and re-group. They say absence makes the heart grow fonder. Maybe Ashley will miss me a little.

I'm so absorbed in my own thoughts I don't even notice Ashley scrolling through her phone until she gasps and sits up to show me what's on her screen. I cup her hand to move the phone a little closer.

"Oh," I say quietly. "I didn't even realize they were announcing that today. Cool."

She gives me an incredulous look, shaking her head.

"Cool?" she scoffs. "You're a World Music Award nominee, and that's all you have to say?"

A slow grin creeps up my face. "No, I don't mean it like that. It *is* cool, I'm just surprised."

She scrolls more and gasps again. "Twice! You're nominated twice!"

I hold my hand out and she gives me her phone so I can scroll through. I look up to see if Zach is at his table, only to find him jogging over to me with Marina hot on his tail. I lean back in my chair and give him a high five. Marina hugs me around the neck from behind.

"Congratulations!" she cries as she grabs an empty chair and pulls it over. Zach beats her to the chair and sits, then pulls her into his lap.

"Yes, congrats to you both!" Ashley pipes in.

"Thanks, Ash," Zach says. "We're especially excited for Rick, though. It's his first *solo* nomination."

Ashley beams up at me. "What?"

I laugh at her adorable reaction. It makes me feel good that she cares this much. Probably too good, but I'll think about that tomorrow.

"Zach and I are usually nominated together since we co-write most Rebels songs," I explain. "But I wrote 'Till the End' by myself. So yeah, it's special."

Ashley wraps her arms around my neck and squeezes. I could die right here. She is the sweetest creature I've ever known. In her arms, I feel like I'm wrapped in my own personal ray of sunshine. I just want more. She moves her lips close to my ear.

"I'm so happy for you," she murmurs. "Congratulations, Rick."

I allow myself this moment to just be in her arms. I know it's only friendship and nothing more, but after that dance, I'll take whatever scraps I can get. If this is what friendship is like with Ashley, heaven help me if she ever lets me out of the friend zone. I open my eyes and find Marina watching me with a big, stupid, love-struck smile on her face. She puts her hand over her heart and makes puppy dog eyes at me and I stick my tongue out at her in return.

Meddling mermaid.

***

It's almost midnight before Ashley begrudgingly lets me carry her to the car, and only after Hillary gives her an earful about the fact that Ashley did enough work on the planning. Apparently, the execution of the whole event is where Hillary actually thrives. She sent us off with a wave of her clipboard.

"I feel guilty, Fireball," I tell her as her father holds the door open for me. I nod my thanks.

Ashley grumbles against my shoulder. "Why?"

"I literally danced you off your feet."

A low giggle is my reward. "I'm so tired, but this was so worth it."

I can't help the smile I get from that tiny giggle. We danced all night. Fast or slow, the song didn't matter. I took every chance I had to hold her in my arms, and I know she had fun. If that's the final takeaway for the evening, it's been the best fake date ever. Except I wasn't faking at all.

The limo driver is waiting for us just outside, the door open. I nod at him as I carefully lower Ash to a standing position. Her dad chuckles behind us, and I step back so they can say goodnight. Ashley smiles sleepily at him.

"Goodnight, Daddy."

He wraps her in a hug. "Goodnight, my beauty. Sleep well. Pretty sure you will."

Another giggle. "Yep."

"Congrats on your fundraiser," she says, stifling a yawn.

"Couldn't have done it without you," he says with fatherly pride. "I'm so proud of you. Now go home and go to sleep."

She nods and takes my offered hand as she slides into the limo. I shut the door and turn back to her dad. He gives me a look as if he's sizing me up.

"You know what you're doing, son?"

I swallow roughly, nodding. "Yes, sir."

He grins then, shaking my hand. "Good. I'm rooting for you."

I smile back at him as I walk around the back of the limo to get in the other side.

"Thanks. I need all the help I can get."

He laughs and turns on his heel, heading back inside with a spring in his step as I get into the car with an already sleeping Ashley...hoping and praying I actually *do* know what I'm doing.

***

Ashley

I wake up in my own bed, wearing a t-shirt I don't remember putting on. I open my eyes just barely to see through the open closet door that my dress is hanging there. My shoes are placed neatly underneath. I honestly don't remember how I got home. I think for a moment, rolling over and noting the time. Almost eleven in the morning. Wow. I slept like a rock.

I remember hugging my Dad goodnight, and then I watched him through the window of the car as he shook Rick's hand. He was still looking at him like a new puppy. Then I just rested my head in the car for a minute and…oh.

Oh.

For a split second, I wonder if Rick brought me in here and put me to bed but I know the answer. He probably carried me. The t-shirt is Marina's. She and Zach left before Rick and I, so they took an Uber back here and let us have the limo. Besides, Rick would never cross that line. He's a gentleman.

I pull myself out of bed and pad to the bathroom on two very clunky, very sore feet. My beautiful shoes performed well. No blisters or anything. I'm simply not used to a night of dancing with a Viking god. And, oh boy, did we dance. He dances so beautifully. I'm pretty sure I was also looking at him like a new puppy as the evening drew to a close. I haven't had that much fun in such a long time.

I turn the shower on and grab a couple towels from the shelf above the toilet. While the water warms up, I scrub the make-up off my face and stare at my reflection. I don't look too bad, considering how hard

I slept. Thank goodness there's literally nothing I have to do today. I just want to curl up somewhere cozy, and think about last night until it's time to fall asleep. Then I can dream about it.

The hot spray of the shower washes the last of the sleep away. I take my time, lathering up my long hair and rinsing it. For a while, I just stand under the spray and let it revitalize me until I'm pulled back into reality. When I finally get out of the shower and put my wet hair up in a towel, I know what Cinderella must have felt like the morning after the ball. No more dancing, no more prince.

I skulk back into my bedroom with a fairly sour expression. Reality sucks sometimes. I reach into my dresser and pull out a pair of dusty blue leggings and a gray sweatshirt that says "I'm a delight" on the front. Not feeling it today, but it's one of my favorites. I throw those on and pull some white fuzzy socks over my tired feet, then pull the towel off my head and put my damp hair up in a clip. Good enough.

I head to the kitchen with the appetite of a bear. My spirits lift as soon as I hear Marina's voice coming from the living room. She's on the phone as I step into view.

"I know, it was so great," she says in a tone that's specifically reserved for Zach. "Hey, Ash is finally awake so I'll catch up with you later, okay? Love you too."

"I love you too, Zach!" I yell loud enough for him to hear as he's hanging up.

Marina laughs as I plunk down onto the love seat and burrow under my favorite throw.

"Morning," I grumble.

"Good morning," my friend replies. It's almost musical. "No tea?"

I prop my head up on my hand. "Eventually, when I have the energy."

She laughs and gets up, then I watch her with squinty eyes as she jogs over to the kitchen and flicks the switch on my electric tea kettle. She jogs back and flops on the couch.

"Where is your energy coming from?" I croak out.

She shrugs. "I don't know. Last night was so fun. I'm madly in love. I'm getting married. Take your pick."

Even in the reality funk I'm in, I can't resist smiling at her. She is freaking adorable and I love her. I rest my head back on the cushions and close my eyes.

"Last night *was* fun."

A pillow bounces off my lap and hits the floor. I open one eye and look at Marina, who's scowling at me like I just said puppies are ugly.

"What was that for?"

She chuffs. "Why did you say that like you're going to a funeral?"

I sit up and look at her squarely. "I didn't."

Marina raises her eyebrows at me as my tea kettle starts to boil. I pull myself up out of the loveseat and head for the kitchen.

"You sounded like someone shot your dog," she calls after me.

I pull a mug out of the cupboard and grab a tea bag. "So it's the dog's funeral I'm going to?"

Marina groans. "Do I have to throw another pillow?"

I laugh and finish fixing my tea, then pace back to the living room and my perch on the loveseat.

"All I said was that last night was fun…and it was."

She lowers her eyebrows. "Then why do you sound so sad?"

I blow on my tea to give myself time to think. Marina stares me down.

"Rick has made me realize some things lately."

More blowing.

More staring.

"I see now more than ever how much I was settling for someone who didn't see me," I say quietly. "But my fake date with Rick wasn't just the best fake date ever. It was the best *date* I've ever had. What does that say about me?"

Marina sighs loudly. "Nothing, Ash. Stop trying to punish yourself."

I nod. "I know. I'm not sure I know how to stop, but I'll try."

"You two were awesome together. I had so much fun just watching you dance."

I groan and flex my feet, then point my toes and relax. "My feet are mad at me. I'm not used to that."

A soft laugh is her only reply.

"And now it's over," I say with resignation. "And real life is back. So maybe that's why I'm a little sad. I need to find a way to cheer myself up."

Marina nods thoughtfully. "Hey. How about I go down to that cute little bakery on Leavenworth and get us some breakfast?"

I gasp. "You'd walk uphill for me? You're the best friend ever." Seriously, the street we live on is legendary for how steep it is. Gotta love San Francisco.

Marina chuckles and makes her way to the door, grabbing her purse off the entry table. "I'll be back after I hike up and down California Street!"

I smile after my friend, then carefully take a sip of my tea. Warmth runs through me, and I sigh. I just need to relax. And focus on the week ahead. I need to get back into my regular routine, that's all. I take another sip of tea and swipe the screen of my cell phone.

Nothing from Rick. No texts or missed calls. That also makes me sad, and it totally shouldn't be because we're not a couple. He doesn't even think of me that way. He literally pointed out there's nothing between us. Can't get more clear than that. Why am I checking my phone like he's my boyfriend?

And what's up with me, anyway? Where's the Dragon Lady when I need her? I shake my head and take another sip. She never comes out for Rick because...well, I'm not sure why now. He treats me with respect, so I've never needed to set boundaries with him. Is there more to unpack here? Maybe there is now.

Now that I've been on a date with him.

Fake date, Ashley. Fake.

Truth is, it felt pretty real to me. And if I'm being honest with myself, I wanted it to be real. He's so gorgeous and thoughtful and interesting. There's nothing I don't like about him. And all the physical affection? Like a drug. But if he says there's nothing between us, there's nothing more to say. I have to find a way to get back to normal.

Maybe this is a sign that I'm finally ready for something more. Going out with Rick woke up a ton of feelings that I didn't allow myself to think about before. Perhaps I should start dating again. It might be just the thing to get Rick out of my system, too, because, let's face it, if he starts dating someone while I have these feelings? Ouch. If I can move on gracefully, nothing has to be awkward between us.

Marina comes through the door just as I start thumbing through dating apps. I look up, surprised to find her carrying a big box with our breakfast resting on top of it. I jump up to help her, taking the box so she can shut the door. She grabs the breakfast items and follows me to the living room.

"What did you buy?" I ask as I set the box on the coffee table.

Marina hands me a bag from the bakery that smells like heaven. Almond croissants. My favorite.

"I didn't buy that. A delivery man was standing in front of the building as I was walking back. It's for you."

My eyes widen. "Me? From who?"

I set my croissant down and pick up the box. Sure enough, my name is on the address label. It's from a courier. I shake my head, unable to think of what it could possibly be.

"I think I know who. There's a card taped on the side."

I flip the box around and find a little white envelope taped there. There's one word handwritten on it: *Fireball.*

I am completely unable to stop the huge smile from spreading across my face as I slide my thumb under the flap and pull a small card out.

Fireball, last night was so fun...but I feel a little guilty about wearing you out. This should help. Rick.

I laugh softly and pass the card to Marina as I start unwrapping the plain brown paper. Marina reads it and grins at me.

"I love him," she says. "He is the best."

I pull the paper away and gasp as I hold up the fanciest foot massager I've ever seen in my life. We both burst out laughing as we read the description on the box.

"Oh, it has heat settings!" Marina exclaims.

"What? We are trying this out right now!"

I pull the box open, and Marina helps me unpack everything. We plug it in and I set it on the floor in front of the loveseat. There are two deep, dark holes where I'm supposed to insert my feet. I take my socks off and put my feet inside. It feels a little weird. There's a soft fabric lining the inside, but I can also feel bumps from the machine underneath. I lean forward and hover my finger over the power button.

"Ready?" I ask Marina.

"Turn it on, I want to know what this thing does!" Marina cries.

I hit the power button, and the machine whirs to life. The massaging element starts rolling what feels like little hard plastic balls against the bottoms of my feet. The heat kicks in pretty fast, and I look over at Marina excitedly.

"Ooooooh!"

She laughs. "Yeah?"

"This thing is amazing."

Marina gets up, steps over to look at the control panel, and starts pushing buttons. The heat and pressure increase, and I groan and fall back against the cushions. This is absolute bliss.

"This is the best thing anyone has ever given me."

I hear a giggle and open one eye to find her holding her phone up. "What are you doing?"

"Taking a picture to send to Rick later," she croons.

I hold my hand out, not willing to move away from this machine. "Not without showing me first."

She drops her phone in my hand, and I hold it up to my face. It's hysterical, but still acceptable. I hand the phone back.

"Acceptable," I mutter. "But don't send it until I have the chance to thank him, okay?"

She nods. "Rick is so sweet."

I heave out a huge sigh. "He is."

She points her finger at me. "There it is again. Where's the funeral?"

I shake my head. "I can't possibly be expected to form a coherent sentence with my feet in the Bliss Maker."

A huge laugh bellows out of Marina. "The Bliss Maker? You've named it?"

I grin. "When this cycle is over, you're next. Then you'll understand."

She stands, picks up my croissant, and hands it to me.

"Until then, eat your croissant and be happy."

I give her a thumbs up and settle back against the cushions. How can I possibly start dating again when I already have Mr. Perfect? Except I don't have him. I shoved him in the friend zone pretty quick, and I don't have anyone to blame for that but me and my feminine rage.

The machine turns off, and I sit up, pulling my feet out and slipping my socks back on. My feet are tingling and warm, and they feel so good. I push it over to Marina with a grin.

"Your turn."

She puts her feet in and starts pushing buttons as I pull up my cell phone and open a text to Rick.

Ashley: You are the sweetest man who ever lived. Thank you for the best foot rub ever.

"Oh my gosh!" Marina exclaims.

"Right?" I say with a knowing grin.

Rick: I'm glad you like it! Are you feeling alright? I didn't want to text you earlier in case you were sleeping.

I think about my reply. I need to be smart. I need to do what is logical and necessary, not what I want to do. I need to step away from my perfect, beautiful, hot man-friend before I come away with a broken heart.

Ashley: Feeling fine, just not used to so much dancing - which was awesome. Thank you so much for being such a good sport last night, Rick. You're a great friend.

Emphasis on friend. I hate myself as I type out the message, but this is the logical and necessary path. Distance myself. He's happy in the friend zone. I'm the one who's getting all weird. Obviously I need to distract myself and start over, so I swipe open the dating app I was looking at and start filling out my profile.

Chapter 10

Two days later, I step into the apartment after work and hear the now familiar sounds of Rick's drill as he works on the bookcases. Despite my best efforts to quell the crush I have on him, my heartbeat still picks up excitedly when he's here. I'm trying to just let it exist, trusting that it'll fade away eventually. Originally, I tried actively talking myself out of these feelings, but I always ended up just listing all the qualities I like about him. That isn't helpful.

"Ash?" Rick's voice booms from the living room.

Honey, I'm home.

No, Ashley. No.

"Hey, you!" I call out as I walk into the living room.

Rick has his back to me, facing the bookcase that's now about half done. The long-sleeved t-shirt he's wearing perfectly accentuates his broad shoulders and muscular arms for my viewing pleasure. His hair is pulled back in the usual man bun. I'm beginning to think it's some kind of antennae that broadcasts his sex appeal even further, reeling me in like some kind of tractor beam. I want to walk up behind him, snake my arms around his waist, and kiss the back of his shoulder.

No, Ashley. No.

He turns to face me, completely disarming the rest of my defenses with a gorgeous smile.

"Hey, buddy!" he says, setting the drill down and coming over to give me a hug.

This is a new thing that developed after the night we danced, and I'm not sure how I feel about it. He keeps calling me "buddy" and "pal". At first, I try to lean into it because it audibly reminds me that we're just friends. We're only ever going to be friends, a fact made even more obvious by the fact that he keeps using those words. It's really just annoying me now, but it's always followed by a Rick hug and I will never, ever turn those down.

I smile, and he pulls me into a warm, strong embrace. I wrap an arm around him, my hand drifting up to the broadest part of his back. Muscles ripple under my fingertips as he squeezes me tighter. I would love nothing more than to just stay here. His familiar, oh-so-delicious piney woods scent welcomes me into hug heaven. At least I'll always have this. He's a hugger.

"How's the bookcase coming along?"

Rick releases me and steps back so fast I nearly smack into him, but I catch myself. He walks back to the bookcase and smacks one of the shelves with his hand.

"This section has been giving me a little trouble, but I think it's okay now."

I take a moment to look at it. "Looks perfect to me."

Just like you.

"Thanks, Ash. I'm happy with it now."

He starts packing his tools up, so I head for my bedroom to drop off my bags, then pop back to the living room and sit in my usual spot. Thankfully, no one got any paste or other substance on me today, and things were relatively peaceful. I did get sneezed on by sweet little Emily Allen, but that was right in the face. My clothes were spared.

"It's my night to make dinner again," I remind him. "Would you like to stay?"

Rick looks up from his tool bag with a grin. "Actually, Marina came up earlier to let me know she's going out with Zach. So you're off the hook. You don't have to cook dinner."

This seems to be happening with alarming regularity. I make a mental note to have a talk with my bestie, the meddlesome mermaid. She keeps trying to shove us together when it's obvious to me she's just wishful thinking.

"Well, I still have to cook for me at least," I say with a wry grin. "But I'll make something simple later."

Rick puts his bag over by the door, then comes to stand in front of me.

"Actually, I meant you don't have to cook at all. Why don't we go grab some food?"

Hmm. The thought of not having a mess to clean up later is very appealing. Add in the chance to spend more time with Rick, and the offer is hard to beat. I look up into those ocean blue eyes of his.

"What are you in the mood for?"

He wiggles his eyebrows at me. "Taco Tuesday?"

I reach up for a high-five, and he lightly smacks my hand. "Sold. Tacos sound perfect."

"Cool," Rick says. "In about an hour? Unless you want to go now."

"No, an hour at least," I say, standing up and heading for the kitchen. "I need to decompress first."

I grab my electric tea kettle off the stand and fill it with water, then put it back and hit the power switch. Rick pulls out one of the bar stools and takes a seat, watching me as I pull my favorite mug out of a cabinet and gather my tea bag, spoon and the milk from the fridge. I hold a tea bag up.

"Do you want a cup?"

He shakes his head. "I'm too hot from working on the bookcases, but thanks."

I nod, then open the tea bag and set it in the mug.

"We should talk about Dad's company retreat," I hedge.

Rick grows serious. His eyes meet mine. "What about it?"

I hear the water in my tea kettle begin to boil. I have to give Rick an out. I'm in complete conflict over wanting him to go and wanting him to stay away. The logical thing is to give him an out and let him gracefully decline, as I'm sure he wants to.

"I don't want you to feel like you have to come," I say in a tone I hope is light and airy. But I don't feel that way at all. "I'm releasing you from any obligation. I'll just say your publicity thing came up again."

Rick gets up to grab a bottle of water from the fridge, then moves to my side of the kitchen island and leans a hip against the counter. His gaze flicks over my face, studying.

"Because you don't want me to come, Fireball?"

My throat goes instantly dry. Because I *do* want him to come, but that is the dumbest idea ever. I shake my head just slightly.

"No, it's not that."

Rick holds my gaze. "So what is it then?"

I chew on my lower lip as I try to think of anything believable. "I know you don't like…"

Uh oh…what's his name?

The corner of Rick's mouth tilts up in a smirk. "Greg?"

"Greg! Yes!!" I exclaim a little too loudly.

Get a grip, Ash.

"The weasel," Rick adds, prompting a laugh from me.

"You really don't like him at all, do you?"

"No," he growls, almost preternaturally still as his deep blue eyes assess me.

"Because he hurt my feelings." It's not really a question. I know Rick cares about me, but sometimes it really does seem like he has bigger feelings.

"No."

I raise my eyebrows at his unexpected response. He takes a step closer and his eyes darken as he looks down at me. I can feel the heat from his body reaching out to mine like a living thing, begging me to take one tiny step closer…into his arms.

"I don't like him because he never *saw* you. Not really. He never appreciated the absolute treasure he had when he had you. I don't like him because he tried to shove you into a mold that he made so he could have what he thought was the perfect woman, but he missed the mark. You were already perfect. He tried to make you less. *That* is why I don't like him."

I gulp down a swallow. Just like that, I'm back to wanting to throw caution to the wind and just go for it. How does he have this kind of effect on me? All logic is gone now. Any words I can think to say feel meaningless after a speech like that, and I find myself wanting to touch him. I could tuck my hand into his, or reach up and stroke my fingers along that sexy five o'clock shadow. Or just throw all caution to the wind and step into his space, wrap my arms around his neck, and see what he tastes like once and for all. His eyes drift down to my mouth as if he's thinking the exact same thing.

Knock, knock, knock.

We both jump at the sound of a loud knock on the door, followed by Scarlet's lilting voice.

"Yoohoo!" she calls through the door. "Open up, I know you're in there!"

I clear my throat and step back. A muscle twitches in Rick's jaw as he turns away and heads to the door.

"I'll get it," he grumbles.

I pour the water into my cup with a pounding heart, trying to process what just happened. I don't even know where to begin. I'm not sure I ever will. What was that? I mean…it was…wow.

Wow.

This is getting too crazy and I am going to end up hurt. I try to focus, but my head feels a little fuzzy.

Rick opens the door, and Scarlet breezes in. She greets him and heads toward me in the kitchen. I stir my tea and try to look as nonchalant as possible.

"Hey, I—" she cuts herself off and stops cold, glancing between Rick and me. "Oh, yikes. Did I interrupt something?"

I raise my eyebrows and shake my head. "Nope."

Rick just frowns.

"Oh, no…were you two having a *moment?*" Scarlet prattles on.

I shake my head again, trying to give her a look that says *be quiet.* But it's Scarlet. She doesn't work that way.

"Because it looks like you were having a moment," she says, smiling at me. "You are three shades of red, dude."

I tilt my head at her, eyes wide and highly alarmed. "No, I'm not… and what's new with you?"

She doesn't answer me. She just keeps looking between us. Finally, her gaze settles on Rick.

"And you look positively grumpy," she says with the air of a detective in a murder mystery. "You're never grumpy."

Rick scoffs. "I'm *not* grumpy."

I clear my throat at Scarlet. Loudly. She finally snaps out of it and pats Rick on the shoulder.

"Well, good," she says lightly. "Because I need a favor."

I point at Rick. "From him?"

Scarlet nods at me as if this is a normal thing she does every day, then whips out her cell phone.

"Marina said you might be able to make these."

She holds her phone up so Rick can see what's on her screen.

"Corbels?" he says, nodding. "Yeah, I can make those. All kinds. I even have a wood lathe at home so I can do wood turning."

Scarlet squeals and jumps up and down. "Can you make these for me? How much would you charge? How long would it take?"

I laugh. "Breathe, girl."

Rick takes another look at the photo. "How many do you need?"

"Four."

"One day, maybe two, depending on what I have going on."

"Okay, and how much do you want?" she asks, biting her lower lip.

He grins at her, and my heart melts. "No charge for the inner circle."

She shakes her head. "Nope. Can't do that...I have to pay you something, c'mon."

He thinks for a moment. "I'll tell you what. You buy the wood, and I'll throw in the labor for free."

Scarlet shakes her head again. "Tempting, but you're still not getting much for a lot of work. Increase your price. A little bit...not a lot."

Rick laughs. "Okay, final offer: you buy the wood, I do the labor. You throw in some of Nonno's breadsticks, and you owe me a favor."

Scarlet laughs. "Deal!"

I smile at Scarlet and blow on my tea. "How's the project coming along?"

She grins devilishly. "Awesome. Designing the decor for my Mom's office is going to do the trick for sure."

I notice Rick's confused look and fill him in about Scarlet's quest to win the ultimate home decorating challenge.

"Well, I'm definitely all in," he tells her. "If you win, my corbels will be famous."

I laugh out loud. "You're already famous."

He tilts his head slightly. "True."

"And nominated for *two* World Music Awards. I'm so proud of you," I say, just slightly gushing. But I *am* proud of him. And happy for him as well.

Rick looks at me pointedly. "Well, if you're proud of me, then I've already won. I don't need the trophy."

Once again, my heart pounds out of my chest, and I feel like one of those cartoon characters with hearts for eyes. I wish he'd stop being so sweet. It's so confusing. Those words could be so romantic if he wasn't calling me "buddy" half the time. But that's what I am: his little buddy. And he's just being sweet.

I have to get control over myself before I get hurt.

"Right!" Scarlet chimes in, making me realize she's still here. I was drifting off to Rick Land. "So you guys continue on with…whatever you were doing, and I'm gonna go work on some stuff."

I follow her to the door, my face heating in embarrassment. I need to nip this in the bud.

"We weren't doing anything," I proclaim, loud enough for Rick to hear. "He's just a friend. There is nothing going on, nor will there ever be. Stop imagining things."

Scarlet chuckles under her breath as she gets to the door, whispering, "Yeah, you were having a moment."

I look over my shoulder to see where Rick is, and he's still in the kitchen. Looking at his phone.

"Scarlet," I grumble out. "He doesn't think about me that way."

She looks at me like I told her I want to shave my head. "You've got to be kidding me. How can you be so smart and not see this?"

"Shh!" I hold up a finger, and she stifles a laugh. "He calls me buddy and pal all the time. He pointed out that there's nothing between us. He absolutely does not want me as anything but a friend. You're imagining things."

Scarlet's expression grows serious, and she pulls me in for a hug.

When she pulls away, she places both of her hands on either side of my head and looks at me with eyes filled with emotion.

"And you're so afraid of getting hurt again after Greg that you would rather not see the man standing right in front of you who would rearrange the moon and every star in the sky for you."

Scarlet swings open the door and steps through it, then turns around and lightly touches my arm. I look at her with a thousand questions on the tip of my tongue.

"Love you," she says quietly, then turns on her heel and heads downstairs and out of the building, leaving me speechless.

***

Rick

I watch Scarlet and Ashley huddled by the door, taking a moment to come to grips with what just happened. As much as I hate to admit it, Ashley's words really stung.

There is nothing going on, nor will there ever be.

Ouch.

I guess that puts it all to rest. The finality of it rings in my ears. Clearly, I need to stop being so delusional. Ashley's feelings obviously don't go beyond friendship and that's that. I need to get with the program or I'm going to make things awkward between us - and that's assuming I haven't already. I thought she might be softening up, but nothing has changed at all. This is just the reality check I needed.

I hear the door close and look up in time to see Ashley headed back to the kitchen, so I shove my pride aside and plaster a pleasant smile on my face. She looks flushed, and she's pinching the bridge of her nose.

"Everything okay?"

She smiles wanly and grabs her mug of tea. "Yeah, I'm just really tired all of a sudden."

I frown at her, suddenly concerned, and then I remember it's not my place - and she's made that abundantly clear.

She smiles apologetically and takes a sip of her tea. "Actually, do you mind if we order in? I don't feel like going out."

More likely, she doesn't really feel like company at all. I take a step back.

"Maybe I should just go home," I offer. "I'm sure you'd probably enjoy some peace and quiet."

She studies me for a moment, and if I didn't know better I'd say I saw disappointment in her expression. Ashley blinks up at me a few times.

"Oh, yeah. You probably have things to do as well. I can just order something for myself."

Against my better judgment, I let my eyes rove over her face. Those beautiful blue eyes watch me carefully. I worry my bottom lip with my teeth, then give her a quick nod.

"Right," I say, snapping myself out of my Ashley trance. "I'll just get out of your way."

I turn away and head for the door.

"Rick?"

I turn back to look at Ashley, who crosses her arms across the front of her chest and watches me cautiously.

"Did I say something bad?" she asks in a small voice. "You seem... well, if I made things weird, I apologize."

I clear my throat.

"No, I just don't want to be in your way," I tell her. "I can't imagine what it's like to manage a classroom of noisy kids all day. You probably want some peace."

She's quiet, considering. As if on queue, my stomach lets out a growl that could wake the dead. I let out a chuckle as Ashley's eyebrows nearly hit her hairline.

"Was that your stomach?"

I grin sheepishly. "Sorry."

"I can't let you go all the way back to Mill Valley with your stomach growling like that," she says lightly, pulling out her phone. "I'm ordering tacos."

She steps into the living room and sits on the loveseat.

"I always order from Big Daddy Tacos," she says hoarsely. "Have you ever had their food?"

I shake my head, slowly wandering over from the kitchen. Staying here and having tacos with Ashley is a horrible idea. I need to get away from her and get my head in a better place. We need distance, not tacos. She smiles up at me and I feel the all too familiar tug at my heartstrings. Bad idea, Rick.

"What do you usually get?" I ask, stalling. "Taco fillings can tell a lot about a person."

Ashley's eyes widen. "They can?"

I nod, feeling my self-respect shrivel up inside me. Grow a backbone, Rick. She isn't interested.

"I'm a grilled chicken kind of girl," she offers. "With a little cheese, light on the lettuce. Spicy salsa. You?"

I feel the corner of my mouth tick up and I fight the smile.

"Usually it's steak and pico," I tell her. "But don't order anything for me. I really should get going."

She definitely looks disappointed, but I can't think why. Ashley puts her phone aside and moves to stand, but I wave her off as I walk towards the door.

"You don't have to see me out, Ash," I tell her over my shoulder. "I know the way. Have a good night."

I grab my tools and slip out the door, hearing her say goodnight just as it snicks shut. Every step I take down the stairs makes me feel better and worse all at once. Better because I'm putting some distance between us, worse because it's not at all what I really want.

Once outside, I toss my equipment into the truck and walk around to the driver's side to get in. I sit back in my seat for a minute, letting out a bitter chuckle. So much for the reverse psychology I was trying to pull by calling her "buddy" and trying to make her think she was in my friend zone. Ashley and I are friends and that's all we're every going to be. Full stop. The sooner I get that through my thick skull, the better.

***

Ashley

I had the hardest time falling asleep last night after behaving like a world class klutz in front of Rick. I was the moth to his flame and then I had to go and mess it up. Watching him backtrack and shove a wall between us was downright painful. Sleep was fitful at best, and now my alarm is blaring me awake. I sit up too fast, realizing I have a splitting headache and a raging sore throat.

No, no, no.

I'm not sick. I can't be sick. I try to stand up, but I'm so dizzy that I have to lie back down again.

I'm so sick.

I fumble around for my cell phone and call work to explain the situation so they can call in a substitute. The school principal can barely understand me because my voice is so hoarse, but she gets the gist of it and tells me to go back to bed. I feel my forehead, and it doesn't feel too hot, but my throat is on fire. I can tell by the silence in the apartment that Marina must have spent the night at Zach's. Even if I had a normal voice, there's no one to hear me plead for water and aspirin, so I try to get up again. Slowly.

Standing doesn't give me as much of a problem, so I walk slowly to the kitchen, get a bottle of water and some juice, then head back to my bedroom. I set everything down, then head to my bathroom to get some painkillers and wash my face. *That* makes me pretty dizzy. I get back to my bed and take the painkillers, then drink down a few gulps of juice.

As soon as I crawl back into bed, I realize I need to stop Rick from coming over to work on the bookcase. Of course, after last night he'll probably rejoice when I tell him not to come. I test my voice and can barely get a squeak out, so I open a text message.

Ashley: Do *not* come work on the bookcases today. I'm really sick. Sore throat, probably a fever coming. I hope I didn't get you sick. Please stay away, but please text me back and let me know if you're feeling okay.

I text something similar to Marina, so she stays at Zach's for a while. Satisfied with that, I drift off into a fitful slumber.

***

I need to wake up from this dream. What is even happening right now? I'm freezing cold and sweating, and someone is calling my name. My head is foggy.

Ashley...

I try to roll over, but everything hurts. I groan, but hardly any sound comes out.

Ashley, wake up...

I recognize the voice.

Rick.

It's Rick. No, it can't be Rick. I told him to stay home.

"C'mon, Ash," Rick's voice sounds gently in my ear. "Wake up..."

I open my eyes carefully and Rick's worried face looks down at me.

"Noooo," I whisper hoarsely. "I told you to stay home, Rick."

"Shh," is the reply I get as he gently strokes my hair away from my face. "There is no way I'm staying away if I hear you're sick."

"Go home."

He shakes his head. "Not happening, sorry. You're not the boss of me."

"Please go home."

Rick lowers his face close to mine, his eyes full of sweetness. "No. And please stop talking so you don't hurt your voice."

"I don't want to get you sick."

He raises his eyebrows in mock concern as if I've just defied him in the worst way. Even as sick as I am, it's funny. Honestly, it's a relief to see him acting normally. The teasing feels like a good sign.

"Stop. Talking."

I manage a feeble smile. "How can I tell you I need something if you don't let me talk?"

He smiles back, and it feels like a gift - especially after the events of last night.

"Are you going to let me stay if I let you talk?"

I nod, and my head goes spinning. "Whoa..."

Rick moves instantly. A cold cloth appears out of nowhere, and he presses it to my forehead.

"Oh, wow...that's nice."

He nods. "See? I'm a good nurse. I'm glad you're gonna keep me on the payroll."

I raise my eyebrows and close my eyes. "Payroll? What am I paying you? Can I afford you?"

"Maybe tacos someday," he replies. "Or just a big hug."

I open my mouth to answer back, and he holds up a hand.

"As much as I adore the direction this conversation is heading, can I ask you to give your voice a rest for a few minutes?"

I nod slowly, and he looks relieved. "Very good. Can I get you to drink some water?"

I nod again and move to sit up. Wordlessly, Rick puts his arm around me and helps pull me up into a half-sitting position. He offers me a cold bottle of water and I take it, managing to get small sips in. My body hurts everywhere.

"If I make a piece of toast, do you think you can eat a little?"

I take a few more sips and hand the bottle back. I sink back to the bed and nod.

"Do you want anything else?"

His eyes are so full of concern. I shake my head and mouth *thank you*, knowing I can't get any sound out of my voice right now. He smiles softly, a hint of something I can't identify behind his eyes, then stands and disappears from my field of vision. I hear water running in the bathroom, and he reappears, putting another cold cloth on my forehead.

"I'll be right back, Fireball," he says gently. "Try to drink a little more if you can."

I nod and watch him walk away, feeling a little too much gratitude that he's here. I felt like such a jerk last night when he all but raced out of here, trying to get away from me. I wasn't prepared for all the feelings that came with it. Feelings of guilt, sure, but also I felt alone without him…like I'd really lost something important. I hated the feeling.

I should send him straight back home. I should insist that I'll go to the doctor and tell him he's crowding me, but I'm facing a very familiar roadblock. I don't want to push him away anymore.

I realize I may be inviting a whole lot of heartbreak at the end of this. Somehow, my heart has changed. I sit up as best I can and take a few more sips of water before settling under the covers and praying I'm not making a huge mistake.

Chapter 11

Rick

I roll over in a bed that's in the middle of the city, not at my home in the woods. When Marina and I got the texts from a very sick Ashley, we quickly got together and made a plan. We met up at the apartment and after we checked on her together, we agreed that I would stay and look after Ash, and that Marina would stay at Zach's. They have a big interview later this week, all about the Mermaid Foundation, and she can't be sick for that. When I asked for fresh bedding for the couch, she put it on her bed instead and told me to stop being ridiculous. So I've set up camp in Marina's bedroom while I take care of Ashley.

Is it against my better judgment? Yep. Am I going to change this self-destructive path I'm on? Nope. Not when she's sick. I'll build my boundaries back up after she's well again.

Last night was all about getting her to drink and rest. I had the local drugstore deliver everything I need to take care of her, and of course, I also have the whole inner circle at my disposal if I need help. And even if I don't need help.

Merry stopped by with a huge order from Nonno's last night. I was completely prepared to just make myself a sandwich or something, but the unexpected meal from Nonno's was a welcome substitution. And the leftovers kept me going as I checked on my patient through the night.

I swing my legs out of bed and throw on my jeans so I can check on her before I hit the shower. Padding down the hall towards her room, I make a mental note to try to get her to eat a little before it's time for her next dose of medication. I step into her room to find her sleeping, looking a little more peaceful than last night.

I shove aside the feelings that curl in my gut at the sight of her. I need to get that in check. It's not gonna happen, Rick.

I gently touch her forehead to check her temp and I'm relieved to find the fever is still gone. It raged through her for a few hours, but between getting her to drink and keeping cold compresses on her, I got it down.

"Rick?" she croaks, rolling over to face me.

"Right here," I say gently. She reaches a hand up in my direction, and I take it. "What can I get you, Fireball?"

She pulls at me and scoots over. "You," she squeaks out. "Hugs."

Yep. This is fine. I'm fine. She's just sick and needy right now. This doesn't mean anything.

I take a seat on her bed, leaning back against the headboard. She lays her head on my chest and drapes her arm across my middle while I hold her. This was standard practice last night, so I guess we're continuing today. It won't continue once she's well because…it just can't now. I do wish I'd put a shirt on first, although she still seems pretty out of it. She probably won't notice.

I reach over to the nightstand and grab the bottle of Gatorade she was working on last night, offering it to her after I unscrew the cap.

"Can you drink a little of this?"

She murmurs something and takes the bottle from me, swigging from it a little too hard. Gatorade splashes, and I grab a tissue and start dabbing her chin and neck. She's still pretty out of it, but she grabs the tissue from my hand and starts dabbing my chest. Or what she thinks is my chest. She's actually very lightly punching me in the stomach with a fist full of tissue as I try not to laugh. I grab another tissue and try to finish dabbing her neck where the liquid splashed.

"Stop fighting me," she grumbles adorably. "I'm trying to help."

"You're doing great, Fireball," I say as I stifle my laughter.

I toss the tissue into the little bin I put next to her bed and hold her while she continues trying to mop up a splash that she's already cleaned up.

"Oh, these are nice," she murmurs as she lays her cheek against my chest.

I look down. "What are?"

She moves her fingers across the flat of my stomach. "These abs right here."

I laugh softly. I hope she doesn't remember this when she's feeling better. She'll be mortified, even if I think it's ten kinds of adorable.

"How many are there?"

Her hand starts to drift lower, and I jolt up, taking her hand and placing it on the bed. I slide out of the bed and ease her head onto her pillow.

"I'll tell you what," I say as I check her for fever again. "Maybe I'll let you count them someday."

She closes her eyes and drifts off, murmuring something unintelligible. I take a moment to just stand here and look at her. I'll get my head in check later. Even as ill as she is, she's beautiful. Her long blond hair is splayed out all around her like rays of sunshine. I smile to myself as I turn back to the hall and go take a shower. A cold one, thanks to the ab-counting incident. After that, I'll get breakfast ready and hopefully, she'll eat something.

What do dragons eat, anyway?

***

Ashley

A feather-light touch brushes across my brow, and I flutter my eyes open after another good, long nap. I look up to find Rick there, looking down at me with concern. Then he smiles, and I smile back as I stretch under the covers. With much relief, I realize my body doesn't hurt everywhere anymore.

"What time is it?"

"Around five o'clock. Almost dinner time," he says. "Are you hungry?"

I think about it for a moment. "I could eat a little something."

He nods. "Good. Anything sound appealing?"

"Not very much. Maybe some toast?" I look around the room. "How long have I been in these pajamas?"

Rick laughs softly, and I smile back at him. "I think I want to take a shower."

He looks relieved. "Well, that's a really good sign if you're thinking that way. Let's just make sure you can stand up without getting dizzy, okay?"

I take the hand he offers to help me sit up, pulling myself up slowly. I feel a bit wonky, but I'm super relieved when I don't get dizzy. I carefully swing my legs from under the covers and place my feet on the floor. I look down to find I'm wearing two different colored fuzzy socks and laugh.

"Wow, I'm a mess."

Rick laughs. "You're not a mess. You're sick. You get a pass."

I nod. "I'll take it."

I pull myself up to a standing position, still not getting dizzy. I look at Rick victoriously.

"Okay, I think I'll give you the space to take your shower in peace," he says, heading for the door. "And I'll go make your toast."

I nod and give him a small smile as he leaves, and then I walk into my bathroom and turn on the shower spray. I pull down two towels, then lower the cover on the toilet and sit down to wait for the water to warm up. I don't feel super wobbly, but my energy level is definitely sapped. And I'm still pretty congested. When steam starts to billow inside the shower, I get up and shut the bathroom door, then strip and toss my jammies in the hamper.

I move slowly and take my time, but I don't linger because I definitely still feel weak. I wrap my hair in a towel, then dry off and grab my robe off the hook and pad into my closet to find something to wear. Leggings, t-shirt, big sweater. I stop for a clean pair of matching fuzzy socks and head back to the bathroom, shutting the door behind me. I get dressed, then comb through my wet hair and get the hair dryer from the cabinet.

Dizzy, dizzy, dizzy.

I know not to lie around with wet hair when I'm sick, though, so I take a seat on the toilet again and plug in the hair dryer. Just a few minutes of trying to hold the hair dryer up has me tired. I set it down with a laugh. Okay, then. I work my hair into a twist at the back of my head and secure it with a clip, then head out to the kitchen to see about that toast.

Rick is coming around the corner just as I get to the kitchen, and we almost run right into each other. He steadies me with two big hands on my shoulders, looking into my eyes to make sure I'm okay. When I look at him, I'm rapidly overcome with gratitude for everything he's done for me over the past two days. I don't ask, and I don't think. I just step into his arms and wrap my arms around his waist. Without hesitation, his arms wrap around me. One hand floats up to cradle the back of my head as I press my cheek to his chest and breathe in. We just stand here for a few minutes, holding each other.

"Are you all right?" he murmurs against my hair.

I nod. "Yep. Just grateful."

His fingers lightly massage my head, and I pull away with a laugh.

"I will pass out from relaxation if you do that right now."

He laughs. "Okay, why don't you go back to bed, and I'll bring your toast."

I chew on my lower lip. "I'd rather be out here for a while. I'm so tired of my bedroom."

He grins at me. "Another good sign. I think you've turned the corner. I can tell Marina you're going to live."

"Oh, ha ha," I tease, letting him lead me over to the living room.

I sit on the loveseat, not at all surprised when Rick pulls the blanket out and proceeds to tuck me in tightly. I just watch him, smiling as he works. When he's done, my arms are pinned to my sides, but every part of me is warm. He ducks down so our faces are level.

"Don't go anywhere," he jokes. "I'll be right back."

I smirk at him as he goes, but my heart returns to gratitude. I don't deserve him at all. While he putters around the kitchen, I have a minute or two to think about the situation. Just a few weeks ago, I didn't want anything to do with a relationship with anyone—including Rick, even though I've always noted his perfect, rugged good looks. Fast forward through a few awkward moments and one heck of a fake date, and I was looking at him like a love-sick puppy, even though he kept calling me buddy and pal every thirty seconds. Now, he's just spent the past two days taking care of me after I was such a jerk….and I'm realizing I may have had the wrong idea. Something's not adding up.

My thought process is still fuzzy, and I smell sausage cooking, which is very distracting. My voice is still not back to normal, so I can't talk to Rick while he's in the kitchen. I have no choice but to just wait patiently…cocooned in my favorite blanket. It's a few more minutes before I hear footsteps, but Rick eventually reappears with a plate and a glass of juice with a straw in it.

"Are you warm enough?" he asks.

Nope. I do not deserve even a shot at this man.

I nod. "Perfectly."

He sits beside me on the loveseat. "Good. Stay there then."

I raise my eyebrows at him. "How am I supposed to eat?"

He shrugs like it's no big deal. "I've got this."

He holds the glass of juice up so I can put the straw in my mouth, and I giggle.

"This is ridiculous," I say before putting the straw in my mouth.

He sticks his chin out. "C'mon."

I keep eye contact with him and take a few sips of juice.

"Done?"

I nod. "Was anyone taking care of you while you were taking care of me?"

He frowns. "No, why?"

"Because I think you've lost your mind."

He laughs. "It's all part of the five-star service I provide."

He spears a breakfast sausage with a fork and holds it up for me. I giggle and nod, taking a bite. My stomach growls in anticipation as I chew and swallow the bite. I think about my next words carefully.

"And do you provide this five-star service to all your friends?"

He tilts his head, thinking. "Well, Zach and Marina have each other for this kind of thing. Sam is married, and Jimmy's had the same girlfriend for ages. They're all taken care of."

I nod. "I see." I take another bite. "So you would provide this service to Scarlet or Merry if they get sick then? Since they don't have boyfriends or husbands, I mean."

I chew and watch his expression in delight as he realizes he's backed himself into a corner. "Well, no. That would be weird."

I nod again, a slow smile spreading across my face. "I see."

He squints at me as if I'm trying to unearth some secret that isn't there. I take the last bite of sausage and chew, smiling at him like I know a secret. I think I *do* know a secret. I think I'm beginning to understand.

"What do you see?" he asks, offering me more juice.

I sip from the straw slowly, swallowing when I'm done. I lick my lips and shrug.

"It's just interesting. Thank you."

Rick picks up the piece of toast on the plate and holds it up. I nod, and he moves it forward towards my lips. He pulls it away abruptly and squints at me.

"What's interesting?"

I shake my head slowly, offering him a secret smile. "Not sure I'm right about it. Maybe I'll tell you later."

He moves the toast to my lips, and I take a bite.

"Thank you," I mutter around the crunchy, buttery bit of toast in my mouth.

He sighs. "I'm glad to see you feeling so much better."

I smile and nod. "Me too."

He smiles, and I take another bite of toast. I chew it slowly, and we just sit here watching each other. I shake my head when he offers me more.

"I think I should stop. That's enough for now."

He nods and puts the toast back on the plate, then he picks up a piece of sausage and pops it in his mouth.

"I'd return the favor and feed you, but I'm all germy."

He laughs softly. "Thankfully, you're less germy than you were when I first stopped by to check on you."

I nod. "Hey, have you even been home this whole time?"

He sets the plate on the coffee table, then turns back to me.

"The first day, once Marina and I decided that I would stay to take care of you, she sat out here so I could run home and pack a bag. I haven't been home since then."

My eyebrows float up to my hairline. "What? I'm so sorry."

He shrugs. "Why? I don't have any pets. There's no one else there. No one's waiting for me."

My expression stills. "What happened to that woman you told me about?"

His gaze flicks over my face, assessing. "What woman?"

"I asked you for details and you said there was nothing to share because she doesn't see you."

He nods slowly. "She doesn't."

I feel like we're circling each other in a verbal dance of double meaning, neither one of us wanting to actually speak the truth.

I tilt my face forward and look into his eyes. "How about now?"

His smile is almost bashful, his eyes seeking. "I think she might be starting to."

I sink in against the cushions. "Sounds like a smart woman."

Rick stands up and takes the plate to the kitchen, then returns to my side. He lightly touches my forehead, checking for fever again. I grin at him.

"I don't think the fever is coming back, Nurse Rick."

He suppresses a smile. "Nurse Rick likes to be sure."

He checks my blanket to be sure it's tucked in, then his gaze comes back to my face.

"How are you feeling?"

"Getting tired," I admit. "Not tired enough to go back to bed yet."

"Do you want to watch TV for a while?"

"That sounds good. You choose. I don't have it in me to make a decision right now."

He laughs and grabs the remote from the end table, sitting back against the cushions. "You may regret that."

I shake my head. "No, I won't."

I pull my arms out of their confines, keeping my legs covered, then lean into Rick's side and wrap my arms around his middle. He looks slightly surprised, but his arm instantly wraps around my shoulders. I smile softly at him.

"Are you warm enough like that?" he asks.

I look at him and nod. "You're like a furnace. This is perfect."

His gaze roams over my face, trying to gauge my feelings. As he turns the TV on, he mutters.

"I think so too."

***

Rick

Judging from the soft snores, Ashley has fallen asleep. That would be perfectly fine if I wasn't somewhat reclined on the loveseat with most of her weight stretched on top of me. I don't think there's any way to get up without waking her, and she needs rest. Plus, she's argued with me every time I've tried to insist she goes back to bed. But I'll need a chiropractor if I don't sit up soon, so here we go. I start pushing myself up, and she groans in protest.

"I'm still watching."

I laugh, pushing further. "No, you aren't."

"Am too."

I sit all the way up and she raises her head to squint at me.

"If you were watching, what was on screen?"

She thinks a moment. "They just caught the lady with five thousand cigarettes in her suitcase."

I laugh again and stand, swooping her into my arms and then just stretching my legs for a second. She cradles her head against my shoulder as I start carrying her to her bedroom.

"That was thirty minutes ago," I mutter against her hair. "You were totally sleeping."

Another soft snore and she's out again. I walk into her room and gently lay her down on the bed, then pull the covers up over her. Unable to resist, I gently place my palm along the side of her face and graze her cheekbone with my thumb. She sighs softly and rolls over. I pull the comforter over her shoulder and turn off the light as I leave. I head back to the living room and grab my cell phone from the end table, opening a text to Marina.

Rick: We're eating, drinking, showering and feeling better over here. I feel pretty good about her progress.

Marina: That's great! How are you doing? Can I bring you anything?

I think about the answer to that question. The only thing I need is for Ashley to realize I don't belong in the friend zone, and there were several moments tonight where I dared to hope that might actually be happening. It still feels too tenuous. Like thinking about it too much or too long will make it fade away and then it will never actually happen. So I force myself to behave as if everything is status quo while there is the tiniest spark of hope deep in the confines of my heart.

Rick: I'm okay, but thanks.

Marina: Zach says to tell you that they got confirmation that the Rebels interview is still on for tomorrow. Do you think I need to stay with her while you're gone?

Rick: Judging by how she woke up this evening, I think she'll be feeling even better in the morning. But you should check with her to be sure.

Marina: I'll do that. Oh, by the way, I think Merry is coming by tomorrow with more food from Nonno's. Text her if you want anything special. And thanks again for taking such good

care of her.

Rick: My pleasure.

I throw myself onto the couch and try to distract myself with the TV. Ash and I stumbled upon a documentary series that highlights the weird things travelers try to bring through customs in various countries, and we had the best time trying to guess what each person was hiding. It's not nearly as fun to watch without her, so I grab the remote and turn it off.

The Royal Rebels have to make an appearance at a radio station here in town to start promoting our new album that'll be out in time for Christmas. That means I have to stop playing nurse long enough to do that, then I plan to head right back here and spend whatever time I can with Ashley. Honestly, I wish we could continue to exist in this bubble for a few more days. Without her being sick, of course. Everything is so easy between us right now. I don't know what's going to happen when the real world creeps back in. And that's what I worry about most. What happens when another creepy guy comes along and brings out the Dragon Lady. Or worse, what happens if we go to this company retreat and Greg the weasel decides he wants another chance.

I stand and stretch, then head to the kitchen for a bottle of water and an apple on my way to take a shower. I can't see what's coming, so I need to be ready for whatever comes…whether that's more of everything with Ashley or having to let her go because she really doesn't see what we could have together.

Chapter 12

Ashley

I hear footsteps coming up the hall, signaling the fact that Rick is awake and coming to check on me. My pulse picks up from excitement, a feeling that's very reminiscent of the time I had a crush on my class valedictorian in high school. Except this is infinitely better because, first…it's Rick…and, second, Rick would never be cruel to me like Tom Bakersten was.

I look up just as he appears in the door frame. His expression goes from happy to see me to curious when he sees the box on the bed in front of me. He steps into the room.

"Morning, Fireball," he says cautiously. "How are you feeling?"

I nod, then blow my nose into a tissue. "Better."

"Yeah? And what's in the box?"

I stare at the box for a few seconds, then look up at Rick. "Yarn."

He looks confused now. "Yarn?"

"My mother's yarn," I clarify.

A sudden look of realization flashes across his face. "Oh…are you all right?"

I nod and smile, waving the tissue. "The nose blowing isn't from crying," I explain. "It's from the mucus demon."

He laughs. "How did you sleep?"

"My sleep cycle is all screwed up now, but I slept fine. I woke up at three am and couldn't get back to sleep. That's why I'm sitting here staring at this box."

Gingerly, he steps forward towards the edge of my bed. I scoot over a bit, and he sits down and leans back against the headboard, wrapping an arm around me as I cuddle against his side. Now, we both stare at the box.

"How can I help?" he asks gently.

I turn my head and look up into his face, watching his eyes take me in. I do the same. My eyes wander, taking in the deep, beautiful ocean blue eyes, the perfectly trimmed stubble that's dusted across his jawline, and the half-smile he's now watching me with.

"Just being here is enough."

His gaze flicks down to my lips and stays there for so long I find myself wondering if he's actually going to lean closer to see if I'll pull away. I already know I won't, but I also know I can't make the first move. If I do and I'm wrong, Despite the shift that's happened between us, I could still ruin a friendship that's become incredibly special to me. If Rick really doesn't want anything but friendship from this, I know I'll accept that decision and find a way to live with it. But I also know for sure…I want more. And I don't want to screw it up.

His throat constricts as he swallows hard, and he turns his focus back to the box.

"What are you going to do with it?" he asks quietly.

I lick my lips as I stare back at the box. "I want to learn how to crochet," I share. "My Mom tried to teach me once when I was a teenager, but I was too impatient. Too interested in other things."

He nods. "You were a typical teenager."

"True, but I wish I'd paid more attention. I remember how easy it was for me to get lost. You're basically holding a little hook and some yarn, and you twist it this way and pull it through that way…and suddenly you have a scarf. It's like witchcraft or something."

We both laugh. I nod at the box.

"Since I've taken the rest of the week off to rest and make sure I'm over whatever this demon germ is, I thought I might try to figure it out. Especially since you're leaving this morning."

Out of the corner of my eye, I see him look over at me with a frown.

"Only for a few hours," he says. "Do you want Marina to come and sit with you?"

"No, I'm okay," I say with a soft smile. "It's not about me needing a nurse. I'm just a little congested now, that's all."

He nods. "What *is* it about then?"

I shrug. "I'll just…miss you."

His gaze locks with mine, and a slow, sweet smile spreads across his face. Part of me wants to look away, but I don't. I wait for him to put up a boundary by calling me buddy…or pal. He doesn't. His thumb makes gentle, lazy circles on my shoulder.

"Sorry if that's…weird."

"It isn't weird, Fireball," he begins, looking more than a little pleased. "It's probably the best thing I've heard in a long time."

I look back at the box. "What time do you have to leave?"

He checks the time on my bedside table clock. "In about an hour. Can I make you breakfast before I go?"

I nudge him with my shoulder. "Let's go make something together. If you keep waiting on me, I'll never want to go back to real life."

He laughs softly and stands, pulling me with him. "Real life is highly overrated."

I put my phone on the charger and follow him out of my bedroom. "I completely agree."

***

Rick

I shake my head, watching Jimmy and Zach trying to one up each other in a spirited argument in the back of the SUV we're riding in. The current debate: whether black licorice is better than red. Zach asserts that they're both of equal merit, and Jimmy insists that all black licorice should be permanently banned. Sam is sitting quietly across from me, holding hands with his wife, Bella, who also happens to be our manager. It works out well because we all trust her implicitly. She's also known in the music world as "Hella Bella" because of the wrath anyone provokes from her if she doesn't get what she wants. For a band manager, it's a great quality to have. The intimate way she and Sam are murmuring back and forth to each other is making me miss Ashley, and I pull my cell phone from my pocket, opening a text message.

Rick: How's the knitting going?

Ashley: It's crochet

Rick: Okay, how's the crochet going?

Ashley: Haven't started yet

Rick: Are you still staring at the box?

Ashley: No! It's in the living room now, and I'm watching beginner crochet videos on YouTube. How did the interview go?

Rick: Honestly? Kind of boring. I'd rather spend the day streaming Customs Watch while you crochet me a scarf.

Ashley: Well, hurry up and get back here. I'll see what I can do.

Bella gasps out loud, and we all stop what we're doing to see what's up. She looks up from her phone and smiles at me.

"Rolling Stone wants to do an article on Rick!" she exclaims.

The guys simultaneously burst into applause, making me laugh out loud. I turn back to Bella.

"Just me?"

She nods. "You've got a solid history as a musician, you're one-quarter of the world's biggest indie rock band, and you've just been nominated for your first solo World Music Award for Song of the Year. They want to do an article and a full photo shoot."

Zach hoots. "Well done, man!"

Jimmy and Sam high-five me, and I just sit here stunned. Wow. I look in Bella's direction again.

"So, how does this work?"

She thumbs through her phone. "They want it out before the awards, so we have to schedule it quickly."

Zach nods. "When are the awards? I never remember these things."

Bella gives him one of her patented *are you kidding me* looks. "Two weeks from Friday. In Los Angeles, since I know that'll be your next question."

Zach flinches and whips out his cell phone, and starts typing.

"Don't bother texting Marina," Bella says quickly. "She knows all about it. I spoke with her last week. She has something on her schedule she can't move, so you'll get dressed and ready to go, here in the city. I've arranged for a charter jet to take you to Los Angeles for the awards. The rest of us can go down the night before."

I snicker, and Bella turns her sights on me.

"Are you bringing your mom again?" she asks.

I think for a moment, then nod. From the first time since we were invited to these awards, my mom has been my plus-one. I wouldn't be a musician if it wasn't for her support. I never would have gone to Julliard and met Zach. None of this would have happened if it wasn't for my mom, but I can't help wishing Ashley was going with me. I would love to see her all dressed up in a designer gown, smiling up at me as we enjoy the evening.

"Rolling Stone wants to do the interview at their offices in New York—and they're much more busy than you at the moment. Tomorrow is the best day for them."

My heart sinks. Real life is determined to pull me away from Ashley. And I won't just be gone for a day if I'm going to New York. I haven't seen my mom or my sister for months. I definitely want to see them, so I'll head up to Connecticut once I'm done. That means I'll have to soak up all the Ashley time I can get for the rest of the day.

I nod at Bella. "What time is the interview?"

"They're squeezing you in, so it's not 'til four o'clock. They'll have a car pick you up at the airport. Your plane lands at three o'clock. Photoshoot first, then the journalist is taking you out for dinner for the interview."

"Okay," I reply, silently grateful I don't have an early morning flight. That means more time with Ashley. "Any advice? What to say or not to say? What to wear or not to wear?"

Bella gives Zach a pointed look, then turns back to me. "I never have to worry about you, Rick. You do you, and all will be well. Unlike some other people we know."

Zach bursts out laughing and so does Bella. They love to drive each other crazy. Sam and I just shake our heads at each other while Jimmy scrolls on his phone.

Rick: Change of plans. Have to go to NYC tomorrow, so this is your last night with Nurse Rick.

Ashley: :-(Well, then get here quick please. I intend to get all the Nurse Rick hugs I can get.

Rick: Oh yeah?

Ashley: I gotta stock up.

Rick: See you in about fifteen minutes, Fireball

***

Ashley

Rick's going to New York. I hate New York. I hate anything that pulls us out of this little bubble we've been living in for the past few days. I want to do something to thank him for taking care of me while I was sick, and I think I know just the thing. I swipe open my phone.

Ashley: Hey, can I get an order delivered super quick?

Merry: Sure! It's slow right now.

Ashley: Lasagna for three, salad, cannoli, and about one hundred pounds of breadsticks.

Merry: Lasagna for three? Who else is there?

Ashley: It's just me and Rick, but he's a mountain. And he's been taking care of me for days. He gets extra.

Merry: Got it. Okay, see you in thirty!

Ashley: Thanks, girl

I don't bother changing clothes or doing anything ridiculous, like putting on make-up. Rick has seen me at my worst and didn't balk, not to mention I'm still getting over whatever this demon germ is. I do, however, head straight for my bathroom and run a brush through my hair. I go back to the living room and take up my usual spot on the loveseat. I've been watching crochet videos since Rick left and I think I'm finally ready to try this.

I lean over and look into the box, eyeing the contents again. For some reason, it's hard to reach in and disturb any of it. It seems silly because Dad and I just opened this box…and we've already disturbed the contents. But I've somehow regressed back to the Ashley who just lost her mom, and I feel like I'm not supposed to touch her things. This is how Rick finds me when he lets himself in with the key Marina gave him.

"Hey, Fireball," he says pensively, somehow sensing that I'm having some trouble with this box.

I look up into the eyes I've come to trust so much. "Hey."

He puts the key and his wallet on the entry table and walks slowly towards me.

"Everything okay?"

I shake my head just slightly. "Not sure."

He nods, coming closer. "Want to talk about it?"

I look into the box. "Part of me feels like I shouldn't be touching her things. Like I'm still the kid who just lost her."

He sits on the loveseat facing me. "That seems like a natural reaction to me."

I turn my head to look at him. "It does?"

He nods. "You probably thought you'd already been through all your mom's things long ago, right?"

I nod.

"So how did you feel when you opened this box at your dad's?"

"Happy?"

Rick's eyes are full of emotion as he smiles at me. "Okay. Anything else?"

"Sad. Like I lost her all over again."

He nods. "Something similar happened to me a few years ago. I understand."

"Tell me," I say quietly, forcing my lip to stop quivering.

Talking about this with Rick makes it real in a way that's different from talking about it with Dad. I realize I was trying to be brave in front of my Dad so he wouldn't get upset.

"You know I wasn't close with my Dad," Rick begins, reaching for my hand. "But my Uncle Dave was there for me a lot."

I squeeze his hand. "Your mom's brother?"

He nods. "He was fun. He loved life. And he tried to fill the void my dad left. One day, he was in a car accident...and he was gone."

I take Rick's hand in both of mine. "I'm so sorry."

"Thanks," he says quietly. "About a year later, my mom found a birthday card he'd tucked somewhere for me, but no one found it. She gave it to me, and I opened it. He'd written how proud he was of me and how he knew I was going to do amazing things with music."

"That's so nice."

He nods. "I felt that way, yeah. But I was also sad for a long time. It reopened the wound all over again, and I wished I'd told him how much I appreciated him when he was still here."

I tilt my head at him. "You were just a kid."

Those gorgeous blue eyes flick to me. "And so were you, Ash."

My lip trembles again, and all I can manage is a faint nod. Rick tugs gently on my hand and pulls me to him.

"Come here," he says softly, squeezing me against him.

I wrap my arms around his waist and breathe him in. Something inside me settles instantly.

"Grief is always hard for me," he murmurs against my hair. "But I try to remember that there's no timetable for it. There's no right or wrong. You're allowed to be sad whether you're eight or eighty. And there's no rush to touch those things. If it feels wrong, then put the lid on the box and put it away until you're ready. And if you're never ready, that's okay too."

I don't say anything. I just let him hold me. And I wonder…is this what love can be like? Someone who is always there, who doesn't judge and just lets you be who you are? I hate thinking about Greg in this moment, but he would have told me how to feel. Or he would have implied that my feelings weren't convenient because we were going to be late for something…or he wasn't in the mood to talk about them. We didn't fit, and I can look back now and see it so clearly. I was really fighting to make it fit. Like a puzzle piece that you're sure is right because it looks so close but…nope. It doesn't fit.

Rick floats a hand up from my waist and rubs my back as he holds me. I have so many feelings, all on the tip of my tongue, but I can't quite say them yet. If I say them out loud, then they're real. And if I feel a certain way and he doesn't, then we have to do something about it. Maybe that ends with not seeing Rick anymore, except for the awkward moments we can't avoid…like weddings and baby showers.

"You're really good at this," I murmur against his chest, praying I'm not drooling on his shirt. I really can't tell.

I feel him smile against my hair. "Thank you."

Knock, knock, knock. Knock. Knock, knock. Knock. Knock.

I pull away from Rick and laugh. "It's Merry."

He looks at me confused.

"She always tries to knock out song lyrics and we never get what they are. Let me get it before she really gets going."

I hear Rick chuckle behind me as I move to the door and let Merry in, who comes bursting into the room with arms full of Nonno's bags.

"I'm here! You will no longer be hungry, my friends. I've come to save you."

Rick grins at Merry and stands, taking the bags from her and putting them in the kitchen. She dances over to him.

"Hey," she says, giving him a poke in the shoulder. "Thanks for taking care of my friend."

Merry wraps her arms around Rick and gives him a hug. He gives her a quick squeeze with one of those little pats on the back we tend to give a person we don't know well. And feel little connection with. I watch them together for a minute in the kitchen and notice how different he is with Merry than with me. It's almost like Merry is his sister. There are no smoldering looks. At no time does he take her breath away. She's bouncing to the living room now, coming to say hello. She's already over the Rick hug she experienced, which boggles my mind because I just want more when I'm in his arms.

"Hello, dah-ling!" she greets me in the overdramatic way she sometimes does. She plops next to me and gives me a hug around the neck.

"Thanks so much for bringing the lasagna," I say excitedly.

Her big brown eyes go round as saucers. "No lasagna."

"What? Why?"

"Nonno said no because that's all the Viking god has been eating while you've been sick," Merry explains. "So he sent chicken alfredo and told me to tell you 'good job, taking care of your big man!'"

Merry laughs after sharing Nonno's message by mimicking his accent. I laugh nervously, my gaze flicking up to Rick's. He looks amused by the whole thing.

"Oh, wow!" Merry exclaims, looking over to the box at my feet. "Is this the box of your mom's stuff you were telling us about?"

I grin. I absolutely love Merry. Everything about her is sunshine and rainbows. She spreads positive energy everywhere. Who else would be excited about a box of stuff like this.

She sits next to me and peers inside, then looks at me excitedly. "Crochet?"

I nod. Her excitement is palpable and contagious as she looks the contents over. She braces her fingers on the edge of the box but is careful not to touch anything.

"So these hooks in this coffee mug," she says, pointing. "They were your mom's."

"Yep," I reply, then add, "It makes me feel like a kid again. When I lost her. I feel like I'm looking through my mom's things and shouldn't disturb them—although Rick has helped me see that's not weird. It's just grief."

Merry wraps an arm around me and squeezes. "Of course it is, and I'm sorry it's made you sad. But it's also a gift, right?"

I smile softly. "I guess."

"Sure, it is," she says, leaning over the box once more. "I mean, who was the last person to use these hooks?"

My gaze flicks over Merry's bright expression. "My mom."

She nods. "Your sweet mom. And now you get to use them. She touched them last, and now you will. It's almost like getting to hold your mom's hand again."

I look down at the box, then up at Merry again. She just smiles brightly, nodding. I look at the hooks. She's right. The last person to touch those was my mom. Something shifts in my heart, and I grin at Merry.

"I've been wondering how we overlooked this box all these years," I share, my gaze drifting from Merry to Rick and back again. "Now I wonder if I just wasn't meant to find it until now."

Rick nods, quiet compassion etching his features. "When you were ready?"

"Yeah," I say in a near whisper. "When I was ready. I wasn't interested in this stuff when she tried to teach me, but now I feel like this is a second chance to be closer to her. Even though she isn't here. I get another chance."

Merry nods. "What a wonderful gift."

I look down in the box and reach for the mug of hooks. When my fingers wrap around it, I feel connected with my mom's spirit in a way I didn't expect. I touch each hook carefully as if they're made of precious materials. Rick steps up next to me and places a reassuring hand on my shoulder.

I remember the YouTube person recommending an H8 5mm hook, so I carefully look through them and my heart pounds with excitement when I find one. I pull it out and squeeze it in my hand, smiling up at Rick.

"This is it," I say happily. "This is the one I need to start learning."

Merry nudges my shoulder with hers. "There ya go. And you're not learning with some random crochet hook you bought at a store.

You're learning with your mom's hook. She's with you."

I throw my arms around Merry's neck, and she squeezes me back. "You're right. Thank you so much."

Merry pulls away and winks at me. "Hey, crochet is hard," she says as she stands up. "So you're probably gonna suck at it for a long time. But then you won't! You'll be awesome. So wait until you don't suck before you make me a sweater, okay?"

I burst out laughing. "You got it."

"All right, I have to get going," she says lightly. "Time to head back to Nonno's so I can ask him to re-open my Nonna's bakery, and he can tell me no, no, and no again. Talk later!"

We say our goodbyes, and she leaves us in the quiet apartment. Just Rick and me. He sits next to me and wraps an arm around my shoulders. We both look down at the crochet hook in my hand.

"You okay?"

I nod and look up at his handsome face. "Thank you for helping me work through all of that."

His eyes roam over my face, and he reaches up to gently tame a wayward strand of my hair.

"I didn't really do anything. You did it yourself."

I shake my head. "You were here for me in every way that matters," I share. "Thank you."

The corner of his mouth turns up slowly. "Anything for you, Fireball."

Chapter 13

Rick

If I look up the word conflicted in the dictionary right now, I won't be surprised to see my face staring back at me from the page. I'm excited about my first solo nomination for a World Music Award and pretty darn excited about the Rolling Stone article. Even more excited to see my mom and my sister when I'm done with the interview, but I'm also going to miss Ashley like crazy. Way more than I probably should.

She pulls away and sits up, looking over her shoulder to the kitchen counter where Merry put the Nonno's bags.

"Are you hungry?" she asks with a half smile. "We should probably eat that soon. Nonno's alfredo doesn't microwave well."

I stand and offer her my hand. "Well, let's go then."

She laughs softly and lets me pull her up off the loveseat. We chat easily as we unpack all the bags. The scent of Nonno's decadent alfredo sauce makes my stomach grumble like I haven't eaten in a week. We dish up our plates, grab drinks, and take everything to the dining table.

"So tell me about this interview," she says as she picks up a bread stick and tears it in half.

I shrug. "They want to do a feature on me since I got my first solo nomination, so there's a photo shoot as well as an article. It's not the cover, of course, but it's still a big honor."

She smirks at me and I lower my fork.

"Don't minimize it," she scolds.

She dips half a bread stick in her pasta to soak up the sauce, then takes a bite.

I give her a defensive look. "I didn't. Did I?"

She smirks again, and I want to take a picture of it so I can carry it with me. Always.

"What would you say if I told you I won the Teacher of the Year award, but it's only the California one…not National?"

I nod slowly. "Okay. I get it."

She grins and spools some pasta around her fork.

"I am so happy for you," she says. "And super proud of you, my super talented—"

She cuts herself off and then becomes overly interested in her pasta.

I tilt my head and smirk at her. "You're not still embarrassed about the beautiful, hot, perfect man-friend thing, are you?"

She shakes her head, still focused on her plate. "Not entirely."

"What were you going to say?"

She shakes her head again. I reach over and steal the last bread stick on her plate. Her eyes nearly bulge from their sockets, and her jaw drops open so fast that I burst out laughing. I love moments like this with her. Every time I think about being away from her for four days I feel like someone has dropped a lead weight on my chest. I wag the bread stick at her.

"You can say anything to me," I remind her. "So what were you going to say?"

"Nothing," she protests. "Just…friend. Isn't that what I always call you?"

I nod. "Sure. Why do you not want to use that word now?"

Her beautiful hydrangea blue eyes instantly flick up to mine, assessing. I school my expression into neutrality, but my heartbeat is riotous. I hold her gaze and remain silent, giving her the space to figure out what she wants to say. She opens her mouth to speak several times, then closes it and looks away.

"I'm just being silly," she says with a shake of her head.

I purse my lips and turn my attention back to my food. For a moment there, I thought she might open up. I clear my throat and start to push away from the table, but her hand closes over mine. When I look at her, she almost looks scared.

"Are you feeling sick again?"

She shakes her head and licks her lips nervously.

"No," she says hoarsely. "I want to ask you something, but I'm scared."

I frown. "You can ask me anything. Always."

Her throat bobs.

"I don't want it to change us," she says. "Like…I don't want to embarrass you or make you feel so weird about it that we can't be friends anymore."

I squeeze her hand. "There is no danger of that. Ask me anything."

She takes a deep breath, and I squeeze her hand again.

"Do you sometimes feel like we could be…*more* than friends?"

I move our hands so they're palm to palm, flat against each other, and look her straight in her gorgeous eyes.

"It's not *sometimes* for me, Ash," I say softly. "It's always."

She bites her lower lip, trying to suppress a smile, but it's too late. I see it. And my heart soars at the sight of it. I smile back.

"Really?" she asks, almost a whisper.

I nod and lace our fingers together. "It has been for quite some time."

She laughs softly and shakes her head.

"I feel like I've been walking on eggshells, trying to figure out what to do about this," she confesses. "I didn't want to ruin our friendship, or our friendships with Zach and Marina."

I stroke my thumb down the back of her hand and grin.

"Well, as much as I love them both, what happens between us is not their business."

She laughs. "Try telling them that."

We sit there for what feels like several minutes, just looking at each other. Smiling at each other. Sitting in the truth of this together. I squeeze her hand.

"As much as I don't want to let your hand go," I tease lightly. "You need to get well. So please eat your dinner so I can go back to monopolizing all of you for the rest of the night."

She picks up her fork and rolls it up with pasta again, and I dig into my plate. Wordlessly, I put the bread stick back on her plate, and her face lights up.

"Thank you," she mumbles around a mouth full of pasta.

We eat in silence for a few minutes. The new understanding we share stretches out between us and binds itself around us.

"So now what?" Ashley asks. "What do we do? What…are we?"

I think for a few moments. "How about we just spend more time together? Away from the lovingly watchful eyes of our friends. We don't have to name whatever this is between us in order to explore it. What if we just give this time to grow into whatever it's meant to be?"

She nods slowly. One corner of her perfect mouth tilts up. "Our secret. I like it."

She finishes her dinner and sits back in her chair, then pats her stomach when she sees me checking out her plate.

"Food baby," she says with a grin. "I'm full, trust me."

We clean up our dinner mess quickly and head back to the living room. Ashley plops down on the love seat in her usual spot, but she pulls me down with her. I instantly wrap an arm around her shoulders, and she nestles into my side. This is so much better than wondering what's in her head half the time.

"How are you feeling?"

She lifts her face to look at me. "Better. Pretty sure I'm going to live, Nurse Rick."

I squint at her. "Thanks to me."

She puts her head on my shoulder. "Yep. Thanks to you."

"Well, if you're feeling better," I say hesitantly. "I know how we can spend the rest of our evening."

"Cuddling on the couch?" she asks sweetly.

I pick up the remote control and pick a music channel that streams ballads, nodding.

"Eventually, but first…let's dance."

I extend my hand, and my heart does some serious flipping as a slow grin spreads across her beautiful face. She takes my hand, and I stand and pull her up and into my arms. I chose a station that streams ballads because salsa dancing around the apartment isn't really a great idea when she's still recovering. The fact that she'll never leave my arms when we're slow dancing is an added bonus.

"When you led me out on that dance floor at Dad's gala, I wasn't sure what to expect," she confesses. "But then you pulled me into your arms with that little tug, and I knew. Instantly, I knew you could dance. And I got so excited. That was so fun."

I spin her around gently and laugh wholeheartedly. "You lit up that dance floor like it was on fire, Ash."

She shakes her head humbly. "*We* did. We did that."

I shake my head and pull her in a little closer. "No, those moves…that red dress…those legs…all you."

She stops moving and grips my shoulders, her fingers compulsively clutching at me.

"Do you think it was inappropriate to do that at Dad's dinner? Did it look bad?"

I frown down at her. "Did your Dad say so?"

"No, not at all."

I nod. "Did anyone else?"

"No."

"Okay, what was the reaction from people when we went back to our table?"

She bites her lower lip and doesn't reply. She just looks up at me with those beautiful, unique eyes.

"Everyone loved it," I remind her. "And it got more dancers on the floor, and the dancing really picked up after that."

She nods. "Okay, you're right. Yeah. Thanks."

I smooth a hand over her hair. "I think the worst thing that weasel did to you was make you think your fire…your personality, and your spirit for life…is something that needed to be tamed. Dimmed."

She nods again. "I can't quite seem to get back to normal. I don't know how to fix this, Rick."

I settle both hands on each side of her face and tilt her head so she's looking up at me. I really, really want to kiss her right now, but I'm not going to. Because it feels a little too fast after we just decided to explore things and because I'm leaving in the morning. Kissing her and then being away from those lips for three days seems like the worst kind of torture.

"I know how to fix it," I say, a gruff edge to my voice.

She watches me curiously as I stroke a thumb across her porcelain cheekbone.

"Let your fire out, baby girl," I say quietly, pressing a soft kiss to her forehead.

The corner of her mouth twitches up. "Why do you always know the perfect thing to say?"

I laugh and pull her into my arms again as we melt back into a slow dance.

"Just lucky, I guess."

Her hand makes lazy stroking motions across the back of my shoulders as we sway to the music. She rests her head on my chest and sighs, and all I can think of is how grateful I am that we've somehow managed to find this space. This tiny middle ground where we've both admitted we want to know what might grow between us. For now, it's enough and my heart begins to fill with something that looks like hope.

***

Ashley

I have mastered the slip knot and the chain stitch. I victoriously clutch the crochet hook in my hand and grin like a kid who just learned to ride a bike. I've mastered the beginnings of crochet, and it's really exciting. Have I mastered the art of not obsessing over the Viking god who is currently three thousand miles away right now? No. No, I have not. I put the hook down, blow my nose for the hundredth time this morning, and resist the urge to check my phone again. I woke up to the most wonderful of text messages waiting for me this morning.

Rick: Morning, Fireball. I hope you rested and slept well, and I hope you're missing me just a little bit. I can assure you that I am missing you a lot.

Ashley: Good morning, my beautiful, hot, perfect man-friend. I am, in fact, missing you.

Rick: Yeah? How much?

Ashley: Must I tell all my secrets so soon? Quite a lot. I

have to walk to the kitchen to get orange juice all alone instead of dancing there with you. And the spontaneous cuddles are severely lacking when you're away.

Rick: Well, I promise to make it up to you soon.

Ashley: :-) How did the interview go? I fell asleep when you were still in the middle of it.

Rick: Pretty well, I think. Although I didn't like the photo shoot part. When it's the whole band, we just have fun together. This time I was alone and it just felt weird.

Ashley: You deserve a little spotlight, Rick. You've earned it.

Rick: They had four different sets of clothes they wanted me to wear for different pictures. It felt like a modeling shoot.

Ashley: I can't wait to see it. I'll bet you look incredible.

Rick: Not as incredible as you looked in that red dress.

Ashley: Rick Archer, you better get home soon so I can hug you for that.

Rick: Now I have something to look forward to during the long flight home tomorrow.

It was the best thing to wake up to. I miss him a lot too. How can I not? But it also feels like we left the friend zone so fast and we're on a runaway train to Awkward Town. *Possibly.* Because no one can predict how this is going to go. My knee-jerk reaction is that we need to slow down, but then I realize…we're already going pretty slow. We haven't even kissed yet. I'm just overthinking it. Again. Probably because every time I think of him, I'm like a purring kitten just looking to curl up in his lap and make myself at home.

I shake myself out of my wayward thoughts and return to the pot holder-sized row of chain stitches in my hand. I took today and tomorrow off of work in order to get this demon germ completely out of my system, so I've decided to focus on learning crochet to keep my focus off the fact that I'm in total Rick withdrawals. Every time

I'm with him, I just want more and more. I was poking around online and found a cute pattern for a scarf that's pretty basic, and I'm hoping to get that started by the end of the weekend.

The whole process of learning to crochet has made me feel closer to my mom in a way I didn't expect. I have countless memories of her holding a crochet hook and working on a project while she, Dad, and I watched TV or spent a lazy Sunday together. The fact that I'm using her hook makes it even more special. I chose the smallest chunk of yarn in the box to learn with. It is a random white ball, anyway, and the other skeins are nicer. I plan to save those for something special since it's yarn my mom picked out for something. And then, finally, when I actually know what I'm doing, I'll finish the scarf she was working on for me.

My phone vibrates on the seat next to me, and I grab it.

Rick: Well, we don't just have to deal with Marina & Zach butting into our relationship. My Mom and sister are now suspicious.

I laugh at his text.

Ashley: Suspicious? What's there to be suspicious about?

Rick: When my sister was here, she had knitting in her bag and I asked about it. So then she wanted to know why I wanted to know about it. She can sniff out a secret really fast and I'm not a good liar. They can both see it on my face if I try to say there's no big deal when I actually care about something or someone.

Ashley: I can't decide whether I'm more scared of your sister's sleuthing abilities or happy that you care about me.

Rick: I'm glad you can't see the stupid grin you just put on my face. But no worries. I'll protect you from my sister until you're ready to meet her. If you ever want to, that is.

Ashley: If she can crochet as well as knit, I might need to stay on her good side. Maybe she can give me some tips.

Rick: She will...or she won't get any more free tix to Rebels concerts.

Ashley: LOL. Wow! What time are you home tomorrow?

Rick: Late. Every time I visit, Mom wants to spend every minute possible together. So I'm taking the last flight back tomorrow night. I'll be there when you get home from work on Monday, though. Only another day or two and the bookcase will be finished.

Ashley: You mean you can't find any other way to work slower than you already have been? :-)

Rick: If it was that obvious I was working slow, why didn't you say anything?

Ashley: Maybe I wanted you to work slow too. :-)

***

My first day back at school has been one for the books. San Francisco is having a rare heatwave, for one, and I intend to soak it all up. But the universe is also trying to send me a message. It's not the kind I expected. The universe doesn't seem to want to remind me to be kind to animals or remember to check the batteries in the smoke detectors in the apartment. No, all the universe wants me to think about is Rick.

As a reward for a good behavior report from the substitute teacher, I let the kids in my class have free creative time this morning. Most of them usually write a story of some kind, or draw a picture. The finished works that were turned in to me before lunch were teeming with Rick reminders. A story in which the main character's name was Rick. Another story had a woodworker with magical abilities create a mysterious bookcase. One student drew a picture of a Viking with long blond hair, and another wrote a poem about a guitar player. Rick, Rick, Rick.

As if that weren't enough, I volunteered for playground duty at lunch today since I was sick all last week. One of the boys who was in my class last year came to say hello and wanted to talk about how much fun it was when Rick came for music day. Thanks, universe.

I'm trying to remain level-headed here. It's something I was sorely lacking during the Greg-pocalypse and I don't want to go through anything like that ever again. So I've been trying not to think about Rick constantly, but everything reminds me of him. Is it National Rick Day and no one told me? Seems like it. By the time school is over and I've gotten my classroom ready for tomorrow, there's a little conga line of Ricks dancing through my head.

As I head to my car, I decide to give normalcy one last effort. What did I even think about before Rick wiggled his way into my heart? It must have been something. I throw my bags in the front passenger seat, start the car, and lower the convertible top to enjoy some of this sunshine. Perhaps a little vitamin D is just what I need.

I pull out onto the street and flick on the radio, singing my heart out to every pop song that hits the airwaves. My spirits lift considerably, and I soon find I'm no longer worried about what my old or new normal looks like. I'm just enjoying my day so much that I nearly miss the turn for the small alley behind our house that leads to the garage.

I make the turn, then slowly pull up the alley, frowning when I see the garage door is open. Did I leave it like that? I hope not. No, I remember Rick is working on the bookcase today. Maybe he was down here for some reason.

As I turn the car into the garage, my jaw nearly hits the floor at the sight in front of me. Not just Rick. *Shirtless* Rick. In a heatwave. Covered in the sheen of his own sweat and working with power tools.

Oh, universe, what are you trying to do to me?

His muscles are bunching and stretching in their own hypnotizing little dance. I slam on the brakes so hard that the tires screech, prompting Rick to look up. He flashes me the sexiest grin I've ever seen, then he and all six of his abs come to greet me. Maybe it really *is* National Rick Day.

Chapter 14

Rick

This could be a little fun. Ashley turned real pink when she pulled her car in and found me working in the garage with no shirt on. Just like me, she can't hide the truth on her face very well, and I am highly flattered by the look I just got. It's probably very similar to the look I had when I first saw her clowning around in that tunnel under the stadium with her friends, trying to get Marina to calm down after the whole viral video thing. She was wearing a sailor suit, so excited to meet The Royal Rebels that she never noticed the dumbstruck look on my face. The same one I always have whenever she's near. I brace both hands on her door and lean in just slightly, smiling down into her gorgeously stunned face.

"Did you just say it's National Rick Day?" I ask.

Pretty sure that's what she mumbled.

She flinches and stares straight ahead. "Nope. Sure didn't. Is that even a thing?"

I smirk. "You tell me. You're the one who said it."

She glances up at me, then straight ahead again, suppressing a smile. "Didn't."

I notice her eyes dart quickly over my chest, so I throw my hands up over my head and stretch dramatically. I throw in a loud grunt for good measure, and she caves.

"All right!" she wails with a little giggle at the end. "I said it. Yes, I did. Now, where is your shirt? This should be illegal."

I laugh and back away, opening the car door for her. "Didn't Marina tell you about your HVAC system?"

She steps out of the car and grabs her bags, then regards me curiously. "No, what's wrong?"

I hold out my hand for her bags, and she gives them to me with a shy smile.

"The heat wave decided to take it out, so the apartment's been boiling since about ten this morning," I say as I follow her into the building. "The repair guy just left about a half hour ago, so it's still pretty warm in there. I came out here to work on Scarlet's corbels and cool off."

She steals a backwards glance at me. "You don't look very cool."

I follow Ashley up the stairs and into the apartment, handing her bags over when she reaches for them.

"Thanks," she says quietly, smirking at me. "I'm going to go put these away and change into something more comfy."

I hover in the doorway and grin. "Okay, I'll go back to work then."

She turns back to face me, an adorable suspicious squint on her face.

"I know what you're doing."

I feign innocence. "Me? What do you mean?"

"This!" She gestures wildly at me. "That. The ticket to the Rick Show."

I laugh out loud. "The Rick Show?"

She tilts her head, stubbornly waiting for me to confess. I feel the corner of my mouth twitch just slightly as I fight to keep a neutral expression. For several seconds, we stare each other down...but her knowing expression finally breaks me.

"Okay, fine," I say lightly. "I can't help it. I love messing with you."

She puts her bags down with a determined look, then walks over and steps right into my space. She tilts her face up to mine and gives me an adorably devious smile.

"Just remember," she murmurs in a tone that sends a thrill up my spine. "Two can play at this game...and you're playing against a dragon."

I grin. "Bring it, Fireball."

She squints up at me, trying to look tough. "You might get burned."

I lean over and move my lips close to her ear. "Yeah," I murmur, "but what a way to go."

***

Ashley

Rick Archer is going to be the death of me, I think to myself as I head to the shelter of my bedroom. My ear is still tingling from where his breath tickled my hair. I was trying to call his bluff, trying to act tough and play the same game he did. Instead, I feel like I will burn alive in my clothes and want to run down to the garage and swear my undying love for him. I'm off my game when it comes to flirting. Actually, that's not true. I have no game when it comes to flirting. Zero game.

Heaving a frustrated sigh, I peel off the clothes I wore to work and throw them in the hamper. I pad over to my dresser. It's still pretty warm in the apartment, so I pull out a light pair of leggings and a t-shirt that says, *That's a terrible idea...what time?*. I change, spray on a little perfume, and then head to the kitchen to grab a bottle of water before plopping onto the loveseat. Rick is nowhere to be seen, so he must have really gone back to work downstairs in the garage.

Probably still with no shirt on. All those abs beckoning to any woman within a thirty-mile radius.

I shake my head and grab my crochet stuff from the drawer in the coffee table.

Focus.

I work my crochet stitches, one after the other, being careful to keep consistent tension on the yarn. The rhythmic movement of my hands as I work lulls me into a state of calm. I'm starting to realize why Mom enjoyed this. I don't focus on everything I have to do or the things that bring me stress in life because this requires focus. When I crochet there's a peace I achieve that I really enjoy.

I hear a key in the lock and the door opens as Rick comes through. He is wearing a ridiculously handsome smile and holding a shopping bag in his hand. He's also wearing a shirt, mercifully. I smile back at him as he walks over to the loveseat and sits beside me.

"I finished Scarlet's project and called her. Before she gets here…this is for you," he says simply, handing me the shopping bag.

"What?" I say in surprise. "What's this for?"

He sits back against the cushions. "Open it, and you'll see."

I dip a hand in the bag and take a peek. Four skeins of yarn are tucked inside. They're so soft. I pull one out of the bag to see it. It's a beautiful light blue with an almost lavender tint to it. One look at it confirms that it's not from a big box craft store. This is high-end stuff. I shake my head at Rick and give him a smile.

"I'm not worthy," I joke, running my fingers over the soft yarn.

Rick scoffs. "You *are*. But I understand what you mean. Save it. For something special."

I put the skein back in the bag. "The color is perfect. I love it."

He offers me another smile, this one slower. Sexier.

"It matches your eyes."

I feel a blush creep up my cheeks. It's impossible not to get all swoony over half the things this man says to me. Without another word, I lean over and sink against his side. I'm rewarded with the now familiar feeling of his arm wrapping around me and squeezing me tight. I rest my cheek against his chest and feel the steady, strong beat of his heart there. I want this to be real. I want this to be more. So much so that I almost feel sad in his arms. I remind myself that we're just exploring now, and that's perfectly okay. It might turn out to be more. We don't have to give it a name right now.

"Thank you," I say quietly. "You didn't have to get me a present, but it's beautiful. Thank you."

He gives me another squeeze. "As soon as I saw that color, I knew I had to get it for you. It's you."

I lift my head to give him an assessing look. "And you just happened to be strolling through some bougie yarn store? What's that about?"

He grins down at me. "I was with my sister, and she needed to go in there, so I went in to see if I could find something for you. Then I got scolded for looking at the wrong stuff, so she pushed me over to the *acceptable* yarn. When I saw this, I grabbed it."

I nod, then go back to cuddle position and snuggle in tight. Rick wraps both arms around me this time and sighs against my hair. This is so nice. Really, really nice. In fact, it's quickly becoming my favorite thing to do. My favorite thing that is quickly interrupted by a knock on the front door.

Scarlet.

I sigh dramatically and push myself off the loveseat to go answer the door. I barely get it open, and Scarlet rams into me, wrapping her freakishly strong arms around my neck and pulling me into a hug.

"Your boyfriend is awesome," she whispers in my ear before pushing me away and running over to Rick.

I laugh and shut the apartment door as Scarlet gives Rick a quick hug.

"You are officially my favorite Royal Rebel, dude," she gushes at him. "Thank you so much, Rick, really. This means a lot."

He waves her off. "It's no problem at all. I can't wait to see what you do with them."

"They're just an accent, really, but I couldn't find anything like what I needed. The fleur de lis you incorporated ties in with the one in the wallpaper on the accent wall."

I step back into the living room and sit in the chair next to the loveseat, prompting a curious look from Rick that I try my best to ignore. But Scarlet smells a rat, and I feel an overwhelming sense of dread hit me square in the chest as she narrows her gaze.

"What are you sitting over there for?" she asks with eerie calm.

I shrug. "I don't know. Why does it matter?"

Her knowing grin runs a chill down my spine. Here comes the reality check that we all get when Scarlet gets this look on her face. I steel myself for her scrutiny, but she turns her attention to Rick.

"To honor our deal, Nonno's breadsticks will be here at your first request," she says in a tone dripping with sweetness. Too sweet.

Rick, oblivious to my terror at my friend's impending truth bomb, nods gratefully.

"So, have you thought about the favor part?" she asks, glancing at me.

Help. Help me.

Rick shrugs. "It's no big deal, Scarlet, really. I was happy to help."

Without missing a beat, she tilts her head in my direction and winks at Rick.

"I know a hot blond I can set you up with. Pretty sure she'd say yes."

"Scarlet!" I cry out.

She giggles. "Dude, you are such an easy target. Relax."

I give her a withering look, and she just widens her grin, then claps her hands together.

"Right. Well, I need to get back to work. If I can grab those corbels, I'll be out of here super fast, and you two can go back to acting like there's nothing going on between you."

Rick stands and chuckles under his breath. "Come on, Scarlet, let's get you those corbels before the Dragon Lady gets you."

Undaunted, Scarlet leans down and gives me another hug.

"Love you, girl," she calls as she follows Rick out the door, shutting it behind her.

I flop back against the cushions in a huff. Scarlet's most endearing traits are also the most annoying ones sometimes. I'm not mad. I'd just rather my relationship status (or lack thereof) not be a source of entertainment. I pick up Mom's crochet hook and run my thumb over it. I'm not in the mood to do anything with it, but sometimes, it helps to just fidget with it.

Rick pops back through the front door and regards me with a sympathetic look.

"You okay?"

I toss my head back against the cushions.

"I wish she wasn't so real sometimes," I grumble, closing my eyes. "But yes, I'm fine."

"Can I distract you by changing the subject?" Rick says, his voice growing closer as he moves into the living room.

"Yes, please."

Suddenly, I'm scooped up in Rick's arms, and I squeal in surprise. He laughs as he sets me on the loveseat and sits beside me. He reaches for my hand and squeezes it tightly.

"I need a favor."

I raise my eyebrows. "Really? Name it!"

He laughs softly. "You might not want to do it. It's a big favor."

I raise my chin. "How big?"

He wiggles his eyebrows. "Huge."

I nod. "Tell me."

He looks down at my hand, then back up at me.

"Before I do," he hedges. "I want you to understand that it's perfectly okay to say no. I don't want you feeling obligated for any reason."

I sit up taller. "You're killing me. Out with it."

He licks his lips nervously.

"Okay, the first part is…I need a date."

My eyes widen, and my pulse is riotous at the mention of a date. I already know the answer to this one.

"First part? How many parts are there to this favor?"

Rick looks up as he considers his answer. "Three."

"Three? Wow. Big favor," I say lightly. "And part one is you need a plus one for something and you want me to do it?"

He nods.

"Done. What's part two?"

He winces slowly. "I need a date for the World Music Awards."

Whoa. What?

"Oh," I mutter, suddenly breathless. "Wow, that is big."

Rick's grip on my hand becomes featherlight. "Too big?"

Something in his tone gets my attention. He's trying to keep a neutral expression on his face, but I can see plainly what this means to him. He's right. Neither of us can hide our feelings very well. I squeeze his hand.

"Is your mom okay?" I ask quietly. "I thought I remembered Marina saying you took her last year."

He nods. "Mom's fine, but she's decided she doesn't want to go this time."

I give him a curious look, remaining silent.

"It's a little suspicious," he adds, "given the level of interest she showed when she sniffed out our little secret."

I feel a smile playing at the corners of my mouth, and I shake my head in disbelief.

"They can't help it, can they?" I ask lightly.

Now it's Rick's turn to squeeze my hand. His gaze rivets me in place. Deep blue eyes rake over my face, lingering on my mouth before tipping back up to my eyes.

"If it keeps pushing us together, do we really mind?" he asks cautiously. "Since that's where we want to be anyway?"

I shake my head. "Nope."

"I know you don't care for the spotlight," he hedges slowly. "This is a big thing to ask. You'll be photographed a lot. We'll have to walk the red carpet. I'll have to talk to reporters. They'll want to know who you are. It's really okay to say no, Ash."

I nod slowly, looking down at our clasped hands as I think it through. It *is* a big ask. I remember the media frenzy that ensued last year when the paparazzi was on the hunt for Marina after we were all in a viral video with Zach. But that situation was different. Marina was intentionally hiding from the media because of her job, and the story was one of a kind. Rick and I are already friends. There were a few mentions of his visit to my school last year by some media outlets. We've been pictured together a few times in the background on various articles about the band or Zach and Marina.

On the other hand, as we both know, neither of us is great at hiding our feelings. Especially me. There is no way I can spend an evening on Rick's arm at an event like the World Music Awards without some reporter snapping a picture of me looking completely smitten. Because I am. And there's just no denying it anymore. I square my shoulders and look up at Rick.

"Do you know what one of your most wonderful qualities is?" I ask softly.

Rick's anxious gaze watches me carefully. "No...what?"

"You're so considerate," I share, giving his hand another squeeze.

"You're kind. And caring. You don't try to persuade me or push me. You let me…just be me."

A muscle ticks in his jaw.

"My answer is still yes," I say. "I'd love to go with you."

Rick smiles ear to ear, and it's a sight to behold. "Yeah? You're sure?"

I nod emphatically. "Yep. Done deal."

He brings my hand to his lips and kisses the back of it. "Thanks, Fireball."

Keep kissing my hand and looking at me like that, and you can have as many dates as you want.

I take a deep breath. "Okay, what's part three?"

Rick stares at me blankly for a moment, then remembers there's a part three. He shakes his head.

"No," he says lowly. "This is good. This is enough."

I frown at him. "No, tell me."

He shakes his head again.

"Rick," I say quietly, giving his hand a gentle tug. "Remember when you told me I can say anything? The same goes for you."

He nods. I watch a range of emotions play over his face as he thinks through what he's going to say, and I wonder what on earth holds this much weight. It almost makes me nervous, but I know in the deepest part of myself that Rick would never ask too much of me. He can't, really, because there isn't much I wouldn't do for him.

"I'm not sure if you noticed," he begins pensively, "but there was one word missing when I told you I needed a date."

I scan his face, looking for a clue. I'm not sure I'm following. He smiles and gives me a nudge.

"Fake."

Oh, right. My heartbeat goes from normal to running from a rabid bear in two seconds.

"Oh," I mutter.

My eyes search his for answers, and I find them all in the gentle circles his thumb is tracing on my hand…and the look in his eyes. That look like I'm the only woman on the planet. I don't even try to suppress the stupid smile that springs up at the realization.

"You don't want a fake date," I say needlessly. "You want a real one."

He just nods, waiting for my response. He looks like he's ready to jump out of his skin. I give him a little nudge.

"You're not scared of the Dragon Lady?"

He laughs softly and shakes his head.

"I found a book called 'How to Date a Dragon,'" he says with a smirk. This man. *Swoon.*

I pull his hand up to my lips and kiss the back of his hand sweetly. His eyes darken and that traitorous muscle in his jaw feathers again.

"Well, it must have worked," I say as I hold his gaze. "Because I would love to go on a not fake date with you, Rick Archer."

Chapter 15

Ashley

"I think it's totally normal," Marina says sweetly, rubbing a soothing hand on Scarlet's back. "You've worked harder than anyone I know on this. For years. We all know how much this means to you."

Scarlet shakes her head and takes another bite of her taco. In a rare breach of protocol, we opted for tacos for this emergency conclave. Honestly, I approve wholeheartedly. We've had so many lately that I was getting pretty sick of Chinese takeout.

"I never fall apart," Scarlet argues.

"We all do once in a while," I say reassuringly. "It doesn't mean anything bad, girl."

"Yeah," Merry says from her spot on the couch. "You're like that taco you're eating."

Everyone stops what they're doing and looks at Merry, who is nodding her head and looking at us like we know exactly what she means. We don't. We rarely do. But she has a point and I'm sure she's going to clear it up any second now. A huge chunk of chicken falls out of Scarlet's taco. Merry points and nods as if that somehow helped. Marina frowns and shakes her head.

"Don't you see?" Merry says, gesturing at the taco mess on the wrapper in Scarlet's hand. "Tacos fall apart, and we still love them."

Scarlet nearly chokes as she bursts into laughter. Marina pats her loudly on the back. I shake my head at Merry.

"That was a good one," I say with a grin. I feel like we should be writing down all of Merry's quips so we can make a book of them and present them to her on a milestone birthday.

"I still think I'm doomed," Scarlet groans. She crumples up the taco wrapper. "But thanks for making me laugh, Mer."

"Well, enough with the doom," Marina says. "How can we help? What can we do to get you through this?"

Scarlet considers for a moment, then shrugs. "You've done it. You're here. Listening to me whine. Now all that's left is for me to stand and deal."

"I still don't think it'll be as bad as you think," Merry chimes in. "You're so talented. Surely, the judges won't be so easily swayed by some suck-up."

Scarlet smiles at Merry, but the defeat behind her eyes is obvious. She got news earlier today that one of her competitors in the decorating challenge is actually the niece of Dara James, one of the most famous interior designers in the country. She's the star of her own TV show, author of at least five books, and the darling of America.

I crumple up my own taco wrapper and take Scarlet's from hers, gathering trash and carrying it to the kitchen. I grab a bottle of water from the fridge and head back to my friends in the living room.

"At the end of the day," I offer gently, "all you can control is you. You can't control her or the judges or any of it. But you can do the best job you can, just like you always do. I believe in you, so cheer up. You've got this."

Scarlet blows me a kiss, and I pretend to catch it. I hate that she's sad over this. She's usually so driven and focused. I guess we all get knocked on our butts from time to time, but Scarlet has worked hard for years. She competes in this challenge every year, and every year, her hopes are dashed. Some day, she just has to catch a break.

"Actually, there is a way for *you* to cheer me up, Ash," Scarlet pings back.

All eyes turn to me. Here comes the dread. This is about Rick, I'm sure. I shake my head at her.

"I'm sure that's not true."

Scarlet throws her hands up in the air. "Just tell me you've finally decided to go for the Viking god, and I can at least look forward to living vicariously through you."

I shake my head again. "This isn't about me. We're here for you. You called the conclave."

She smirks. "If I called the conclave, I set the rules. I'm making room for you. Let's talk about you."

"I don't need help, but thanks."

Marina snorts, and I shoot her a look as if to say don't start. I don't expect the traitorous blow to come from sweet Merry, but it does.

"Yeah, what's the latest on Rick? You guys are so cute together."

It's on the tip of my tongue to deny that there's anything going on, but at this point, I'm fairly sure Rick has told Zach that he asked me to be his date for the awards. If that's the case, Marina knows, and I'll never get away with it. My nervous gaze flicks over my friends, all of whom are watching me expectantly.

"Okay, if I give you an update, can you please not make a big deal out of it?"

A small, tortured sound chokes out of Merry's throat. It's asking a lot of her, our unicorn, to not make a big deal about something. She's the most extra of us all, but I know she'll at least try for me.

"Rick and I have been getting closer," I say hesitantly. "And I don't want to make a big deal of anything right now. I don't want to jinx it."

Scarlet looks at me incredulously. "You have got to be kidding me. Jinx it? Gregzilla was the jinx."

Marina looks at me squarely. "Talking about it would clear things up for you."

I shrug. "Maybe, but I want to keep my feet on the ground this time. I don't want to get excited and carried away. That's how Greg mowed me down."

Merry shakes her head in disbelief. "How can you be anywhere near Rick and not be carried away? I've seen the look you get. You're kidding yourself, Ash."

Scarlet smirks at me. "Truth from the unicorn. You guys are perfect for each other. Tell me you see that."

I open my mouth to deny it and then falter. If I say it out loud, then it becomes a real thing between more than just Rick and me. It becomes something I need to deal with. Keeping it between me and Rick has been safe. Even though it feels fast on one hand, it's also starting to feel like hiding, not talking about it with the people closest to me. Not a secret in a good way, but a secret like it's something to cover up. And I'm realizing it's not something I want to cover up at all. I actually want to shout it out loud for the world to hear, and it's just like my inner circle to help me figure this out.

"Hey," Marina says with a look that tells me she understands exactly how I feel. "It's okay to be excited about someone who makes you feel good. Gregzilla never made you feel this way."

I laugh out loud. "Rick calls him The Weasel."

Merry sighs. "It's official. He can't get any more perfect."

I smile to myself. No, he can't.

"Okay, I like him," I offer, somewhat antiseptically.

Scarlet rolls her eyes. "Duh. Try again."

Merry looks at me in exasperation. "We *all* like him."

I cover my eyes with my hands as the truth bubbles up from within.

It crashes through every stupid boundary I've built up and comes pouring out of my mouth.

"Okay, I really like him. Like *really*. Probably crazy about him. I can't stop thinking about him, and I'm a hopeless mess."

Marina abandons Scarlet and shoves herself in next to me.

"Not a hopeless mess," she scolds gently. "But hopefully ready to go on an actual date with one heck of a good guy."

I can't help the smile that blooms on my face. "He *is* a good guy, isn't he?"

"Absolutely," Scarlet chimes in. "There was always something about Gregzilla that made me want to punch him so bad."

Marina nudges me. "Are you going to tell them the whole thing?"

I laugh softly. "We're going on a real date."

"Yes, girl!" Scarlet yells, holding her hand up for a high five. I give it to her. So much for not making a big deal, though.

Merry claps her hands together. "When, when, when?"

I take a deep breath. "That's the scary part. I'm his date for the World Music Awards."

"Whoa!" Scarlet exclaims as Merry squeals loudly. Marina laughs out loud at their reactions.

I nod. "I can't decide if I'm crazy or stupid," I say slowly. "But I know, at least when it comes to Rick, my answer is always yes."

"So, does this finally mean we can stop acting like there's nothing between you two?" Scarlet asks dramatically, making me laugh out loud.

"Is that what you've been doing?" I ask. "Because you're terrible at it."

She laughs in turn. "Okay, maybe I am, but I'm still relieved. You guys are so cute together. Don't hide it."

Merry takes a sip of her drink. "So, what are you wearing to the awards?"

I gasp at the question. I never even thought of that part. I have nothing appropriate, and certainly nothing made by any famous designer. Just as I feel panic rising, Marina jumps in.

"We're going dress shopping together, Ash," she says, giving me a side hug. "Don't freak out. We'll find you something."

I nod, silently wondering how I'll pay for it. I mean, I could ask my Dad, and he would give me the money without batting an eye. I try not to do that, though. It's important to me to stay independent, but it's also important to me that I don't embarrass Rick by wearing something off the clearance rack that wouldn't be appropriate. There's a designer rental boutique in town. I've passed it a million times. Maybe they'll have something.

"Hey," Marina says, nudging me. "Don't worry about it, I mean it."

"Can we go too?" Merry asks wistfully. "You can't leave Scarlet and me out of it even if we're not going. I want a vote."

I grin at my friends. "I think that would be fun."

Marina nods. "This Saturday, ladies? Brunch and shopping?"

We all nod, and I sink back against the cushions. It'll be okay. I'm not going to overthink any of it. The dress. The date. Rick. It'll all be okay because I have the best inner circle ever. They've got me, and I've got them. It's really going to be okay.

***

"I'm not even trying that on," I argue as Merry shoves a polka-dot jumpsuit at me. She pulls it away, looking slightly offended.

"Polka dots are so cheerful," she half argues.

"She doesn't want to look cheerful," Scarlet counters. "She wants to look beautiful. Which, luckily for her, is pretty easy."

"Aww," I say lightly, giving Scarlet a nudge. "Thanks."

We've been here just twenty minutes and Merry seems bent on

finding the winning dress like there's some kind of contest. Marina giggles beside me and takes a sip of her champagne as we wait for the saleswoman to come back to us with what she assured us were stunning dresses perfect for our body types and coloring. Scarlet motions from her spot on the chaise next to me.

"Merry, sit down with us and stop fussing," Scarlet whispers.

Merry abandons her search and sits in a plush chair near us, ignoring her glass of champagne.

"No one knows you like your friends," she argues. "I bet I can find something better."

I smile at her. "It's not a contest."

She shrugs and watches the saleswoman as she comes floating back to the seating area with several dresses in her arms. Her name is Meredith, and she is all things polished and professional. As soon as we hit the foyer and checked in for our appointment, she gushed an appropriate amount at Marina and discreetly informed me that Rick had called her and taken care of the bill in advance. She begins arranging the dresses on a hanging rack nearby, then runs her hand over a lovely green floor-length satin gown.

"Ms. MacArthur, I thought this would look lovely on you," Meredith says as she pulls the dress off the rack.

It's a beautiful dress, but I'm not sure that shade of green will work with Marina's gorgeous red hair. She takes it with a nod and heads for the dressing room. Then it's my turn, and I'm disappointed when the first dress she reaches for is red.

"Ms. Roberts, this will show off that beautiful hair of yours."

I smile kindly at her. "Thank you so much. Actually, I just wore a red dress to the last event I attended with my date. I'd love to try on any other color."

To my horror, she reaches for a sparkling gold dress that's not my style at all. Merry shakes her head immediately.

"Nope," she says with a syrupy smile. "Not her style at all."

Meredith's smile falters as she gives Merry a look, then she turns her perfectly coiffed head to me.

I nod. "I'm afraid she's right. Not my style, but thank you."

She tilts her head and flips to the final dress, which is a pretty black satin one. The neckline and hem are dusted in little black rhinestones, giving it a little extra flair. Merry makes a noise, and I turn to her before she can object.

"I will try this one on," I say quickly, taking the dress with a smile and heading back to the dressing room just as Marina comes out wearing the green one.

I was right. It's a beautiful dress, but it doesn't quite complement Marina. I can see by her expression that she agrees, but she walks forward to show it off.

"It's a beautiful dress, but…" Scarlet says, tilting her head. "Wrong shade of green for you."

"Big time," Merry chimes in.

Meredith nods. "I do agree. Let me go see if I can find something a tad darker."

She disappears into the store, and I continue back to the dressing room with my dress. Marina stays to chat with the girls. I change into the dress quickly, relishing in the feel of slipping into such a well-made dress. It's very pretty, and as I look in the mirror, I see definite possibilities. I smooth my hands over the bodice and walk out to the waiting area to show my friends.

"Oooh! That's very pretty," Marina says with a smile.

Scarlet nods. "It looks good on you. What do you think?"

Before I have a chance to say anything, Merry chimes in.

"It's black."

We all look at her. Merry stands and comes over to me, gesturing at the dress.

"You look really nice in this dress. But it's black, the same color a bunch of other women are going to be wearing. And it's not your best color."

Meredith returns with more dresses for Marina and rakes her gaze over me. "That looks lovely."

Merry gets up quietly and disappears into the store. I smile at Meredith.

"This is a definite possibility," I say. "I'd also love to try on some different colors."

"Of course," Meredith says with a smile, then she pulls a dark green satin gown out and holds it up to Marina. "This color does compliment you very well, Ms. MacArthur. What do you think?"

I nod. "That's gorgeous!"

Marina takes the dress and holds it up. "This is definitely more like it."

"You try that on while I find something for—"

"Found it!" Merry says excitedly, rounding the corner with a beautiful cornflower blue gown.

Marina and I gasp.

The dress in Merry's hands is drop-dead gorgeous. The bodice is tight-fitting lace with a deep v-neck and long sleeves. The floor-length skirt is chiffon of the same color, flowing softly from the waistline. Tiny crystals are beaded across the skirt in a random pattern, giving it just the right level of sparkle.

Meredith nods her approval. "I think your friend found a winner. You'd better go try it on."

I grin and take the dress from Merry, heading back to the dressing room. I carefully remove the black dress and hang it up, then slip into the blue dress. I instantly love it. It fits like a glove, although the neckline dips lower than anything I've worn before. The skirt makes me feel like a fairy princess. The hem drags a little, but that will be resolved if I wear the right heels. I pop out of the dressing room and head back to my friends. The chorus of oohs and aahs I'm greeted with only confirms the fact that I've found the dress. I spin in a circle.

"Now *that* is a dress," Scarlet says emphatically.

Meredith nods. "And I think a four-inch heel should manage that hem. Are you okay with that?"

I nod confidently. I've never had a problem walking in heels. I just don't do it often. I'll make a point to wear some around the house after work every night to get used to them. Marina squeezes my hand.

"You look gorgeous," she says, turning back to the dressing room to try on the dress in her hands.

"Thanks, girl," I say as I follow her back to remove this beautiful dress.

I change quickly, leaving my dress on a hanger, and join my friends in the waiting area as Marina finishes up. Scarlet gives me a fist bump.

"Well done, dude."

Before I can reply, Marina comes out of the dressing room looking absolutely breathtaking in the green satin dress. The sleek lines complement her shape well, and the simple cut of the dress is very flattering.

"Oh, wow," I say, motioning for her to spin. "You should wear your hair down. Show off the red."

She nods and smiles at Meredith. "I think this is it."

Scarlet holds up her glass of champagne. "Cheers to efficient dress shopping, ladies!"

Merry is positively gloating from her perch in the chair to my right. "Rick won't know what hit him," she says quietly.

I take another swig of my champagne, hearing Rick's voice in my head murmuring *what a way to go* and suddenly I can't wait for next Saturday night.

Chapter 16

Ashley

"Aren't you glad I fought you about this now?" I ask Marina as she grins at her reflection in the make-up mirror. She nods excitedly.

I hired a hair and make-up team to help us get ready for the awards tonight. I plan to do the same for Marina's wedding as a gift, so this was good practice and the results are fantastic. Her hair looks like satin, flowing freely down her back and providing a beautiful contrast against the deep green of her dress. A beautiful rhinestone clip is secured in her hair, adding a little extra sparkle. Her make-up is perfect as well, turned up just a little for this formal occasion. She and Zach will definitely get a lot of media attention tonight. Their love story still gets a ton of media coverage, especially at a music awards show like this.

"You guys look so beautiful," Merry sighs happily from her perch on my bed. "This is so fun!"

Scarlet is sprawled out next to her, taking photos with a huge grin on her face.

"This is the best slumber party we've had in a long time," she says. "We get all the glamor but we don't actually have to go anywhere. We can stay here in our jammies and watch it on TV."

Marina laughs. "Part of me wishes I could join you. This is fun, and I'm so proud of Zach and the guys, but I'm always up for a sleepover with my girls."

I step into my shoes and take a last look in the mirror. The skirt on this dress is full like a ball gown, and there are layers of chiffon that kind of float. I'm having a hard time understanding how this is all going to work. I shoot Marina a confused look.

"How am I getting on an airplane like this again?"

Scarlet scoffs. "It's a private plane, dork. It's not like you're shoving yourself into row 33 on a Patriot Airlines flight."

Marina smooths a hand down her dress. "If it's the same kind of plane Zach and I took last time, it's got about eight very large, cushy seats. There's plenty of room."

"Okay, get together so I can get your picture!" Scarlet pops up on her knees on my bed as Marina and I pose together.

"Can you text those to me so I can send one to my Dad?" I ask.

Scarlet nods.

Marina turns to me excitedly. "I texted Zach and they're on the way down. Ready?"

I nod shakily. "Yeah, just give me a minute to gather my wits," I say breathlessly. "I'll be out there in a minute."

Marina smiles knowingly. "Your first real date. With a *good* man. I'm so happy for both my friends."

I shake my head. "Don't jinx it."

"Are you kidding? No one can jinx this," Scarlet adds. "You're so obviously meant to be."

Marina takes one more quick look in the mirror. "All right, I'm heading out there to get some pre-award show kisses."

Merry flies off my bed and beats Marina to the doorway.

"Let us go first!" she yells. "They totally won't appreciate these jammies if they see you two first. Don't steal our thunder."

A laughing Scarlet follows close behind. They're wearing pajama pants with guitars all over them and matching Royal Rebels t-shirts to show their support. I hear Zach making a fuss over them, followed by a crash…which means Merry attempted to slide in her socks again. She thinks she's great at it, but half the time, she ends up ramming into furniture. I say a silent prayer that nothing's broken, both in the apartment and on her.

Since we're spending the night in LA after the awards, our apartment will be empty. Merry and Scarlet decided to crash here since they wanted to see us off. Since Jimmy and his girlfriend went down to LA yesterday with Sam and Bella, they were nice enough to take our overnight bags with them, so we don't need to worry about it. Marina steps in front of me and puts her hands on my shoulders.

"You look more beautiful than I've ever seen you before, girl," she says sweetly.

I hug my friend, careful not to mess her up. "You look pretty amazing yourself."

"Thank goodness for this lip stain stuff," she says. "Zach is definitely kissing me when he sees this dress."

I laugh out loud. "Well, duh!"

"Okay, I'm going to go see the guys," she says. "See you in a few minutes?"

I nod and turn back to the full-length mirror as she leaves. The make-up and hair girls are packing up their supplies as I check my reflection one more time. They made me glow, and I still have no idea how they did it. I understand there was highlighting involved, but the technique was fascinating to watch. And I've never used lip stain before, but this stuff is amazing. My lips look perfect, but there's nothing to rub off. Zach will definitely be able to kiss away on my friend, and he won't ruin a thing.

My hair is in a loose, soft updo with little rhinestones pinned throughout. They complement the ones dusted across the skirt of my dress and bring the whole look together. I went for simple, single pearl studs on my ears. My mother's. Dad gave them to me on my eighteenth birthday, and I only wear them on special occasions.

I pick up my evening bag off the dresser and retrieve my phone. Quickly, I send the photo of Marina and me to my Dad.

"Thanks again, you guys," I say to our hair and make-up wizards. "You've done such a great job."

"Have a great time!" Audrey says sweetly. The others just smile back at me and wave as they keep packing. "I promise to text you the link for that lip stain."

I smile my thanks and leave the bedroom, walking out into the hall towards the sound of my friends excitedly chattering away. My phone beeps almost immediately, and I swipe my screen to see a text from my Dad.

Dad: Oh, my precious girl. How beautiful you are.

Ashley: Thanks, Daddy. Wish me luck.

Dad: Luck? That boy is half crazy about you already. You don't need any luck. When he sees you in that dress, he's yours. End of story.

Ashley: Ha ha. Okay, I have to go. I love you!

Dad: Love you too, my gorgeous girl. I'll be on proud dad duty...watching on TV.

I tuck my phone back into my evening bag and continue down the hall. When I get to the living room, I see Zach fussing over Marina in her gorgeous dress. She's in his arms, of course, smoothing a hand down the front of his black suit. He's wearing a black dress shirt as well, and his vibe is very much true to his rebellious reputation.

As soon as my eyes find Rick's, time stands still. Rick is in a charcoal black suit, and he looks so beautiful. The suit is perfectly cut to accentuate his broad shoulders and tall, muscled frame. His hair is slicked back with some kind of product and pulled into his usual man bun. That gorgeous stubble of his is groomed perfectly as well. He's wearing a white dress shirt with no tie, and his collar is open just enough to see a bit of his muscled chest.

His eyes follow me as I move closer on legs I can no longer feel. I don't even know how I'm propelling myself forward, but I make my way straight for Rick until I'm standing right in front of him. His eyes glisten just slightly.

"You look…" his voice fades away as his eyes flick over my face.

He shakes his head as if waking from a dream, and I fight back a smile. Seems like I look pretty good if this is his reaction.

Zach whistles and steps forward, planting a friendly kiss on my cheek. I smile back at him, but my eyes drift right back to Rick. He shakes his head just slightly, then lifts his hand to reveal a gift bag I didn't even notice. He passes it to me.

"I could have brought you flowers," he says quietly, "but I wanted to make you something special."

I slowly reach for the bag without breaking my gaze from his. "You made me something?"

He steps back with a grin as I gingerly reach into the bag and remove the tissue paper. Marina steps over to help, and I hand her the wrapping. I reach back into the bag and my fingers grip smooth wood of some kind. I pull my hand out to find the most beautiful yarn bowl I've ever seen. My eyes flick back up to Rick's for a moment as I smile and inspect the treasure in my hand.

From the red tint in the wood, I'm guessing it's made from some kind of cherry wood. The bowl is the typical shape of a yarn bowl, with the traditional curved cut along the side that allows a single strand of yarn to pass through while knitting or crocheting. But there's a tiny detail added that makes this bowl extra special. Where the curved cut line should usually end with a little swirl to hold the yarn as it exits the bowl, this one has a tiny dragon embellished on it. As if the dragon is pulling the yarn out of the bowl. The craftsmanship is beautiful, and it's the nicest thing anyone has ever made for me. I turn the bowl in my hand to admire it more, and my name is intricately carved into the other side.

"This is so beautiful," I say with misty eyes.

Zach, Marina, Scarlet and Merry all move closer to admire the bowl. I hold it up for them and turn it around so they can see all sides. Zach pats Rick on the back.

"Did you turn that with your wood lathe? That's excellent, man," Zach says.

He gives it one more admiring glance before pulling Marina back into his arms.

"That's so pretty, Rick," Merry says with a sniffle. "So romantic."

Rick gives her a nod. "Thanks, Merry."

"Gorgeous work, dude," Scarlet says as she drags Merry over to the living room sofa.

I cradle the bowl in my hands as if it's the most precious thing in the world. It's really beautiful. The tiny dragon stares back at me, and I smile up at Rick.

"Let me just put this in my room, and we can go."

Rick nods, still watching me with that mesmerized look as I walk back to my room with the bowl. I pass the hair and make-up team on their way out of my bedroom with all of their equipment. I'm alone when I step into my room, and I hold the bowl up once more to have a look at it. The wood is so smooth. The finish is almost like glass. I run my fingertip over the tiny dragon and smile to myself. There is no end to Rick's thoughtfulness. He's going to steal my whole heart by the time the night is over.

I carefully place the bowl on my dresser and walk back to the living room. Our hair and make-up angels have left, and Rick's eyes are riveted to me as I return to him. I smile shyly and spin.

"Do you like my dress?" I ask quietly.

I feel like a princess in this dress, and I never want to take it off.

He swallows hard and nods, looking me up and down.

"I have no words, Ash," he says huskily.

His smoldering gaze is like a brand on my skin.

I let my gaze rove over Rick from head to toe. "Me either. You look extra handsome tonight."

Something catches Rick's attention over my shoulder, and the corner of his mouth tips up. I turn to find Merry and Scarlet, in their matching Royal Rebels jammies, sitting on the edge of their seats on the sofa watching us. They're rapidly shoving popcorn into their mouths, and Merry has the same expression she gets when she watches Hallmark movies. I turn back to Rick.

"Shall we?" I say breathlessly.

Our hands just sort of float up and find each other. Rick laces our fingers together as we move to join Zach and Marina at the door.

"You kids don't stay up past your bedtime," Zach teases as he steps into the hallway with a laughing Marina.

"Yes, Big Daddy!" Scarlet calls back.

I wave at my friends as I follow Rick towards the door. Merry looks absolutely love-struck. She's so cute. Scarlet throws an arm around her shoulder and gives her a squeeze.

"Love you guys!" Marina calls over her shoulder.

The four of us step into the hall outside the apartment door as I pull it closed. Rick puts a light hand on Zach's shoulder, getting his attention. Zach turns to look at Rick while Marina tries to tug him down the hall.

"We'll be right along, okay?" Rick tells Zach and Marina. "I just need a minute."

Curiosity takes over as Rick watches them disappear down the hall, leaving the two of us alone just outside my apartment door. We're still holding hands, but Rick feels like a ball of energy that's going to explode at any moment. Is he tense about his nomination? Maybe he gets stressed out about awards shows. I put a gentle hand on his arm.

"Rick, are you all right?" I ask quietly. "What's wrong?"

As he turns to me slowly, he pulls me into his arms as I look up at him with concern. With one arm around my waist, he raises a hand and brushes his fingers along my cheekbone.

"I've never seen you looking so beautiful, Ashley," he says in a voice thick with emotion. "I don't deserve you."

I relax against him and place my palms against his chest. Muscles ripple under my fingers as I smile up at him.

"You certainly do," I argue sweetly. "I worked really hard to look like this. Now I'm worthy of my beautiful, hot, perfect man-friend."

His eyes darken as he gives me a wicked, sexy grin that has my pulse pounding in my veins. He smells fantastic, too. That piney woods scent, mixed with soap and Viking energy, is intoxicating. His gaze flicks to my mouth.

"You look perfect whether you're all dressed up or covered in paste from some kid at school," he says in a low growl.

I smirk. "What about coughing and sneezing from some demon germ?"

That muscle feathers in his jaw as he smirks back. "Even then."

I laugh softly. "That is so untrue, but thank you for being so sweet."

His hands are solid and warm against my back as I look up into his handsome face, so serious.

"I need one more thing from you," he says softly, "or I'm not going to be able to focus on anything tonight."

I nod, waiting. "Anything."

He reaches up and palms my cheek ever so gently.

"I need to kiss you, Ashley," he murmurs. "I know I should wait until the night is over, but I've thought about nothing but kissing you from the moment you stepped out in this dress. I can't possibly get through tonight unless I kiss you right now."

My throat tightens with emotion at his words. He is going to completely wipe all other men off the map for me, there's no doubt. I feel my eyes line with silver as I look up at him and give a wobbly nod.

"Yes," I say breathlessly.

That's all the permission he needs as he brings his other hand up to palm my other cheek. I slide my arms around his waist as he lowers his mouth to mine, stopping just short of my lips. A little whimper escapes my throat, and he dips down to bring our foreheads together.

"There's no going back after this, Fireball," he murmurs. "You know that, right? If I kiss you, we're crossing the border of the friend zone for good. I won't be able to go back to the way things were."

I wrap my arms around Rick's neck, pressing closer, and smile up into his eyes as I give his man bun a gentle tug.

"Rick Archer, if you don't kiss me right this second, I'm going to pull you out of the friend zone by that man bun of yours," I murmur, rubbing our noses together for good measure.

He grins. "So I don't have to stay locked up in there anymore?"

I shake my head. "I'm gonna burn it down. There's no going back."

Finally, Rick lowers his mouth to mine and I am instantly lost. His lips are soft and warm, firmly taking possession of mine in sweet exploration. I sigh against his mouth, opening for him as our kiss deepens. His kiss is everything I need, and I never want this to stop. I wrap my arms tighter around his neck as our bodies press together. A tremor runs from my head to my toes just as Rick pulls away with a ragged breath.

His arms wrap around me again, steel bands keeping me upright as my knees wobble. My heart rate is racing wildly as I cling to him. I take a deep breath.

"Wow."

He nods, leaning forward to plant a soft kiss on my forehead. Outside, a horn honks twice. Rick smirks, then looks down at me.

"I guess we have a plane to catch," he says, eyes drifting back down to my mouth briefly.

I nod, reluctantly pulling away as Rick laces our fingers together again. I squeeze his hand.

"Do I look okay?" I ask.

I don't want to let go of his hand, even to grab the compact in my evening bag to check my face.

His gaze runs over my face, and he grins again. "You look perfect, Fireball."

I laugh softly. "Then let's get going, handsome."

We walk down the hall to join our friends in the limo that will take us to the airport. With my lips still tingling from Rick's kiss, I fight the urge to skip alongside him while my friend zone goes up in flames behind me.

Chapter 17

Rick

"Are you feeling okay about this?" I murmur to Ashley as we wait for the car door to open.

Zach and Marina are busy looking out the window on their side of the limo. They're more used to this attention than Ashley, who has been looking out the car's window like a deer in headlights as the limo slowly moved up the street in front of the theater. Now it's time to get out and walk that long red carpet ahead of us, and I'm praying she isn't full of regrets already. She turns away from the window to look up at me.

"Are you worried I'm going to run already?" she asks with a glint in her eye.

I shrug. "I'm not sure I could blame you. This is a lot."

She leans closer, and her perfume nearly teases me into oblivion.

"It *is* a lot. But you're totally worth it," she says. "I'm grateful to have Bella running interference, but I also know you've got me. You're not going to let me down."

Her words make me grin. "You sound so sure."

She nods. "Do you remember telling me you want someone who

shows up for you?"

"Yeah."

Ashley tilts her head at me. "That spoke to me. Because I didn't have that before. And you have always shown up for me, even when you were locked up in the friend zone."

I nod but remain silent. The limo rocks just slightly as the driver and our security team exit the vehicle, getting ready to open the door.

"You deserve someone who shows up for you, Rick," she says softly, nodding at the fans and media chaos just outside. "I'm not thinking about them. I'm here for you."

She leans forward and kisses me softly, then pulls away before we get carried away in it. Her eyes are luminous as she grins up at me.

"Ready when you are," she says just as our team opens the doors to the limo.

Zach steps out first, and the wall of fans along the red carpet go insane. He flashes them a smile and waves, then turns back to the car to help Marina get out. More cheers from the fans when they see the famous mermaid from last year.

As soon as they step away from the car and onto the red carpet, I step out of the car. The Royal Rebels always arrive together, so the crowd goes crazy again when they see me. I smile and wave, then turn back to help Ashley out of the car. I know from experience that the car pulling up behind ours carries Sam, Bella, Jimmy and his date. The Royal Rebels have arrived.

I reach for Ashley's hand immediately, then look down to gauge her expression. She just smiles up at me and squeezes my hand as if to say I'm all right. I squeeze back, and we begin walking the red carpet that leads into the theater where the World Music Awards will take place.

It takes almost an hour for us to walk the fifty-yard distance from the street to the theater entrance, but we're used to it. Reporters from every major news agency line the red carpet, waiting to interview us.

Bella already coached us on how to handle any questions we don't want to answer about who Ashley is and the status of our relationship, so we're as prepared as we're going to be.

With Zach and Marina just ahead of us, we get several requests for Zach to run back and pose with me. This prompts both of us to yell at Jimmy and Sam to get in the photo as well, so we're causing our own version of chaos on the red carpet. It's a thing we're known for, though, and our fans love us for it. Whenever things get crazy, I notice Ashley just laughs and steps aside with Marina to watch. When we're ready to move up to the next reporter, Ashley appears at my side and slips her hand into mine. Heaven.

When we get inside the theater, I'm relieved that we only have one reporter asking where my Mom is and if Ashley is my girlfriend. I responded honestly by saying Mom had other plans but is doing well, and then I moved us along without commenting on the girlfriend remark. I would love to say yes, but this is our first date, and I've probably set the record for first-date craziness. If by some miracle she's still not freaked out by the end of the night, it's still pushing it to call her my girlfriend after one date—even if I've known for a while, she's the only one for me.

We find our way to our seats, and the eight of us are split up so that the cameras can get all four of The Royal Rebels in one shot. Zach and I are in front with Ashley and Marina, and Sam, Bella, Jimmy and his date are right behind us. It's a busy night for us tonight. We're presenting the award for the Best All Female Band, we're performing "All You, All Day, All Night", and we're up for two awards: Best Music Video and my solo nomination for Song of the Year. I'm glad Ashley has Marina to be with while I'm backstage or on stage.

Before we know it, the lights dim, and everyone takes their seats. I reach over and take Ashley's hand, lacing our fingers together. She wiggles in her seat excitedly, beaming up at me before leaning in to say something. I lower my ear so she can whisper.

"I'm so excited for you," she says. "This is so fun!"

I quietly let out a sigh of relief. It's not too much for her, and that means a lot. If it was too much, it would still be okay, but to have her here and with me…and not put off by it all…it's amazing.

During one of the breaks, a production assistant comes to take us backstage so we can get ready to perform. Ashley and Marina stand up to stretch their legs as we leave, and I can't resist pulling Ashley into my arms for a kiss. Her hand slides up the side of my face, and she pulls me closer, threatening to completely disintegrate my resolve. We pull apart and she smiles up at me.

"Knock 'em dead, my beautiful, hot, perfect man-friend."

I grin widely as the guys drag me away. "You got it, Fireball."

***

Ashley

Marina and I applaud with the audience as the Master of Ceremonies announces The Royal Rebels. The stage's backdrop magically disappears in three different directions, revealing the whole band on a moving platform that slowly propels forward as the audience cheers loudly. All the guys smile and wave as they play the intro to "All You, All Day, All Night". There's energy in this audience that's different from regular fans. I've seen the guys play at charity events and regular concerts, but we're surrounded by music celebrities right now, and it's wild. To my left, Elton John and Eminem are on their feet cheering. To my right, Taylor Swift is dancing with Dua Lipa and Ed Sheeran. I'm not sure I'll believe myself later when I remember this moment. How did I get here?

Rick makes eye contact and winks at me, and I instantly feel like a thirteen-year-old girl at her first concert. I scream and cheer along with the rest of the audience. Just before he starts singing the lyrics, Zach pulls the mic up to his mouth and looks at one of the TV cameras.

"This one's for Merry and Scarlet!" he growls, then laughs along with Rick, Jimmy, and Sam, who all wave at the camera.

Oh my goodness…they're probably screaming at the tops of their lungs right now. Marina and I look at each other, wide-eyed and screaming, then get up and dance to their performance with the rest of the audience. Near the end of the song, Zach jumps off stage and runs along the front row, getting a few music stars to sing different lines of the lyrics into the mic he's holding. My eyes are mostly on Rick, though, who's just having the best time playing his guitar and laughing along with the guys as they do what they do best. Every once in a while, Rick locks his gaze with mine, and it instantly feels like we're the only two people in this giant theater. Be still my heart.

We all sit down when the performance ends, and more awards are presented. My phone and Marina's start vibrating like crazy. I'm sure it's Merry and Scarlet, but we can't have our phones out during the show, so we're forced to ignore them. Two random people run out and sit in Zach and Rick's seats, which would have confused me if Marina hadn't forewarned me. Being a seat filler is literally a job, and the production company pays people to dress up in formal wear and stand on the sidelines waiting for spaces to fill. They're under strict instructions not to bother celebrities by asking for autographs and selfies, and it's fascinating that this is a job that exists. I had no idea.

It seems like forever before the next break happens, and when it does, I'm disappointed that Rick hasn't come back. The Rebels are presenting the award for Best All Female Band soon, so they opted to stay backstage. The lights are up in the audience for a break, so Marina and I swipe open our cell phones to see the hysterical mass of texts from our friends.

Merry: OMG!

Scarlet: Did that...just...HAPPEN?!?!?!

Merry: Move over, Marina. I'ma marry Zach!

Scarlet: I seriously almost peed my pants. That was EPIC.

Merry: Nonno's bread sticks for life. All of 'em. That was so fun!

Marina and I giggle together as we read through the messages.

Ashley: Please do not pee on our couch. Go pee on your own couch!

Scarlet: Might be too late, might not be. You'll never know. :-)

I roll my eyes and laugh out loud. That girl is ridiculous.

Merry: You both looked so beautiful in the red carpet coverage. I can't wait for you to see yourselves on the news!

Marina: We can all watch it together on our pee-free couch when we get back. Right, Scarlet?

Scarlet: *eyeroll*

Marina and I laugh again, then put our phones back into our evening bags as the lights dim and the producer announces that the show is starting up again. People scramble back to their seats just in time, and the Master of Ceremonies comes out to announce the next presenters. Three awards are presented and accepted before The Royal Rebels take the stage again, this time to present the award for Best All Female Band.

"It's our honor to present the award for Best All Female Band this evening," Zach says in his trademark gravelly British accent.

Rick leans over to the mic next. "Each of these bands is a force unto its own, brimming with talent and creativity."

"And the nominees are," Jimmy continues, "The Crazy Daisies."

Sam leans over next. "Dogwood Dreamers."

Zach and Rick look at each other and say in tandem, "And Finnster Sisters."

The guys make a joke of passing the envelope back and forth until

Sam grabs it and rips it open. The audience laughs as Sam holds the card up for all the guys to read. They all nod, then lean in together and yell into the mic.

"The Crazy Daisies!"

Applause erupts as the members of The Crazy Daisies jump from their seats and hug each other, then climb the stairs up to the stage. They hug all the Rebels as well, and then their lead singer steps up to the mic to give their thank you speech. I'm not sure I care for how much their drummer is latching onto Rick, but he's being a good sport about it. As they exit, she wraps a perfectly manicured hand around the back of his neck and pulls his head down so she can whisper something in his ear. He keeps a smile plastered on his face but clearly says no to whatever she says, and I feel an insane amount of triumph at the disappointed look she wears all the way off stage.

When the final break of the evening happens, I'm overjoyed to see Rick walking up the aisle toward me. Zach stops behind him to visit with the lead singer of Train. Rick hugs Marina before scooting into our row, and I pull him into my arms. Just the feeling of his arms wrapping around me is sheer heaven. It wouldn't matter if we're at a star-studded awards show or standing barefoot on a beach. This man's embrace sets my heart on fire. We sit in our seats, and I lean over to whisper in his ear.

"So what did The Crazy Daisies' drummer ask you?"

Rick throws his head back and laughs out loud, making me giggle.

"I knew you wouldn't miss that," he says, then he leans over to whisper the rest. "She invited me to do things a gentleman doesn't discuss with a lady. I politely declined."

He laces our fingers together, then brings our hands to his mouth to kiss the back of mine. Swoon. I smile up at him and rest my head on his shoulder.

"I'm having the best time," I say with a sigh.

Rick's hand comes over to softly cup my chin, and I look up at him and into that perfectly handsome face.

"I'm so glad to hear that," he murmurs just loud enough for me to hear.

I raise my mouth just a bit, and he brings our lips together in a soft, sweet kiss. As much fun as I'm having, I almost wish we weren't here. I wish we were somewhere quiet. Alone. So I could make out with him all night long.

"You guys were so great," I say with a huge grin. "Merry and Scarlet freaked. I'll show you the texts later."

Rick laughs again. "Zach told us he was going to do that right before we went on. I wish we'd been able to see their reaction. I'll bet it was hysterical."

"Merry says the whole band gets Nonno's bread sticks for life."

"Oh, then I'm definitely glad we did it."

I laugh, then quiet down as the lights dim and everyone takes their seats again. Marina plops into her seat next to me and reaches across me to tap Rick on the arm.

"Good luck, my friend," she says with a huge smile.

Rick nods at her. "Thanks, Marina."

"Pssst!" Zach says, waving a hand at Rick. He gives him a thumbs-up and a wink, making Rick smile.

The audience quiets down, and I squeeze Rick's hand. He looks down at me with those beautiful ocean-blue eyes.

"Whatever happens," I murmur, "I am so incredibly proud of you. You are amazingly talented, and 'Till the End' is a beautiful song."

He steals a quick kiss as the Master of Ceremonies comes back on stage.

"Thank you, Fireball. That means the world."

We turn our attention to the first presenters, who just happen to be The Crazy Daisies. As they begin naming the nominees for Best

Music Video, Rick leans over to whisper in my ear.

"If the Rebels win this, will you come with me on stage in case she gets grabby?"

His smile is positively devilish, and I laugh softly. I crook my finger to get him to lean down to me.

"You're on your own, handsome," I whisper, my lips tickling the shell of his ear. "But if I see her touch you, she'll face my dragon fire."

He suppresses a laugh and nods. "I feel completely protected."

We listen to the nominees being listed, applauding for each one, including The Royal Rebels, of course. The lead singer of the Daisies rips open the envelope.

"The winner is…Flight Fifty One!"

We all applaud, of course, but I'm disappointed for the guys. The members of Flight Fifty One take the stage, looking stunned and hugging each other fiercely. Zach stands up and whistles, starting a standing ovation that ricochets through the whole theater. Now we're all standing and applauding, and the band members are in tears at the podium. I know from listening to Zach and Rick talk about it, that this is the band's first nomination for a music video after a very tumultuous year. They had to work incredibly hard just to get the video produced, and the band ended up directing it themselves because they were so dedicated to their vision. The lead singer motions for everyone to sit and places a trembling hand over his heart as he bows in thanks.

"To win this award is amazing enough," he says in a voice choked with emotion. "But to have artists like Zach Adams, Elton John, and so many of you stand for us? That means everything."

The audience erupts in applause again, and I feel a little added moisture in my own eyes at how moved they are at their win. I can't imagine how it must feel to work so hard at something and then be acknowledged in this way. And I'm surrounded by people from all walks of life who've worked their entire lives to make it to this level of success. It's incredible.

Each band member takes an opportunity to step up to the mic and say a few words, and the next presenters take the stage. The award for Best Solo Male Vocal is announced next. Ed Sheeran wins and gives a gracious thank you speech before walking off stage with the presenters. Next, Elton John takes the stage to announce Song of the Year, and I feel like I'm about to have a heart attack. Elton Freaking John…announcing the award Rick is nominated for. Holy cow.

I squeeze Rick's hand as Elton John walks up to the podium.

"When you win this thing, do I have to behave, or can I scream my head off?"

His whole face lights up. "If you have that kind of faith in me, I've won something way better than a trophy, Fireball."

I keep an iron grip on Rick's hand and place the other one on his arm as Elton John names each songwriter and song up for the award. The envelope is torn open, and Elton grins and nods as he leans over the mic.

"Rick Archer for 'Till the End'."

I jolt in my seat and cheer my head off, right alongside Zach, Marina, and everyone around us. Rick's expression is a combination of humble, grateful, and overwhelmed as the theater erupts in applause. He stands and pulls me up and into his arms. I wrap my arms around his neck as he crushes me against him and buries his face in my neck. I just hold him, squeezing tight and letting him hang onto me as long as he needs to.

He pulls away just enough to smile down at me, and then our lips come together in a celebratory kiss that has my toes curling in my shoes. He gently lets me go and makes his way to the stage, accepting congratulatory hugs from Zach, Marina, Jimmy, Sam and Bella on his way. I sit and beam with pride as he takes the stage and accepts his award, then steps up to the mic.

"The first person I will always thank is my Mom," Rick begins, his voice already breaking. "She was the first person to see I had musical ability, and she always encouraged it. That's even more incredible when you consider that she was a single mom raising two kids without any kind of financial support. So, Mom…thank you. I couldn't have done any of this without you."

The audience erupts in spontaneous applause, and Rick pauses until we are quiet.

"I'd also like to thank my sister, Kate, for being one of my biggest cheerleaders. I love you, sis. But this especially wouldn't be possible if I hadn't met a certain sarcastic musical genius-slash-wanna be duke," he growls into the mic, prompting laughter from everyone, including Zach. "Or an insanely talented drummer with an unhealthy addiction to Pop Tarts and a heck of a bass player who's neater than freaking Mary Poppins."

More laughs from the audience, including me. I love how close the guys are. They remind me a lot of me, Marina, Merry and Scarlet. Family more than friends. Rick holds his award up, tears gathering in his eyes.

"Zach, Sam, Jimmy…I love you more than I could love any brothers by blood. Thank you all for this incredible honor. I will never forget tonight as long as I live," he croaks, then takes a deep, stabilizing breath. His eyes meet mine and the world stops spinning.

"And finally…to someone very special to me. Fireball…I hope you always look at me the way you have tonight. *You* are the song my heart sings."

And just like that, Rick Archer walks off the stage with his first World Music Award *and* my heart.

Chapter 18

Rick

Hours later, our entire group is at the official after-party and having a blast, but if I'm being honest, I just want to be alone with Ashley. We've stolen a few kisses from each other whenever we can, but it's not enough. Everywhere I look, the newly awarded are being schmoozed to death by reporters, influencers, and anyone trying to climb the ladder in the music industry. I'm ready to go, but then I look out on the dance floor at the dragon princess I brought with me, and I want her to have all the fun in the world tonight. Right now, she's dancing with Sam, who is a horrible dancer, but no man can resist Ashley tonight. She's danced with music legends, boy bands, and, of course, me.

As if on cue, her eyes meet mine from across the room as the song ends, and she excuses herself to come back to me. I watch her with a secret smile on my face, one she gives right back to me. As soon as she's near enough, I pull her into my arms.

"Thanks for dancing with Sam," I say quietly. "Bella will owe you for a year."

Ashley makes a face. "She doesn't want to dance with her husband?"

214

I laugh out loud. "She's worse than he is! I saw them dance together one time. It looked like they both had a horrible rash and were itch-twitching."

"Oh no," Ash replies, laughing softly. "Poor Bella."

I shake my head. "She's the smart one. She knows she can't dance. Sam simply doesn't care."

Ashley steals a glance at Sam, who is now wrapped around Bella at the bar.

"Well, anyone who loves to dance has a special place in my heart," she says adorably. "I'll dance with him any time."

I raise my eyebrows in jest. "Am I going to have to talk to him about trying to steal my girl?"

Ashley's angelic face lights up as she laughs. For a moment, I wonder if I should have said that. Maybe it sounds too possessive. We keep saying we'll go slow, but everything about this feels so right, and it's hard not to just lean into it. I feel like she does the same, but I'm not sure how she feels about it. Is she scared at all? Does she want to slow down more? I'd love to talk to her about it, but the time and place for that is not at a party for the World Music Awards.

"You're awfully serious all of a sudden," she says, standing on her toes for a quick kiss. "What are you thinking?"

I look out at the room full of celebrities and entertainers. "That I'm so glad you came with me tonight, and you're not intimidated by any of this."

"And?"

I shrug. "Honestly? I just want to be alone with you."

She pulls away to look up at me. "You do?"

I laugh out loud. "Is that bad? I just won the biggest award in my career, I'm in a room full of the music world's elite, and I just want to go somewhere quiet and be with you."

She smiles softly and steps away, tugging at my arm. "Let's go."

I pull her back into my arms. "What? You're having such fun dancing with everyone."

Ashley shakes her head and wraps her arms around my neck. "I've had an amazing time, but I am more than ready to go somewhere and be alone with you. That's what I want too."

I don't even bother fighting the stupid grin on my face as I text our security lead and head to the table where our group is sitting, Ashley's hand secured firmly in mine. I hear a soft giggle escape from her as I hurry us over to our friends. Zach looks up just as I slap him on the shoulder.

"We're going, my friends," I say as I scoop my award off the table. "It's getting late."

Marina looks at her phone. "Oh, please, it's only nine o'clock!"

Ashley feigns a yawn. "I'm so tired, though. Goodnight, you guys. Have fun."

Marina gives us the side-eye and giggles to herself. I make her get up for a hug, then we make our rounds at the table saying our goodbyes. One of our bodyguards meets us at the door and walks us to the waiting limo. I help Ashley get in, then move to the other side and get in beside her. I make eye contact with the driver in the rearview mirror.

"Can you give us a second?"

He nods with a smile and pulls out his phone as I turn to Ashley.

"Did you want to go anywhere in particular?"

She chews on her lower lip as she thinks for a moment.

"I love this dress, but I'm really just ready for some comfy clothes," she says with a sigh. "If that's okay."

I wrap my arm around her and pull her close, kissing the top of her head. "It's more than okay."

I look back up at the driver. "Can you just take us to the hotel, please?"

"Yes, sir."

He raises the privacy screen, and Ashley and I are in our own little world as we move through the glittering City of Los Angeles. She snuggles in tight and I'm not sure this night can be any more perfect.

We're back at our hotel in no time, holding hands and walking through the lobby, pausing briefly so the concierge can congratulate me, then waiting for the elevator. We step inside and I press the buttons for both of our floors.

"I'll go get changed and come back down to you, okay?"

Her frown is interrupted by a yawn. "You don't mind hanging out in my room?"

I pull her back into my arms as the elevator whisks us up to her floor.

"I have a feeling we're going to be talking and kissing all night," I say, stealing another kiss, "and I don't want you to have to leave my room and go to yours…so we'll hang out where you can just go straight to bed, and I'll make the trek upstairs."

The elevator stops at her floor, and she reluctantly pulls away.

"Don't take too long. I'm looking forward to the kissing part."

She throws me a devastatingly beautiful smile and floats down the hall to her room, leaving me in the elevator with my jaw on the floor.

***

Ashley

Now I really know how Cinderella feels. Except I'm not worrying about coaches turning to pumpkins at midnight, thankfully, and I get to make out with my prince.

I swipe my card key to open the door to my room and pop off my shoes as soon as I'm inside. Then I head for the giant closet in this massive suite Bella booked for me. I told her not to give me anything fancy, but of course she didn't listen. Zach and Marina are in a suite. Rick is in a suite. Everyone else is in a suite, so apparently, I get one too.

I carefully remove my dress and hang it up, taking a moment to admire it again. It's such a beautiful dress. It's the prettiest thing I've ever owned, and now I have a night of amazing memories to go with it. I pad out to the dresser and grab a pair of leggings, a sweater, and some socks, then head to the bathroom. Carefully, I remove all the little rhinestone pins in my hair. Then I get to work taking my hair out of the updo. I feel a little guilty about destroying the hard work that went into creating my look tonight, but I want to fully relax and not worry about these pins or messing up my hair. Once I have it down, I run a brush through it and slip into my clothes just as there's a knock at the door. Rick.

I run to the door and swing it open. Rick is wearing a faded Royal Rebels t-shirt and a pair of sweats, and the combination is every bit as sexy as the suit he was wearing earlier. I reach for him as he steps into my suite and pulls me into his arms. I fist the soft t-shirt in my hands and grin up at him.

"Cuddle clothes," I murmur. "Well done."

He laughs softly and cups my face in his hands, lowering his mouth to mine in a soft, slow, oh-so-sexy kiss. I sink against him and completely surrender to his kiss. We're finally alone. No one waiting in the car for us. No schedule to follow. No party to attend. Just us. We break off our kiss and I squeal loudly as Rick hoists me up over his shoulder in a fireman carry and drops me on the sofa in the living room. I laugh out loud as he stands in front of me with a mischievous grin plastered on his face.

"Okay, cuddle time for sure," he says. "But are you hungry at all?"

I don't even have to think about it. "Yeah, I didn't really eat much."

He nods. "What are we hungry for? I'll eat anything, so you choose."

I raise my eyebrows in challenge. "Anything?"

He grins again. "If you wanted pizza from New York, I would fly us there right now to get it."

I laugh under my breath. He's joking, of course, but I don't doubt him either. He is a romantic, and I'm here for it.

"No need to travel that far for me," I say, "but pizza does sound good."

He pulls his cell phone from his pocket. "Toppings?"

"Pepperoni, sausage, and extra cheese?"

"Done," he says, hitting a button on his phone and holding it up to his ear. "Tony? Hey, bud."

I recognize the name of the concierge downstairs immediately. He rushed to congratulate Rick when we were walking through the lobby, and it was clear they've had a fond relationship for quite some time. Rick orders the pizza, along with sodas and champagne, then hangs up and sits with me. Like a magnet, I lean in and wrap my arms around his waist as he pulls me close.

"Better," he says.

"Alone," I add. "Finally."

"But you had fun tonight?" he asks. "Really?"

I bounce up into a sitting position, facing him, and take his hand.

"I had a blast," I say excitedly. "And I am so proud of you."

The corner of his mouth twitches up. "Yeah?"

I nod. "I love that you're so incredibly talented but very grounded. You're humble. And kind. And…a very good kisser."

A slow, sexy smile spreads across his lips. "Yeah?"

I nod again. "A very good kisser. A+."

He leans forward and nips at my nose. "I love getting good grades. Especially from hot teachers."

I laugh softly, and he steals my laughter with a kiss. His lips tell me everything I need to know. With every touch, every kiss, he feels like a man uncaged…released from the friend zone once and for all, and he's on a mission to make sure I never want to lock him back up. His kisses are intense in their exploration and worshipful in a way that nearly moves me to tears.

My phone vibrates on the small coffee table. Then again. And again. We break off our kiss so I can swipe open my phone and look.

Merry: OMG!

Scarlet: Dude, are you near a tv?

Merry: You really need to be near a tv, Ash.

Scarlet: Channel 8, girl!

I hold my phone up so Rick can read the messages. He frowns, grabs the remote and turns the TV to channel eight. An entertainment tabloid news show pops up, and my stomach lurches when I see footage of Rick and me walking the red carpet tonight. At the bottom of the screen, a banner scrolls by that says, "WHO IS SHE?"

"Rick Archer, lead guitarist of The Royal Rebels, stunned fans tonight at the World Music Awards by walking the red carpet with this unknown beauty," the reporter says.

I snort a laugh, and Rick looks at me with a too-serious expression. I squeeze his hand and keep watching.

"I didn't even know he was dating anyone, Sharon," an off-screen reporter pipes in. "He usually takes his mom to big events."

The reporter on screen nods excitedly, scrolling through her phone and waving it at the camera. "I know, which is extra adorbs, but now he's dumped mom, and I'm proud to share I've figured out who this mystery beauty is."

I frown at the screen. "Who says 'extra adorbs'? That's ridiculous."

Rick hits pause and looks at me with a worried expression. I stare back at him, waiting for him to say something, but he's just watchful. Like he's waiting for me to freak out. Then I realize he had a front-row seat for all the drama between Zach and Marina when they first met.

Marina had a job at a very conservative law firm, working for a viper in high heels, and she actively tried to hide from reporters in order to not get fired. I squeeze Rick's hand again and lean forward, looking into his eyes with concern.

"Are you worried about me freaking out?" I say with a soft smile. "I'm okay."

He nods, but his expression tells me he doesn't quite believe it. "Really?"

I tip my chin at the TV. "C'mon, let's see if she figured out who the unknown beauty is."

Rick laughs under his breath and hits the remote, and the TV comes to life again.

The on-screen reporter scrolls through photo after photo of Zach and Marina on her phone until she finds a picture taken of all of us from last year. The photo shows Zach and Marina kissing on stage, and there's me, Merry, and Scarlet standing in the background at a mic near Rick…singing backup. She does a pinch zoom on the screen and holds the phone up.

"Boom!" she yells, then lets out a cackle that makes my skin crawl.

The camera switches to show three reporters at a desk in the network's main studio, all leaning forward to look at their monitors so they can see the photo better.

"Rick's new love is none other than Ashley Roberts," the reporter declares. "Best friend of our favorite mermaid, Marina MacArthur."

"Aww!" one of the anchor reporters gushes. "They could be friends in law!"

The only male reporter makes a face and rolls his eyes. "That's a stretch, Deb."

One of the other anchor reporters pulls up an iPad and zooms in on a still shot of Rick and me inside the theater, and my heart nearly stops. I'm saying something to him, and he looks absolutely smitten.

If you looked up the word besotted in the dictionary, you'd find this photo.

"Look at this guy, Mark," she says pointedly. "He's in love already. I'll fight you on that, buddy."

I grin stupidly as Rick jams his thumb on the off button. I wiggle in my spot until I'm facing him again.

"I'm okay, Rick," I say reassuringly. "This is totally different from Zach and Marina."

"Yeah?" he mutters, still looking worried.

I reach over and take his large hand in both of mine.

"I don't have to worry about my job like she did," I begin, "and I'm also not the control freak she was."

He starts to smile a little. "This really doesn't bother you?"

I shake my head. "Nope."

He nods slowly. "May I ask why?"

"You can ask me anything," I say with a big smile, leaning over for a quick kiss. "I don't care what these people say about me. I actually find it a little sad that they make a living by analyzing something like this. It's a normal moment between two human beings who are—" I stop short for a moment, then laugh softly, "clearly crazy about each other."

His eyes darken, and he begins to lean forward slowly. My eyes dip down to his lips, and I lick mine in anticipation.

"You're crazy about me?" he growls out as the corners of his mouth tip up.

I nod. "As much as you are about me."

He bumps our noses together and nips at my lower lip. "That's awfully presumptuous, don't you think?"

I shake my head. "I see you, Rick Arch—"

Rick's mouth comes crashing down onto mine, and I brace my palms against his cheeks as he kisses me senseless. This man's attention threatens to completely undo me, and as he pushes me back onto the cushions and deepens our kiss, my last thought is *what a way to go.*

***

Ashley

Ashley: OMG emergency conclave…now!
Scarlet: Dude, you're still in LA. You know that, right?
Marina: Ash? You okay??
Merry: Video call, ladies. Ash, send us a video call…

I send a video call invite and wait for all three friends to appear on screen. Marina appears first, rushing through her suite from the bedroom to the living room and sitting on the couch. Scarlet has a paint smear on her cheek and looks like she's in her mother's office. Merry looks like me: sitting up in bed and completely disheveled.

"Ash, what is it? What's wrong?" Marina asks, her expression full of concern.

I shake my head, still panicking a little over the nightmare I just woke up from.

"Rick…"

I shake my head again, feeling more and more ridiculous as I realize I just worried the heck out of my friends because of a stupid dream.

"What, sweetie?" Merry says gently.

"He was bored," I mutter, closing my eyes. "With me."

Marina looks relieved and sad all at the same time. "Oh, Ash, did you have a nightmare? I'm coming up there right now. Give me two minutes."

Marina disconnects.

"Stupid Gregzilla," Merry mutters. "I hate that guy."

"Whoa!" Scarlet says with a laugh. "That's pretty serious for you, unicorn."

Merry scoffs. "Well, I do. He's such a jerk. Rick didn't actually say that to you, did he?"

I shake my head immediately. "No. It was a nightmare."

Scarlet and Merry both heave a sigh of relief.

"But it made me think," I admit. "What if that happens, you guys? I've been so stupid. We kept saying we'd go slow, but then we sped up. I don't know what to do."

A soft knock sounds at my door, and I take my phone with me as I answer the door and let Marina in. She wraps me in a hug immediately, and I squeeze back. Hard.

"Okay, okay," Scarlet says. "We can't see over here."

I let go of Marina, and we move into the living room. I prop the phone up on a small sculpture on the coffee table, and we both sit on the couch so we can see Merry and Scarlet.

"You guys saw the pictures they were analyzing on that show last night," I continue, replaying it all in my head. "You saw the look on Rick's face."

"Oh yeah," Scarlet says in an almost growl. "Most women would kill to have a guy look like that at them."

Marina nods. "Merry texted me a screenshot. He is so adorable."

I feel my lip tremble. "He is. And he's good. And kind. And beautiful. And..."

My friends wait for me to finish my sentence, but I'm not sure I can. I take a deep breath.

"And?" Merry says encouragingly.

My throat bobs as I choke out the words. "And what if he stops looking at me like that?"

"Oh, girl..." Scarlet says gently.

Marina throws an arm around my shoulders and squeezes. "Not possible."

"No way, Ash," Merry chimes in. "Think about it with your brain...

not the part of you that Gregzilla broke."

Marina nods and rocks us gently back and forth. "I agree a thousand percent. This is Gregzilla rearing his ugly head and nothing more."

I choke out a sob. "I hate that jerk."

Scarlet hoots. "Well said!"

Marina squeezes me again. "Take a deep breath."

I do as she says and slowly exhale. Then I do it again.

"Now tell us about the nightmare," Marina says.

I recount the whole dream from our first date last night…that morphed into us sitting at a fast food stand, ignoring each other so we could scroll through our phones. Then the dream changed again, and I wore the red dress to Dad's gala, but Rick wouldn't dance with me. He was bored and pouting at the table because he had to be there with me.

"Does that sound like Rick in any way?" Marina asks.

I shake my head. "No."

Marina nods. "Okay, then how about you and I get dressed and go out to breakfast so we can talk this through?"

I feel a few tears fall and drop my head onto Marina's shoulder.

"I'm so sorry I woke you guys up for this," I say hoarsely. "It was just a panic attack."

Scarlet scoffs. "Panic attacks are nothing to make light of. You did exactly what you should have done…you called us. We've got you, girl."

I nod slowly. "Okay. Okay, thanks."

Marina smiles at me softly. "Okay, Merry and Scarlet, I'm going to get her up and out of here for a while, and we'll be home this evening."

"You want us to come over?" Merry asks. "We were planning to be packed up and out of your apartment, but we can meet you there."

I shake my head with a wobbly smile, grateful for my friends.

"No, I'm okay, really," I say. "I'll be okay if I just get some air and talk it through. We can catch up later."

"Okay, let us know if you change your mind," Scarlet says. "Love you guys!"

Merry waves and blows a kiss as she disconnects, and I end the call on our side. Marina wraps me in another hug.

"All right, let's get ready and go somewhere good," she says. "I think pancakes are in order."

I laugh softly. "Panic-cakes."

Marina smiles brightly. "Now I know you're okay because you're cracking jokes."

I offer another feeble smile as I head to the bathroom to take a shower, and I wonder how okay I really am.

Chapter 19

Rick

Something is different about Ash, and I'm not sure what to do about it. We had a perfect evening at the World Music Awards last week, especially when we had the chance to be alone together. Finally. We stayed up until two in the morning, just talking, laughing, and kissing each other senseless. When she started fighting sleep, I pulled myself away so she could go to bed. I went back up to my room with a huge, stupid grin on my face.

She went out to breakfast with Marina, so I didn't see her again until we left for the airport to fly back to San Francisco. Her eyes were puffy, and I don't think it's because we stayed up all night. There was a sadness about her that wasn't there the day before. She's still physically affectionate but has pulled away from me a little. It's almost like she's under some kind of cloud. Like maybe Greg the Weasel has entered the picture again somehow. Every time I ask what's wrong, she says she's fine. She isn't. Not at all.

Tonight, we're in the apartment along with Zach and Marina as Marina throws a little cocktail party to celebrate the completion of the bookcase. I love that Marina always finds something to celebrate, but I think this is another chance for her to throw Ashley and me together. I won't be complaining about that.

Even though we've been back to normal for a week now, I haven't asked Ashley on another date. We've spent time together as I was finishing the bookcase, but I've felt this funk in the air between us, and I'm trying to wrap my head around what it is. Plus…she works hard all day, and the kids take a lot of energy to deal with. I feel like asking her to go out on a date in the middle of the week isn't super considerate. Thankfully, it's Friday night, and she doesn't have to work tomorrow…so I'm hoping Zach and Marina pull their usual disappearing act and leave us alone. That'll give me time to finally get to the bottom of this and to talk about the upcoming retreat for her Dad's company. I'm still planning to show up for that, and she hasn't told me any different.

Marina pours us each a glass of champagne and serves them up, and we all drink to the new bookcase. It's all in fun, and she lets us tease her about how excited she is over it. The bookcase covers the entire wall, and she and Ashley have already artfully arranged their books, art, and other possessions. It looks great, and I'm happy I could create something they love in the space where they spend so much time.

Zach brings a tray of appetizers into the living room, and we all follow the food. Ashley pulls me over to the loveseat and I pull her against me as we settle onto it together. Marina watches with a satisfied smile, which is normal. Everything *looks* normal. But something is off.

"Rick, where did you decide to display your World Music Award?" Marina asks as she settles next to Zach.

"In the study with my guitar collection," I reply, "and it looks pretty darn good."

Zach lets out a gravelly laugh. "So proud of you, brother."

I nod my thanks, and Ashley tilts her mouth up to my ear.

"Me too."

I turn my face so our noses are nearly touching and smile down at her. I search those beautiful eyes for any sign of what could be wrong, but she seems okay right now.

"Thank you," I murmur, placing a soft kiss on the corner of her mouth.

"So, what's the next song you're working on?" Ashley asks me.

I grin down at her. "Zach and I are working on a few together, but I'm also writing one by myself...called 'That Red Dress.'"

Ashley's whole face lights up. *There she is.* There's my girl. That twinkle in her eye is back.

"Where'd you find the inspiration for that?"

I rub our noses together and whisper, "I wonder."

I'm rewarded with her soft laughter, and it's enough for now.

***

Ashley

Rick Archer is crazy about me. How did I get here? And how did I ever dare to question his heart? Even when he was locked in the friend zone, Rick showed up for me more than Greg ever did - and we were *engaged*. Rick showers me with affection. If I need anything, he's there. And now he's writing a song about the red dress I wore the night of our fake date? How could I let a nightmare shake my confidence in the attraction between us? What is even wrong with me?

True to form, Marina and Zach just made their excuses and went upstairs to his apartment after a couple hours. Now Rick is in the kitchen making me a cup of tea and grabbing a drink for himself, and I'm realizing what an idiot I was for even trying to compare him to stupid Greg. But, speaking of Greg, Dad's company retreat is next week, and I need to talk to Rick about it. If he still wants to go.

My phone vibrates on the coffee table, and I grab it quickly. I swipe it open to find a notification from the dating app I downloaded a few weeks ago. Ugh. I forgot I even downloaded the thing. Another #WhatWereYouThinkingAshley moment. I click it and find a message from some guy named Dan, whom I'm about to disappoint.

Hey, beautiful. I'd love to meet up and see what we have in common. You have the most beautiful eyes I've ever seen. Can't wait to see them in person. Love, Dan.

Yeah, no. Sorry, Dan, it's never gonna happen.

"Whatcha lookin' at?" Rick says, right behind me as he passes my tea over my shoulder.

I jump so high my phone nearly flies out of my hand. I hit the snooze button, and the screen goes dark. I take the mug from him. He steps around the loveseat and sits beside me, then opens his bottle of water.

"Nothing important," I say as I put my phone down.

"Okay," Rick says. "Can we talk about what's been bothering you lately?"

My nervous gaze flicks to his. I think of feigning surprise for a split second, but I can't pull it off. I could never have been an actor.

"I didn't realize it was that obvious," I say with a low sigh.

He nods, and his throat bobs. "Something's been different since the morning after the music awards. I can't figure out what it is, though. If I've done someth—"

I reach out and take his hand, shaking my head emphatically.

"It's nothing you've done," I say as I squeeze his hand.

He eyes me pensively but remains silent.

"Nothing at all," I say.

"Then what is it?"

I set my tea on the coffee table and turn to face Rick squarely. A nervous muscle ticks in his jaw.

"This is going to sound so stupid…"

Rick brings a hand up and smooths a strand of my hair with his fingers.

"Not to me."

I take a deep breath, ready to share the depths of my stupidity.

"I had a nightmare, and it made me ridiculous."

The corner of his mouth twitches as if he's fighting a grin, and I give him a half smile.

"A nightmare? When? About what?"

"The night of the awards," I say lowly. "We stayed up all night, and it was…so perfect. The awards, the after party, but especially our after party for two."

A slow smile is his only response.

"The late-night pizza, the talking…and especially the kissing."

Rick's expression goes from intrigued to puzzled in two seconds.

"You had a nightmare because of the kissing?"

"No!" I nearly jump out of my seat. "No, not at all. The nightmare was about Greg."

"So I kissed you, and you thought of Greg?"

I lunge forward and bring my mouth to his so quickly that his eyes widen in surprise, but he recovers quickly. His strong arms wrap around my waist and pull me into his lap as I wrap my arms around his neck and take control of his mouth. He can't draw the wrong conclusions if he can't talk. That's my theory.

I sink against Rick, reveling in the feeling of being wrapped in his solid embrace. A low growl escapes his throat, and I smile against his mouth. Now I have his attention. I break off our kiss and put my palms on either side of his face, forcing his gaze up to mine.

"Are you going to listen to me now?"

He nods. "Yes, ma'am."

I laugh softly and begin to scoot off his lap, but his arms hold me still.

"Mm mm," he murmurs with a shake of his head, making me laugh again.

"That night was everything," I say with quiet emphasis. "It was perfect. And I guess I got a little scared because I had a nightmare that you became...indifferent."

He frowns.

"Bored," I clarify. "With me."

Another low grumble from Rick. "I really hate that weasel."

I lower my forehead to his. "I'm sorry. I don't know what I was thinking. It just really freaked me out."

He tilts his head slightly and brings our lips together. Slow. Soft. So, so sweet.

"It's okay," he breathes against my lips.

I pull away. "It's not okay, and it won't happen again."

His eyes rove over my face. "You left with Marina that morning..."

I nod. "To talk things through," I share. "I scared the hell out of everyone with a video emergency conclave, then she came to my room, and we went out to breakfast."

He nods, absorbing my words. "Are you all right now?"

I smile, and he smiles back. "I'm in your arms. I'm more than all right."

That earns me a kiss that stops time. I don't even know how else to describe it. Nothing else matters but the feeling of this man's lips devouring mine. If we stay like this forever, I don't even care. *What a way to go.*

When we finally break off the kiss, I press my forehead to his. "Forgive me?"

He pulls back and frowns. "There's nothing to forgive."

I let out a sigh of relief and wrap my arms around his neck. He pulls me tight, and I rest my head on his shoulder.

"I do not deserve you," I murmur.

"I'll be the judge of that," he replies gently, rubbing a hand down my back.

"I just want to stay here all day."

He chuckles, and his breath tickles my hair.

"Might be hard to do some things, but I can live with it."

I squeeze him harder. "We don't need to do anything. Just this."

He laughs again. "Yes, ma'am."

A sudden realization has me pulling away enough to look at him.

"Actually, we do need to do something," I say. "We need to talk about the retreat."

He nods. "Okay."

I wiggle off his lap and he lets me this time. I don't go far.

"Do you still want to go?"

His watchful eyes flick over my face. "Do you still want me to go?"

I smirk. "That's not an answer."

He reaches over and takes my hand. "Of course I do. If you want me there."

"I don't want you to feel obligated," I say quietly. "You were kind of having a verbal duel with the weasel when you said you'd go."

Rick throws his head back and laughs, and it's the best thing I've heard all day. I giggle proudly.

"Fireball, you're just the best thing ever."

I give him an easy smile. "Back atcha."

He leans over to rub our noses together. "I still want to go."

I nod. "Okay, so I should tell you more about it then," I say. "It's a lot."

He smirks. "I think I said the same to you about the World Music Awards, so go for it."

I laugh softly.

"It's three days of awkward social interactions and pretentious networking," I begin, rolling my eyes. "But Dad likes me to go, and there's nothing I wouldn't do for him. It's at Felicitas, a super bougie country club in the wine country. We'd get there on Thursday night, then spend the weekend doing various activities like swimming, golfing, and having breakfast with a hundred finance geeks."

"Wow," he says with the sexiest grin ever. "That sounds awesome."

"You can totally back out if you want, Rick," I say emphatically. "It's not very fun."

He smirks again. "So my choice is A: stay home and have a weekend without my Fireball, or B: spend a weekend at a bougie country club and go swimming, golfing, and eating with my Fireball and a hundred finance geeks?"

I giggle. "That's about it."

In one deft movement, he reaches over and sweeps me back into his lap. His lips brush mine just enough to tease me.

"I choose B."

His eyes darken as he brings our lips together softly. Passionately. A tremor runs through me from my head to my toes, prompting a growl from Rick, and I think…just maybe…I may finally have some fun at this retreat.

***

Rick

I mentally curse the traffic on the Golden Gate Bridge this morning as I crawl slowly into San Francisco with what feels like thousands of other vehicles. This isn't how I thought I'd spend my morning, stuck in commuter traffic, but here I am. Why? Because I was kissing my girlfriend until the wee hours of the morning and left my wallet on the table in her entryway like an idiot.

Actually, she's *not* my girlfriend. I don't get to call her that, especially when she's on a dating app and keeping her options open, which is killing me slowly. I hate that I saw her phone screen last week. I wasn't trying to read it over her shoulder. It was just really in my face when I popped over her shoulder, and now I can't unsee it.

I don't understand what's going on right now, but I know I'm the one she chose to go to her dad's retreat with, so I'm guessing I'm at least at the top of the heap. Not that there's a heap.

Ugh.

I could wait until tomorrow when I pick Ashley up to go to the retreat, but I need my credit card before then. Because, just to prove that I'm completely lost over this woman, I found the perfect present for her. And I'm giving it to her, even if she's not all-in like me.

Traffic speeds up just long enough to give me hope, and then it grinds to a halt again. Just like my relationship with Ash. I sigh in frustration. She sure kisses me like she's all-in, though, and that's what's so confusing. Why is she on a dating app?

I could ask her, but it isn't really my business. We've never talked about this. We've never agreed to be exclusive, so she has every right to see other guys if she wants. I just thought we were further along than this. I am, anyway. I definitely am.

I hem and haw over a thousand ridiculous scenarios, briefly interrupted by five minutes of terror as a San Francisco police car rolls up behind me and tails me all the way off the bridge. It would have been my luck to be pulled over when I had no driver's license or identification, but he mercifully went in another direction once we got into the city.

It's ten in the morning on a Wednesday, so parking spaces are actually available in front of the building that houses Zach's apartment, Marina and Ashley's apartment, and the offices of the Mermaid Foundation on the ground floor. I park quickly and head to the Mermaid offices first to see if Marina's okay with me retrieving my wallet. Ashley's at work, so I know she won't be home.

The Mermaid Foundation's offices are something else. Scarlet outdid herself when she decorated this space as a gift for Marina. The walls are painted three shades of blue, starting with the lightest shade at the ceiling and gradually getting darker as it goes lower. Deeper, like the ocean. The furniture and other decor are all ocean and mermaid-themed, giving it a fun and welcoming vibe. I barely get in the door, and I hear Marina.

"Rick!" she exclaims as she heads over and gives me a huge hug.

"Hey, Marina, sorry to bother you."

She shakes her head. "No bother at all. What's up?"

"I left my wallet in your apartment last night," I say with a sheepish grin. "Is it okay to run up there and get it?"

She waves a hand at me. "Of course! You don't need to ask."

I scoff. "Yeah, I do. What if you were upstairs just getting out of the shower or something? I don't need a punch in the jaw from my best friend after he finds out."

Marina laughs out loud. "Good point. Go on up. I'd get it for you, but I've got a meeting in a few minutes."

I shake my head. "No, it's okay. I'll run up really fast and be out of here before you know it. Thanks, Marina."

I hug her goodbye and leave the office, then trot up the stairs to the third floor where their apartment is. I pull my keys out and let myself in. My wallet's not on the entry table. Hmm. That's weird. I'm sure I left it right here.

I step further into the apartment. Could I have left it in the kitchen? I must have. A quick glance at the living room tells me it's not on any of the tables in there. I head back to the kitchen. It's not on the island or any of the counters. Could I have left it in the guest bathroom?

I take a few steps towards the guest bathroom when Ashley, with her face completely covered in some kind of colored goo, comes bounding out of the guest bathroom and slams right into me. Her face fully impacts my chest. She screams like she just saw a ten-pound spider, and I reach out to steady her before she falls. She flails a bit before she realizes it's me.

"What are you doing here!" she yells, clutching her chest and panting over the shock.

"What are *you* doing here? It's Wednesday!"

She paces over to the kitchen and pulls out a bar stool, perching on it as she catches her breath.

"Emergency renovations at the school," she says. "It's closed for the rest of the week, remember?"

Oh. Yep. She did tell me that. She told me that the bathrooms were flooded, and they had to dig up something…she told me. I was half listening, half obsessing about Dan, the dating app guy and whether he'll get to see her beautiful eyes in person. Those same beautiful eyes that are now looking at me in shock and confusion.

"Oh *no!*" she yells suddenly, apparently realizing that she's covered in goo. She runs into the guest bathroom, and I hear the faucet turn on.

She sputters. I hear scrubbing. I wait patiently, looking down at my ruined shirt. I pull it tight against my chest to see how bad the damage is. It's a white shirt. It's a goner. I hear Ashley gasp and look up to see her staring at my shirt in horror.

"Your shirt is ruined!"

I shrug. "It's okay, Ash. I have other shirts."

Her lower lip pops up in an adorable pout. "But that's one of my favorites."

I raise my eyebrows. "You have favorites?"

A devilish little grin. "Any time you wear a Henley with those shoulders, those arms, and that chest, it's a gift to all woman-kind, Rick."

I laugh out loud. Noted. I need to go buy more Henleys.

"What was that stuff on your face?" I ask.

She blushes.

"I was all puffy from staying up too late, so I was using a face mask to try to reduce it," she says. "It was supposed to be part of my super relaxing at home spa day."

I suppress a laugh. "Until I broke into your apartment and scared you to death."

"Something like that," she says, grinning up at me. "But I got my revenge."

I look at her curiously, and she nods at my chest with a little giggle.

"There's an almost perfect impression of my horrified face stained on your shirt."

I laugh and head to the guest bathroom to look in the mirror. Ashley follows and watches as I stretch the shirt out to get a good look. Sure enough, there is a clear imprint of a face on my shirt. Big eye sockets, nose imprint, wide-open mouth frozen in horror. It's hysterical. Our eyes meet in the mirror.

"I am never getting rid of this shirt."

Her eyes go wide. "Don't be ridiculous."

I grin at her in the mirror. "I'm not being ridiculous. This is my favorite shirt. My awesome Ashley shirt."

She rolls her eyes at me and puts a hand on her hip. "Nope. Not happening. That shirt needs to go."

I just keep grinning and carefully pull her against me so I don't stain her clothes with face goo residue. I plant a kiss on top of her beautiful head.

"It's my new favorite thing," I murmur against her hair. "You can't take it away from me."

And that's how The Great Ashley Shirt War began…

Chapter 20

Ashley

"You did what?" Marina asks in a supremely exasperated tone.

I cringe, flipping through the stupid dating app that's still on my phone. "It was way back when I was still in denial. I forgot all about it, honestly."

Scarlet shakes her head at me from her spot on the couch. "Dude."

Merry hovers over my shoulder. "Delete it already. It's bad mojo."

I scroll through the app settings, finally finding the option to delete my profile. Poof! Gone. Then I flip over to my apps manager and delete the app. I hold the phone up to show everyone.

"Gone."

Marina chuffs. "And you don't think Rick saw it?"

I shrug. "He didn't say anything to me. I don't think he was looking at the screen."

She gives me an incredulous look. "Of course, he wouldn't say anything to you. He's a sweetheart."

He is. I really hope he didn't see that message from creepy Dan. Creepy Dan, who means absolutely nothing to me. I'd ask him about it, but then what does that look like? We haven't talked about making things exclusive between us. I don't want to seem clingy.

Hey, Rick, just asking...can I be your girlfriend? Forever?

"What time is he getting here?" Scarlet asks. "I want to show him the pictures of his corbels in Mom's office."

I look at the clock in the kitchen. "Any minute now."

"You did a great job, Scarlet," Merry says encouragingly. "It's in the bag this year."

Scarlet grins. "Thanks, Mer. We'll see."

I see Marina out of the corner of my eye and turn to her. "Are you going to scowl at me for the rest of my life? I made a mistake."

She purses her lips. "Yeah, I know. I'm sorry...I just really want you two to end up together. You're perfect for each other."

I flop down on the loveseat with a stupid smile on my face. "Well, for once, I'm not going to argue with you on that. He is perfect. And beautif—"

The sound of a key in the front door halts my rambling, and Zach walks into the apartment. Rick is right behind him. Both men tower in the doorway, and Zach gives us all a knowing look.

"Wow," he growls. "Could you ladies look more guilty?"

"We don't know what you're talking about," Merry declares with a syrupy, innocent smile.

Zach laughs. "No, but I do," he says, nudging Rick. "I'm just glad I'm not the topic of conversation this time. Good luck, bud."

Rick looks around the room and smirks, then heads straight for me with a look that is borderline feral.

"Well, as long as you're talking about me anyway," he says, leaning over me and bringing our lips together in a kiss that sends a chorus of hoots and hollers erupting from my friends.

I laugh softly against his mouth as he pulls me up off the loveseat and into his arms. Sheer heaven. I wrap my arms around him and hold him tightly. He's like a mountain. A big, huggable mountain that smells amazing and kisses like a dream.

"Get me away from these women," he whispers into my ear, making me laugh again.

I pull away from him. "I won't let them get you, don't worry."

Merry lets out a growling noise and wiggles her eyebrows at Rick, prompting a worried look from him that furrows his brow. I fight back my laughter as I grab my purse and slip my hand into his.

"Let's go before Merry gets ideas," I tease. I wave at my friends. "Bye, guys!"

Scarlet leaps up from the couch. "Wait a minute!"

She trots over to Rick and hands him her phone. He takes it and looks at the photos of her Mom's office as she reaches over and scrolls for him. He nods appreciatively.

"That looks awesome, Scarlet," he says. "I can't imagine what could beat that. I love how you used the corbels for decorative shelving. It looks great."

She takes her phone and grins proudly. "Thanks. And thanks for the help."

"Anytime." Rick steps over to the entry where my bag is waiting and picks it up. "Ready, Fireball?"

I nod and join him, turning back to wave at my friends again. "Have a great weekend, guys!"

"Hey, Rick," Merry calls as we step out into the hall. "Remember Greg's gonna be there. Probably a good idea to walk around with no shirt on. A lot."

I nudge him forward. "Don't turn your back," I tease as I close the door behind us. "She can smell fear."

***

The gentle, green rolling hills of California's wine country go by as I

241

relax against the passenger seat of Rick's truck. We're almost there, and it's been a fun drive so far. We stopped at a little market just off the roadside and bought some snacks, including this delicious Port Salut cheese that I couldn't resist. And a loaf of sourdough. I know from past retreats that there are small refrigerators in the suites, so the cheese will be fine. I didn't think to ask Dad's assistant, Tammi, whether she was able to get Rick a suite instead of a regular room. I'm sure she's done her best. She does an amazing job coordinating this retreat every year.

Rick steers the truck up the long, winding, tree-lined driveway of the country club. A sprawling complex of cottage-style buildings appears dotted against the beautiful green landscape. Black shutters adorn all the windows, and spring flowers bloom in beautiful containers artfully arranged against the buildings. True to form, I see Dad sitting on the wide, wrap-around porch in one of the white rocking chairs as he chats with a handful of the executive leaders who report to him. His face lights up when he sees me, and I wave at him. Rick gets out and comes to open the door for me.

"I hope you're ready for a little hero worship," I tell Rick as I slide out of the truck. "Dad has had a slight obsession with you since the World Music Awards."

Rick laughs softly, kissing the top of my head.

Swoon.

I love it when he does that. It's so sweet, especially from a giant man like him. He grins down at me.

"I can handle it."

Dad ambles down the porch steps to greet us. Rick gets a firm handshake and a hearty slap on the back, and I get wrapped in a dad hug. I kiss him on the cheek.

"Hi, Daddy."

"Hello, beauty," he says. "Did you have a nice drive?"

I nod. "I bought some cheese at a little market, so I want to check in and get it in the fridge. Have you seen Tammi?"

"She's at the check-in desk, honey," Dad replies. "Go on in and get settled. We'll catch up at dinner. Good to see you, Rick. Welcome!"

Rick nods at Dad as he pulls our bags out of the truck and hands the key to the valet.

"Glad to be here, sir."

I head up the porch stairs with Rick following close behind and find Tammi seated at a special check-in desk for events. Dad always buys up all the rooms, so the entire country club is full of executives and management from his firm. Tammi smiles at us as we approach, her bright blue eyes darting between me and Rick.

"This must be the famous Rick Archer," Tammi gushes, extending a hand to him and blushing a hysterical amount when he takes it. "Welcome to our little retreat."

I laugh under my breath. There's nothing little about this place or the budget it takes to put on this retreat every year. Tammi checks something on her clipboard and pulls two brass keys on Felicitas branded keychains out of a drawer. She checks them both and hands one to each of us.

"You're in suite number three fourteen," she purrs. "Enjoy your stay."

I shoot her a confused look. "What room is Rick in?"

"Three fourteen, honey."

I nod. "Okay, what suite am I in then?"

Now it's Tammi's turn to look confused. "Three fourteen, of course."

"What?" I whisper. "Tammi, no. I asked you for two rooms."

She shakes her head. "No, you didn't."

I stare at her, wide-eyed. "I certainly did."

She shakes her head. "You certainly didn't."

I decide not to argue. "Okay, well…it's not like that, so can you please give him his own room?"

Tammi's troubled gaze darts between me and Rick a few times.

"Honey, we're booked to the gills," she says quietly. "There are no other rooms available."

"There *have* to be," I say with equal quiet.

Rick leans forward. "Ladies, I can go to a hotel."

"No," Tammi and I say in unison.

I look up at Rick. "This place is massive. There are no hotels nearby."

I turn back to Tammi. "You didn't think to ask?"

Tammi nervously looks at Rick, then turns to me. "It's Rick Archer," she whispers loudly. "I didn't even consider that you weren't...you know...how can you resist *that?*"

"Tammi!" I exclaim as Rick bursts out in laughter.

Rick takes me by the hand and begins tugging me away.

"It's okay, Ash," he says confidently. "We'll figure it out. Let's go."

Tammi smiles apologetically as Rick guides me towards the elevators. The suites are on the third floor, so it doesn't take long for the elevator doors to open and let us out. I follow the signs to our suite and open the door, holding it open for Rick to bring in our bags. I let the door close and head inside to assess the situation.

Yep. Just like I remembered: a king-sized bed and a loveseat in the small living area. No couch or chair that folds out into a sleeper. I turn an apologetic glance at Rick.

"I'm so sorry, Rick," I sputter. "I know I told her to give you a room of your own."

He smirks at me, and I immediately recognize the look he's got in his eyes that he's playing with me.

"I think you did it on purpose."

Now it's my turn to smirk. "Do you now?"

He nods. "Pretty sure."

I laugh softly, then stomp my feet in frustration. "What are we going to do? You can't sleep on that."

I gesture at the little loveseat. It's way too small.

He shrugs. "I go camping sometimes. I'll sleep on the floor."

I gasp. "You will not. That's not fair."

Rick leans over to kiss my forehead, and I look around the room as if a better solution will miraculously materialize. He roots through our bags from the market and finds the cheese, then steps over to the mini bar and puts it in the fridge. I smile my thanks.

"Okay, final option," Rick says, putting his hands on my shoulders and giving me a little squeeze. "I fake appendicitis or something and just go home. You can ride back with your dad, or I can come get you, saying I feel much better."

I step into his arms and sigh against his chest. Those big arms wrap me in a warm embrace.

"Not an option," I say quietly. "I want to spend time with you."

A large hand comes up to cradle my head against his chest. "Music to my ears."

I steal a glance up at him. "So now what?"

He's thoughtful for a moment. "They were serving appetizers in the lounge downstairs. Why don't we go get you a snack? I think you might be a little hangry. Then everything will look better."

I adore this man who just wants to feed me, hold me, and kiss me all the time. I let Rick usher me out of the suite and downstairs, lured into an optimistic outlook by the feel of his hand at the small of my back and the delicious array of treats we find downstairs. The opening night dinner is in a few hours, so I make up a mini charcuterie plate while Rick gets our drinks from the bar. I find a couple plush chairs by the big stone fireplace and settle in. Rick finds me easily, and hands me the water I asked for.

He sits, and we eat in silence for a few minutes…just watching the fire. Finally, he turns to me.

"So what's tonight? Anything special?"

I nod. "The opening night dinner," I reply with a grand sweep of my hand. "Everyone in the grand ballroom as Dad kicks it off with a motivational speech. There's a group dinner every night that we'll need to attend."

Rick nods. "I love the passion your dad has for his company. It's nice to see."

"He's a good leader," I say, "and a fair boss."

"And tomorrow?"

"They'll all start grouping up for golf, and wine tasting," I explain. "We can do what we want since we're not interested in networking, thank goodness."

"That doesn't sound too bad," he says. "What would you like to do?"

I grin. "I'm really boring."

He throws his head back and laughs. "There is nothing about you that's boring."

"Even if I want to stay in the lounge and cuddle up with you all day?"

He raises his eyebrows and grins. "That doesn't sound boring at all."

"It doesn't?"

"You've been to this retreat every year for how many years?" he asks, not really expecting an answer. "I'm betting you have the perfect spot scoped out."

I nod.

"We can cuddle up all day," he begins. "Go for a walk or two. Feed each other pancakes in the morning. Curl up in front of this fireplace. I don't care, as long as it's with you."

I pick up a piece of cheese from my plate and pop it in my mouth, unable to find the words to answer something so romantic. I don't want to spoil it with lesser words.

"Now, about the room situation," he says quietly. "We will do whatever you're comfortable with. But if you say there's no hotel nearby, and you won't let me sleep on the floor, then you're going to have to let me sleep on the loveseat. And I will be fine."

I frown at him. "I feel terrible about it."

He reaches over and takes my hand in his.

"Why do you beat yourself up so much?" he asks softly. "I really wish you wouldn't."

I shrug. "Old habits, I guess."

"Speaking of old habits," Greg's voice sounds behind me, "good to see you, Ash."

I turn instantly and give him the dirtiest look. Rick, however, that's another thing altogether. It's like all the energy around him changes. That telltale muscle ticks in Rick's jaw, and he looks at me with lethal calm...and smiles.

"Excuse me for a moment, Fireball."

He stands and turns in one lithe movement, then walks around to the back of the chair where Greg is standing, stepping into his space. Rick's a good five inches taller than Greg, so he has to crane his neck to look up. He frowns up at Rick.

"Hi Greg," Rick grumbles, squinting better than Clint Eastwood ever did.

"Yeah, hi...Rick, is it?"

"You know my name, Greg, don't try to act tough," Rick growls. "Now listen. We're all here to have a nice weekend. And I don't want it to start off on the wrong foot, so we'll go over basic manners right now. If you ever speak to my...Ashley, like that again, you'll be doing it with a much less perfect-looking nose. Do we understand each other?"

Greg looks at Rick, his mouth in a twist. He steps away.

"Relax, guitar hero. I was just making a joke. See you guys at dinner."

He acts tough enough, but he walks away a little too quickly, and I can't help but give him a good sneer as I watch him go. Rick sits back down and wraps my hand in his again.

"So," Rick says, turning back to me. "Dinner tonight. Tell me more."

I nod. "Seating isn't assigned, but Dad always wants me to sit close."

"Of course." He flashes me a devilish smile. "Dancing?"

I laugh. "On the last night, yes. The final dinner is kind of a big party. And I plan to monopolize all of your time."

"And what about Greg?"

I furrow my brow. "What about Greg?"

"I just figured if we're here and he's here…you might want to poke a stick at the weasel."

I giggle, then shake my head. "I don't care about him. At all. I would love for this weekend to just be about us."

"Us," he parrots, the corner of his mouth tilting up. "Sounds like a perfect weekend to me."

***

Rick

I'm trying my best not to stare as I wait for Ashley in the bar area. The weasel is having a heated argument with his girlfriend, and it's taking all my resolve not to walk over there and offer to pay for an Uber to get her away from him. I can't hear the conversation, but I'm getting enough from facial expressions. Whatever the thing is that's upset her is not a priority for him or even an issue. I can tell the expectation is for her to just deal with whatever it is. She's not getting any support from him. I can't imagine Ashley ever being with someone like this.

"Is this seat taken?" Ashley purrs at me as she pulls out the bar stool next to me.

I'm on my feet in an instant, reaching out to wrap her in a hug, but then I see what she's wearing. I step back and give her a good, long look as my heart hammers against my ribs. Heaven help me.

Ashley is wearing a strapless red dress that hugs her body in ways that have me thinking all kinds of thoughts. Her long blond waves have been pulled back into a high ponytail, which brings even more attention to her beautiful eyes. I hope no one else speaks to me at dinner because I won't be able to take my eyes off her.

"Ashley," I murmur. "How am I supposed to focus on anything else with you looking so beautiful?"

She beams at the compliment and leans in to kiss my cheek, but I turn at the last minute and claim her mouth. I feel her smile against my lips as I wrap my arms around her and pull her against me. She snakes her arms around my neck, and a little moan escapes her throat. Remembering that we're at her father's company retreat, I reluctantly break off the kiss and let her go, linking our hands together.

"Right," I say quietly. "Should we go to dinner before your Dad bans me for groping his daughter in public?"

She giggles, then leads the way through the spacious main lounge to a grand archway on the other side. There's a cocktail reception happening in the foyer, with various guests milling around and chatting, and the doors are open to the main dining room as well. I can see a stage set up with a podium, and the room is full of round dining tables that seat six each.

"Open bar. What would you like to drink?" she asks as we approach one of the little bars set up around the foyer. She smiles at the bartender. "I'd love a margarita."

I look at the beers on display, then nod at the bartender and tap the bottle of a local IPA.

"Hey, man," I say lightly. "This one any good?"

He nods, then does a double take. Ah. He recognizes me.

"Oh wow," he says as he mixes Ash's margarita. "Rick Archer? This is so cool! I'm a huge fan, man."

I smile politely and glimpse at his name tag. "Thanks, Eric. That's always nice to hear."

He hands Ashley her margarita with a smile.

"Have a taste and make sure you like it," he says. "I can't have Rick Archer's girlfriend thinking I make weak margaritas."

Ashley laughs softly and gives it a sip. "This is delicious. Thank you."

"Uh," Eric sputters, popping the top off the beer I pointed to. "It's a really good one to answer your question. I love it."

He hands me the beer with a smile, and I nod my thanks. I set the bottle down for a moment, and pull a twenty out of my wallet to drop in his tip jar.

"Thanks so much, man," Eric says. "I can't believe I met Rick Archer. This is incredible. Are the other Rebels here too?"

I laugh softly. "Sadly, no. You're stuck with just me."

He shrugs. "You're my favorite anyway. I used to play guitar once upon a time. You're really amazing. And congrats on the World Music Award!"

I reach out and shake his hand.

"Thanks a lot, man," I say genuinely. "I was really proud to win it."

He nods. "I love that song."

"You said you used to play guitar," I say curiously. "Not anymore?"

He shrugs it off, but I see regret in his eyes. "Life got in the way, you know? Marriage. Kids."

I step aside while someone stops by for a drink. He pours a glass of wine and hands it to them with a smile. I reach back into my wallet and pull out one of the guitar picks I always carry for fans. I hand it to him.

"Being a father is one of the most important jobs there is," I say quietly. "Pick up that guitar and play for your kids, man."

He takes the pick and his expression is the same as if I handed him a thousand dollars. He looks at the logo.

"Oh wow," he says excitedly. "You make your own guitar picks?"

"Only for me and the fans I meet," I say with a grin. "You can't buy those anywhere."

I feel Ashley's thumb caress my hand where our fingers are laced together, and I look down to find her smiling sweetly up at me.

He nods thoughtfully. "You're right. I'm gonna do it. I'm gonna dig my guitar out of the attic and start playing for my girls. I never thought about it that way. Thanks, man."

"It was nice to meet you, Eric," I say as I move away with Ashley. "Thanks for the chat."

He nods at me, and I walk away with Ashley.

"I didn't know those are special guitar picks," she says. "You really can't buy them anywhere?"

"Nope," I reply. "They're nothing special, but I'm very particular when it comes to my picks. So when the Rebels started doing well, and I had a little money, I had these made. I don't have any interest in marketing them because they really aren't a big deal, but I thought they'd be a cool thing to give away to fans they can't get from just anywhere."

Ashley stops just inside the dining room and holds her hand out to me with a grin.

"Do I get one?"

I laugh softly and pull my wallet out of my pocket, showing her the three remaining picks tucked against my credit cards.

"Pick a color, Fireball."

She grins like a kid at Christmas, reaching immediately for the red one and holding it up for me to see. I nod my approval, and she leads me to the head table where her dad is holding court with a few of his staff. He sees us approaching and stands to greet us. For a brief moment, he looks like he has a hard time getting out of the chair, and

I look at Ashley. She doesn't seem to notice, and he seems fine now.

"There's my beautiful girl," her dad says proudly, wrapping her in a hug.

"Hi, Daddy," Ashley says happily, planting a kiss on his cheek.

Her dad turns to me, and we shake hands.

"Rick, do you golf?" her dad asks.

I shake my head. "Never played, sir."

He laughs. "Not much time for rock stars to golf, I suppose. Well, that's okay, I can teach you the basics."

"Daddy," Ashley scolds gently. "What if he doesn't want to play?"

"I'm happy to give it a shot," I say lightly. "But I hope you don't expect much. I could be a real disaster."

Her dad and his companions laugh at the joke.

"What's this?" Greg's weasely voice sounds behind me. "Are we golfing tomorrow?"

Ashley's dad looks less than thrilled, and I feel way too happy about that.

"*We* aren't, Greg," her dad says. "I've invited Ashley, Rick, and Kevin."

The companion, whose name is apparently Kevin, nods at Greg with a look on his face like he's rubbing it in. Greg is clearly out of favor.

"Bye, Greg," Kevin says with a smile.

Ouch.

Greg smirks and moves away, giving me a look as he goes. Creepy dude.

Ashley tugs at my hand, and I smile down at her.

"Let's find our places."

"Lead the way, Fireball."

***

Ashley

"It's okay to tell him no," I say to Rick as he gathers his bathroom stuff together. "Do you even like golf?"

He shrugs. "How would I know? I've never played. I really don't mind, Ash. It's okay."

I nod and watch him disappear into the bathroom to change for bed. I flop on the bed and look around the room again, wishing there was a better alternative for him than that tiny love seat. I even had Tammi check with the hotel management to see if they had a cot or any kind of air mattress. Nothing. I shake my head and pull out my phone.

Ashley: You guys aren't going to believe this. Tammi didn't reserve a room for Rick. It never occurred to her that we weren't...you know.

Merry: Going boinky boinky?

Scarlet: OMG...

Marina: Merry, honestly. LOL.

Scarlet: So what's the plan?

Ashley: There's no hotel anywhere near here. He's going to sleep on the loveseat.

Merry: That doesn't sound very comfy for someone as tall as Rick.

Ashley: No, it sure doesn't. I feel terrible.

Marina: Girl, you can share. No one's there to judge you...

Rick comes out of the bathroom, so I snooze my phone and put it on the nightstand. When I look up, I can't believe my eyes. He's wearing a pair of sweatpants, a mischievous grin, and the stained-up Henley with my face imprinted on it.

Chapter 21

"What are you wearing?" I gasp, laughing so hard I nearly fall over.

Rick grins and struts around the loveseat like he's oh-so-proud. He rubs a hand on the front of the shirt.

"I love my Ashley jammies."

I grab a pillow and throw it at him. Hard. He catches it one-handed.

"Thanks! I needed a pillow."

"Rick, you can't be serious," I cry. "I can't believe you kept that stupid shirt."

He laughs. "Why? I love it. It's cozy and comfy…and it has your face on it."

I roll my eyes. "Thank God it doesn't actually look like my face. It could be anyone's face."

He nods. "But we know whose face it is."

I shake my head. "Please get rid of that. It's so embarrassing."

He frowns. "Why is it embarrassing?"

"Because…" I open my mouth and try to make the same face that's on the shirt, and I'm rewarded with a huge laugh from Rick.

He sighs heavily. "You're adorable."

I try to get serious, but he just looks so ridiculous. I school my expression into a sober one and snap my fingers.

"Not kidding, get rid of that thing. It's horrible."

I set my jaw and fight against the laughter threatening to bubble up.

He raises his eyebrows in challenge. "Okay, if you say so. I'll take it off and—"

Rick pulls the shirt up, partially revealing his killer abs, and I yelp.

"No, never mind!"

He stops but doesn't drop the shirt. The abs are still staring at me. My throat feels dry all of a sudden.

"You can keep it for now."

He smirks at me and lets the shirt go. "Thanks."

I watch as he steps over to the large armoire and opens it, pulling out the extra blanket on the top shelf. Guilt hammers at my heart.

"Rick?"

He drops the blanket on the loveseat and looks up at me.

"Please let me sleep there," I plead. "You can't even stretch out."

He walks over to me and sits on the edge of the bed, taking my hand in his.

"I will be just fine. Please don't worry about it," he says, kissing me lightly on the mouth. "Besides, you're not a shrimp. You're what…five foot nine?"

I nod.

"You're not stretching out on that thing either," he says. "Better me than you."

"That makes no sense," I argue. "I'm five inches shorter than you."

"Are we going to have our first fight over who has to sleep on this loveseat?"

I gasp. "No! That's crazy. Come here."

I pull him to me and kiss him softly. He frames my face with his hands, holding me exactly where he wants me, taking his time. We pull apart and I put my head on his broad shoulder, sighing.

"If we're gonna fight, it'll be about that stupid shirt," I mutter, then snicker.

He laughs out loud and kisses me once more, then springs off the bed and heads for the loveseat.

"All right, we'll save that for another day. I need to get some sleep if I'm going to learn how to golf and not embarrass myself tomorrow."

Rick fluffs up the pillow and lays it on one end of the loveseat, then pulls the hair tie out of his hair, and my skin feels like it's going to catch fire. I've never seen him with his hair down before. He really does look like a Viking god. His hair is beautiful. It's thick and healthy looking, lying just past his shoulders. I desperately want to dive my hands into it.

"What did you say?" he asks with a smirk.

I shake my head, finding myself unable to speak.

"Did you just call me a Viking god?"

"Nope."

He laughs and shakes his head, then lays down and pulls the blanket over himself. His legs hang off the armrest almost to his knee.

"That does not look comfortable."

All I see is his hand pop up so he can give me a thumbs up.

"In my mind, I'm in the Bahamas," he says. "Sleeping in a hammock on the beach."

I just sit there for a minute, feeling horrible. This is a king-sized bed. Surely, we can—

"Are you going to turn out the light or stare at me all night, Fireball?"

I hear a light chuckle come from the loveseat.

"Sorry," I mutter, leaning over to hit the light switch.

I roll over and shove a pillow under my head. I last exactly three seconds before sitting up in the dark.

"Rick?"

"Yes, Fireball?"

"We're adults, right?"

I hear a smirk in the dark. "Mostly."

I laugh softly. "I can share."

Rustling from the loveseat. "What?"

"This is a king-sized bed," I reply. "I can share. We cuddled on my bed when I was sick, and nothing happened."

Another smirk. "Well, you did get a little frisky. You just don't remember."

I hit the light switch. "I did what?"

He sits up and peers over the loveseat at me with a grin. "You were trying to count my abs."

I smack my hands over my face.

Of course. Of course, I did that.

I hear Rick laugh.

"Fireball, I'm only teasing."

I peek through my fingers. "You mean I didn't actually do that?"

He scoffs. "Oh, no, you did it. But it was really cute. And you're right: nothing happened."

I stare at him for a minute. "If we share this bed, do you promise not to tell me any other embarrassing things I've done that I don't know about?"

He raises his hand like a scout taking an oath. "I promise."

I offer him a half smile. "Then will you please come here and be comfy with me?"

Rick stands and grabs the pillow, walking slowly over to the bed.

"You're sure you're comfortable with this?" he asks seriously for a moment.

I nod and reach out for his hand, tugging him onto the bed. His hair falls in his eyes, and I resist the urge to brush it back. He reaches up and brushes it away, muscles bunching and flexing as he moves. He sits on the bed and puts the pillow down, watching me closely.

"I trust you more than any other man I've ever known," I say quietly. "No one else has made me feel more treasured or special than you."

He offers me a soft smile. "Then let's get some sleep, okay?"

I nod and lean over to turn off the light. I feel him stretch out on the bed, and he reaches for me as I scoot under the covers. His arm wraps around my shoulders as I rest my head against his chest. Heaven. Am I ever going to be able to sleep alone after this?

Rick's lips graze the top of my head as he plants a light kiss there. I feel his body relaxing into sleep already.

"Good night, beautiful," he murmurs.

I smile against his chest.

"Good night, my beautiful, hot, perfect man-friend."

***

Rick

There's an angel on my shoulder. That's what she looks like as I watch her sleeping, lips softly parted. I think about how different we are, and my heart lurches, skipping a beat. Ashley guards her heart, which I understand now more than ever, especially when I'm so uncertain about how this will go. I don't know how smart it was to climb into this bed with her last night. Perhaps it would have been smarter to wake up with a sore back than to line up for a possible broken heart.

Her whole experience with the weasel was traumatizing. That's obvious. But does she regret losing him? Is it possible? She says she doesn't care about him, but could there be feelings she isn't ready to acknowledge? Possibly. I'm not sure it's feasible to know what her heart wants. I don't think she knows either. Not if she's kissing me like she does, but has a profile on a dating app. An active profile, which is the important part. She's getting messages. I don't know what she wants, and that's starting to scare me.

I'm torn about what to do. I could ask Marina, but that feels childish if I'm not ready to ask Ashley. But as I lie here holding the only woman I want to hold for the rest of my life, I'm worried about what happens if she decides I'm not that person for her.

She stirs, and I lean my head down to kiss her forehead. She grumbles, then stretches, and finally, her eyelids open, and she focuses those beautiful blue eyes on me. A shy smile plays across her face.

"Good morning, my beautiful Fireball."

"Morning," she says hoarsely. "Did you sleep okay?"

I nod. "You?"

She closes her eyes. "So good. You're like some kind of cozy drug."

I laugh softly. "Well, that's something, I guess."

Ashley rolls over on her stomach and rests her chin on my chest, smiling up at me. I rest one hand on the curve of her hip. The air around us feels charged somehow. Weighted.

"What's in that head of yours?" I ask softly.

She smiles brilliantly. "About a dozen tiny Ricks, dancing around in that stupid shirt."

I laugh out loud and roll, pinning her to the mattress as she squeals. I'm careful not to put too much weight on her as I lean down to rub our noses together.

"And what about your heart?"

She bites her lower lip and raises one delicate hand, smoothing her fingers down my jawline.

"You're so tuned in to everything when it comes to me," she says almost reverently. "Don't you know what's in my heart?"

I shake my head slowly. "I wish I did. Can we talk about it?"

She frowns and pushes against my shoulder. I roll away and let her sit up.

"Maybe I should ask what's in that head of yours," she says with concern, taking my hand in hers. "Tell me."

I hesitate, and she squeezes my hand. "Please."

I sit up and turn so I'm facing her. "I need to ask you something, but it's not my business. And I'm afraid it might change things between us if I ask it."

Just saying that much has my heart pounding fiercely, but I also feel the weight of it lifting. Her expression is sober but from concern. She isn't upset. Or scared.

"I can't imagine anything you could ask me that would be that bad," she says with an encouraging smile. "Whatever it is…ask me."

I gulp down the lump in my throat. "I saw a dating app on your phone and can't stop wondering why it's there. Even though we've never said we'd be exclusive."

I don't expect the reaction I get. I don't expect the bright, wide smile that lights up the whole room. It gives me hope.

"If that's your question, I'll be more than happy to put your mind at rest, Mr. Archer."

A smile teases at the corners of my mouth. "Please do."

"I downloaded that app about a thousand years ago," she says. "The day after our fake date, to be precise. I decided I should start dating again. To get *you* out of my system."

My eyes rove over her face. "I see."

"I thought you didn't see me as anything more than a friend," she explains, focusing on our joined hands. "I didn't think anything else was possible. You're my beautiful, hot, perfect man-friend, and there would be nothing worse than having a front-row seat when you start dating some gorgeous model. Especially when I started catching big feelings for you after our fake date. So I created my profile, thinking I could force myself to date."

I nod but stay silent. She's on a roll.

"But then I got sick. And you put everything on hold to take care of me," she continues with raw emotion. "I forgot all about that stupid app until that night we were together, and I got a message from some random guy."

"Dan."

She nods. "I thought you might have seen it, but I wasn't sure…and to ask you if you did or try to explain when we never said we were really committed seemed needy."

I smile slowly. We're a real pair when it comes to communicating.

"I didn't want you to think I was moving too fast," she says softly, "or being clingy."

I reach for her, reverently placing my hands on either side of her face and claiming her mouth with mine. I don't need any more words. I need *her*. I put all my feelings into this kiss. With this kiss, I show her just how much she is wanted. Desired. Needed. A little whimper escapes her throat as I pull away.

"Let's be clear," I say, my voice rough with passion. "I'm all-in, Ashley. I don't want anyone else. I don't want to keep my options open. I only want you."

She nods, and her lip trembles. "Me too. That's exactly what I want, too. Just you, Rick."

Ashley wraps her arms around me tighter and surrenders completely to my kiss. I'm agonizingly slow in my exploration, diving my fingers into her hair and taking possession of her mouth. She sighs against my lips, and I pull her into my lap in one deft move. She smiles against my lips as I kiss the corners of her mouth, then switch to her nose, her cheeks, her eyelids, and her forehead. Her eyes are darkened as she pulls away just slightly.

"You are the best kisser," she murmurs sexily, those darkened eyes flicking down to my lips and back up again.

"I aim to please, Fireball," I say against her mouth just as her stomach makes a loud, low grumble.

I pull away and smirk at her as she bites her lip self-consciously.

"I think we need to feed the dragon, my angel," I say, laughing as I lightly smack her hip. "Let's go get you some breakfast."

Her stomach growls again, not even giving her the opportunity to object. She laughs then and slides off my lap with a defeated sigh.

"Okay, I call first dibs on the shower," she says, bolting for the door and making me laugh. "Then straight to breakfast and back here."

"Oh, do we have a tee time with your dad already?"

She flashes me a devilish grin. "Nope. I just want to spend as much time as possible kissing my boyfriend."

With that, she disappears into the bathroom, and I'm left with another big, stupid grin on my face.

***

Ashley

I take two strips of bacon off Dad's plate and put them on mine, then add a container of Greek yogurt to his plate. He makes a face at me, then looks at Rick as if he's going to save him. Rick averts his eyes and focuses on his slice of sourdough that's crawling through the restaurant-grade toaster.

"Daddy, that's too much salt," I say as we walk to our table. "You know what the doctor said."

He sits across from me as Rick pulls my chair out. I smile up at him as I put my plate down and sit, and then Rick takes the seat beside me.

He frowns at me. "I'm on vacation. I can't have a little salt on vacation?"

I give him a firm look. "I left you two pieces. That's enough salt."

The three of us are distracted all at once by raised voices on the other side of the dining room. What a surprise to find that it's coming from Greg and his poor, unfortunate girlfriend. She looks really upset. I exchange looks with Rick. Dad turns to see what's going on and scoffs.

"She deserves better," he grumbles, prompting a giggle from me.

"We should try not to stare," I murmur.

Rick slips a hand under the table and takes my hand in his. I meet his gaze and give him a secret smile.

"You two are so cute," Dad says, chuckling as he munches on a strip of bacon.

I give Dad a curious look, and he shrugs, grinning at both of us.

"This is a different kind of happy," he says cryptically. "You told me you were happy with Greg, but it was invisible. This is a happy you'd have to be blind not to see."

Rick grins and nods but stays silent. I laugh softly under my breath.

"Well, I'm glad—"

Greg's girlfriend, Janine, bolts up out of her chair and runs from the dining room. She looks over at our table as she goes, wiping a tear from her cheek. I'm half tempted to run after her to make sure she's okay, but I see Tammi is already on the way. Probably more appropriate anyway. Greg stands, and I avert my eyes. It doesn't do any good. I can see out of my peripheral vision that he's heading this way. Rick stretches a territorial arm around the back of my chair.

He steps over to our table, looking rather sheepish, and Dad frowns up at him.

"Greg, I wish you were as good at getting new accounts as you seem to be at upsetting your girlfriends," Dad grumbles. "What's the problem now?"

"Sir, I'd like to apologize for that," Greg grovels. "I was just trying to be honest with Janine, but she took my candor personally."

I can't help the smirk on my face, but then Greg turns to me.

"Ashley, can I have a word?"

Slowly, I look up at Greg. "What do you want?"

He twists his mouth into something resembling a smile. "Privately."

"No." I don't even have to think about it. Not interested.

He nods impatiently. "Please."

Rick leans forward. "The lady says no, Greg."

I notice Dad dabbing a little sweat off his brow with a napkin and frown. "Daddy, are you okay?"

He nods. "Sure, sweetheart. Just hoping Greg gets to the point so we can get on with our breakfast."

"Fine," Greg stammers. "If you insist, I can say what I have to say here."

I glare up at him. "Or you could just leave without saying anything since I don't care about anything you have to say."

"I think you'll care about this," he says confidently. "I was wrong, Ashley. About a great many things. Seeing you again has rekindled all the feelings I had for you, and I've realized what I lost."

I shake my head at him. "Stop talking."

Dad slams his fork down on the table in exasperation.

"I want you back, Ash," Greg declares in front of everyone. "And I'm not taking no for an answer."

Chapter 22

Ashley

I shoot Greg a warning glare, and then I lean forward to get a better look at my dad.

"Daddy, are you sure you're okay?"

Greg looks worried. "Actually, sir, you are looking a little pale."

Tammi wanders back into the room at the perfect time, and I flag her down to look after Dad. I stand up and jab a finger into Greg's shoulder.

"Step outside," I mutter. "Right. Now."

I turn to see Rick standing as well, and I motion for him to follow. The three of us step out of the dining room and into the lobby. Two tries at a relationship with this jerk, two break-ups because he was bored. I feel all the wrath I never got to let out boiling up. I whirl around and put a finger right up in Greg's face.

"You are the most impossible and ridiculous man I have ever met," I say calmly. "You are delusional if you think I would ever get in a relationship with you again."

Greg puts his hands up as if in surrender. "Ash, you know what we had was so good."

I shake my head. "No, what *you* had was so good," I counter. "What I had was a self-centered, egotistical, insensitive jerk who never saw me."

He frowns. "I saw you all the time. You even lived with me during the mermaid stuff."

I close my eyes against the headache I know is coming. I feel Rick's solid warmth behind me. He stays out of the fight because he knows it's not his, but I know he's there if I need him. One word from me and Greg's nose will totally be less than perfect.

"You don't get it," I blurt out. "And it's not my job to help you get it. I do not want you in my life, and I certainly don't want a relationship with you."

"I can't walk away from you, Ash," he says with pleading eyes.

"Um, pretty sure you can," I reply curtly. "You've already done it twice."

"I'll do whatever you want."

I nod. "Good. Then go. Leave right now. Never speak to me again."

He briefly looks over my shoulder at Rick like he wants to punch him but wisely decides to turn away. To my relief, he walks away from us towards the cottages. Hopefully to pack up and get out.

I sag backwards against Rick's chest, and he wraps his arms around me, pulling my back against the solid wall of his chest. I tilt my head back to look up at him.

"Thank you."

He frowns. "I did nothing, Fireball. I literally just stood here."

I turn and wrap my arms around his neck. "But I know all I had to do was say the word, and you would have come to my rescue."

His lips graze mine. "You don't need to be rescued. Especially when you let your fire out, Dragon Lady."

I laugh softly and pull away. "Let's go check on Dad. I don't like how pale he was."

We walk arm-in-arm back into the dining room to find Tammi sitting next to Dad. They're easily chatting and the color seems to be returning to his face. Rick and I sit back down.

"Daddy, what's going on?"

He sighs and shakes his head. "Nothing, sweetheart. I just really don't like that kid."

Tammi and I exchange secret looks, neither of us believing him.

"Do you have any chest pain or pressure? Maybe we should call a doctor."

He shakes his head and takes a drink of water.

Rick leans over, eyeing Dad soberly.

"How about any jaw pain? Or your shoulder or arm?"

Dad smiles feebly at both of us.

"You kids are sweet," he grumbles. "I'm not having another heart attack. I think I just need to lay down and take a break."

I nod. "Okay, why don't you go do that and I'll check in on you at lunch?"

Tammi taps him gently on the arm. "Let's go, Dave."

Dad nods and stands up, letting Tammi follow him to the elevators. I give Rick a worried look, and he scoots close and wraps his arms around me. I lean against the solid wall of his chest.

"What a morning," I say with a heavy sigh.

"No kidding," Rick murmurs. "The music world doesn't have this much drama."

I giggle and plant a kiss on Rick's cheek.

"Can we get out of here for a while?" I ask with a frustrated sigh. "This morning has been absolutely crazy."

He frowns at my plate. "Have you had enough breakfast?"

"Not even hungry after all that," I explain. "There's a cute little village just east of here. Can we just go walk around and get a change of scenery?"

He nods. "Let's go, Fireball."

"I just want to grab my purse first."

Gratefully, I get up and walk with him to the elevators. He laces our fingers together as we walk, and my heartbeat feels suddenly jumpy and giddy. I'm holding hands with a Viking god who just happens to be my boyfriend. My beautiful, hot, perfect man boyfriend? No, that's doesn't quite work. I'll think about it.

We get into our room and Rick heads for the bathroom. I'm heading to the loveseat to get my purse when I'm struck with an idea, so I just kind of hover around until Rick closes the bathroom door.

I spring into action, quietly rushing over to the dresser and easing open the drawer where he keeps his pajamas. *Victory!* I pull out the horrible Ashley shirt just as the toilet flushes. Yikes! I run over to the armoire and stuff it behind my suitcase quickly. I'll find a better home for it later. I rush back to the loveseat and sit down. When Rick emerges from the bathroom, I'm calmly smoothing a hand over my hair and smiling at him. Ha ha.

"Ready?" I ask breathlessly, taking the hand he offers as we head for the door.

"Let's go get some fresh air, Fireball," he says, smiling at the very woman who just stole his favorite shirt.

***

Rick

I'm watching the most beautiful woman in the world have a religious experience over a cookie, and I can't stop smiling. We found a little cafe in town with a display of baked goods in the window that she couldn't pass up, so we found a table inside to grab a snack. And now she has her delicate hands wrapped around a steaming mug of coffee with a gallon of cream in it, still talking about the maple cream sandwich cookie I bought her. The thing was the size of my hand, and it's already been devoured.

She sits back and pats her full tummy, grinning at me as I laugh and shake my head.

"That cookie didn't have a chance," I say, taking a sip of my coffee.

"Isn't it a biscuit if I'm having it with coffee?" she asks. "I thought Zach said that."

I smirk. Zach and his British roots trying to complicate things again.

"You're in the state of California," I say dryly. "In the USA, Fireball. That is a cookie, no matter what you drink with it."

She giggles. "You're such an easy target."

"But you're still crazy about me."

She nods, and her beautiful hair flows over her shoulder. "So crazy."

I pull the box out of my jacket pocket that I've been holding onto since we left our room and place it on the table in front of her. She looks down at the five-inch square box and the red bow atop it, surprise blooming on her face.

"I got you something," I say quietly. "I couldn't stop thinking of you when I saw it."

Ashley leans across the table to kiss me, which I gladly accept. One kiss turns to two, which turns to three. She picks up the box and admires it.

"I love it," she says as she pulls the bow off.

"Most people wait until they open something to say that," I tease.

Her fingers pause as she starts to open it. "I don't care what it is. I love it because you gave it to me."

My heart squeezes at her words. Beautiful. Adorable. Sweet. Wonderful. How did I get this lucky?

Ashley pulls the top off the box and gasps at the silver chain inside. She holds it up to get a better look at the tiny dragon charm hanging from it. Tiny rubies and citrines simulate the fire it's breathing, giving it a little sparkle.

"Rick, this is so beautiful," she gasps.

I smile gently. "Just like you."

She admires it closely for a few more moments, then opens the clasp and puts it on in one deft move. I lean forward and reach for the tiny dragon, my fingers gently brushing the soft skin over her collarbones. Ashley's eyes follow my movements as I reach for her and pull her in for a soft, slow kiss.

I love kissing dragons…

***

Ashley

Rick laces our fingers together as the valet drives away with his truck, and we ascend the steps into the main lobby of the country club. We've had a wonderful afternoon together, poking around quaint little shops, stealing kisses, and, oh my goodness…that cookie. And just to put extra sweet icing on the cake, this dragon charm necklace is so beautiful. And thoughtful. And I just keep realizing over and over again how lucky I am that I decided to use my dragon fire for something productive…like burning down the friend zone. I am teetering on the edge of falling in love…and it's wonderful.

"There you are!"

I look up to find Daddy rushing towards us, looking a little breathless.

"Dad? Are you okay?"

He pulls me into a hug, and I hug him back, but he looks tired. Worn out.

"Daddy, didn't you rest at all?"

He nods and waves me off like I'm making a big deal out of nothing. I'm really not so sure.

"I'm fine, honey," he grumbles. "Stop fussing. I needed to get out of that room. Are we still golfing?"

Rick and I look at each other like deer caught in headlights. Golf doesn't seem like a good idea when I consider the pallor of Dad's complexion.

"Baby, would you mind taking our stuff up to the room?" I ask as I put a hand on Rick's arm. I don't miss the way he grins at the endearment. "I'm going to grab a drink with Dad."

Rick nods, then reaches down to plant a soft kiss on the corner of my mouth. I give him a reassuring smile and mutter, "Thirty minutes". He nods again and heads off to our room.

"All right, let's go," I say to Dad, looping my arm through his. "We're getting some water and having a chat."

Dad chuckles. "Water? How exciting. But if I get to hang out with my girl, I'm okay with it."

We pick a table near a window that overlooks the gardens leading to the golf course. It's not mealtime yet, but there's an array of snacks on display and a self-serve beverage station.

"Would you rather have juice?" I ask. "How about a snack?"

He looks over at the display and then back at me. "I see a lot of food you're not going to let me eat, so I'll leave it to you. If you find something I can have, I'll eat it."

"Deal," I say quickly, giving him a quick kiss on the cheek.

I grab a tray and pour two glasses of ice water, then get Dad a small glass of juice. When I poke around the snack display, I grab a bag of popcorn, an apple, and a freshly baked snickerdoodle cookie. I head back to our table and set everything down. Dad immediately locks onto the cookie, then he eyes me suspiciously.

"Eat the apple, and you can split the cookie with me," I say with a no-nonsense flair.

"You drive a hard bargain, tough guy," Dad jokes.

He takes a sip of his juice and leans back in his chair.

"I'm worried about you, Daddy. You're more tired than normal, and you keep going pale."

He nods. "I know, kiddo. I think all the excitement has been a little much, that's all. I promise I'm okay."

I give him a skeptical look. "I'd feel better about that if you'd let a doctor give you a quick check-up."

"Honey, I'm fine. Really."

I nod and stay silent. I don't want to be bossy and demanding, but he nearly died last year. He's all I have in the whole world. The thought of losing him is more than I can stand.

"I'll tell you what," he offers, covering both my hands with one of his. "You and Rick go golfing with me this afternoon as planned, and I'll lie low for the rest of the day. Deal?"

"And you'll tell me if you feel weak or weird or anything?"

He smirks. "I'm a finance geek, honey. I'm always weird."

I roll my eyes, and we both laugh. He takes a big bite of his apple and raises his eyebrows at me as if I should applaud the effort.

"Yes, I'll tell you. I promise. I just want to have a little fun with my baby girl and her new man."

I curse myself for the gigantic smile that blooms on my face.

"He's so amazing, Daddy," I say quietly. "I'm crazy about him."

Dad laughs softly. "It wasn't too long ago, you were bullishly telling me you weren't ready and you didn't want anything to do with men."

I shrug. "There are normal men," I begin. "And then there's Rick. He's one of a kind."

Dad nods. "That's obvious to anyone who sees you together. He would do anything for you, my beauty. I can see that myself. As a loving father, I can tell you it means the world."

"That night at the music awards…" I shake my head. "It was the most amazing night I've ever had."

Dad takes another big bite of the apple and chews it.

"I had so much fun watching you on TV," he says brightly. "You looked like a princess in that dress. And the commentary from some of the reporters was a crack-up. I can't believe people get paid for those jobs."

I laugh. "I know. Rick was worried that I wasn't going to react well to all of it, but I just think it's funny. I don't care what a bunch of strangers think of me."

Dad nods. "You're like your mom, baby girl. You're strong, and you can take care of yourself."

"Am I really?" I ask quietly. "I have a teenager's memories of Mom. Am I really like her as an adult?"

Fine little lines appear around Dad's eyes as he smiles at me. "Oh yes. Very much. That's why I knew Greg wasn't the one, honey. He was just a lesson you had to learn so you could find real love."

I pause for a moment, letting Dad's words settle on me. I never thought about it like that. I've always wished I could have avoided the whole Greg fiasco altogether. Both of them. To me, they were a mistake I made because I was being stupid. But Dad's right: I did learn from it. If I hadn't been jilted by the bad choice, it may not have been as easy for me to see the good choice right in front of me.

I think about the kids at school. Do I think they're stupid at the beginning of the year? Of course not. I create lessons and they learn. Greg was just a lesson. Any woman could have fallen for him. There's nothing wrong with me or my ability to make decisions. Greg was just the wrong man for me. The right one is upstairs. Waiting for me.

"Daddy, thank you," I say as I plant another kiss on his cheek. "I never thought about it that way, but you're right. He was just a lesson I had to learn. And now that I've learned it, I'll never repeat it again."

Dad smirks. "I'm thankful for that. What a weasel."

"Daddy!" I whisper. "Have you been talking to Rick?"

He just winks at me. "Absolutely," he says. "That kid's future son-in-law material."

I feel a flush coming up my cheeks with such force I know my whole face must be beet red, which of course is perfect timing…because here comes Rick right on time. He grins at me and takes the chair next to me.

"What are you two talking about?" he asks, leaning over to kiss me.

"You," Dad says without missing a beat. "Can't you tell?"

I give Dad a look and he just chuckles. Rick makes a point to look at my face, his grin bemused.

"I can," he says quietly. "Looks like it was a good conversation."

"If you two are done embarrassing me, are you sure you feel well enough to golf today, Dad?"

He nods, then nudges Rick. "It's good to have an ally, son."

"Oh, boy…" I'm going to have to watch these two.

"Do we need a tee time?" Rick asks. "How does this work?"

Dad slaps Rick on the shoulder.

"It's my retreat, son," he says, standing up and stealing the whole cookie in front of me. "It's tee time when I say it's tee time."

Dad waves the cookie at me as if to say, "Cheers!" and takes a huge bite.

I'm somewhat relieved at the spring in his step as he leads us out the door towards the golf course.

***

By the time we're on the ninth hole, I'm watching Dad more than I'm watching anything else. He insisted on walking instead of taking a golf cart like he usually does. It's not a super warm day, but he can't stop sweating, and something about him just feels off. Like he's trying to put on a good face around Rick, but if it was just the two of us he'd be telling me we're done because he needs a break. Rick and I keep exchanging secret looks, and I know he's getting the same vibe I do.

"Hey, Daddy…" I say in a tone of voice I reserve only for him. "Is it okay if we just make it nine holes today? I'm a little tired. We can do all eighteen tomorrow if that's okay."

I don't miss the relief in his eyes at my suggestion. He thinks about it and nods.

"Sure, honey," he says. "If that's what you want, we can do—"

"Ashley!"

We all turn towards the trees to see where that came from. I don't see anyone, but I think I know that voice.

"Ashley!"

Yep. There's Greg emerging from the tree line that runs parallel to the clubhouse. Rick rolls his eyes, and Dad mutters something under his breath. Seriously.

I hold my hands up as if to say, "What!" I'm not yelling back at this guy.

He breaks into a run, and the closer he gets, I can see he's spooling up for more drama. It's not real, though. Nothing is with Greg. He's putting on a show. Trying to manipulate me again. He reaches for Dad's hand and shakes it as soon as he's close enough.

"Mr. Roberts, please," he pants. "Please help me show Ashley that we belong together."

Dad tries to pull his hand away and Greg keeps hold of it, making Dad yank away from him. He stumbles and nearly falls over.

"Hey!" I yell, stepping between him and Dad. "Don't touch my dad."

Greg looks from me to Dad to Rick and back again.

"Look at what a cozy picture you make, all golfing together," he says in a tone meant to sound anguished. "Out with the old and in with the new, huh?"

Dad scoffs. "Have some pride, Greg. Come on now."

"Greg, leave us alone," I say firmly. "Leave *me* alone. This has gone too far."

He shakes his head. "I can't. I can't let you go. I can't let him have you. I can't stand the idea."

Rick remains calm and quiet behind me, but I feel him there.

"Greg, this is now over the line," I say plainly. "You have no business here. Your behavior is extremely inappropriate. You need to leave. And you need to get some help."

"There is no getting help," he mutters. "Not without you. Is this really what you want, Mr. Roberts? This?"

Greg points to Rick, who is now standing with his huge arms crossed over his chest and looking as angry as I've ever seen him. Dad steps closer to Rick.

"Greg, it's time to go," Dad says. "I'm going to have Tammi set an appointment for you that I want you to keep, son. I think you need to talk to somebody."

"That's your answer? Therapy?" Greg laughs. "So you're just going to give her over to this guitar guy and let her live her life going from motel to motel? Do you care so little for your own daughter?"

I chance a look at Rick, and he's just squinting at Greg now. Judging from the motel comment, I don't think Greg's ever really heard of The Royal Rebels. He doesn't really like music. Or art. Or...anything but money and status.

"Greg, that's en—" Dad begins. "I'm not going to waste my breath."

I take a step towards Greg. "What gives you the right to speak to my dad that way? Or anyone? If you don't leave now, I'm calling—"

"Ashley," Rick says behind me.

"Just a sec, babe," I say. "Greg, I'll call Security. I mean it."

"Ashley!" Rick exclaims, making me turn around just in time to see Dad collapsing into Rick's arms.

Chapter 23

"Daddy!" I scream as he falls.

"No!" Greg yells right behind me.

Everything seems to happen in slow motion, but also all at once. Dad sags against Rick, his face slackened as he goes down. Rick reacts quickly. He catches Dad, then lowers him gently to the grass. He pulls Dad's hat off, then reaches down to loosen his belt.

I fall to the ground at his shoulders, moving to lift his head. I'm halted by Rick's firm but gentle hand on my arm.

"Ash," he says with calm authority. "Don't move his head. Okay, baby? You with me?"

I nod, watching as Rick assesses the situation around us. He has Dad's wrist in his hand, taking his pulse.

"Scoot behind his head so you're blocking the sun, okay?"

I nod and do as Rick asks, shielding Dad's face from the sun. Greg paces all around us, muttering what sounds like a prayer under his breath.

"Greg," Rick calls quickly. "Can you bring his golf bag over here?"

Greg bolts over to the bag and brings it to Rick.

"Can you look for a towel or something we can use to cool his head?"

Greg starts digging and finds a small towel fairly quick. He holds it up victoriously. I nod at my pink water bottle, lying forgotten on the ground.

"My water's still cold," I say in a wobbly voice. "Over there."

Greg runs to get it, making quick work of soaking the towel in cold water and handing it to me. I dab Dad's face, then place it across his forehead as he stirs.

"Good work, Greg," Rick says, still keeping his fingers on Dad's pulse. "Run to the clubhouse and get help, okay?"

"What's going on—" Dad murmurs as Greg runs for help.

I put my hands firmly on his shoulders. "Stay still, Daddy. You passed out."

Rick moves his face into Dad's line of sight.

"Sir, are you having any pain anywhere?"

"No," Dad sighs. "Just…dizzy. Can't catch my breath."

Rick nods. "No arm pain? Jaw pain? Chest?"

"None."

I begin to cry. I don't want to, which makes it even worse. I'm trying to hold it back as much as I can, but I feel tears pouring down my cheeks, and I'm starting to shake.

"Daddy…"

It feels like hours go by. Sirens finally pierce the quiet around us. The sound of help. Greg is back with a golf umbrella to make more shade for Dad, who begins to try to sit up at the sounds of me sobbing.

"No, Daddy," I manage to choke out. "Stay still. Please…"

"Ash," Rick's calm voice tries to soothe me. "You're doing so good, baby. Help is coming. It's gonna be okay."

I focus on the cloth on Dad's forehead and on the rapid rise and fall of his chest, just trying to keep myself as together as possible as the ambulance pulls up and three EMTs come running our way. I'm pulled away by Rick as they go to work, and I collapse into his arms, sobbing my heart out. His hand comes up to cradle my head as he rocks me back and forth.

"It's okay," Rick murmurs. "He's okay. His pulse was fast, but it's steady. It might be stress or heat, but I don't think he was having another heart attack."

I just nod, clinging to Rick's waist and watching the EMTs move Dad to a stretcher. His shirt is open, and he's wired up to an EKG machine. One of them watches the screen on the EKG monitor while another has a stethoscope against Dad's chest, listening. Rick keeps rocking me, holding me tightly. More time ticks by as they work.

"See your dad sitting up, babe?" Rick says quietly. "They wouldn't let him do that if it wasn't good news. It's gonna be okay."

I nod again, my sobs slowing. Rick strokes my hair with one hand, just rocking me and holding me tight as we watch the EMTs work. They're talking to Dad, but I can only pick up bits of the conversation.

"...pretty strong..."

"...just dizzy...crazy kid..."

"...drink some water..."

"...my daughter..."

One of the EMTs steps over to us.

"Ma'am," she says, offering me a kind smile. "Your dad's okay. He's just as worried about you as you are about him, I think."

I just nod dumbly as Rick holds me.

"The EKG shows no heart attack," she continues. "It appears to be an anxiety attack or maybe some kind of heat sensitivity."

"No heart attack?" I parrot, my voice quaking. "You're sure?"

She nods. "I'm sure. His heart is fine. His pulse was a little weak when he got here, but we've got him drinking water and talking now. It's strong and will likely level out once we get him inside and cooled off even more."

"Okay," I say shakily. "Do we need to take him to the hospital?"

She purses her lips. "We recommend that just so he gets a full check-up, but he's already told us he's not going. I do recommend he sees his regular doctor as soon as possible."

I pull away from Rick enough to face her. "And you're sure it wasn't his heart?"

She smiles gently. "Very sure. Do you have any other questions?"

I nod, wiping my tears away. "What does he need now? What kind of care?"

"Rest. Calm. Quiet," she offers. "No drama. Who's the crazy guy he was talking about?"

My gaze darts over to Greg, who's pacing by the clubhouse.

"He won't be a problem," Rick replies, glancing down at me. "We'll talk to him."

"Actually, can you stay for a minute?" I say to the EMT, almost growling. "He's going to need you when I'm done with him."

The EMT glances up at Rick and then smiles, apparently realizing I'm no real threat to anyone. Rick squeezes me and looks down at me with a gentle smile.

"There she is," he says sweetly. "There's my Fireball."

I smile feebly at the EMT. "Thank you so much."

She nods and smiles as she steps away, then turns back for a moment. "Oh, he also asked us to tell you he collapsed from bacon withdrawals."

I close my eyes for a moment and shake my head.

The EMT laughs. "I'm not telling you to feed him more bacon, but if his sense of humor is intact, that should make you feel better."

I nod my thanks, and she walks away to help her colleagues pack up.

Tammi comes walking quickly out of the lodge, followed by a club employee with a wheelchair. The EMTs help Dad off of the stretcher and check his vitals one more time. He's given the all-clear, so we take him inside the lodge. As soon as we're inside, I tell the employee to stop so I can break away from Rick and kneel in front of Dad. He looks humbled, but he has color and the report from the EMT is enough for me to not worry about his heart.

"I want you to let us take you to the hospital, Daddy."

He chuckles softly and strokes my cheek with his hand.

"Honey, you know if we do that, we're going to be in the cold emergency room with me hooked up to machines all night," he grumbles. "So I'm not going to do that. But I will ask the club to send out their private doctor to check me out. Is that a deal?"

Relief washes over me, and I nod. "That's a deal."

Tammi doesn't wait to be asked. She flits off to make it happen. It's one of the reasons we all love her. Rick watches me carefully for a moment from behind the wheelchair.

"Are you okay alone here for a minute?"

I nod and watch as he steps away to where Greg is hovering near the entrance. I watch him flag Kevin over, one of Dad's right-hand men, and the three of them appear to have a calm conversation. It ends with Greg shaking Rick's hand and walking away with Kevin, looking rather sheepish. Rick heads straight back to me and Dad, gripping the handles on the wheelchair and nodding at me.

"Ready when you are."

I just stand there for a minute, looking up at him with no words. Looking at this man who is my calm in a storm where I thought I was losing my Dad. My entire world was crashing down around me and there was Rick…helping my Dad, keeping me steady, and handling the situation with calm and such care. I nod at Rick and we head to the elevators.

We're silent as we take Dad to his room. We're joined fairly soon by Tammi, who brings the doctor on call, and we all step out into the hallway to give Dad some privacy. Rick keeps a steady arm around me, planting the occasional kiss on my head and just being there for me while we wait. Finally, the doctor opens the door and asks us to step back inside.

With Dad tucked into bed, the doctor puts all my fears at ease. It really was an anxiety attack, likely brought on by the excitement of the retreat and the extra drama caused by Greg's theatrics. The doctor offers me a sedative to help me sleep, which I politely decline. A glass of wine will do the same thing for me. Weirdly, I can handle a lot of margaritas but red wine knocks me right out.

We stay with Dad and eventually decide to have a light dinner in his room, just the four of us. When he finally starts trying to kick us out at 8 pm, I make sure he's all set up with water and a snack before Tammi and Rick pull me out of the room. I hug Tammi fiercely, thanking her for being the saint she is, and she heads off to her room after making sure I promise to get some rest as well.

By the time Rick and I get to our suite, I feel like every muscle in my body is ready to give out. We step inside, and I immediately turn and pull him against me. Steel bands wrap around my waist and crush me against him. I stand on my toes and kiss his cheek, then move my lips near his ear.

"Thank you," I whisper. "Thank you, thank you, thank you."

He rocks me back and forth again, and I feel overwhelming gratitude for this wonderful man in my arms. My heart is so full, but I can't put it into words right now, and exhaustion is creeping up on me quickly. His lips brush my hair, and he begins walking me toward the dresser.

"I'm so glad I was there, Ash," he says. "Why don't you change for bed…you must be tired."

I nod and pull away to grab my pajamas from the dresser, then retreat into the bathroom to change. By the time I come out of the bathroom, Rick has a huge glass of red wine sitting on my side of the bed and I laugh softly.

"I'm not sure I'll even need that," I say, stepping in for a kiss. "But thank you."

I grab a candy bar I had in my purse and crawl into bed, ripping it open as Rick opens the dresser to get his pajamas. Oh…oh, yeah. I take a bite while I watch him root around in all the drawers for the Ashley shirt. He steps into the bathroom to see if it's in there, then comes back out. One look at me tells him I've done something with the shirt. I fight a losing battle with the guilty smile on my face.

"Ash," he says in a humorously ominous tone. "Where is my Ashley shirt?"

Wordlessly, I point to the armoire with a sweet smile. He opens the door and pokes around until he finds it, holding it up victoriously and heading to the bathroom to change. I take a big sip of wine and then finish the candy bar. I hear the shower turn on in the bathroom and grab my cell phone from the nightstand to send a quick text to the girls. I'm brief, but I share what happened and make sure they understand Dad's okay. Then I plug my phone into the charger and settle against the pillows, closing my eyes just for a moment while I wait for Rick.

***

Rick

I roll over and find a cold spot in the bed where Ashley should be. I grumble, reaching my arm around to make sure she really isn't here. She isn't, and judging from the silence in the suite, she's gone somewhere. Probably to check on her father after the drama of yesterday.

I sit up and hit the switch for the bedside lamp. Ashley's phone is still charging on her side of the bed, so I can't text her. I have a choice to make. Stay put and wait for her to come back, or go looking for her. I get up immediately and get in the shower because there's no decision, really. I'm going to find her and be at her side if she needs anything.

I keep seeing her face when her father collapsed. I can't get her look of utter desperation out of my head. In the ensuing aftermath, my mind was set on helping Ashley take care of her father and just being there for both of them. But this morning…there are things to say that I didn't have the space to say to her last night. Everything was too raw. Now? I don't want another minute to go by without her knowing that I will move heaven and earth to make her world a better place. I will not rest, I will not falter, and I will never stop showing her how much she means to me. Because I love her. More than anything in the world.

I'm out of the shower, dressed, and walking out the door of the suite super quick. I head to her dad's room first, but I don't knock. She may not be with him, and he may be getting some much-needed rest. I put my ear to the door, knowing that I'll hear her if she's in there. My girl likes to raise her voice when she lectures her dad. No sound at all, so I head for the elevators and cut through the lobby on the way to see if she's having breakfast with her dad. I find her dad, but no Ashley. He sees me immediately and flags me over.

"Good morning, sir," I say, giving him a gentle but firm handshake.

He gestures for me to sit in the empty chair at his table, so I do. I'm relieved to see some color back in his face this morning.

"Good morning, son," her dad says. "I wanted to say thank you again for everything yesterday. But especially for taking care of my girl."

I nod. "I'm glad to see you looking better this morning. How are you feeling?"

"Much better," he says, stabbing a spoon at a bowl of oatmeal with a grimace. "But I'd rather this was bacon."

I laugh softly. "Ashley's orders?"

He nods. "I guess I need to start calling her *our girl*."

"I hope that's true, sir," I say quietly. "Have you seen her this morning? There's something very important I need to tell her."

Her dad grins from ear to ear, and I swear it takes years off his face. "Ain't love grand?"

I chuckle under my breath.

"After she took all my bacon away, she went off to find Tammi somewhere," he tells me, then points toward the courtyard. "That way."

I stand immediately and clasp his hand. "Thank you, sir. Enjoy your breakfast."

He smirks. "Of course I won't."

I chuckle again as I head for the lobby and the courtyard on the other side of it. I'm almost to the door that opens to the large, well-manicured space when I see her. But she's not alone. She's sitting on a bench with Greg. And they're holding hands.

The sight of it punches a hole right through my heart. She's smiling slightly while he's talking, passionately gesturing with his free hand. He must be painting a very pretty picture because she's soaking it all up. She nods and laughs, and I feel like I'm not even looking at the same woman anymore. Where is the Ashley who never wanted to see him again? Where is *my* Ashley? Where's the Dragon Lady when I need her?

The answer is a simple one: gone. The evidence is right in front of me. I shake my head as I watch them, not wanting to believe the truth that's playing out right before my eyes. He raises her hand to his lips and kisses the back of it, and I feel sick to my stomach. She clasps his hand with both of hers, speaking to him with such emotion. They both stand, and he pulls her into his arms. I'm frozen to this spot. As much as I want to move, as much as I want to go pack up and get out of here, I stay.

I'm so riveted by their spectacle that I don't see the country club employee step in front of me and open the door to the courtyard, bracing a wedge under it to keep it open so they can begin carting food somewhere. Both Ashley and Greg look over at the door, where I am now visible just inside. I prepare myself for Greg's sneer and haughty attitude. To my surprise, that's not what I get.

He smiles slightly and waves. Then he turns to Ashley to hug her again before turning away and walking in the opposite direction. And Ashley…she positively glows as she smiles at me, hurrying up the path and through the doorway, straight into my arms. I'm so stunned as her arms wrap around my neck that it takes me a minute to process.

"What's going on?" I ask with quiet calm.

Ashley puts her palms on either side of my face and smiles warmly.

"I'm thinking that was something of a shock to see," she says. "So let me clearly communicate what that was. He apologized. I allowed it. He listened. I encouraged it. And then we said goodbye. He will not be darkening my doorstep again, and I wished him well."

I look at her incredulously. "That's what I saw?"

She nods, clear adoration in her eyes. For me. "That's what you saw. That's all it was."

Gingerly, she raises her lips to mine and presses a kiss to the corner of my mouth.

"Are you okay?" she asks. "I'm replaying it all in my head, and it probably looked like something else for a minute."

I nod. "It did."

She smiles and nips at my bottom lip.

"Well, I'm here to tell you that there is nothing else," she murmurs. "There is no dating app. There is no Greg. There is only you, my beautiful, hot, perfect man-friend. Because I'm in love with you."

And I'm done. I pull her firmly against me and bring our mouths together in a crushing kiss that has her gasping. I kiss her, and then I kiss her again, and again, and again. My hands are in her hair as

I worship her mouth with mine, and she clings to me as if her life depends on it. Finally, I pull away...just enough to look into her remarkable eyes.

"I love you too, Ash," I whisper, stealing another kiss. "So, so much. So much it hurts."

She shakes her head at me, and it's her turn to steal a few kisses. Soft ones. Slow ones. Incredibly sexy ones.

"I don't deserve you," she purrs into my ear. "But I'm selfishly going to keep you anyway."

I lightly dot kisses on her cheeks, her nose, and across her forehead as she laughs softly.

"Ahem," Tammi mutters as she walks behind us. "Get a room."

I laugh under my breath as she keeps walking, heading into the dining to check on Ash's dad, most likely. I pull Ashley against me, cupping her head as she presses her cheek to my chest.

"What an excellent idea," I say against her hair.

I can feel her smiling as she pulls away just enough for us to walk arm-in-arm toward the elevators.

"So what will we do for the rest of our day?"

She pulls me into the elevator and kisses me again as she hits the button for our floor.

"Kiss, crochet, snack, repeat," she purrs against my mouth.

We're rudely interrupted by the ding of the elevator as the doors open. She pulls me down the hall as I frown.

"Do I have to crochet?" I tease. "Can I just watch you?"

She laughs softly as we enter the suite. "Or you could read a book."

"I could see if they get 'Customs Watch' on TV here."

She turns to me with a huge grin. "Perfect."

I smile down at her beautiful face, thinking...I couldn't agree more.

Chapter 24

Rick

What. A. Weekend.

Overbooked rooms. Jerk ex-fiances. Wall-to-wall finance geeks. A life-changing maple cream cookie. Heart attack scares. This was the least relaxing retreat I've ever been to. But…it ended well. Because there's an angel sitting next to me, who won't let go of my hand. And she loves me.

Traffic is light this afternoon as I steer the truck over the Golden Gate Bridge to take Ashley back to her apartment. As we approach the north tower, I squeeze her hand, and she looks over at me.

"Isn't this right about where it all started?" I ask, nodding ahead.

Ashley looks at the bridge and grins, nodding. "Right….there!"

I laugh.

"If you guys hadn't been stuck in traffic with us…"

"If Merry hadn't had the idea to sing a sea shanty in the middle of the bridge…" Ashley continues.

"If Zach hadn't heard Marina singing…"

Ashley laughs softly. "And if Marina hadn't been all dressed up as a mermaid…"

I kiss the back of her hand. "You were the cutest sailor I'd ever seen."

"I'm kind of glad we're not doing the singing gigs as much anymore. We're getting too busy with our actual careers, which is totally fine with me."

I frown. "I hope you won't stop singing, though."

"Oh, no…I love to sing. I just don't need to perform."

"Well, I think after our performance at the engagement party, people will be clamoring for more."

She laughs, and it's almost musical. "That was weeks ago. Pretty sure that ship has sailed."

"Do we want to do an encore at the wedding reception?" I ask with a devious grin. "They can't stop us."

She doesn't even hesitate. "Oh, definitely. And maybe we elevate it a little. Get more people involved."

"They'll love it."

She nods. "They totally will. And we have a while to come up with a really good plan."

"We'll need lots of planning sessions together."

More nods. "Lots. It's important to think through every detail."

"Yep."

"Know what helps me think?" she asks.

I shake my head, but I think I know.

"Kissing," she tells me. "Lots and lots of kissing."

I laugh as I pull into a spot in front of her building. I throw it in park immediately.

"Well, if that's what it takes," I growl, reaching for her. "We'd better get started."

***

Ashley

I knew I'd have a hard time sleeping once I got a taste of snoozing next to a Viking god. I've been back in the city for two nights now, and I can't get comfortable. I can't settle down. There's something about Rick that grounds me. The bed feels too big without him.

I know I'll get back to normal eventually, but it's still frustrating, especially when I need to be awake and alert at work. It probably doesn't help that I'm excited about Daddy's news too. He called me last night to tell me he's decided to retire. Life is too short, he says. He wants to travel more and enjoy life. He'll still be active for about a year, and he'll still be the owner, but he won't be steering the ship. He wants to focus on the Have a Heart Foundation and take more time for himself.

I roll over and grab my cell phone, swiping the screen and starting a new message.

Ashley: I miss you so much. I can't sleep.

Rick: I miss you too, Fireball. So much. Everything okay over there?

Ashley: Yeah, my brain just won't turn off...and the bed feels so big without you here.

Rick: No, you just miss seeing me in my Ashley jammies. Admit it.

Ashley: Absolutely not.

Rick: Big facts.

Ashley: You know I'm just going to steal that shirt again.

Rick: You can try.

Ashley: LOL. Do the Rebels still have to go to New York next week?

Rick: Yep. But I was thinking...what if you met me out there for the weekend? I could take you up to Connecticut and you could meet my family. If you're ready for that. If it's too soon, that's okay too.

Ashley: No, it's not too soon. Not for me. Do you think we can set our own rules when it comes to timing things? Maybe slower works for some people, but we were friends first. I think we're allowed to do things the way we want.

Rick: You're the boss, Fireball. I'll have Bella reach out to set up your flight.

Ashley: How exciting! Now I really won't sleep.

Rick: Sorry, baby. I wish I could help more. Maybe it's time for a big glass of wine.

Ashley: Not a horrible idea.

Rick: Hey...

Ashley: Hey...

Rick: I love you.

Ashley: I love you, too. xoxo. Can't wait for dinner tomorrow night.

Rick: Get ready, baby...I'm wearing a Henley.

Ashley: You say the nicest things...

Rick: Sweet dreams, angel

I pad out to the kitchen to pour myself a glass of wine, unable to get the smile off my face. Not gonna lie, I'm not even trying. Dad is retiring and will be taking better care of himself. I am in love with the most wonderful soul in the universe. And I'm heading to New York to meet his family. I'm even getting better at crochet. Things are looking up for the Dragon Lady.

*** Six Months Later ***

Rick

It can't get any better than this, can it? I'm having a hard time picturing anything better than watching my girlfriend, my mom, and my sister, Kate, laughing hysterically in my kitchen. They're putting the final touches on the appetizers while I prep everything I'll have going on the grill. Well, until Sam gets here and takes over because I don't know what I'm doing. His words, not mine.

In less than thirty minutes, my house will be converged upon by everyone near and dear to Ashley and me. She thinks it's so we can all plan a side trip to London that many of us want to take when we're in England for Zach and Marina's wedding in six months. I'm sure we'll talk about it, but that's not the real reason for this get-together. It's actually a surprise party for Ashley's birthday…which isn't until next week, but that's the genius of it. She doesn't suspect a thing. We're even hiding a birthday cake, made by Merry, in the guest room that Kate's staying in. Her presents are secreted away in the room my mom is staying in, and everyone else has been instructed to leave their gifts on the porch when they arrive tonight. Kate will grab them as we're all sitting down to dinner, and we'll pull the big surprise after that.

"Daddy, no!"

Ash's dad walks by and steals a few pieces of salami off the meat and cheese tray on his way to the couch, and I catch Ashley in my arms when she tries to chase him down. I pull her back against my chest and brush my lips against the shell of her ear.

"Let him have it," I murmur, relishing in the shudder that ripples through her. "He passed his latest physical with flying colors."

She relaxes against me and gives me a quick kiss.

"Gross," Kate blurts, laughing as my mom smacks her playfully.

The doorbell rings. Early birds. That has to be Zach and Marina. She is never late, and Bella has come to love the effect it has on Zach. Ashley rushes off to get the door, and my mom comes over to give me a hug.

"I'm so happy right now," she says, patting me on the chest. "I adore her. And I love how happy she makes you, son. You two are perfect for each other."

"Thanks, Mom."

"Hey, let go of my girl!" Zach growls, pulling my mom away from me.

"Zach!" Mom cries out, pulling him in for a big hug.

Marina flits in, grabbing me for a hug before saying hello to Kate on her way to Ashley's dad…and the chaos has begun. I take the stuff for the grill and pop it into the fridge so I can spend time with everyone before cooking time begins.

Before I know it, the doorbell rings again. Then again. And again.

I'm getting a hug from Hella Bella when I hear Scarlet's voice in the house. She lost the interior decorating contest again, and it hit her pretty hard this time. There were two emergency conclaves called to support her during the first few days. The silver lining is that the shelves she designed with the corbels I made her earned a little air time on the season premiere of the show, and the story was picked up on our local news, too. Scarlet got quite a few new clients as a result, and she's been dubbed the Corbel Queen by the inner circle. Her business is looking up, even if her morale took a hit.

I head to my bedroom to grab something I made for her, and I nearly trip over Ashley's overnight bag next to my bed. Something catches my attention, and I look closer. Yep. My Ashley shirt is rolled up and tucked into Ash's bag. *Beautiful thief.*

I laugh softly and pull it out of her bag. The Great Ashley Shirt War has been a thing for six months now, and it just makes me love her even more. We keep stealing it from each other. I grab a white t-shirt from my drawer, roll it up and shove it in her bag in the same spot. Hopefully, she won't discover the switch until she gets back to her apartment tomorrow. I tuck the Ashley shirt under my bed where it should be safe. Hopefully. The woman is both gorgeous and resourceful.

I head back to the party and find Scarlet, pulling her off to the side after getting my hello hug and fist bump. I didn't bother with wrapping it or anything. It's not much. I hold it out for her, and she grins as she takes it from me.

"Dude, what?" she says, grinning ear to ear as she holds up the crown I made from a hunk of wood I had in my stockpile. She turns it, inspecting every side with an admiring glance.

It's fairly intricate in detail, which was a challenge for me, and engraved along the side and painted in gold are the words "Corbel Queen". She runs her fingers over the lettering and hugs my neck, making me laugh.

"This is way better than winning some decorator showcase," she says with a wink.

"Yeah, right!" I exclaim, then turn serious for a moment. "Scarlet, I hope you know how much we all support you. Any time you need corbels or whatever you think I can make, I'm on it. Don't give up."

She nods. "Thanks, Rick. You're still my favorite Rebel."

Scarlet runs off to show Marina and Ashley while I head over to say hi to Jimmy and Sam, but a hundred and ten pounds of positivity lands on my back. I know it's Merry without having to look, but I make a show of spinning around and freaking out about it while she squeals. She jumps down and high-fives me for being a good sport.

Ashley breaks away from chatting with her dad when she sees me, slowly working her way towards me with a smile meant only for me. She steps into my open arms as I lean down for a kiss. With her friends and family surrounding her, she is all sunshine and light right now.

"They're already arguing about whether Big Ben is the name of the clock or the tower that holds the clock," she mutters, shaking her head. "Is there anything you want to see when we're in London? I'm prepared to fight for it."

I laugh out loud. She would, too. It's one of the things I love most about her.

"I've been quite a few times while the band was on tour," I reply. "I'm all yours. You're the boss. We'll do whatever you want to do, my love."

She tilts her head back and looks up at me with those strikingly beautiful eyes. "How did I get so lucky?"

I kiss her slowly, and a sweet little sigh escapes her throat. I'm the lucky one. I'm reminded of it every day. Merry tugs Ashley out of my arms to look at some ridiculous video Sam is showing everyone, and I see my opportunity. I need to talk to Marina, preferably without Ashley seeing. I wave at her and motion for her to come to me, making sure Ash can't see me.

"What's up?" Marina asks as she approaches.

I wag my head towards the hall. "Got a minute?"

"Always," she says, following me into the hall and then into my study.

"I need you to do me a favor," I say quietly. "But not right now. I need the favor when we're in England."

A conspiratorial grin takes over my friend's face.

"Tell me everything."

✻✻✻

Ashley

As Rick comes around the corner into the dining room holding a birthday cake after dinner, everyone starts singing happy birthday and my jaw drops open. What is happening right now? My birthday isn't until next week. Rick's face is illuminated by birthday candles as he mouths *I love you* at me, and my eyes fill with tears. I blow out the candles and shake my head at everyone.

"I can't believe you guys! This is such a surprise. I love every single one of you."

Marina and Kate disappear briefly, then return to the dining room with armloads of birthday presents. I gasp, helping to keep some from falling off the table.

"You were all in on this? How long have you been planning it?"

About three different people answer me at the same time, and I can barely discern the replies among the cacophony of chatter coming from my friends and family…but I gather this has been in the works for a while. I take a good look at the cake and beam across the table at Merry.

"Merry, I know this was you…it's so pretty!"

She wiggles her eyebrows at me as Rick hands me a cake knife and has me cut the first piece. It seems a shame to cut such a work of art, but I know Merry would be insulted if we didn't eat it. It's a beautiful eggshell white colored frosting base with beautiful red piped roses all around the base. Edible pearls of varying sizes are tucked in as well. In beautiful writing, it says "HBD Ashley". Merry is such an artist with anything baked. I hope someday Nonno finally says yes and lets her open that bakery she wants.

Rick turns the cake cutting over to Kate and Marina, who serve up slices of the delicious Italian creme cake. I'm given several orders to start opening presents, so I do. A gift card to a fancy yarn store from Kate. Some very cute clothes and accessories from the inner circle. A necklace to match my Mom's pearl earrings from Dad, which has me shedding a few tears. Finally, Rick hands me a heavy box that's about the size of a placemat. What on earth?

I plant a kiss on his cheek and open it to find a brand-new, extremely fancy laptop. I look up at him in surprise. All heads turn in his direction to see what he says. He shrugs.

"When you told me you were thinking about writing a children's book, I thought you might need a better laptop than the dinosaur you've been using," he says quietly. "I don't know much about laptops, but apparently, that's a really good one."

I nod, laughing. "Yes, I think I could probably launch satellites with this thing."

Everyone laughs, and I get up and wrap my arms around the love of my life. He smiles down at me and moves his lips next to my ear.

"Happy birthday, baby."

"Thank you, my beautiful, hot, perfect man-friend."

He kisses me, then dips me like he did on the dance floor the night of our fake date. Everyone cheers. I love this man so much.

Naturally, Scarlet is the one to bring us all back to reality.

"Enough kissing, more planning!" she yells, whipping out a notebook that has a London cityscape on the cover.

"Oooh, yes, please!" I say as we all head to the living room to chat. "I definitely have a list of things I don't want to miss."

Zach grins at me, then pulls Marina down next to him. "I wish I could be there to show you ladies around myself, but I will be…very busy."

He nuzzles her neck and kisses her, throwing Scarlet into a fit.

"Oh my gosh with the kissing," she barks. "I'm going to get the hose from the yard and spray you two."

Merry clucks at her. "C'mon, Scar, you have to admit…love is grand."

Scarlet frowns at her. "I don't have time for love."

Marina raises her hand. "That's what I said."

I raise my hand. "Me too!"

Scarlet looks at both of us and rolls her eyes, making me chuckle under my breath. Wow. When love hits her, it's going to have to be pretty big to get her attention.

"Well," Merry chimes in from her seat on the couch next to me. "The way things are going for me, I'll end up being the crazy cat lady."

I nudge her. "That's because you have to go on *second* dates. And then maybe even a third or a fourth."

She feigns shock. "Is that what I've been doing wrong? Thanks!"

I giggle to myself as Rick passes a coffee cup over my shoulder and hands it to me, then kisses the top of my head and heads back to the kitchen. I look inside the cup, and it's a splash of coffee with a ton of cream. I make a love-stricken face and show Merry.

"Aww!" she gasps. "Nonno would totally call him a keeper."

Scarlet taps my knee with her pen. "Dude, top five London things on your list...Go!"

"Oh, um..." I conjure up the list I've been keeping in my head. "Westminster Abbey, Tower of London, Buckingham Palace, Harrod's, and I want to get fish and chips in a pub."

Scarlet begins making a list, and Merry starts naming her top five. I look around and see everyone conversing easily with each other. Kate and Rick have cleared the dining table, and I head in there. Scarlet makes a face at me.

"I'll be right back, I promise..."

Rick pulls me into his arms as soon as I'm in range, and I wrap my arms around his neck.

"A bougie laptop," I say with a grin. "That is a very pricey gift, sir."

"If you're going to write, you should have the best tools available," he says matter of factly. "All I did was give you an upgrade."

I smile up at him. "I am so grateful for you. What a thoughtful gift."

He smiles his trademark Viking god smile and lowers his head to mine.

"Your dreams are my dreams too," he murmurs, "because I want all your dreams to come true."

I brush my lips against his, my heart full, and whisper, "One dream has already come true...because I have you."

Chapter 25

Somewhere in the English countryside just outside London…

Ashley

I watch the future Duke and Duchess of Wendly, aka Mr. & Mrs. Zach Adams, walk down the aisle of this ancient church in the English countryside, happy tears streaming down my face as they go. Behind me, Scarlet wipes a tear from her cheek, and Merry already has the hiccups. Standing behind her, also as a bridesmaid, Hillary nudges Merry's arm to make sure she's okay. Merry just nods happily and hiccups again.

I make eye contact with Rick as we walk toward the aisle together and follow Zach and Marina. Love shines bright and true in his eyes as he grins at me, and I'm reminded yet again how very lucky we are to have found each other. I take the arm he offers and give him a quick kiss as we head down the center aisle of the church and out into the beautiful day ahead. Behind us, Scarlet and Jimmy are followed by Merry and Sam, with Hillary and Marina's brother Max bringing up the rear. Max also walked Marina down the aisle, but Zach felt strongly that his future brother-in-law was a groomsman so Max pulled double duty.

As I pass her, I grin at the Duchess of Wendly, Zach's mother. She reaches out to squeeze my hand, and I squeeze back. She is such a gracious and sweet person. She's already a mother figure and good friend to Marina, and I'm grateful for my friend that such a wonderful relationship has formed with her new husband's mom. She's welcomed our entire inner circle with open arms.

Outside, the courtyard erupts in cheers as the bride and groom exit the church and head for the car that will lead the procession to Allenton Hall, Zach's family estate. The Duke and Duchess are hosting the reception there. The bridal party has also been staying there this week, and it's been a surreal experience to stay in such a beautiful home that feels like a real-life Downton Abbey.

As Zach and Marina's car drives away, Rick and I are the first to get in the large van that will transport the bridal party. The parents and other family, including my dad, Scarlet's mom, and Nonno will be in a second van.

We scoot in close, and he wastes no time pulling my mouth to his to give me a proper kiss. Everyone else shuffling in behind us makes an assortment of noises ranging from amused to disgusted, but we don't care.

With everyone safely seated and belted in, the van begins moving down the road. We've done everything we can to warn Zach's family that, while the wedding service was very much Church of England, the reception will have a lot of American influence. Including a very extra, over-the-top bridal party entrance to the reception area. We're all dancing in to, what else, Bruno Mars' "Marry You". Marina and Zach had no such desires, though, so they're doing a more traditional entrance.

Merry gasps, and I turn to find her looking over Scarlet's shoulder at something on her phone. Scarlet's grin is absolutely predatory.

This has to be about the decorating competition for this year. She's lost it a few times now, and she's the most determined person I know. I lean forward as she turns her phone toward me.

"A warehouse?"

She nods. "There are four of us who have formed a friendship of sorts. We're all talented but with limited funds, so we've decided to put our money together to transform this giant empty warehouse into our projects."

Rick squints at the screen. "How does that even work?"

"It belongs to my friend Brad's dad, who agreed to let us use it for this. It's got good bones," she explains. "The warehouse has walls that divide it into four fairly equal-sized sections. We're drawing names to see who gets what section, and we're gonna go for it."

"It sounds really ambitious," Rick says.

"The space each of us will get is enough for us to create two whole rooms to showcase our talent," Scarlet continues. "If I can't win it that way, I'm just not going to apply again. I'll focus all my energy on building my business independently and leave it at that."

"Well, you know you can count on me for the woodworking stuff," Rick says. "If you're planning things far ahead, it's probably a good idea to clear it with Bella to make sure we won't be traveling, but otherwise, I await your next assignment."

Scarlet grins widely. "You're the best!"

Merry hiccups again, then blows her nose into a little handkerchief she's been carrying with her bouquet. I smile softly at her and she waves a hand to signal she's fine.

"I'm just so happy for them," she cries. "It's so romantic. And then there's you two…"

Now she's gesturing wildly at me and Rick.

"…you never would have happened if they hadn't gotten together, which makes it even more romantic…"

Scarlet snickers, then looks out the window. "She'll stop crying eventually."

Merry just nods and blows her nose again. Behind me, Max and Hillary are catching up. I hear them talking about the pictures they're showing each other on their phones. She's talking about the trip she just took with her boyfriend, and Max is talking about the kids he coaches. Everyone's got something exciting going on in their lives. That may be why I've been feeling a little restless lately.

I love the kids I'm teaching, but I'm starting to feel like it's a grind lately. Kids are always awesome, but it's becoming the same challenges with parents…the same struggles with funding. I'm starting to not love it as much as I once did. That's why I've been taking classes on writing children's books. It could be a fun, new way of helping kids grow into good people.

The van pulls into the front drive at Allenton Hall and we all get out. Merry, Scarlet, Hillary and I all smooth out our dresses and check each other for wardrobe malfunctions. Marina ended up opting for a very light, almost dusty lavender color for our dresses. The v-neckline plunges into a pleated bodice, and the chiffon skirt has a high-low hemline…so it comes to our knees in front but tapers to the floor in the back. Silver strappy heels add a little flair.

The wedding coordinator, a terrifying woman named Hilda, rallies us immediately and ushers us around to the side of the estate as guests begin coming up the drive. She claps her hands at us, taking us to where Zach and Marina are waiting for us with the photographer. I step closer to Rick and smooth his tie with the palm of my hand. The groomsmen are all in traditional morning suits, and all of them look striking.

"You look so handsome," I murmur, letting my gaze rove over him appreciatively.

Rick grazes my lips with his, and I suddenly wish I could pull him behind one of the giant potted topiaries out here in the garden.

"You two!" Scary Hilda yammers at us. "No time for kissing, please!"

Looking appropriately shamed, Rick and I head over to join the group.

"Yes, no time for love…we're at a wedding," Rick mumbles, making me laugh out loud.

We take pictures for an hour before Hilda decides we've earned a reprieve. Tuxedoed waiters enter the garden, carrying small bottles of water and little finger food snacks that were obviously chosen for the mess they won't leave on any of us. Still, it's nice to be able to have a little something before the reception starts. Maybe Hilda has her good points.

After a thirty-minute break, we're ushered to one end of the enormous white tent where the reception will be held. The setting inside is magical. Ficus trees in giant pots are dotted around the interior border of the tent, covered in white twinkle lights. White tablecloths adorn the tables and candles are everywhere. It's simple and elegant.

Since we're in the UK, we line up at the tent entrance to welcome the guests as they enter. I meet Zach's extended family, several members of the aristocracy, and quite a few celebrities. Finally, all the guests are in and seated. Hilda ushers us right back out of the tent so we can do our very American bridal party entrance.

The DJ starts up the music and we hear the intro for Bruno Mars' "Marry You". Hilda begins rushing around, putting everyone in order as we wait to be announced. I grab Rick's hand excitedly and he smiles down at me.

"This is so fun," I say breathlessly. "I'm so happy for our friends, and so grateful to spend this day with the man I love."

Rick leans down for a kiss.

"No kissing!" Hilda yells as the DJ announces Max and Hillary's entrance to the reception tent.

Wedding guests cheer and clap along as they dance into the tent, boogie around the dance floor, then take their places at the wedding party's table. Next are Merry and Sam, then Jimmy and Scarlet. Hilda gives Rick and me a look before it's our turn and I burst out laughing. That's probably not going to earn me any points.

"And now let's give it up for the bride and groom's besties," the DJ yells. "Ashley and Rick!"

Rick and I burst into the tent, waving and throwing our hands around to get everyone applauding. Then, as rehearsed, I throw my bridesmaid bouquet to Merry as the DJ mixes "Marry You" into "Fireball" and Rick and I take off down the dance floor.

We dance for just a bit of the song, then we take a bow and head to the table where the rest of the wedding party awaits. The DJ fades "Fireball" out and fades in the Rebels' hit "You Are My Heart". The song has extra special meaning to Zach and Marina, and my eyes fill with tears.

"Now, ladies and gentlemen, please stand and welcome Mr. & Mrs. Zach Adams, the future Duke and Duchess of Wendly," the DJ says rather sweetly as our friends enter the tent.

Everyone in the tent stands and applauds as Zach and Marina walk in, looking like love personified. I don't think it's possible for two people to look happier than they do right now. Zach leads her to the center of the dance floor, and walks her in a circle so everyone can see how beautiful she looks.

"They're so beautiful together," I say with a little sob, wrapping my arm around Rick's waist as he pulls me in tight.

He kisses the top of my head. "They really are."

We watch our friends spellbound until they join us at the table.

I smile brightly at Zach. "Hey, bestie-in-law."

He laughs out loud and pulls me in for a huge hug.

"Not only do I gain a beautiful wife today, but a beautiful bestie-in-law. I'm a lucky man."

Rick steps forward and pulls Zach into a back-slapping dude hug, and then everyone takes turns greeting our friends. Tuxedoed waiters are already moving about the tent, setting plates down in front of guests. We all take our seats and I finally have a moment to talk to Marina.

"How are you doing?" I ask. "Do you need anything?"

She giggles. "No, thanks to you and that ridiculous thing you're wearing. You're the perfect maid of honor, Ash."

I laugh out loud. After we were fitted for the dresses, I went back to the dress shop where we got them and bought a matching shawl. Then, being the resourceful and crafty person all school teachers have to be, I made a sort of sleeve that fastens around my upper thigh like a garter. It has little pockets that I hand-stitched to hold anything Marina might need, like aspirin, hand lotion, you name it. I even have a granola bar in there. No one can see it because the skirt of the dress is full, and the pockets are only on the outer thigh portion of it so I can't accidentally sit on anything. It's a genius invention that also had the inner circle writhing on the floor from laughter as we were getting ready this morning. I'm pretty sure I've secured a place in the maid of honor hall of fame.

Dinner is delicious, and soon Zach and Marina are called to the cake table to cut the first slice. The DJ starts up the dance music as our bride and groom head back to the table for a bit. Couples begin to hit the dance floor, and Rick begins pulling me in that direction.

"C'mon, baby," he croons at me. "I've got my girl in a beautiful dress in this fairyland setting. I'm dancing with you every chance I get."

I can't argue with that logic. I step into his arms and let him guide me around the dance floor.

"I'd love you anyway," I say with a grin. "But I love how much you love dancing."

He smiles down at me. "It's a happy thing," he muses. "That's what my mom always says. And the world needs more happy things. You can't be mad while you're dancing."

After a few dances, I drag Rick off the dance floor for a break. I'm overjoyed to find a large piece of cake at my place, and I happily dig in. Jimmy leans over and nudges me with his shoulder.

"You don't know how hard it was for me not to eat that, Ash."

I point my fork at him with a smirk. "If you steal my cake, you unleash the Dragon Lady."

Jimmy and Rick both laugh out loud, and I shrug.

"It's all she's good for now," I say, stealing a kiss from Rick. "I don't really need her for anything else."

Rick gives me a secret smile, and I mouth *I love you* at him. He winks, then turns away as Zach grabs his attention. I look around at my friends, and my heart swells. I am happier than I probably have a right to be, but I'll take it. I'll take it all.

The dance music ends, and the DJ plays a series of chimes to get everyone's attention.

"Can I get all you lovely single ladies up here on the dance floor, please," he croons. "It's time for the bride to toss her bouquet!"

He immediately begins playing Beyonce's "Single Ladies". Merry, Scarlet and I bust out laughing. They get up quickly and start moving towards the dance floor. I look over at Rick with a smirk.

"I'll be right back," I say, planting a soft kiss on his gorgeous mouth. "Save my place for me?"

Rick places his hands on either side of my face and brings me in for a slower, softer kiss. His beautiful blue eyes meet mine, holding my gaze for a few seconds.

"Always."

Swoon.

Merry comes back and tugs at me. "You can't squeak out of this, it's tradition!"

I laugh as I stand and follow her. "I wasn't trying to squeak out of anything. Is that even a real thing?"

Nearly twenty women are on the dance floor by the time Merry and I get out there. I plan to focus on not falling down in these heels, so I won't be dashing left or right for this thing. Scarlet looks at both of us with a wry grin.

"If it even comes near me, I'm karate chopping it in the other direction."

I laugh out loud. "Wow, you may be worse than me when I was the Dragon Lady."

Merry nods. "You're a little scary right now, Scarlet."

Everyone applauds as soon as Marina appears on the dance floor. She looks so beautiful in her simple but elegant dress. Zach's mother had it commissioned for Marina as a gift. She flew Marina here for a mother/daughter-in-law long weekend for the fitting. Marina was able to pick the style, fabric, and tailor it to her specifications. There is a beautiful hand-embroidered mermaid on the small train. It blends in with the design, so it's not obvious at all, but she knows it's there.

Marina smiles, then looks at the group of us clustered against the stage where the DJ is and shakes her head.

"Nope," she says. "You ladies stand where I am, and I'll be against the stage. I don't want anyone falling backwards into it."

We move to the center of the dance floor, as she says. With all of us facing the stage, the wedding guests don't have much to look at but our backs. Marina grabs me, Scarlet, Merry and Hillary and brings us front and center of the group.

"The photographer's going to take pics," she explains. "I want us all in the same area, girls."

The photographer gets up on the stage with the DJ to take some candid photos, so Merry naturally starts clowning around. Before we know it, we're all doing the choreography to Beyonce's "Single Ladies" while the wedding guests laugh and cheer. Finally, the music fades out.

"All right, everyone, you know the tradition," the DJ croons into the mic. "Whichever lucky lady catches the bouquet is the next lady to get married!"

"I'm out!" Scarlet yells in jest, running away until Merry chases her down and brings her back.

Marina moves into place and holds the bouquet up for show, then she turns her back to us and makes a few practice moves with her bouquet arm. Scarlet and Merry are causing some kind of ruckus nearby, but I'm seriously just focusing on not looking like an idiot by tripping on my dress or something. Dance? Sure. Catch moving projectiles? Nope.

"Here it comes!" Marina cries out, swinging her arm up...but she doesn't toss the bouquet.

Marina turns to face us. Her smile is so beautiful and her eyes are full of emotion. Then she walks straight for me. I start backing away and to the side to clear the path, but she grabs me by the shoulders and hugs me.

"No, my beautiful friend," she whispers at me. "You stay right here. I love you."

Marina hands me her bouquet, leaving me speechless as she steps past me. I whirl around to ask her what's going on, and all the other women have left the dance floor. No one else is there...except Rick. On one knee...with a ring in his hand.

The tears are instant. My lip begins to tremble, and my hand floats up to cover my mouth. All the wedding guests are applauding like crazy.

Rick looks up at me, his eyes full of love and a lifetime's worth of promises. A tear falls down his cheek, and I immediately want to kiss it away, but I can't move.

"Ashley Marie Roberts," Rick says in a voice thick with emotion. "My Fireball. You are everything to me. Everything. And I don't want to live another minute in this world unless I know you're going to be mine for the rest of my life. Will you marry me?"

I'm nodding between sobs, but it takes me a few seconds to find my voice.

"Yes!" I squeak out, and he's off his knee in an instant.

Everyone cheers as Rick slides the beautiful ring onto my finger and then scoops me into his arms. I hold him tightly as he spins us around, and move my lips next to his ear.

"I love you so much," I whisper, kissing the side of his head. "More than anything."

He sets me down and wraps those strong arms around me, holding me tight.

"I love you too, baby," he whispers, rubbing our noses together. "Thanks for saying yes."

I laugh out loud. "There is no other answer. Not for me. Thanks for asking."

He raises his eyebrows. "You may regret it. I'll never give up my Ashley shirt."

I giggle softly. The DJ starts playing a ballad, and couples begin joining us on the dance floor. We're already in each other's arms, so we start dancing.

"Your dad's going to be so happy this is all done and over with," Rick tells me. "He was having a hard time keeping it a secret."

I look over his shoulder to what Marina calls "the parents' table". My Dad is wiping tears away as he chats happily with Scarlet's mom, Nonno, and Zach's parents.

"I'm surprised you told him," I say with a shake of my head. "He's terrible at secrets."

Rick grins. "I had to ask his permission first, Fireball. Things like that matter to him."

I look up at him in wonder. He even included my dad. He really is perfect.

"I'm so glad you're mine," I whisper.

He captures my mouth in a sweet kiss. "I've been yours since the moment I saw you, Ash."

I laugh softly. "Well, I'm sorry it took me so long to catch up, but I'm here now."

"There's plenty of time to make it up to me," he purrs into my ear.

I shoot him a mocking glare. "Oh?"

He nods slowly. "All the kisses I want for the rest of time…and hands off my Ashley shirt."

I throw my head back and laugh, then reach up and give his man bun a little tug.

"If it'll make you happy, baby," I say with silver lining my eyes. "Yes, and yes. Always."

The End

Want to see Rick and Ashley tie the knot? Get their wedding scene free when you join my reader list. Grab some tissues!

Read Rick and Ashley's Wedding: From Friend Zone to Forever now!

Paperback readers, scan this code to grab your bonus content now:

Scarlet's next.

She's spent years building her design business and dodging romantic entanglements. Then a fire destroys her project—and a certain firefighter won't stop checking in on her.

Andrew runs toward danger for a living. Scarlet runs from feelings. This should be a disaster.

But slow burns have a way of catching fire when you least expect it.

Start Running to the Rescue now!

Sneak Peek: Running to the Rescue

Chapter 1

Scarlet

All men can be sorted into three categories. Dangerous in a good way, dangerous in a bad way, and meh.

Am I being a tad too judgy? Yes.

Do I care? No. Not at all.

I don't have time for boys, men, or anything in between. Two of my closest friends, Marina and Ashley, love to tease me about their similar feelings about men and relationships until they got bit by the love bug. Marina is now married, and Ashley's engaged. They think it'll happen that way for me as well, but nope. Not happening. And the living proof of it just walked in the door.

His name is Black Leather Jacket, and he's been coming to my coffee shop almost every morning for about a month now. Well, it's not *my* coffee shop in the sense that I own it. It's my coffee shop because it's right around the corner from the beat-up old warehouse I'm temporarily living in. This coffee house is my first stop every morning when the sun rises, and it's safe...or safe-ish...to leave the warehouse.

Right now, Black Leather Jacket (or BLJ for short) is ordering his usual green tea latte.

Gross.

As soon as he has it in hand, he will walk purposefully over to the table in the corner against the window. He'll sit there and sip away with a very zen-like look on his face, watching the busy city of San Francisco wake up. He may scroll through his phone occasionally. Pretty boring, if that is it. But it's not. Every once in a while, he looks in my direction…our eyes meet…and the whole world slows to a halt. Not cool.

"Is that him?" my friend Merry whispers excitedly from across the table.

I give her a look that says hush, and she makes a face at me.

"He's way over there," she whispers. "It's not like he can hear me."

I shake my head slowly. "Not sure I agree, Mer. He might have superpowers."

"Nope," she says succinctly, flipping her shoulder-length dark brown hair over her shoulder. "People with superpowers are very rare. We aren't just standing around on every street corner."

I lift my eyebrows. "*We?* So you have superpowers?"

She smirks. "Duh. You too. Hence…the we."

I giggle. "And what is my superpower exactly?"

Merry smiles warmly. "You can take the ugliest warehouse ever and transform it into a fairytale bedroom."

"*And* an elegant, beautiful library," I add with a wink, then I bob my chin at her. "Your superpower is…?"

Her eyes go as round as saucers as she whispers, "Buttercream."

I snicker and shake my head, looking away and right into the warm, brown, I-see-into-the-depths-of-your-soul eyes of Black Leather Jacket. He holds my gaze, as always. He doesn't smile like a hundred other men would, looking for an opening. He doesn't nod. He doesn't do anything but look at me. Not in a creepy way, but in a…hey, I see you, way that completely unsettles me. And I do *not* like to be unsettled. I have an iron grip on settled.

"Wow…" Merry mutters.

When I finally break my gaze away and look at her, she's staring into her coffee. I nudge her foot with mine. She gives me a stern look and nods.

"I see what you mean," she murmurs. "I looked away, so I didn't get caught in the big brown-eyed tractor beam too."

I turn to face Merry fully, so I'm not tempted to look back at BLJ.

"But it's not creepy, right? He doesn't smile or anything, but it's still not creepy."

Merry snorts. "No, it's the opposite of creepy. He's dead sexy. He's got an energy about him."

I nod and take a sip of my coffee. I don't know why this guy gets under my skin like he does. It's been bothering me so much that I dragged Merry here to give me a second opinion. Although perhaps I should have dragged Marina or Ashley. Merry is such a positive, happy little unicorn, and I doubt she'd be creeped out by Jack the Ripper.

"So go talk to him," Merry murmurs as she breaks a piece off her cookie.

"What?" I whisper. "Why on earth would I do that?"

Merry shrugs and pops the piece of cookie in her mouth.

"Do *you* feel creeped out?" she mumbles while crunching her cookie.

"No."

"Harassed? Icky?"

"No."

She leans forward and whispers, eyes big.

"Do you see the hotness?"

I click my tongue. "Could anyone *not* see that hotness?"

I glance back at BLJ for a moment. I think it's possible that even his muscles have muscles. The guy is cut. His hair is perfect. His jaw is always freshly shaved. And those eyes. They make me want to go swimming in their depths.

Merry shrugs again. "So, what's the problem? Other than this violation of baked goods sitting in front of me."

She points to the cookie and shakes her head at it like it slapped her in the face.

"No, I'm not looking for a relationship, you know that," I reply. I say it a lot. "I just…I don't know. I wanted a second opinion because I wasn't freaked out."

Merry frowns at me. "You were worried because you *weren't* freaked out?"

I nod. "With the staring."

"Yes, well, now that I've seen him…he's not really staring, is he? He's just looking. Straight into your soul."

"Yes, but why?"

She shudders. "I could ask the same about this cookie. Why?"

I laugh under my breath. "Still a big no from Nonno on the bakery?"

"Yep. I'm not sure Nonno even knows how to say yes. I'm still not giving up."

"Good," I say with a reassuring wink. "You'll wear Nonno down. I know you will."

Sweet Merry. She works miracles with anything that's baked. She makes beautiful pastries, cakes, and cookies. It's her passion. For years, she's been limited to using an old, unloved spare oven in her grandfather's Italian bistro. He's allowed her to sell grab-and-go desserts from a small bakery case in the restaurant's entry, which he thought she'd grow weary of. Instead, it only inspired her, and she's been begging him to let her re-open her grandmother's little bakery next door for ages. But dear Nonno, as we all call him, can't seem to let anything new grow in the shadow of her Nonna's memory. He'd rather let it sit unused, a partial storage facility for his restaurant.

I love Nonno like my own grandfather. He's a grandfather figure to all four of us. There's something else going on here because he is usually nothing but big pasta sauce smelling hugs and loud kisses on the cheek. He gets positively grumpy when the bakery comes up.

"So, what are you gonna do?" Merry asks, rousing me from my thoughts.

I'm confused for a moment.

"About tall, dark, and sexy-not-creepy over there?" she clarifies.

I risk a glance over my shoulder. BLJ is frowning at his phone, scrolling. Even when frowning, I have to admit the guy is gorgeous. The black leather jacket he's always in isn't a biker-style jacket. It's a coat. A blazer. Today, he's wearing it with blue jeans, black suede boots, and a dark gray t-shirt that looks tailor made to hug his chiseled freaking chest. I force my gaze back to Merry's.

"Nothing at all."

Merry looks disappointed, but not at all surprised.

"Then why are we here?" she mutters. "Let's go shopping or something."

I smirk at her. "You have to have money to shop, Mer. I'm really trying not to spend anything I don't have to."

She leans forward with a smile. "You are going to win this whole thing this year. Everyone else should be petrified of your determination."

I laugh softly. I love that Merry is such a cheerleader for her people, and I'm lucky to be counted as one of them.

"Thanks, Mer."

"So, how long do you have to work on your two rooms?"

"Almost two months," I reply with a tight smile. "It'd be more than enough if I hadn't gone a little crazy with the details. I'm committed now, so there's no going back."

She nods. "Our paint party will help, though?"

"Definitely. I'm not too proud to accept all that help."

Merry, Ashley, Marina, and I were all out to lunch last week when Merry volunteered the whole group to come and paint my two rooms in the warehouse. As if that weren't enough, she volunteered *the men folk* to move the furniture I'm using too. In this case, the men folk also happen to be The Royal Rebels...a world-famous indie rock band. Zach Adams, the lead singer, is married to Marina, and Rick Archer, the lead guitarist, is engaged to Ashley. Sam and Jimmy, the other two band members, were thrown in for good measure by Merry, but cooler heads prevailed.

There are a ton of reasons why The Royal Rebels can't move furniture and perform manual labor for me, mainly to do with the insurance on their very valuable persons. Plus, I can't even imagine the chaos that would erupt if they were identified and fans started showing up.

Zach offered to pay for professional movers to take care of moving everything for me, which was incredibly generous, but that's who he is. It's why we all love Zach. Rick, my favorite Rebel, has volunteered his awesome woodworking abilities for my use and abuse. Last year, he made me a set of gorgeous corbels that I designed and turned into shelves. They got some air time on the Home Network's TV show about the competition, which helped me tremendously. Because of it, I now have a fairly steady stream of interior design customers.

"What kind of details did you get obsessed with on this project?"

I grin. "Embroidery."

Her eyebrows shoot up to her hairline. "What? Where?"

"The library room. I'm putting in mock windows, and I want it to look like it's twilight outside, so I was messing with the lighting for that when the idea hit me. I found these gorgeous sheer curtains on clearance, but they needed a little extra something. So I'm embroidering white flowers and vines onto them and running some little silver threads through it to give it a little sparkle."

"You don't think you have superpowers…but you can pick up embroidery just like that?"

I laugh. I'm resourceful and scrappy. I'll find a way. I always have. It's just what I do.

"How's your mom doing?" Merry asks.

I nod. "Good. *Really* good. First vacation she's taken in ten years. I get a huge dump of pictures every morning when I wake up. It starts my day off with a big, stupid smile."

Merry opens her mouth to ask the question I know is coming next, and I hold my hand up to stop her.

"No, she doesn't know I'm living in the warehouse," I say quietly. "And no, I'm not going to tell her."

She shakes her head. "Momma's not gonna like that…"

I scoff openly. "Our apartment is too far away, and I don't have a car. Taking the bus is not an option," I explain. "It's fine in our bougie neighborhood, but the closer the bus gets to the warehouse, the freaks start boarding. I tried it once. It's not safe."

Merry looks at me incredulously.

"It's not safe to take the bus in this neighborhood, but sleeping in an abandoned warehouse in the same neighborhood is?"

"The warehouse is secure. There's an alarm that I set when everyone leaves. And, while we're talking about it, I might as well tell you that I'm not going to tell Marina or Ashley. This needs to be our secret."

Merry frowns. "Why? We don't keep secrets from each other."

She's right, we don't. Guilt hits me in the gut like a sledgehammer.

"This is going to sound ridiculous, but you have to hear me out."

Merry nods and stays silent.

"If I tell them, they're going to intervene," I explain calmly. "Especially Marina. She won't be able to help herself. She'll insist on having a security guard here to protect me or something, but I'm fine. Really. The warehouse has been empty for ages. Brad's dad says there have been no break-ins for over a year."

"He's the owner?"

I nod. Brad is a friend and one of the other designers on our little team.

"I don't want to be a burden to my friends, and I don't want this to be a big deal," I continue. "But I do take my safety seriously, I promise. I did some research on crime in the neighborhood. Retail theft, carjacking, and muggings are all on the rise here. The warehouses on this block haven't been impacted. The local criminals are more interested in robbing the liquor store than some empty warehouse."

Merry shakes her head at me. "That doesn't make me feel any better about you living there."

"What if we implement a check-in system while I'm staying there?"

She eyes me warily. "Like what?"

"I'll promise not to go out after dark, and I'll text you every night when I lock up," I offer.

"And first thing in the morning when you wake up," she adds.

I nod. "Agreed. And believe me, I want out of the warehouse as soon as possible. It's no fun living there."

She makes a face. "What about showers?"

"Ah," I say, scrunching my nose. "I'm not sure what this warehouse was used for previously, but the bathroom has an open, tiled area with a sprayer attached to a hose hanging from one wall. It's cold, but I can tough it out. It's only a few weeks."

Merry sits back in her chair. "That's a lot of cold showers in the pursuit of fame and glory."

I laugh softly. "Hopefully, that's how this story ends. Fame and glory."

Merry's eyes flick over to the offensive cookie and back to me.

"All right, c'mon," she says, standing and stretching. "Show me this warehouse and get me away from that horrible cookie."

I stand and turn around to grab my bag off the back of the chair. BLJ is gone…and again, I wonder where he went.

***

Andrew

She's back, and this time she has a friend with her. I focus on the menu board in front of me, but she fills my peripheral vision. City Girl, or CG as I call her, is a mystery to me. She doesn't belong in this neighborhood. That much is clear. So what is she doing here?

My favorite barista, Rosa, tells me she comes in every morning. Even weekends. She sits at the same table every time and orders a black coffee.

Gross.

Most of the time, she has a sketch pad on the table with her. I wonder what's in it, way too often. Does she just love to doodle, or is she an artist? Every time she walks in the door, I'm full of questions that are never answered.

"Green tea latte, please," I tell Alfie, another barista here, at the counter when it's my turn.

He smiles and rings me up, then I step to the side and wait.

This place has only been here a few months, but I love it. It's part of a revitalization effort in this part of the city, which I'm grateful for since I spend a good amount of time in this neighborhood as a fireman for Engine 14. We work twenty-four-hour shifts every other day, so having a nice place to grab a latte in the morning is a luxury I enjoy having. I just wish the rest of the neighborhood would hurry up and revitalize as well because some parts of it are pretty sketchy.

Which brings me back to CG. She doesn't look anything like most of the locals here. I noticed her right away, and not just because she's pretty. If I looked up the word *driven* in the dictionary, I'm pretty sure I'd find her picture. Right next to mine. I recognize it in her because that's how I live my life. With purpose. From her determined walk to the fierce glint in her gorgeous blue eyes, this woman's on a mission, and I find myself far too curious about what it is.

"Andrew," Rosa says with a smile as she passes my latte to me over the counter.

I smile my thanks and head to my favorite corner.

I steal a glance over at CG's table, and her friend is looking in my direction with undisguised curiosity that's almost feral. She looks away immediately. They're talking about me. That's confusing because everything about CG screams *go away*. It's why I've never approached her. She's clearly not interested in anything but whatever's in that sketch pad. Someone like that doesn't want some random guy in a coffee house sliding into the seat across from her to talk about the weather. She couldn't care less for cheesy pick-up lines. But what *does* she care about? I really want to know.

My phone vibrates in my pocket, and I pull it out to read the text.

Jake: Hey, kid. You at that fancy coffee house?

I smirk at my phone.

Andrew: Yep. You want your usual?

Jake: Well, if you're offering…

I chuckle under my breath. Captain Scheffler, or Jake as we all call him, is an old family friend. My dad's best friend, actually. They were fire cadets together. Earned their chops as firemen together. Until one day, when an arsonist tried to take out a high-rise office building, and my dad never made it out. I was five years old. A lot of kids who lose a parent early in life barely have any memory of them. Jake made sure that didn't happen for me. He's been a constant in my life ever since, and I owe him a lot. When I first joined the fire department, I was over the moon excited to be assigned a position under him. Especially at Engine 14, where he and my dad were first assigned as new recruits.

I look over in CG's direction again. Half a second later, she looks my way, and our gazes lock. This happens frequently. Whenever my gaze drifts to her, she looks. It's as if our subconscious minds seek each other out. I can't seem to look away when it happens. I want to smile at her, but I feel like it'll be perceived like I'm hitting on her. She looks away before I have a chance to do anything, and I return my focus to my phone.

Andrew: I'll be back soon. Just needed to stretch my legs.

I return to the article I was reading about an arsonist in Florida. Fire fascinates me in all forms, but it's deadly and must be respected. While my mom loves watching documentaries about serial killers, I'm immediately pulled into anything about arsonists. I guess we all have our hobbies. Either that, or we're the weirdest family ever.

I take another sip of my latte and start scrolling through my social media accounts. I don't spend much time on it, but a local reporter named Kevin Starbuck has been trying to focus the public eye on this neighborhood. He's written some great human interest stories lately, all involving local residents and businesses. Some struggling, some new. I've never met him, but he gets mad respect from me for trying to make a difference.

I look over towards CG and her friend again. Wow. Her friend really doesn't like the cookie she's trying to eat. What a face she's making. I laugh under my breath and gulp down the rest of my latte, then head over to the order counter, where Rosa is already smiling at me.

"Almond croissant again?" she asks with a grin.

I nod, then watch as she bags it up. I tap my credit card and take the bag from her.

"Thanks, Rosa," I say as I pace toward the door.

I turn and push my back against it so I can steal one more glance at CG. She doesn't notice, and I step out onto the sidewalk in the waking city, wondering if I'll ever get her attention.

About the Author

Dianne Oren enjoys writing fun and swoon-worthy romantic comedies. She's also a self-professed embroidery nerd, an iced coffee addict, and an avid reader. She lives in Texas with her husband Kevin, two horrible puppies named Duke & Daisy, a house panther (black cat) named Finn and a tiny gray potato tornado named Rebel (calico cat).

You can connect with me on:

- https://dianneoren.com
- https://www.facebook.com/DianneOrenOfficial
- https://www.instagram.com/dianneorenofficial

Subscribe to my newsletter:

- https://dianneoren.com/subscribe

Also by Dianne Oren

How to Date a Mermaid

Marina has spent her entire life swimming against the current—and she's finally close to the future she's worked so hard to earn. A job at the city's most prestigious law firm is her first step toward law school, where she plans to fight for kids in crisis just like she once was. One slip-up could cost her everything, and her notoriously strict boss doesn't tolerate distractions—or bad press.

So of course, the one spontaneous moment Marina allows herself lands her in a viral video with a world-famous rock star…while she's dressed as a mermaid and singing in public.

Determined to protect her future, Marina plans to disappear—until her meddling friend tells Zach exactly where to find her. When he shows up at the library where she's singing to children and curious onlookers start pulling out their phones, the two are forced into a hasty escape. One impromptu dinner later, Marina finds herself agreeing to the one thing she swore she wouldn't risk: dating him in secret.

Zach promises to protect her identity. But the more time they steal together, the harder it becomes to keep their worlds separate—and the harder it is for Marina to ignore the truth. She's not just hiding from the media; she's hiding from a future that scares her more than any viral video—one where she lets someone in.

With her carefully planned future on the line and her guarded heart opening against her will, Marina must decide whether to keep chasing the life she planned…or take a leap toward the love she never expected.

Running to the Rescue

Scarlet

I have six weeks to win the Home Network's Decorator's Showcase and the $250,000 grand prize. I've entered this contest three years running. This year, I'm living in an abandoned warehouse in a sketchy neighborhood just to make it happen.

I don't do distractions. I don't do spontaneous. I schedule everything—including my love life.

So when I meet Andrew, a firefighter with an annoyingly perfect smile, I feel the attraction. But I shut it down immediately. I ask him if he'd like to have coffee. In six weeks. When the contest is over.

He laughs. Says he'll wait.

Then a fire destroys my project three weeks before the deadline.

Andrew is the one who pulls me from the blaze. A news photographer catches the moment—my face lit by flames, half-covered in ash, Andrew carrying me out. The headline: "The Phoenix and the Fireman."

I tell everyone I'm done. There's no time to start over.

Andrew—and my meddling friends—disagree. They replace my equipment, rally support, and offer up the fire station as my new location. I can redesign their kitchen and living room. It's perfect. It's also impossible to keep things professional when Andrew is there. Every. Single. Day.

Andrew

I used to be like Scarlet—career-obsessed, scheduling life down to the minute. Then I lost a friend. He died while I was too busy climbing ladders to pick up the phone.

I won't make that mistake again.

When Scarlet asks me out for coffee in six weeks, I know exactly what she's doing. Putting life on hold for ambition. I've been there. It doesn't end well.

Then I pull her from a fire and everything changes.

She wants to give up. I won't let her. My crew and I offer her the fire station, and she throws herself into the rebuild with the same relentless focus that's going to burn her out.

I'm not backing off. She asked for six weeks. I'm giving her every reason to change her mind.

Merry & Bright

Merry

A runaway car. A twisted ankle. A very serious police officer who keeps calling me ma'am.

I'm turning thirty—not eighty—and Officer Nicholas Bright is not amused by my objections. He's buttoned-up, stoic, and completely unprepared for my nonstop commentary…until I finally make him laugh.

He insists on driving me home.
Then he keeps showing up.
"Just checking in."

I'm a baker—specifically, a Christmas-cookie maximalist. When Nick mentions that his adopted grandmother used to bake with him every Christmas, something shifts. She has Alzheimer's now. Most days, she doesn't remember him at all.

So I suggest cookie decorating.

And somehow, I end up going with him.

Nick

I don't believe in optimism. Life cured me of that.

Merry is sunshine and chaos—too cheerful, too talkative, and far too determined to see past my badge and dark sunglasses. I tell myself we're just friends. I have nothing to offer her. My grandmother is slipping away, and Christmas—her favorite season—feels like salt in an open wound.

Then Merry comes with me to the care home to decorate cookies. And for a few precious minutes, my grandmother remembers me.

I break every boundary I built. I don't care anymore.

I want Merry. And I want more than friendship. For the first time, I'm willing to risk my heart to get it.